The TSUNAMI FILE

Other Works by Michael E. Rose

Novels:
The Mazovia Legacy
The Burma Effect

Non-fiction:
For the Record

Plays:
Gallery
Lotto Cantata
Gameshow

Children's Literature:
Kangaroo Christmas

The TSUNAMI FILE

Not every victim is found to be innocent ...

MICHAEL E. ROSE

McArthur & Company
Toronto

First published in Canada in 2008 by
McArthur & Company
322 King St. West, Suite 402
Toronto, ON
M5V 1J2
www.mcarthur-co.com

Library and Archives Canada Cataloguing in Publication

    Rose, Michael E. (Michael Edward)
    The tsunami file / Michael E. Rose.

    ISBN 978-1-55278-705-2

    I. Title.
    PS8585.O729T88 2008   C813'.6   C2008-900301-2

Design: *Mad Dog Design*
Author photo: *Matt Dunham*
Printed in Canada by *Webcom*

The publisher would like to acknowledge the financial support of the
Government of Canada through the Book Publishing Industry Development
Program (BPIDP) and the Canada Council for our publishing activities.
The publisher further wishes to acknowledge the financial support of the
Ontario Arts Council for our publishing program.

10 9 8 7 6 5 4 3 2 1

For Sheryle . . .
Journalist. Friend. Wife.

"I cried by reason of my affliction unto the Lord, and he heard me. Out of the belly of hell cried I and thou heardst my voice, for thou hadst cast me into the deep in the midst of the seas, and the floods compassed me about. All thy billows and thy waves passed over me..."

The Book of Jonah

"The importance of being able to fix human personality, of being able to give each human being an individuality differentiating him from all others, under conditions which will ensure that this individuality can be convincingly and quickly ascertained in spite of all efforts that may be made to confuse it, cannot be over-estimated."

SIR EDWARD R. HENRY,
Classification and Uses of Finger Prints, 1900

PART 1
Phuket, Thailand — March 2005

Prologue

Frank Delaney on assignment in Thailand. Journalist on this occasion, not spy. Not yet. What does he see? Squat steel shipping containers sitting in silent rows on stony level ground. They are old, weathered. Some are white, some pearl grey. Faded markings and logos and serial numbers from the sea-freight companies that once used them are still inscribed on the corrugated rectangular sides and the sturdy double doors, which are tightly closed against Phuket's intense tropical heat and light.

There are dozens of these containers in the deserted, barren compound. From afar, there is nothing that immediately indicates their contents. They sit silent in the new day's burgeoning heat, for Phuket in the month of March at sunrise is already hot. They reveal, for the moment, nothing.

Tall, slender palms sway in the slight breeze outside the compound's fenced perimeter. Inside, low temporary electrical poles among the container corridors support many strands of black cable. From these poles, single strands of cable pass to the backs of each container, then down to small air-conditioning units that hum quietly at ground level, the sound all but obscured by the rustle of palms and by the breeze itself.

Here and there on the rough gravel pathways are old-fashioned medical gurneys, little more than sturdy stretchers on oversized wheels. These give an observer the first hint of what goes on in this forlorn place, when the day begins.

There are several large tents to one side, khaki military tents with small flags haphazardly flown from makeshift standards. On one tent, first in the row, a flag of Sweden flutters fitfully. On another, Australia's flag, and on the rest flags of Germany, United Kingdom, Netherlands, other nations.

Through the slightly parted flap of one of these tents can be seen two sets of rubber boots, one set white, the other powder blue. On a cot in the dimness behind the boots lies a ball cap of the type worn by a policeman, perhaps a soldier. These items, too, give a hint of what goes on in this place when the day begins.

On the opposite side of the compound, well away from the tents, are some temporary flat-roofed structures with white metal walls and small windows. Air-conditioning units behind them are tethered to black electrical cables, as with the shipping containers. More medical gurneys are ranged near the entrance doors to these small buildings, alongside green rubbish containers on wheels with bright yellow plastic liners showing beneath their hinged covers.

A passenger jet takes off from the airport in the near distance, its muted roar breaking the dawn spell of this strange and lonely scene. Delaney turns to watch it go, squinting against the brilliant sun and the steel flash of aircraft wings.

Casually dressed people begin to arrive in the compound, individually, and in small groups, most of them incongruously cheery and talkative in such surroundings. They take little notice of Delaney standing outside the compound fence. He carries no notebook, no camera. The arrivals, however, carry small overstuffed backpacks, battered sports bags, official briefcases. They greet each other and remark on the weather and make small talk as colleagues do in any workplace on any workday morning anywhere in the world.

Many languages are used for these morning workplace greetings. Men and women, but mostly men, enter the tents and reappear in spotless medical garb. Blue surgeons' smocks and caps, white lab coats, rubber boots. Some have surgical masks bunched at the ready on their necks; some carry rubber gloves. Most of these people are Europeans. Some Thai workers in overalls and some uniformed Thai police also appear.

The place suddenly takes on an air of macabre hustle and bustle. Steel container doors are swung open. White vapours waft out, the cold dry air from inside meeting the hot moist air outside in a sudden ghostly mix. Within the dimness of the containers being opened appear rows of rough wooden bunks. On the floors is a mixture of sawdust and sweating corrugations of ice.

On each bunk, in large blue or white plastic bags, lie the dead. Perhaps fifty bodies per 40-foot container—fewer in the 20-foot variety. Dozens of these containers, row upon row, hold hundreds of bodies. These are the tsunami dead, those with no names—battered and drowned and rendered anonymous by the giant waves of December 24, 2004, which heaved chaos on Thailand and on the region for thousands of kilometres around.

Thai workers help European colleagues load some of the numbered body bags onto gurneys for the short journey to the low mortuary buildings. Inside, Delaney knows, with bodies laid out on stainless-steel pathology trays, flanked by gleaming instrument tables and trolleys and examination gear, experts in medical smocks will peer and prod and scrape and slice and sample and test and record all through the day; day after day, week after week, month after month. They are seeking history, certainty, identity.

Along with each body bag will come a plastic-wrapped forensic file containing particulars of where each body was found and any obvious clues as to identity noted at the time of discovery, any clues as to who this human form might once have been.

It is the job of these pathologists and scientists and experts and police officers from around the globe to seek obscure signs in the bags of bones and flesh, to read signs from fingers and teeth and blood and marrow, and to discover, if they can, something certain about former identities, former lives.

At day's end, when the gruesome work stops once more and the last rigid finger or putrefying remnant of finger has yielded a print, when the last dental X-ray has been taken and the last tissue or bone sample has been labelled and carefully sealed away, when the last notes have been taken as to scars, tattoos and body piercings, as to watches, rings and pendants worn, the multinational teams will disperse as from any workplace the world over, making plans for meals, for drinks, for various evening excursions.

The bodies will be transported again to their places, for how much longer no one knows. Container doors will swing tightly shut once more. The interiors will fall silent and dark, the nameless forms on comfortless bunks abandoned to their fates once more.

These are the tsunami dead, rendered nameless by the catastrophic waves and the subsequent action of water and sunlight and insects on their skin and features and any other sign of who they were or one day might have been.

Chapter 1

Jonah Smith was a fingerprint man. But he hardly knew himself in Thailand. He had been transformed. Friends and colleagues, especially no-nonsense former colleagues from Scotland Yard and his current colleagues at Interpol back in France, would surely have mistaken him for someone else.

He had, for example, bought himself a bicycle. Not new, not fancy—Chinese-made, black in colour. It had cost him 800 Thai *baht* and a few minutes of heavy negotiation with a grinning local seller who had taken to cruising the Phuket area after the tsunami in a red pickup truck loaded with bikes of dubious origin and in various states of disrepair. Smith had not owned a bicycle for decades, not since he was a skinny boy in short pants in Yorkshire. But he now rode his jangling, creaking, disreputable machine each day from the Bay Hotel, where the Interpol team and some of the Thai disaster victim identification people and senior police had been billetted, to the Information Management Centre in Phuket Town. It was a cheery if somewhat sweaty and bumpy ride of about five kilometres.

Smith had also exchanged his navy blue Interpol Incident Response Team golf shirt—all the Disaster Victim Identification teams in Phuket had been issued similar no-nonsense policelike shirts, emblazoned with their countries' flags or the logos of their home police departments—for some wild floral shirts in bright yellows, green, orange. These local shirts were cooler and far more practical in the intense heat and humidity, and Smith liked the way the sleeves and collars flapped extravagantly in the breeze as he pedalled to work six days a week. He was transformed during those rides, for a time, from forensic expert and finger-print man to all but carefree tourist.

His skin, too, had been changed by the Thai air and sun. It had had little exposure to the sun in the years he worked for the police. For 15 years he took the London Underground each workday from his dim ground-floor flat in Highbury; as often as not he had to run through rain the short distance from St. James's Park station to the forbidding glass-fronted office build-ing set back behind the famous revolving Scotland Yard sign. In London he might not see sunshine for days at a time. In Lyon he had been too busy in the depths of the Interpol headquarters to take much advantage of the southern France sunlight. Now, in Thailand, his skin was toasted brown, cleared of all blemishes, rejuvenated. His thinning curly hair had been bleached a slightly lighter brown, as were his eyebrows and his blossoming new mustache.

He was, in fact, healthier and happier than he ever remem-bered, despite being, as he sometimes had to remind himself, in the direct aftermath of one of the greatest natural disasters of all time, surrounded by death and destruction, by hundreds of unidentified bodies and by the frantic relatives of the dead, by police and forensic experts from around the world, by worried Thai officials and worried foreign diplomats, and trying, prying journalists.

The fact of the matter, he would often think as he rode his rickety bike to the IMC of a morning, was that for a fingerprint man the Phuket disaster site was a little bit of paradise.

He was 43 years old, at the peak of his professional exper-tise. He had been seconded by Scotland Yard to Interpol in

France five years earlier. He had had a very good run at Interpol and in Lyon despite, or perhaps because of, his wife having refused to leave London and join him there. He had helped spearhead Interpol's effort to move more decisively onto the world stage for forensic identification, despite heavy competition from the ambitious DNA types inside Interpol and out, and he had been a natural choice, when the agency's Incident Response Team was hurriedly formed in the hours after the tsunami hit, to be sent out to Phuket to lend a hand.

Almost three months later he was still at it, still counting his blessings as each day another file of postmortem data hit his desk in the IMC building and each day he peered at fingerprints hour after hour, on paper and on computer screens, using his hard-won expertise to match patterns of arches, loops and whorls to the story of who the victim truly was.

It was work he had loved from the first day he walked into Scotland Yard's eighth-floor fingerprint division as a civilian trainee in 1984—during the heyday, the height, of its power and prestige in the London Metropolitan Police. Sir Gerald Lambourne, the legendary division head, had retired a year earlier, but Jonah Smith nonetheless joined at a time when a good fingerprint man was still the object of unconditional respect in police circles and among the public at large. The mystique of a good fingerprint man's knowledge and skills were still the stuff of legend.

Smith had loved that world from the very first days and weeks of his lengthy training. He had loved walking amongst the dark wooden file cabinets that in those years held the millions of fingerprint cards compiled by Scotland Yard to date. He had loved learning the venerable Henry Classification System, despite its Victorian-era quirks and complexities, and he had loved peering for hours through a magnifying glass at fingerprints, sometimes hundreds in a session, trying to discover the true story of someone's identity or their crimes or their manner of death.

He had loved visiting crime scenes with police officers in those years, dusting furniture and window frames and mirrors and mundane household objects for finger marks. He loved extracting a usable mark from a challenging surface, loved bringing his findings back to the Yard and plunging into the drawers of cards, before all of these had eventually been committed to computer files, to find out just who was who and what was what.

"The time I like best is the moment immediately after you make an identification," he would tell all who would listen in those years, would tell his wife in the years when she still listened to him enthuse about his work. "For a little while, for a very short while as you sit with the prints spread out on the table, you are the only person in the entire world who knows exactly who that person really is."

Smith had immersed himself completely in the fingerprint world, in the worlds within worlds on the tips of everyone's fingers. No two prints alike, ever, anywhere, despite what the doubters of recent years and some ill-informed American defence lawyers had begun to say as they tried to cast doubt on the system, and despite what the arrogant young DNA types continually tried to make out as they jockeyed for position in the global forensic identification arena.

Smith had carefully fingerprinted himself as a young trainee and kept those prints on two dog-eared evidence cards all these long years. He still studied them from time to time, watched closely for any slight changes in his own fingertips, much to the irritation of his wife. Fiona had always insisted that he was obsessed, and perhaps she was right. She had in any case refused to allow him to make a set of her fingerprints.

Smith regretted this. He would have liked to study her prints at length, alongside his own, for some outward manifestation of what it was that led to the disastrous marital mismatch he was only now beginning to accept. Sometimes, when he allowed himself to think about such things, he wished that fingerprints could tell him a little more than just someone's name.

Smith stopped asking Fiona to share any of his secret wishes and professional enthusiasms soon after their unborn baby girl died. Things had simply gone too silent between them for such non-essential requests, and now too many years had passed for him to begin asking her for much of anything at all.

He still very much enjoyed studying his own fingerprints, however. He examined the old set of evidence cards as a sort of relaxation or mediation when he was alone. He studied them for signs, patterns, clues as to who he was or might have been. Smith had, as well, developed the idiosyncrasy of staring at the patterns on the tips of his fingers when he was concentrating, or pondering a problem or speaking about a complex subject to a colleague or friend. His own fingerprints were classics of the composite variety—in his view the most beautiful of all prints. His own fingerprints combined the most interesting features of the straightforward common arch pattern, with some frequent loops and the occasional flamboyant whorl.

Smith also always carried with him on overseas assignments a few of his favourite fingerprint texts. They were no longer of any real use in his work. All was now computerized. The Automated Fingerprint Identification System had, it must be admitted, taken some of the mystery away from the classification work but it was still based, fundamentally based, on the system devised in Victorian times by the pioneers—Galton, Faulds and the great Sir Edward Henry. No matter where Smith went on assignment, no matter how far from home he found himself, he always carried with him, at a minimum, one of his several prized early editions of Henry's *Classification and Uses of Finger Prints*, Sir Francis Galton's classic text, and perhaps Faulds's *Dactylography*.

The Henry volume sat even now in pride of place on a shelf in Smith's living room at the Bay Hotel, alongside the Galton and the Faulds. Even if he did not consult Henry often, the book was always there as a silent testimony to the shining history of fingerprint science and of the service it had rendered to humanity in general and to Smith and his professional life in particular.

Smith empathized entirely with the Victorian suspicion of anonymity and of uncertainty. He would happily read and re-read the various textbooks and histories of fingerprinting, and he embraced, as the British had done in colonial outposts and in England itself, the need for a swift and sure method of identifying individuals as waves of international migration and domestic movement and social change intensified in what had too rapidly become a society of strangers.

But in the tropical society of strangers—living and dead—that was Phuket after the tsunami and the other affected countries throughout the region, and to which Smith and the other forensic experts had gravitated each for their own personal or professional reasons, there was, Smith thought as he pedalled his bike through the heat and humidity, not just tragedy but challenge, stimulation, inspiration, pleasure and, yes, sometimes even joy.

Jonah Smith was not normally a very gregarious man, but among the transformations he had undergone in Phuket, among the changes to his previous identity, was a newfound or possibly long-forgotten pleasure in the company of friends.

He liked now, for example, to meet his new Dutch friend, Stefan Zalm, at the Whale Bar in Phuket Town for ice cold Thai beers after both of their workdays had ended. He liked to compare notes on identifications made, technical troubles encountered, rumours heard, scandals and diplomatic machinations underway, and the various misdemeanours and misadventures of the police who had gathered in such large numbers in Phuket after the disaster.

Zalm was at his usual place at the end of the long dark bar on that March evening, sipping Singha beer from a small sweating bottle and looking every bit the earnest young Dutchman, the earnest young Dutch dentist, that he was. His skin was still like a boy's, his hair blond and wispy, though already receding noticeably at the sides despite his being only 35 years of age. Though finished work for the day, he still wore his white team shirt, with the flag of his country emblazoned on both shoulders.

Zalm waved to Smith and called out to the Thai barman. "Another Singha here, Prasan, please. Thank you."

The barman, impossibly slender, implausibly feminine, came immediately with the beer, placing it before Smith as he sat down, then putting his hands together and bowing his head slightly in the *wai*, Thailand's elegant sign of greeting and respect.

"*Khun* Jonah, welcome once again to the Whale Bar, welcome," the barman said in the broad tonal drawl of Thais speaking English.

Smith raised the beer bottle in a toast. "My pleasure, Prasan. Cheers."

Prasan glided back down the bar to serve a group of Belgian DVI officers already shouting and red-faced despite the pre-dinner hour. Zalm, too, raised his bottle in a toast.

"Our heroic efforts have ceased for another day," Zalm said, taking a short sip of his beer. "You have made dozens of identifications today, Jonah, of course."

"Of course," Smith said.

"You will soon begin to tell me the entire history of the development of fingerprint technology by your Englishmen predecessors. I will grow bored by this. We will drink much more beer before I am able to stop you."

"Maybe not tonight, Stefan. I'll spare you that ordeal tonight," Smith said.

"Perhaps, for once, it will be my turn to tell you the entire history of the development of forensic dentistry?"

"The Case of the Matching Molars," Smith said. "Coming

to a cinema near you. Starring Dutch dentist and international film star Stefan Zalm?"

"Not yet, my friend. Not yet."

"No IDs today?"

"Today one only," Zalm said. "We are slowing down. One elderly woman from Italy. Very badly decomposed."

"But not the teeth, of course. Intact as always. Miraculous."

"Exactly. Yes. Teeth intact. Always. Not like fingers. But the Italians have taken all this time to locate her dentist over there. Almost three months, if you can imagine. The dental X-rays were sitting in Milan all this time. A perfect match, it was obvious to me immediately. Two big fillings side by side right rear, she had, and some nice caps. Very nice work. Milan has good dentists."

"And bad systems for storing X-rays, it seems," Smith said.

"Exactly. Yes," Zalm said.

The Belgians at the end of the bar hooted and shouted and jeered. There was the sound of breaking glass. More hoots and jeers.

"A bit early for that, even for the Belgian police," Smith said.

"They are only a few bodies away," Zalm said. "Only a few missing Belgians left to identify and then they can go home. They are happy tonight."

"Bastards," Smith said.

"International solidarity," Zalm said. "Fuck you, our missing countrymen have all been identified, and so we go home."

"Bastards," Smith said. "If all of us did it like that . . ."

"Exactly."

They drank in silence for a moment.

"And you?" Zalm asked eventually.

"Three today," Smith said. "One particularly difficult one. Very bad antemortem marks from Denmark. Taken from a CD cover back there. CDs are usually good for this, as you know, and the Danish technician did his best back there but the marks were smudged badly in this instance, very badly smudged, and he only got three fingers off the cover, two of them partials. I was able to make the match, but it almost made me blind."

"The heroic fingerprint man," Zalm said.

"I suppose."

"The Identification Board will ask for corroboration for that one," Zalm said. "If there is any doubt. They cannot afford any more false IDs."

"There's no doubt in my mind," Smith said quickly. "It was a perfectly good match. Fourteen points of similarity. Ridge minutiae even a police cadet could spot without a magnifying glass. There's no doubt."

"Smudged AM marks, three fingers only. They will want more, the Board."

"Teeth," Smith said. "Of course."

"Of course. Then she can go home for a nice burial."

"He. He, in this case."

"Let me look at his X-rays tomorrow," Zalm said.

"If there are any."

"Then you will have to wait until they come from Denmark."

"If they come."

"Yes."

"Bastard," Smith said. "And when they come you'll claim the identification for yourself."

"Of course," Zalm said. "And for the glory of Dutch forensic dentistry."

The other friend Smith had made in Phuket was Concepción. Much more than a friend, in fact. For the first time in his married life, Smith had acquired a lover.

She was Spanish, from Madrid, from a family of doctors— a civilian expert in victim identification from bones. She had spent years, literally, in Bosnia after the Yugoslav civil war left thousands of buried corpses with no names. Her work with the United Nations Mission in Bosnia-Herzegovina had established her reputation in certain international circles. When the tsunami struck, she was immediately on a plane from Sarajevo.

Smith, and all the other police gathered in Phuket, called her Conchi. She was young, 34, much younger than Smith. She was single, and beautiful in the heartstoppingly dark, glowing, smouldering way that only certain types of Spanish or Italian women can be. Smith knew a lot of the other, younger police in Phuket fancied her and he knew they wondered why she would go with a too-tall, too-thin, bespectacled British fingerprint man clearly past his prime. He wondered about that sometimes, too.

She loved him "for now" she said. "For now, for now, Jonah, that is enough, no?" she would always say, laughing, when he inquired as to her feelings for him. She seemed unperturbed that he was married, even less perturbed after he told her a little, not too much, of how it was with he and his wife.

"And she will not come with you to lovely Lyon?" Conchi would say. "She is crazy, crazy, no?"

On workdays, Conchi still liked to wear her sky blue UNMIBH shirt, with United Nations flags festooned, even though officially she was part of the Spanish police team in Phuket. Her years with the UN mission in Bosnia had been intense, requiring that she and other determined investigators wallow around in rubber boots in muddy farm fields or forests or barns, excavating graves and searching, like Smith in his way, for history, identities, the endings of sad life stories. But she had loved it, was proud of it, wanted people to know if it. She loved her work very much, as he did his.

For the first time in his life, Smith could enthuse as long as he wanted to about the job he did. She would not sneer at his enthusiasms, as Fiona had learned to do. Conchi carefully examined the fingerprint books in his little apartment at the Bay

Hotel, looked closely, many times at the fingerprint diagrams in the Henry text, at the many varieties of prints, at the arcane coding system with its trailings of numbers and letters, and she would sip at her beer and smile.

"He was smart, this Henry, no?" she would say.

Conchi understood the feeling one got when an identity was confirmed. They would talk about it sometimes, in his giant hotel bed after making love or sitting as they liked to do on his balcony at sunset overlooking the hilly island silhouettes in Chalong Bay.

Smith would watch her drinking beer on his balcony. He would marvel at her lovely olive skin, far darker than his now was, even though she carefully protected herself from the sun. He would watch closely as she sipped her beer or her coffee, marvel at the ruby red lipstick stains she left on his glasses and cups, marvel at the urgency of his feelings for this young woman who loved him for now. He loved her for now, too, and, he would think ruefully, most probably for longer than that as well. But he was a man without illusions, neither about the disaster area of his own marriage nor about the possibility that Conchi could one day pull him from the debris.

She let him take her fingerprints, late one humid night as they both sat at the dining table, inches from a revolving floor fan, sweating and suffering in the tropical heat. Smith thought Conchi looked grand in her sarong in the tropical heat, with small beads of sweat poised on her forehead, her small shoulders, her chest.

"Fingertips slightly moist. Perfect, perfect for this work," Smith said as he inked them on a stamp pad.

"Oi, oi, oi, Jonah you are too rough," she cried out as he rolled her fingertips one after another onto Bay Hotel stationery. "I am not under arrest, this is not London in a stinking police cell—you cannot abuse me in this way."

"Perfect, perfect," Smith said when he examined the set of

prints as they dried. "I'm the best in the business, especially with uncooperative prisoners such as yourself."

They peered together at her prints under a magnifying glass, on the dining table under a light abuzz with insects. Her fingertips were tiny, but full of graceful arches. Her prints were quite unlike his own.

She peered through the examiner's glass at his prints on their aging Scotland Yard cards, then back at her own. Back and forth, back and forth, quickly, as a good fingerprint technician would.

"Not a match," she said finally.

"Yes," he said. "A perfect match."

"No, Jonah," she said. "Even I, a bone expert girl, can see this. Not a match."

"We shall see," he said. "There are some definite points of similarity. Ridge minutiae. Worth further examination."

"The Board would not accept this identification."

"Corroboration required?"

"Yes. Bones. DNA perhaps. From my marrow. Get me my little saw."

"No," Smith said. "DNA no. Teeth maybe."

"Yes," she said, flashing her wonderful smile full of wonderful teeth. "See, see mine now," she said, laughing.

Her small shoulders shook as she laughed, at his dining table in his hotel room in her sarong in the heat of a Thailand night in the aftermath of disaster. Smith's heart pounded like a schoolboy's.

"Perfect," he said. "Perfect."

Into this situation came the problem.

Smith at first dismissed it as a simple error, an oversight, a minor clerical lapse. It was natural, he reasoned, that such errors would occur in this place, with hundreds of strangers working under difficult conditions, under intense pressure from their home countries to make identifications and repatriate citizens for burial, using different standards of police work, or of filing and classification, with the chronic lack of proper equipment and the heavy workload and the sheer number of unidentified bodies.

It was a fact, not widely known, that in the early days after the tsunami, when grieving families and harried diplomats from all over Europe swarmed throughout the disaster zone and bodies were still lying in rows in temple courtyards or hospital parking lots in the sun, before refrigerated shipping containers had been procured to store bodies and before any semblance of a rigorous forensic system had been established and before filing systems of any coherence had been put into place, that some foreigners' bodies had been wrongly identified and sent to the wrong countries and the wrong families and the wrong grave sites for burial.

In these few sad cases, after the actual body of a loved one had subsequently been identified and it was clear that another body previously airlifted out of the disaster zone was in fact someone else, police and diplomats would have the heavy task of informing a family somewhere far from Phuket that the body they had buried after a tragic Christmas holiday in Thailand was not who they thought it was at all.

Mistaken identification like this was not the problem that began, slowly at first and then with ever more intensity, to preoccupy Jonah Smith as he worked alongside his international forensic colleagues in Phuket.

On any given day, Smith arranged his work into a series of small piles on his desk in the Information Management Centre. The cases in some of these folders he considered current, routine, not terribly difficult. These were cases in which the antemortem and postmortem data were good, clear, straightforward.

This would usually involve a clear and complete set of AM fingerprints, possibly from government or police records in the missing person's home country, if a particular country took fingerprints of citizens applying for certain types of employment or for certain licences and permits. Or, if certain individuals had police records or court convictions and had subsequently been reported missing in the tsunami, AM prints would also be easy to obtain.

Then, if a body found after the tsunami yielded up good clear postmortem prints, if the effects of sun and heat and other factors had not caused bloating or skin slippage or decay before PM prints could be taken by the teams of pathologists that descended on Phuket, and if good postmortem prints could be obtained, then Smith's job was relatively easy.

Enter scanned images of the AM prints into the AFIS computer system, enter the scanned PM prints, run a search for possible matches, peer more closely at the various possibles the system put forward, peer even more closely at ridge minutiae and various other details and, presto, a match. Some of the easiest of such early matches of routine AM and PM fingerprints, in fact, were of convicted European pedophiles who had left their home countries to prowl Phuket for prey. The police DVI teams at the disaster scene were all too happy, when court documents and AM fingerprints for known pedophiles arrived in Phuket, to close cases for such unlamented missing persons.

In a pile of other folders on his desk, Smith kept cases not quite so straightforward. For these, the sweating forensic pathologists from Sweden or Denmark or Spain or Australia working at the mortuary compound near the airport could not obtain good-quality fingerprints, even when they thrust a dead hand into boiling water to try to raise dehydrated ridges for inking, even when they entirely removed from a corpse the conical skin of decaying fingertip and slipped it onto one of their own gloved fingers to try to roll the macabre remnant onto an ink pad and obtain a usable print that way. Or perhaps police in Copenhagen or Brussels or New York or any number of other cities where ill-fated tourists had lived were not able to obtain good AM finger marks from a missing person's criminal record, or from a CD collection back home or a photograph album or a collection of Bavarian beer mugs or animal figurines or off a neglected corner of a bathroom mirror. Perhaps the AM marks they could lift were badly smudged or only partial. Perhaps there were no such AM marks to be had at all.

In such cases, people like Smith would have to cooperate more fully with those experts of competing forensic persuasions. With the Stefan Zalms of the world, for example. Perhaps bits of dental evidence about crowns, or fillings or missing incisors could be combined with bits of evidence from finger marks on a prized Bavarian beer mug and a poor-quality mark from a finger or two on a corpse in a numbered body bag in a shipping container in a fenced compound in Phuket, Thailand. Perhaps these bits of information might yield a match that would persuade the Identification Board to officially declare a person dead, located and dead, and cleared for repatriation by air.

Perhaps. But perhaps none of this was enough. Perhaps the pathologists would also have to saw into the femurs of the dead, perhaps they would have placed a section of thigh bone in a sealed plastic container and shipped it off to a laboratory in Sarajevo or Vienna or Tokyo for DNA profiling. Perhaps, after many weeks—for DNA profiling is tricky and expensive and often takes many weeks if it is to be done from bones—that particular profile would match a profile obtained by police at great effort and expense from sweat on a victim's clothing in Munich or in Paris or Dublin. Or from stray hairs on a victim's comb or dried saliva on the once-licked flap of an envelope, a letter he or she had sent while alive to a relative now desperately anxious for word that the departed had been identified.

Perhaps all of these elements would come together and even the files considered very difficult could be closed.

Smith was familiar with all such scenarios, accepted them as part of the work he and others had been assigned to do. He had had his share of successes in such cases. The tsunami file that worried him, however, the problem that began to preoccupy his mind, was in a different category altogether.

Smith had examined the file in question many times. It was a particular challenge; it intrigued him. He had returned to it often to study details on the pink Interpol Missing Persons Form which the international police teams had agreed to use in the days immediately after the tsunami.

Caucasian male, body very badly decomposed. In salt water for days before being washed up in mangroves after that, in an isolated area many kilometres from the tourist beaches. Then baked by the sun for many more days before recovery teams spotted it; filthy, obscenely bloated by corpse gases, with very bad skin slippage, bad insect damage, much sand embedded in the face, eyes missing.

So facial recognition was impossible, despite there being hundreds upon hundreds of photos of missing tourists pinned to the so-called Wall of Hope outside Phuket's main hospital by frantic people looking for the lost, and despite the hundreds of other missing persons' photographs cascading down on the Phuket DVI site from police departments around the globe.

No identity documents were found with the man's naked body, obviously. No jewellery was worn, or at least none had survived the deadly battering by tidal wave. One tattoo, however, was apparent. Not large, very old, very faded, on a forearm. It said simply: *Deutschland.*

The body bore no other distinguishing marks or discernable scars or surgical incisions. There were no deformities of the bones. This man had not been crippled or badly injured in his lifetime. The round head was bald, all but bald. The examining pathologist had indicated on the Interpol form that the dead man was at least 55 years of ago, probably between 60 and 70. The examining dentist had found only a very few fillings, despite the victim's age; the man had been blessed in his lifetime with relatively sound teeth. The postmortem dental X-rays were in the file but no available antemortem X-rays had so far been found to match. A bone section had been taken from the man's right thigh, and then carefully examined and catalogued, perhaps by Conchi herself, but a DNA profile had not yet been completed by European or Japanese labs.

The fingerprints that pathologists had managed to lift from this body were very poor quality indeed. The first layer of skin on the hands had slipped away. What was left of the fingertips yielded, despite boiling water treatment and other measures, all but indecipherable smudges. Smith saw through his examiner's glass some faint whorls here and there on a few fingers, but little else. The AFIS computer, when he ran these prints, yielded no possible matches. None at all. So this case would be a particular challenge.

But there were many such challenging identifications to make in Phuket. Smith did not find this unusual or troubling. What he found troubling was the following: it became clear to him, over the course of many days as he returned somewhat obsessionally to this file to peer again at the faint fingerprints and to run them again through the AFIS system in the vain hope some possible matches would be produced or that some new AM marks might have been entered in recent days, that someone had been tampering with the documents.

At first he thought it was his own mistake, his own faulty recollection of what the file contained. At first he thought he had confused its details with those in the dozens of other documents he looked at in any given week. But, no, he decided no. There could be no doubt. He became convinced that someone was tampering with this file in particular.

A page from the pathologist's examination transcript, for example, Smith one day discovered to be missing. Forensic pathologists call out their findings and observations as they work, while a tape recorder runs. This ghoulish commentary of injuries noted and of distinguishing marks apparent yields a written transcript to be placed in a file. Smith could not remember from his first reading of the transcript exactly what was said on the missing page, but it was clear to him that a page was indeed gone. The transcript pages were numbered, in this case, from one to six. Page two was definitely gone. On reading the preceding and subsequent pages it appeared to Smith that the pathologist might have been describing the appearance of limbs and hands, but this was not clear.

More troubling still was that when Smith returned to the file another time, some of the fingerprints themselves were gone. The Phuket pathology teams, in lifting prints from the dead, used rectangular gummed paper labels pressed against the fingertips. The labels were then stuck onto the postmortem forms for inclusion in the victim's file. Three of these labels, Smith saw when he returned to the file one day, were missing, pulled away from the page in question. Seven prints remained, none of those usable at all. The three that were gone, Smith was certain he recalled, had been poor but of possible, just possible, use if good AM marks could be obtained and if someone like him applied all his skills and the best AFIS electronic enhancement methods.

The last straw, for Smith, was when the file itself disappeared altogether. He was willing to acknowledge that the filing system set up in Phuket was far from ideal. In the chaotic early days just after the disaster there was no real filing system at all. Gradually, as DVI teams and Interpol arrived on the scene and agreed on procedures and as Thai clerical staff arrived from Bangkok and as cabinets and stationery and tags were brought into use, a system of sorts was established.

Files could be borrowed by investigators such as himself and were to be returned after use to a central storage area. Officially, this was to be at the end of each working day but many on the police teams kept difficult files, or incomplete identifications, on their desks for days at time. The file of the man with the

Deutschland tattoo was one such item that Smith himself had frequently kept on his desk overnight.

No, perhaps the missing file folder was not in itself the last straw. The last straw was when Smith, annoyed that the paper file had disappeared, opened up the AFIS system to retrieve the scanned electronic copy of the prints that he had used previously to seek possible matches from the growing bank of antemortem fingerprint data. He could not immediately remember the dead man's body bag number, of course, but he found that after some searching in his notebook. He also remembered approximately what week he had first implemented the AFIS search and he was confident he would recognize the exceptionally poor quality prints, especially because the set had shown only one or two faint whorls on three fingers and the other seven were mere shadows, of no forensic use at all.

He flicked through series after series of AFIS images that he and others had entered into the system around the dates in question. He saw evidence of his many searches, his system interrogations, all with body bag code numbers and other details intact. He saw many, many fingerprints pass before his eyes on the computer screen. But of the record of his search for matches to the *Deutschland* prints, and of the scanned versions of the missing original prints themselves, and of any reference whatsoever to body bag PM68-TA0386, he found no trace at all. It was as if he had never created such a search request. It was as if an electronic search had never taken place. It was as if fingerprints had never been lifted from the *Deutschland* corpse at all.

Jonah Smith was a fingerprint man. And he hardly knew himself in Thailand. But one thing that would never change, despite his new habits and new style and his new colleagues and his new Spanish lover, was his dogged determination to do things right, to do his job as he had always done it—methodically, thoroughly, completely. He was not a man to lose a file or to compromise an investigation or to allow a possible identification, any possible identification, to remain unresolved.

However, the real problem before him this time, the fundamental question, Smith thought over and over again—as he rode his bike to work or as he sat on his balcony at sunset looking at islands or as he lay awake beside Conchi on the nights when she stayed with him until dawn—was not the technical difficulty of the identification itself, or even the details of exactly how the file had gone missing. The fundamental question was the following: *Why would anyone want to prevent the body of a tsunami victim from being identified?*

Chapter 2

The Information Management Centre in Phuket Town had been set up in a disused wing of the cavernous Thai Telecommunications building. The centre was a busy, even a cheery, operation most days, incongruously so given the grim events that preceded its creation.

Over the weeks and months, police and civilian staff who were rotated through the disaster zone from many countries had added the little human touches to be found in any busy office anywhere. Pictures of family were taped to computer terminals. Little animal figurines graced some desktops, along with flowers, boxes of tissues, bottles of mineral water, plastic containers of takeaway food. There was much animated conversation in a variety of languages, much cross-cultural banter, frequent laughter and smiles.

The IMC was like almost any busy police office anywhere, like almost any office of any sort anywhere—crammed with desks and filing cabinets and photocopiers and phones, and with personalities, personal histories, ambitions, rivalries and insecurities.

Smith's large metal desk was in one corner, among those assigned to the Interpol staff that had come out from Lyon. For the moment, the team comprised two perpetually disgruntled French civilian data compilers, Nicole and Sandrine; Ruth

Connolly, the tough-talking Irish press officer; Werner Eberharter, Interpol's portly Austrian deputy team leader, nearing the end of his police career; and Janko Brajkovic, the grim-faced team leader, seconded too many years previously to Interpol from the Croatian police, nowhere near retirement but in no hurry whatsoever to leave his dream sinecure in southern France for a return to Zagreb and the nightmare of Balkan policing. He had been treating the Phuket assignment as an unexpected beachside holiday.

The young French compilers worked with pursed lips at their computer terminals all day in an apparent state of controlled rage. They, like so many of their countrymen and women, were never at ease anywhere except in France. Smith often heard them complaining between themselves in French about their Interpol travel allowances, their hotel rooms, the local food and water, the Thai clerical staff at the IMC, and any number of other things that did not at all live up to their Gallic expectations.

Eberharter and Connolly were not at their desks when Smith came in. Brajkovic was at his, however. He was in a foul humour, clearly hung over, and drinking coffee directly from a red Thermos flask when Smith approached him with his problem. Brajkovic rarely used a cup or a mug for coffee-drinking purposes.

"What, what, what?" he growled when Smith came near. His desk sat under a giant powder blue Interpol flag pinned to the wall behind him. "Leave me alone, Smith. I am in a bad way."

Brajkovic had a very young Thai girlfriend, like many of the expatriate police at the tsunami scene, and his nights were long and arduous. His professional specialty at Interpol was stolen motor vehicles. His personal specialty was girls of barely legal age.

"Janko, I need a word," Smith said.

"Please, Smith, I am in a bad way. No troubles, OK? Please? Go find some bodies, make fingerprints, do something else. Send cadavers home, leave me alone." Brajkovic slurped coffee, wiped his handlebar mustache and his chin. He suddenly raised his left hand high above his head in a hearty greeting as a smiling young Thai clerical assistant walked by the Interpol area with her arms full of wire in-trays destined for desks somewhere else.

"There goes a nice one, Smith," Brajkovic said. "See, behind you. I must examine her for identifying marks at once."

He pretended to get up to go, and then sat down again.

"Janko, there's a problem, I'm afraid," Smith said.

"No, Smith, no," Brajkovic said.

"Yes," Smith said. "A file has gone missing. At least one. Perhaps more. But one I know of. A German victim, I think."

"Smith, don't joke, please. A file missing. Who gives a damn? Please. We are in Thailand. It is like this out here. We are lucky there are any files out here at all. Go back to your desk, go back."

"I was working on this one myself. I had the file on my desk and now it's gone."

"Talk to the fucking Germans then," Brajkovic said. "They have taken it. The bastards only want to identify their own people anyway. Talk to them, not to me."

"I'm sure it wasn't the Germans," Smith said. "They would-n't have known it was on my desk. And, Janko, also, the AFIS file search I created has been deleted from the system."

"Bullshit," Janko said. "You fucked something up. You hit the wrong key, your hand shakes too much with lust for little Spanish tarts, who cares? Create another AFIS search and don't bother me with such things. I'm going for a piss."

Brajkovic stood up. His deeply pockmarked skin glistened with sweat. He did not look well at all.

"I think I am going to be sick," he said. "This goddamn Thai food every night, every night, every night, is going to kill me. You will have to ship me back to Zagreb in a box."

Stefan Zalm was by his desk in the dental forensics section. He was fiddling with an aging turquoise portable dental X-ray apparatus on squeaky wheels. It looked vaguely Soviet in design and vintage.

"They send me this stuff to fix, Jonah," Zalm said, looking up. "What do I know about this sort of thing? They send it all the way over from the mortuary site and think I can fix it."

"Pathologists can't fix these machines, so you'll have to," Smith said. "They think you've probably got one just like it in your surgery back in The Hague. You're the expert."

"Not in this. I am not a technician. And this is junk. They need to just get new equipment. Why do they bother sending this over to me?"

Zalm sat down behind his desk. It was covered with X-rays and files, in no apparent order. A plaster mould of someone's lower dentures served as a paperweight.

"Sit, Jonah," he said. "Why do you visit me during the day anyway? There's no beer here."

"I spoke to Brajkovic about the missing file," Smith said.

"Oh, Jonah, please, not this file business again," Zalm said.

"It's important," Smith said.

"One file among hundreds. There are still about sixteen hundred unidentified bodies in those containers by the airport. You think one file has gone missing. Be sensible, Jonah."

"It was on my desk."

"Among how many others? How can you be sure? Look at my desk. Look at this. Look. Look at everyone's desk around here. It is not like Europe here, Jonah. We are working like the Thais work much of the time."

"No, Stefan. We have a system in place now."

"A system, Jonah, please. Don't be foolish."

"I've decided to go to the operation commanders." Smith said.

"Fool, fool," Zalm said. "They will throw you out of the

office. They have too much to worry about already. Do you think they care about a fingerprint man from Interpol who has lost a file?"

"I didn't lose that file," Smith said gravely.

"OK, OK," Zalm said. "So it has been mislaid. Someone borrowed it from your desk and didn't give it back. They brought it to the Whale Bar by mistake and got drunk and now it's in a rubbish bin somewhere. Some Belgian policeman ate it for a bet."

"Something isn't right about this, Stefan. I've decided to see Braithwaite and Colonel Pridiyathorn about this."

"Jonah, I am telling you as friend, those two are too busy with other things to bother about a missing file. They still have all those unidentified bodies. They have families from Europe camped out here for months waiting for bodies to ship home to bury. Waiting, waiting. They have the international media and the local media asking questions every day about mistaken IDs, about how long all of this is taking, about how many millions of euros it is all costing. Pridiyathorn's people in Bangkok are going to fire him if he doesn't wrap this up soon. Braithwaite's own government, your own damn British government, is on his back every day, every day, to hurry up. The Brits are the worst. Do you think the commanders can care about one missing file? They've got the whole operation to run. Not just your part."

"If files start to go missing like this, we will never finish the work, Stefan. The commanders should know when there has been a breach."

"It's not a breach, Jonah. It is a missing file."

"And my AFIS search? That and a missing file? And the missing pages before that?"

"Jonah, you are an experienced Scotland Yard man. You are my friend. We drink together. You tell me about your wife. I know your girlfriend. I am telling you, don't be crazy. The commanders don't care, they can't care about this. They will each kick you in your ass. Relax. Work on other files."

"No, Stefan," Smith said. "Braithwaite said he could possibly see me this afternoon. Pridiyathorn may be available too."

"Fool," Zalm said.

At lunchtime, Smith liked to get out of the IMC and take a walk through the buzzing streets of Phuket Town. He usually ate at a little roadside noodle stall whose Thai owner was growing richer by the day with the lunch money of foreign police officers. Sometimes Smith would meet Conchi and walk with her to the waterfront where fishermen used to spill their catches onto the pavement for sorting. There were few fishermen now, after the tsunami. Most had given up; the local industry had all but collapsed, after rumours circulated among superstitious locals that deep-sea fish had eaten bodies of the tsunami dead.

Conchi was not in the Spanish DVI section, so Smith walked out of the management centre alone into the steamy heat of the day. The Norwegian woman, Ingrid Stokke, was there again today, on a crumbling concrete bench under a tree, waiting for an investigator, any investigator, to come out so she could ask for a progress report in the search for her missing daughter. Today Mrs. Stokke looked very bad indeed.

"Officer Smith, Officer Smith, one moment please," she said, getting up quickly from her bench.

She looked worse each time Smith ran into her. She had been waiting in Phuket since the day after Christmas, when her daughter, eight years old, had been washed out to sea among hundreds of other victims from the beach near their hotel. Her eleven-year-old son had been badly injured but found alive. Mrs. Stokke's husband had flown back to Oslo with the boy for the urgent surgery that was needed in a properly equipped European hospital. She had stayed on, and was slowly going insane with anxiety and grief and regret.

"Mrs. Stokke, are you all right?" Smith said.

"What news, Officer Smith? Is there news for me today?" she said.

"None that I know of today, Mrs. Stokke," he said. "I can check for you if you like."

It is what all the DVI people had learned to say to Mrs. Stokke each day when she accosted them, asking for news. Identification of the children's bodies, especially the very young, was difficult. Their small hands were often in very bad condition due to bloating and skin slippage, and good fingerprints could not be taken easily. Their teeth contained relatively few fillings and dental X-rays did not help much, if they existed for the missing children at all.

In any case, Smith and others were now convinced that Charlotte Stokke's body had been washed far out to sea. The child could have ended up anywhere. There were reports that the bodies of some Phuket victims were now washing up on beaches in the Maldives, thousands of kilometres away.

"Have any new bodies been located, Officer Smith?" Mrs. Stokke asked.

"A few, over the past couple of days," he said. He paused for a moment. "Adults. No children, I'm afraid."

Mrs. Stokke began to cry softly, as she usually did. She took off her small wire-rimmed glasses and stood crying in the busy street, her head hanging between her bare sunburned shoulders. Her floral cotton tank top was soiled and creased. Smith knew she needed grief counselling in a bad way. He had gently suggested to her many times that she should speak to some of the European counsellors who had come to Thailand to help. He was never sure she had taken his advice.

"Perhaps you should go back to your hotel to rest," Smith said. "Rest is important at times like this."

Rest is important. It is what he had said many times to Fiona after she came back from the hospital when their baby had died. Fiona had cried often in those days, too. Like Mrs. Stokke, her eyes had had the same blank, faraway look of the grief-stricken, of those who have faced tragedy and cannot get tragedy out of their minds.

Fiona carried their dead baby inside her for almost three months. The doctors had insisted on allowing the pregnancy to go to term even though the fetus, their tiny daughter, was dead. Smith never understood why doctors would inflict such torture on a woman. The torture had slowly broken Fiona's spirit, it had changed her fundamentally. It changed their marriage fundamentally. It changed everything.

Smith himself, for years afterward, would think endlessly about his dead daughter. He would fantasize about what she might have looked like as she grew up, what sort of person she might have become. He wondered if she would have been pretty and smart and happy. He even wondered about her hands and fingers. He fantasized, or used to, about what sort of fingerprints were developing inside the womb when she died. Even at the early stages of fetal development, unborn babies have faint prints on their tiny fingertips. Smith used to think for hours about his daughter's tiny fingers.

For some reason, today, he said to Mrs. Stokke: "I lost a daughter once. My wife and I know a little about how you must feel."

Mrs. Stokke looked up at him through tear-filled eyes, too sad to share anyone else's grief. She ignored what he had said.

"I need to see my Charlotte," she said. "Even if it is just her body. I can't just leave her out in the sea. I need to see her body. At least this."

Smith had never seen his dead daughter's body. He was never sure exactly what the hospital did with the fetus after Fiona's body had at last expelled it. There had been no postmortem identification process required in that particular disaster scene.

"We're doing everything we can, Mrs. Stokke. I'm sure we will find your daughter for you eventually," Smith said.

"But she will be dead," Mrs. Stokke said.

Smith paused. "Yes," he said. "After all these weeks, I'm sorry to say you will have to expect she will be dead."

"That is what Sergeant Vollebaek says to me all the time," she said.

Magne Vollebaek was a Norwegian missing persons detective who came out to Phuket periodically with antemortem information from Oslo about little Charlotte Stokke, and others. He had made it his mission in life, it seemed, to help the Stokke family as much as he could, to speed the identification of their daughter as much as he could. Smith had spoken to him many times, about various AM finger marks Vollebaek had come up with so far for the missing girl. None had matched any of the children's bodies at the mortuary site. And now there weren't many children's bodies left at the site.

"Sergeant Vollebaek is a very good policeman," Smith said. "He's doing all he can. We're all trying to help you."

"I know that," she said. "I am grateful for what you all do here."

"You should get some rest," Smith said. "Rest is important at times like this."

Smith had eventually stopped saying that to his wife when their daughter went missing in the womb. Fiona could never rest after the baby died. He and Fiona were never at rest as a couple again. She blamed him somehow, Smith came to realize. In her mind, crazed with anxiety and grief and regret, Fiona came to believe that Smith had failed in some way, had failed to protect their baby in some way, had failed to advise her of some necessary precaution. It was as if she thought the wife and the unborn child of a Scotland Yard man should be automatically protected from disaster.

Every day during the Thailand DVI operation, there was a formal meeting of representatives of all the international teams.

This took place in a large meeting room in the management centre, with participants seated at a giant horseshoe of adjoining tables carefully fitted out with bright blue cloths, black microphones, fresh notepads and pens, bottles of mineral water. Behind the tables at the front sat the joint commanders and other senior Thai and international officials, under a banner designed specifically for the operation, emblazoned with the words *Thai Tsunami Victim Identification Operation—TTVI* and the bizarre image of a stick figure running away from a stylized killer wave.

These meetings had become routine. They were conducted primarily in English and all went very slowly as Thai translators repeated every word for local police and officials. The spokesman for a country's DVI team would make a report or raise a problem or an issue that needed to be discussed. The reports usually involved the need for some piece of equipment or more funds to finance the expensive identification and repatriation effort the beleaguered Thai government had been saddled with after the tsunami struck.

Smith occasionally sat in on these meetings, had in fact acted as spokesman for the Interpol team when Brajkovic or Eberharter were away or hung over or otherwise indisposed. Today, he attended in the hope that Braithwaite or Colonel Pridiyathorn would see him afterward about his concerns.

As he walked in to the meeting hall and took his place at a row of observers' chairs at the side, away from the main tables, the Austrian team leader was speaking.

"We respectfully request that new computer servers be obtained for the heavy volume of incoming AM data," the Austrian representative said, leaning toward his microphone. "We believe that the current servers are without sufficient capacity for this work and that this is leading to inefficiencies. We believe that as more and more DNA profiles begin to arrive . . ."

Braithwaite cut the Austrian off from the head table.

"Noted," he said. Braithwaite was a tough Detective Chief Superintendent from Scotland Yard, and Smith knew him well. His angular features, tiny teeth and beaklike nose made him look like a bird of prey. He had a formidable reputation in London for tenacity in major crime investigations. He had been sent out to Phuket as part of the frantic efforts by a British government under intense domestic pressure to account for all 121 of the British missing as soon as possible. Braithwaite took his Thailand assignment very seriously indeed, as if his career depended on it. It quite possibly did.

The Austrian team leader looked aggrieved.

"Noted, thank you," Braithwaite said again.

He turned to Colonel Pridiyathorn, a career Thai police-man who had been given the similarly uninviting assignment by Thailand to help coordinate, with Braithwaite, the entire DVI operation. More than four thousand drownings altogether and tourists from 35 countries missing.

"Colonel, can you approach donor countries to see what can be done?" Braithwaite said.

"Yes, I will see to it," Pridiyathorn said gravely, noting the request on a yellow legal pad. His face was heavily lined. Smith doubted the colonel had been getting more than four hours' sleep a night since December.

Pridiyathorn wore a green Thai police uniform, complete with holstered sidearm. Braithwaite was in a generic blue police-man's shirt, not London Metropolitan Police issue, with the added feature of special button-on "TTVI IMC Commander" insignia on the epaulettes. Thai designers had been very busy making up banners and regalia after the disaster.

"Thank you, Austria," Braithwaite said. "Other issues?"

Smith thought for a moment of raising his hand to describe the problem of the missing *Deutschland* file, but did not. A face-to-face session with Braithwaite would be more effective.

"Transport services could use a new fax machine," said an

American voice. "Ours has packed it in."

"Noted," Braithwaite said, looking over to Pridiyathorn, who entered the request on his pad. "Anything else?"

No one else in the hall raised their hand.

"Good," Braithwaite said. "Now, confirmed identifications?"

Smith daydreamed as the various teams droned on about identifications made. After some initial mistakes in January, a proper coronial system and the Identification Board had been introduced in Phuket, with checks and double-checks and cross-checks so that all identifications were solid. As the month of April approached, no foreigner's body left Phuket before the most senior Thai officials and the DVI commanders themselves were convinced the identification was correct.

Detective Chief Superintendent Adrian Braithwaite of the London Metropolitan Police had one of the very few enclosed offices in the management centre. It had likely belonged to the man who ran the telephone exchange in the building years ago. The fact that it was enclosed meant that the modern air-conditioning system installed in the main working areas did not help out much in Braithwaite's space. A small Toshiba cooling unit had been installed in the window facing onto the street, and a revolving floor fan near the door. Both hummed steadily, but Braithwaite was still suffering.

His face was beaded with sweat and he regarded Smith contemptuously across his large red-hued wooden desk, another relic from the previous occupant. Braithwaite's blue shirt was randomly mottled darker blue with dampness. His large malodorous cigar dribbled ash.

"You're not actually a sworn police officer, if I remember correctly, are you Smith? You're a civilian, if I remember correctly," Braithwaite said as he tried to unload cigar ash into a souvenir FBI coffee mug he kept on his desk for that purpose.

Smith knew that if Braithwaite was playing the civilian card, the time spent that afternoon explaining his concerns about the missing file had been wasted.

"Yes, sir. Twenty-one years this year."

"That long," Braithwaite said.

"Yes, sir."

"I suppose after all those years, civilian employees of the Met Police could be forgiven for thinking they can somehow acquire investigative skills by osmosis."

Braithwaite tapped his cigar, hoping Smith would take offence.

"I've worked alongside police officers on a lot of difficult cases," Smith said.

"Have you now," Braithwaite said, plugging his cigar back between his lips.

"Yes, sir."

"Well, let me tell you about how things are in this particular little case I have been assigned to solve," Braithwaite said. "There is the matter of a tidal wave killing twenty thousand people all around the Indian Ocean, that big body of water a little way off Brighton Pier. As you have been working alongside sworn police officers on this particularly difficult little case, you will be aware that there are still some fifteen hundred unidentified bodies here in Phuket alone, which makes it one of the biggest forensic disaster scenes in history, along with, let's see, Bosnia after the unpleasantness over there when Yugoslavia was falling to bits. Or, of course, that other bit of unpleasantness back in Europe, the Holocaust."

Smith said nothing, simply waiting for the tsunami of Braithwaite bile to recede.

"You're not Jewish are you, Smith? No offence intended," Braithwaite asked with a tight smile.

Smith said nothing.

"I have been given the unfortunate task of overseeing along

with my esteemed Thai police colleagues the whole damn identification process, from start to finish. From start to bloody
finish," Braithwaite said, gathering steam now. His cigar ash
glowed red.

"I have problems and cock-ups and catastrophes every
bloody day here in this sweltering office in this godforsaken little
southeast Asian country," he said. "Every day of my bloody life
now there is some major cock-up. I am not even going to begin
to give you details of the problems I have running this operation,
Smith, as you are not a sworn police officer. I am just going to tell
you that I have no time to waste whatsoever. I have no time to
talk to a civilian Scotland Yard fingerprint technician who after
mislaying a file, one file out of how many, fifteen hundred or so,
comes into my office on the hottest day in history and begins
yammering on about some bloody conspiracy theory he has
hatched over too many Singha beers at the Whale fucking Bar
about how someone has taken the time, as we all have time on
our hands here, to remove pages from a pathologist's report and
then to remove fingerprint evidence from that same file and then
to tamper with an AFIS computer file and to then steal . . ."

"I did not say steal, sir," Smith said.

". . . and to then steal a file from under the noses of some of
the most experienced police officers from, what, two dozen countries who have been foolish enough to volunteer or to be
volunteered for this most thankless investigative task."

Braithwaite's face had become very red.

"I strongly believe something odd is happening with this
particular file, sir," Smith said.

"Something odd is happening in this goddamn cubbyhole
of an office, Smith," Braithwaite said. "Too many people are
coming in here to whine to me about minor problems they face
in their work. If you have lost a file, or if some little Thai secre-
tary has lost a file, that is a very, very small problem compared to
the ocean of problems I am facing here each and every day, along

with Colonel Pridiyathorn and some other very, very senior sworn police officers who are trying to get a big job done."

"I'm sorry you feel that way, sir," Smith said. "Every identification is important."

"What on earth is that supposed to mean, Smith?"

"With respect, sir, I don't believe we can just say 'oh well' when a file goes missing. Any file."

Braithwaite looked like he was going to spontaneously combust in the heat and in his rage.

"Are you accusing me of saying 'oh well' about something, Smith?"

"Not accusing you, sir," Smith said.

"Who are you accusing, exactly? And what are you accusing someone else, not me, of, exactly?"

"I am not accusing anyone for the moment," Smith said.

"For the moment," Braithwaite said. "What is that supposed to mean?"

"I would like to get to the bottom of this if I can," Smith said.

Braithwaite was so incensed he stood up behind his desk and jammed his cigar into the ash mug on his desk.

"Smith, let me be clear about this. I want you to listen very carefully to this. I want no pathetic amateur sleuthing going on during this operation, no bullshit wild goose chases over a minor clerical error. What on earth can you be thinking of? There is nothing to get to the bottom of in this, Smith. A file has been mislaid or lost. This happens in a place like this. It will turn up or it will not turn up, but I want you to cease and desist immediately with these harebrained conspiracy theories and get on with your work. I know the Secretary-General of Interpol personally. He has been out here on a visit and I know him from the old days anyway and I'm warning you, Smith, that if you persist in wasting my time and your time when you are out here in Phuket I will pick up the phone and have your ass hauled back to Lyon so fast your head will spin. I was never clear how you finagled that cushy little secondment to Interpol anyway and I can see now that it's gone completely to your head. You're a fingerprint technician, Smith. You're not a police officer. You know fuck-all about investigations and I will not have you trying to get to the bottom of anything except the pile of fingerprint IDs sitting on your desk. Are we clear on this, Smith? Because I want you to be very clear on this. And I now want you to get the hell out of my office."

Smith stood up.

"I'm sorry you feel that way, sir," he said.

"Out," Braithwaite said.

Smith stood up. "Sir," he said.

"And, Smith," Braithwaite said. "If I hear of you bothering Colonel Pridiyathorn or the Germans or anybody else with any of this nonsense, after our little attitude meeting here today, I will have your guts for garters. Before I have your body shipped back to France. Or London. Or wherever. Understood?"

Smith did not intend to immediately ignore Braithwaite's orders, but he had to pass the German DVI section on the way back to his desk. Three of the team were there, in their identical spotless white golf shirts, two standing, one sitting, and all intently studying what looked like a series of numerical DNA data on a laptop computer. Smith knew one of them by name, Peter Hamel, a bearded Landeskriminalamt officer from a small city in some northern German state. The other two, Smith had seen almost every day but had not got to know.

Hamel looked up, grinning as Smith walked by.

"Professor Smith, Professor Smith," Hamel called out, nudging one of his colleagues with an elbow. "Have you located by any chance the missing *Deutschland* file?"

Smith had approached Hamel when he first started trying to locate the file. Hamel, however, had been interested only insofar as the missing person in question had a tattoo that almost certainly made him a German national.

"Have you?" Smith said.

"Not our responsibility, Professor," Hamel said. His hand wandered as it always did to the bad comb-over he used, ineffectively, to cover his sunburned balding pate. "We are models of German efficiency in this section. We are not prone to, how shall I say, file loss."

Hamel's colleagues chuckled. Smith looked over his shoulder, hoping Braithwaite would not see him with the German team so soon after their meeting. *I am becoming paranoid,* Smith thought.

"Or erection loss," one of the other Germans said. All three of them laughed extravagantly.

"Did you lose anything else lately with your little Spanish sweetheart, Professor?" Hamel said. "She would be a challenge for someone of your age, I would imagine. Lose anything else lately, Professor?"

"Send her over to the German section if you feel you need assistance in this regard, Herr Professor," said a German with the name "Krupp" embroidered on his team shirt. "We can be of assistance in this regard, with a lovely little woman like this."

"Krupp," Smith said. "I would have thought you and your team would be more concerned that a file probably pertaining to an unidentified German body has gone missing."

"We are most concerned, Herr Professor," Krupp said. "It is a most unfortunate matter. We have in fact informed our team leader about this and you will be happy to know that another pathological examination of this body has been deemed appropriate."

"Simple," Hamel said. "A file is lost by Interpol and we Germans will compile a new one. Simple."

Smith stood silently for a moment, resisting the urge to argue with them or to repeat his concerns. He turned away and walked back toward his section, saying nothing.

"Lose anything else lately, Herr Professor?" Krupp called out after him. "Any other difficulties of a more intimate nature you wish to discuss with your colleagues?"

That night, Smith lay awake for a long time after he and Conchi had made love. She was staying overnight at his hotel more frequently now. He wondered where all of this business with Conchi might lead. *Nowhere*, he thought. *Nowhere*. He wondered whether Fiona was lying beside someone in their cramped bedroom back in London. She had not called him or emailed him at all during his time in Phuket. He sent her occasional emails with news, for form's sake.

Conchi slept soundly, face down, uncovered from the waist up. Her bare back moved up and down rhythmically as she dreamed. Smith lay on his back with a hand behind his head on the pillow. His head was spinning a little from the Mekong whisky they had drunk after dinner. His head was spinning as he analyzed his encounter with Braithwaite and tried to decide what, if any, his next steps should be.

While they were eating dinner at his small table, Conchi had said again, as Zalm had done many times, as Braithwaite had warned him so forcefully, to simply let it go.

"Jonah, Jonah, Jonah, relax," Conchi said. "Why do you want to identify this one body so much?"

"It's what I do, Conchi. I find out who people are."

"You make too much of one thing."

"I know. I do. That's how I am, I suppose," he said.

"Yes, Jonah. Good boy. You see this about yourself," she said.

"But you love me anyway, correct?" he said. "For now."

"For now, yes," Conchi said, smiling at him over her tiny glass of Mekong.

Sometime after Smith at last fell asleep that night, very late, someone pounded ferociously on the hotel room door. He woke with a start; Conchi woke with a start. He heard shouts from the other side of the door. It sounded like someone shouting in German.

"Jonah, what is this now?" Conchi said, sitting up and pulling a sheet to her shoulders. She was dazed by sleep and the sudden awakening. "Who is this in the middle of the night?"

She seemed truly frightened. Smith got up and wrapped himself in a towel. The pounding at the door continued. It was definitely someone speaking German, cursing and grumbling it seemed, in German. He heard his name called out as well.

He looked through the peephole of the door.

"Who is it, Jonah, at this time of the night?" Conchi called out from the bedroom.

Smith recognized who it was. It was Becker, a pathologist Smith knew by sight. A civilian who had come out to help the German DVI team with the identification effort. Becker was older by far than most of the other pathologists who had gathered in Phuket—in his late fifties or early sixties. Smith had heard it said that he was one of the most senior and respected pathologists at Frankfurt's main military hospital.

Smith opened the door. Becker stood swaying slightly in the corridor, an angry bulldog of a man—small, muscular despite his age and possibly dangerous when aroused. He held in one hand a bottle of Chivas Regal whisky and an unlit pipe. He had food crumbs in his tightly trimmed grey beard. A pair of wire spectacles was perched precariously on his shining bald pate.

"At last you open your fucking door to me, like a man," Becker said. "I will come in now."

"No, just a minute. No," Smith said. "What's all this about?"

He stood firmly in the door frame, blocking Becker's way.

"I will come in to this apartment," Becker shouted.

"Who is it, Jonah?" Conchi called from the bedroom.

"What do you want, Becker?" Smith said.

"It is what you want, that is what I have come to discuss man to man with you, you British *scheissker* bastard. It is what you want," Becker said, swaying slightly.

"What do you mean, for heaven's sake," Smith said.

"You know exactly well what I mean, *scheissker* bastard," Becker said. "I am here to discuss your plot to discredit me and my team and my country. You want to make us all look like imbeciles."

"What are you talking about?" Smith said.

"You know, British bastard, what I am talking about," Becker shouted. "You know you have spread lies, for what reason I cannot imagine, about me personally and my colleagues, with the commanders. And maybe now the press. Is that next, British bastard?"

"Becker, be quiet, be quiet. It's late, people are sleeping."

"Too bad, too bad, too bad. I will wake them all up to tell them what you the bastard have done. You are spreading lies about me and that file, you will stop this immediately. Immediately you must stop this campaign against me or I swear, Smith bastard, there will be trouble. I am accustomed to dealing with people like you; I have been a medical doctor for forty years now. Do you think some British bastard can ruin my reputation in a few days? Bastard, bastard."

"Becker, you're drunk. Go home to bed."

"You will stop this campaign immediately, do you hear me? We Germans do not lose files, we do not tamper with files, you will stop this campaign against me immediately or there will be trouble."

"You're drunk," Smith said. "Go home to bed."

He closed the door firmly and attached the burglar chain. Becker stayed for a while outside the door grumbling in German and hurling accusations. Eventually, Smith heard him moving away from the door and the corridor fell silent.

Smith and his Spanish girlfriend watched from their balcony on the sixth floor as Becker came out of the hotel. Conchi had wrapped herself in a sheet. They watched as the aging pathologist strode purposefully out from under the driveway awning and straight to a white Toyota in the parking area. Few of the international DVI staff ever drove cars in Phuket. Almost everyone used local minibuses or taxis or they were ferried around in Thai police vehicles or walked or rode bikes.

Becker did not look up. He strode quickly to the car, no longer swaying, no longer carrying a bottle. He reached into his pocket for car keys, opened the driver's door and got in without hesitation or difficulty. He started the engine, waited a moment and drove off slowly, signalling a left turn as he exited the hotel grounds.

"Is that him?" Conchi said.

"Yes," Smith said.

"Are you sure he was drunk?"

Smith watched as Becker's car lights disappeared in the darkness.

"The good doctor sobers up very quickly indeed," he said.

Chapter 3

nto the belly of this beast came Frank Delaney, information gatherer. This is how he preferred to think of himself nowadays. A simple gatherer of information. How he eventually used the information gathered, and on whose behalf, depended very much on circumstances. He had grown comfortable with such professional and moral ambiguities.

The last time Delaney had gathered information in Thailand was in early 2001. The ambiguities of that little misadventure almost got him killed by the Burmese military and had almost got Kate Hunter killed, just at the stage in their on-again, off-again relationship when he was finally letting down the last of his defences. He had neither expected nor wanted to be back in Thailand so soon.

Like most of his journalistic and spying assignments in recent years, the Phuket business came to him by accident, through no particular inclination of his own. Usually these things started because someone had an unanswered question. Sometimes it was an ordinary person, sometimes an editor, sometimes it was a spy, often it was Canada's national spy service itself asking, more or less officially, for assistance. In all cases, people with questions were attracted to Delaney because it was his special talent to find answers on behalf of others.

If he was lucky—and Delaney had no illusions anymore about how much his journalistic and other information-gathering successes had to do with luck—he found answers to questions that were far bigger than the players initially realized.

Delaney was in Phuket for *International Geographic* magazine, his main outlet for freelance stories and income at this stage of his erratic career. He had burned almost as many media bridges in Canada as there were left to burn. The bridge to the Canadian Security Intelligence Service was smouldering, if no longer in full flame. The Thailand and Burma business of 2001 had cost him his columnist's job at the *Montreal Tribune,* and his sometime handlers at CSIS had shunned him for almost a year afterward, ostensibly because he had ignored their orders not to publish what he found out about a bizarre, ill-fated plot to kidnap Burma's pro-democracy leader, Aung San Suu Kyi.

But *International Geographic,* based in Washington and therefore comfortably removed from Canadian media and spy service machinations, had a long history of taking on people like himself with a lot of experience in trouble spots around the world and with few family or other ties to prevent them from accepting assignments that required week after week on the road. The magazine paid exceptionally well, did not quibble about expenses, always provided Delaney with the best photographers and gave him a very good spread when he was actually ready with a story. This time, they had told him to take as long as he needed to produce the definitive piece about the international disaster victim identification operation after the tsunami.

Delaney had been on the story now for almost six weeks. He had travelled to Indonesia to have a look at what was going on there after the waves crashed through Banda Aceh. In that case, once the authorities assured themselves there were few, if any, Western victims, they simply began piling bodies in mass graves and refusing most offers of international DVI assistance. Delaney had subsequently been to Sri Lanka and the Maldives, badly hit, yes, but not like Thailand. Now he was in Phuket to report on the biggest, and most politicized, of all the postdisaster operations in the affected region.

Delaney first encountered Jonah Smith, appropriately enough, at a brief funeral ceremony near the TTVI mortuary compound, with its long rows of refrigerated shipping containers crammed with bodies. Smith was standing beside him under an awning in the hot breeze, watching a profusely sweating priest in white robes reading prayers in Swedish and leading shell-shocked relatives of the dead in mournful Nordic hymns as they stood before five coffins, each draped with their country's flag.

Whenever bodies of foreign nationals were officially identified in Phuket, they were placed in simple wooden coffins, appropriate flags were obtained, religious officials summoned and send-off ceremonies hastily arranged. Casually dressed police officers from the international teams were pressed into service as pallbearers.

This time, five Toyota station wagons in various colours waited to transport coffins to the airport for the long flight home to Stockholm. The Thai drivers stood to one side under the meagre shade of a palm tree, smoking cigarettes. The tall thin man Delaney would soon come to know as Jonah Smith watched the ceremony solemnly, polishing his spectacles with the end of his Hawaiian-style shirt while family members wept tears of sorrow and relief. Delaney's photographer, a young pony-tailed American freelancer named Tim Bishop, snapped pictures with a telephoto lens from a discreet distance away.

"Family?" Delaney asked.

"Police," Smith said, putting his glasses back on.

"DVI?"

"Yes. I'm a fingerprint man."

They watched together as the pallbearers loaded Toyotas with the dead. A middle-aged couple in immaculate white resort wear clasped each other tightly as the coffin nearest them was lifted into one of the cars. Delaney scribbled a few words in his notebook

"Reporter?" Smith asked.

Delaney felt the familiar pang of ambivalence, and of caution, when someone asked that question now. *Yes,* he thought. *Usually. Whenever I am not renting out my services to spies.*

"Yes," he said to Smith. "Don't be alarmed."

"I'd be out here, too, if I worked for a newspaper and not for the police," Smith said.

"I'm with *International Geographic* magazine. For this story, anyway. . . . Frank Delaney."

He extended his hand. Smith shook it.

"Jonah Smith."

"British," Delaney said. "Right? Scotland Yard?"

"Yes. But living in France. I'm working for Interpol now."

"Ah, Interpol," Delaney said. "Lots of your guys out here."

"Yes," Smith said.

They watched as the hearses headed out in convoy toward the airport. The couple in white did not move. They just stood gazing out wistfully until all the cars had disappeared. They still did not unclasp their arms from around each other's shoulders. The priest approached them and said something softly in Swedish. Still the couple did not move.

"There is a lady, from Norway," Smith said as they watched the grieving Swedes. "She has been waiting here ever since Christmas for a chance to see her daughter off like this. She hangs around the management centre in town and asks every copper who comes out why they haven't found her little girl. Every day. Just about every day, for three months."

"And will you be able to find the girl?"

"She may already be found," Smith said. "Charlotte is her name. The hard job is picking her out from among all the bodies in the containers over there behind that fence. The way things are going."

Delaney wasn't sure what Smith meant by that last remark, although it would become all too clear in the days to come. Nor could Delaney at that early stage accurately read everything in the dark expression that suddenly came over Smith's face. It showed sadness, resignation, weariness; perhaps frustration, perhaps even anger. Delaney had seen a range of emotions displayed in the aftermath of the tsunami, had dutifully scribbled his observations about these in his reporter's notebook. But this was something different.

Delaney met Bishop at the end of each day for a debrief and to look at photos and plan the next day's reporting. Bishop was sitting in the bar of the Metropole Hotel, where most of the international media stayed when they came in for the tsunami story. As Delaney arrived, a BBC TV crew was heading out through the revolving glass doors, fumbling with cameras and microphones and aluminum equipment cases. They were doing up a big documentary report, it was said, with carte blanche access to all areas. The word in the hotel bar was that the UK government, very keen to get the word out that it was doing all it could to find British bodies, had leaned hard on the British DVI commander to play ball with the BBC.

Bishop was not like most of the photojournalists Delaney had worked with in war zones and disaster zones for more than two decades. Bishop was 31, and of a new breed—healthy, clean-living, well-adjusted, compulsive only about the work. He was a vegetarian and neither drank nor smoked. He jogged each morning no matter where he was on assignment, except if someone was likely to shoot at him while he ran. He spent almost all of his time on the road, working for any magazine or newspaper or news agency that wanted pictures. Delaney knew that Bishop kept a small apartment somewhere in a rundown part of Paris but was rarely there. He was looking at photos on his Macintosh laptop when Delaney came into the freezing air conditioning of the hotel bar.

"Hey Frank, I got some real good shots of that funeral service this morning," Bishop called out when he saw Delaney approaching. He pushed the computer over as Delaney sat down at the low round table. "Have a look at these. Might be a cover shot in there somewhere."

Bishop picked up what looked like a lemonade and slurped at it contentedly through a straw. He took a piece of ice in his mouth and crunched it energetically. A waiter came over. Delaney ordered a beer.

"Bit late in the day for lemonade, isn't it Tim?" Delaney said.

"Funny guy. Bit early for a beer?"

Delaney liked Bishop, had worked with him a number of times. But it was their assignment together in Iraq that had cemented the relationship. Delaney got himself, and Bishop, into bad trouble in 2003 and bad trouble always creates an unbreakable bond between journalists, if the troubles end happily and sometimes even if they don't. Delaney and Bishop had been lucky. They had refused to swim along with the media tide and wait for briefings or official "embeds" with U.S. troops gathering for the Iraq invasion. Instead, they rented a four-wheel drive in Kuwait and simply drove it deep into southern Iraq just hours before the fighting started.

They were eventually arrested by a squad of very, very agitated Iraqi soldiers. They never saw their rental car or their computers and photo gear again. They were interrogated and slapped around and shouted at for two days, accused of spying for the invaders, and then they were driven all the way across Iraq, under heavy bombardment, to be placed under house arrest at the Palestine Hotel in Baghdad. Why they were not simply executed in the desert, Delaney could never understand. Bishop had handled the situation well, hadn't panicked, and when it was over it gave both of their careers a big boost—Bishop early in his career; Delaney much nearer to the end of his own. Delaney got a strong story for *International Geographic* and Bishop got great pictures in Baghdad, after the Americans arrived and he had managed to buy himself a new camera.

Delaney's misadventures in Iraq had also given things a boost between himself and Kate Hunter. There is nothing like a life and death assignment, Delaney had found, to attract a new lady friend or to paper over problems with an existing one. He and Kate had had a very good stretch after the Burma debacle, right through until mid-2002. She had battled past the defences he erected after Natalia died, well before Kate came along. He had battled past his own defences as well, after Burma, and after he had once again led a woman he thought he might be in love with into danger. He got past blaming himself for Natalia's death and stopped swimming against the tide of his relationship with Kate.

For a while, it worked. Then Kate, as he expected, wanted more, wanted domesticity and almost-marital bliss. When she didn't get it, she hooked up with a policeman who worked with her at the RCMP and she lived with him in Montreal for more than year while Delaney played globetrotting journalist and, increasingly, spy. She threw herself into her police work, more and more important after the 9/11 attacks, of investigating sources of terrorist funding with Canadian traces. Delaney threw himself back into whatever his information-gathering skills yielded in the way of clients, journalistic or otherwise. But his near-death experience in Iraq had given both of them a jolt and now he and Kate were back on again as a couple. Just.

Bishop didn't bother with women, it seemed. He took pictures in hell holes, drank lemonade and jogged. He never talked about his family back in Boston and Delaney never brought it up. The pictures Bishop had taken that morning at the funeral were excellent. He had gone in tight, to the emotions on the faces of the Swedish mourners and the priest.

"What's up for tomorrow, Frank?" Bishop asked.

"I'm going to put in a request to interview a Scotland Yard fingerprint guy, so we'll probably need some head shots of him and some of him working at a screen, or whatever," Delaney said. "I think that will come off. Still waiting for word on whether I can get Braithwaite, the commander."

"OK," Bishop said. "I may go back over to the mortuary site tomorrow morning until you hear. Do up some arty shots of the containers, maybe."

"Dinner?"

"A quick one maybe," Bishop said. "I want to Photoshop some of these pics from today. I've got emails to write. And there's a documentary on CNN tonight I want to watch."

"Party animal," Delaney said.

"The guys in fedoras are all dying off, Frank. Too much hard living."

"I've never worn a fedora in my life."

"Stop the presses. Hold the front page. Sweetheart, get me rewrite," Bishop said with a grin.

"Fuck off, Tim."

"You've got no one to play with anymore."

"Thank you very much."

"It's the twenty-first century," Bishop said.

"Unfortunately," Delaney said.

Interpol's press officer was having another shouting match with the Kendall man. Delaney had seen her do that the first day he arrived in Phuket. This time, Ruth Connolly was shouting at the Kendall man under a tree just outside the management centre. She didn't seem to care who overheard.

"You guys are not even police officers, for fuck's sake," Connolly roared. "I've told you over and over to back off and stop issuing press releases. I won't have it."

It was the same issue Delaney had heard Connolly shouting about on the day he arrived. She had been given the unenviable assignment of coming out to Phuket from Lyon to wrest control of the media machinery from Kendall International, a giant company that specialized in postdisaster relief logistics. Kendall was based in Australia but active all around the world. The company had put their people on planes in the first hours after news of the tsunami broke on agency wires. Before the world's police had got to Phuket to help with the massive DVI effort, Kendall had signed lucrative contracts with the Thais for high-priced pathology equipment, body bags, refrigeration units, coffins, food services, transport aircraft—anything the overwhelmed Thai officials needed or were told they needed.

Kendall's media team was savvy, aggressive and effective. Before Connolly arrived, they had the all-important first few days with the world's media all to themselves. They issued press releases one after the other extolling their company's services and they called press conferences in which their people had sat alongside senior Thai police and military, reassuring the world that everything that could be done was being done.

Interpol, and a score of national police forces, now badly wanted a piece of the media action to satisfy their home constituencies that they were front and centre on the scene. Months after the disaster, however, Kendall's PR chief, a weather-beaten former Australian television journalist named Gary Clarke, was doggedly standing his ground, if only because his job now paid him many times what he could ever dream of earning in the media, and his job very much depended on success in places like this.

"You can't stop a global company or any company for that matter from issuing a press release if it bloody well wants to, Ruth. Even Interpol can't stop us from doing that," he said.

"You guys make me want to puke," Connolly said. "You're just out here peddling your wares and you've got the Thais by the short and curlies. If you want to issue a press release even remotely connected to this police operation, you come to me first. I've been telling you that for weeks. How do you know what I might have planned for the damn media on any given day?"

"I don't have to coordinate my media strategy with yours, Ruth," Clarke shouted back

"Your strategy is just to make your bloody shareholders rich," Connolly shouted.

"And yours is just to make Interpol look good," Clarke shouted back.

"I'm representing all the teams here, Gary," she said.

"Bullshit," Clarke said.

They both noticed Delaney at the same time.

"Are we on the record here, my friends?" Delaney said with a smile, and coming closer. "May I quote you on some of this perhaps?"

"Fuck off, Delaney," Connolly said, reaching into her shoulder bag for a cigarette. "We're on the record when I say we're on the record."

Clarke lit a cigarette as well.

"Ms. Connolly is practising her inimitable scorched-earth policy of media relations," Clarke said. "She'll have me arrested next."

"I'm thinking about that very thing," Connolly said, taking a ferocious drag on her foul-smelling Thai smoke. She was tall, busty, broad-shouldered and strikingly attractive. She wore an Interpol baseball cap and her long auburn hair was tightly tied back. Delaney thought when they met for the first time that she would make an outstanding undercover drugs officer. Perhaps she had done such work in Ireland in her pre-Interpol incarnation.

"What do you want from me now anyway, Delaney?" she said. "Nobody still reads *International Geographic* anymore, do they? Except in dentist offices?"

"I'll leave you to your fate," Clarke said to Delaney. "Ruth, shall we leave this for another day?"

"Just keep your overpaid spin monkeys off their typewriters from now on," she said.

Clarke laughed as he moved off. "Good luck, Delaney," he called out over his shoulder.

Connolly watched intently as Clarke got into a gleaming emerald-coloured Land Cruiser with Kendall logos emblazoned everywhere.

"He is one scumbag," she said bitterly. She laughed, however, as she looked over at Delaney. "Off the record, of course."

"Ah, the politics of international police cooperation," Delaney said.

"They're not even fucking police," Connolly said bitterly. "That's what gets my goat."

"Not everyone can be police," Delaney said.

"Pity," she said. "Now what are you going to bother me about today, Delaney? Can't you see I'm busy alienating the global business community? Haven't you got enough for a little magazine story yet? You've been prowling around here for days and days."

"I'm still waiting for my interview with Adrian Braithwaite," Delaney said.

"I've made the request," Connolly said. "He's a busy man."

"And I'd like to talk to a fingerprint expert now. One of your guys actually. Ex Scotland Yard, now at Interpol."

"Smith," she said.

"Jonah Smith. That's right."

"He's not the brightest spark, our Jonah," she said. "Fantastic at what he does, but . . ."

"Dull?" Delaney said.

"Yes, rather."

"This is not for TV, Ruth."

"Lucky."

"What do you think?"

"What about a DNA person?"

"Fingerprints are yielding a lot of identifications around here. Or so I'm told."

"By Smith, for example."

"And others."

"OK, let's make a deal," Connolly said. "I'll give you Smith, but you talk to one of the DNA guys as well. Keep the peace between the warring camps."

"I would have asked you for a DNA angle at some point anyway, once I get a handle on these things," Delaney said.

"If you haven't got a handle on things after this long, Delaney, you'll never get one. If you don't mind me saying," Connolly said with a giant smile. "How complicated is it?"

"That's what I'm trying to find out."

"OK, well, you can talk to Smith," she said. "But I'll find you a DNA man too. OK?"

"All right," Delaney said. "A two for one sale. Plus Braithwaite thrown in."

"Braithwaite will cost you, my dear Mr. Delaney," she said, batting her eyes in a poor imitation of a screen vamp.

"You wouldn't be flirting with a member of the press, would you Officer Connolly?"

"Good gracious, no," Connolly said, smiling ever more broadly. "Never. Those days are gone."

"You're the second person who's found it necessary to remind me of that in two days," Delaney said.

"There is a message in there for you somewhere," Connolly said.

Delaney didn't get to sit down with Smith until two days later. And Smith didn't tell Delaney about the blackmail attempt until very late in the interview. Delaney didn't think Smith had purposely saved that bit for last. He could see that Smith was a methodical man, far from dull as it turned out, but someone who wanted to set things up properly. First explain background, procedure, situations properly, before going off on any tangents, no matter how important. He had done all of that for Delaney at length, providing outstanding material for a magazine story, before diverting a journalist's attention to missing files, and to blackmail.

The interview took place in the management centre, in a bare anteroom well away from the other DVI team members. Delaney had first been given what amounted to a short course in the history of fingerprinting from Victorian days to the present moment. He sensed that Smith had given his little potted history many times before, whenever an unsuspecting listener had been snared.

"So you see, the issue in those years was actually trying to keep track of everyone," Smith had said. "Not just criminals, but people who were suspect in a more general way. Migrants, strangers, foreign born staff, people who didn't fit into the mould of middle-class Victorian society. The authorities were very keen to develop a way to keep track of these people and fingerprints were a very effective way to do that. Who was actually who, who was entitled to what, what sort of record a person had. First out in the colonies, and then more and more for police work back in England."

As they talked, Smith constantly sipped mineral water from a small bottle. He sweated heavily in the heat and, it appeared, in his intense enthusiasm for the topic. Delaney drank tea that a young Thai policewoman had brought him.

"But they gave up, eventually, on the other matter of trying to use fingerprints as a way to actually predict who might be liable to commit criminal acts," Smith said. "They'd been searching for a long time for ways to do that, the Victorians, with analysis of facial characteristics and measuring skull shapes and limb length or whatever, and then with fingerprints. But eventually they gave up on all of that. There's no recurring pattern anyone's ever been able to determine in criminal fingerprints."

Delaney sipped tea, wrote in his notebook. He let Smith ramble on.

"But then of course the whole business of using fingerprints to identify dead bodies is another issue altogether," Smith said. "In a different category. As you've seen out here in Phuket."

"I'd like to get into that aspect a little further now," Delaney said. "The technical side of it, getting prints from the corpses you can use in your work, that sort of thing."

This launched Smith into yet another lengthy monologue about the pitfalls and trials of obtaining quality finger marks from deteriorating bodies, and of obtaining quality antemortem marks from home countries. Delaney scribbled notes. Smith enthused, stopping occasionally to refuel himself with water.

"In the end, though," Smith said, "at the end of the day, it comes down to the skill of the individual fingerprint examiners. The AFIS system is very good at winnowing down thousands of fingerprints to a handful of possible matches. Computers are fast, but they're dumb. It's the experienced fingerprint examiners who make the final determinations, always. If they're any good and if they do their work properly. You can never eliminate the human factor."

Smith paused for a moment, allowing his captive listener to appreciate this fully.

"And it also comes down to very rigorous record keeping," he said. "In a big operation like this in particular."

"I take it things are going well now that the proper systems are in place out here," Delaney said. "You're getting a lot of fingerprint matches now."

"Yes, lots," Smith said. "Far more than DNA and dental combined, at this stage." He smiled ever so slightly.

"That's not always how it goes, is it?" Delaney said. "In New York City after 9/11, for example, it was almost all DNA, wasn't it?"

Delaney had been in New York in the months after the

World Trade Center attacks, on assignment for CSIS and a Canadian magazine at the same time.

"Oh, well, sure, there it had to be DNA in that case because you had mostly just body parts, most of the bodies in New York were broken up, pulverized," Smith said quickly. "It's very different here. Fingerprints are still the thing."

"That's good news for you," Delaney said.

"Of course there are always some hitches," Smith said. "In a big operation like this."

Delaney's journalistic radar was immediately activated.

"I see," he said. "Can you give me some examples?"

Smith hesitated. He peered at Delaney through his thick glasses. All good fingerprint specialists, he had explained to Delaney early in the interview, had ruined eyes. If they didn't, he had said, they mustn't be looking closely enough at their files.

"You running into problems?" Delaney asked again.

"It's natural to have some problems in any big disaster operation, with teams coming in from all over the world," Smith said.

"But?"

Delaney knew, after dozens, hundreds, of interviews with officials and experts and politicians of all persuasions that something important was coming, that his interview subject wanted to say something significant, perhaps share a secret. He knew the tone shifts and the signals all too well.

Smith hesitated again. He ran his hand over his sunburned forehead and his thinning curls. He stared at his fingertips.

"Look, Delaney," he said eventually. "Can we go off the record for a bit? Or whatever you lot like to call it."

"Fine with me."

When a police officer proposed confidentiality, Delaney knew from experience, something important was coming.

"Off the record," Smith repeated with a small smile. "Rather dramatic, isn't it. Melodramatic."

"Not always," Delaney said. "Not always. Necessary some-times. Depending on the story. What's up?"

"Well, look," Smith said finally. "The fact of the matter is that I'm upset about the way certain things have been handled around here. The fact is, I'm not happy and I've had a word with the senior people out here and they have, quite frankly, done nothing to solve what I see as a serious problem."

Delaney knew when to wait and listen, when not to inter-rupt an interview subject who is about to share a secret.

"Look, I know your work a little," Smith said. "I saw that article you did a few years ago about Aung San Suu Kyi and that crazy plot to kidnap her, or whatever it was. Quite a story. You were working for *Asia Weekly*."

For the Canadian spy service actually, Delaney thought.

"I wrote it for *Asia Weekly*, that's right," he said to Smith. "But I was actually a staffer at the *Montreal Tribune* at the time. My editors there weren't too happy with that little freelance effort of mine and we parted ways right afterward. To put it politely."

CSIS not too happy either, Delaney thought. *To put it politely.*

"Well, I've run into something out here that may interest you, given the sort of investigative reporting things you do," Smith said. "I've come across something odd and I think it's an indication of a larger problem that may, to be really frank about it, get in the way of some of us doing our jobs properly, which as you know is to get all the bodies out here identified and back to their families as quickly as we can. The fact of the matter is I'm upset because the senior people here, some senior people anyway, are ignoring what I've told them and I'm upset about that. Not happy at all."

For Delaney, and those like him in the information-gather-ing trade, there is nothing better than an unhappy official. He did not attempt to fill any of Smith's silences. Unhappy officials will generally fill those if left uninterrupted.

"I've worked for the police for twenty-one years," Smith

said, continuing what Delaney could see was going to be an extended apologia before allowing himself to betray a secret. "I've rarely spoken to the press in all those years and never once felt the need to go off the record or reveal anything confidential about an ongoing investigation or anything else for that matter."

Delaney waited.

"I've thought about this a lot since they told me you'd requested this interview," Smith said. "I'm still not quite sure this is the right thing to do."

"I can see that," Delaney said.

"Is it that obvious?"

"Yes."

Smith laughed bitterly. Delaney could see he was having second thoughts.

"Here's what I think we should do," Delaney said. "We'll go off the record, completely. You tell me what it is that's bothering you about the operation and then we can decide together how I use it or whether I use it. If you have any misgivings about things in any way after you've told me what's on your mind, I won't use what you give me in my article. Not directly. But in situations like this, I tell people that I'll use what they tell me to try to get the information from another source and if I get it again in that way I can use it in the piece. And, at that stage, I can also use what you have told me directly, but still off the record, if you're feeling more comfortable. How would it be if we started off like that?"

The deal clearly worked for Smith. He launched immediately into a detailed tirade about the missing *Deutschland* file, about the missing elements of the file he had observed before it disappeared completely, about the brush-off he got from various DVI colleagues, and from Adrian Braithwaite. He told Delaney about the late-night visit from a possibly drunken Horst Becker. And eventually he told him about the blackmail note. Once Smith decided to tell Delaney the story of the file, he told it all.

"What did the note say exactly?" Delaney asked eventually.

"Well, it basically said if I didn't stop asking questions about the file, there'd be trouble. I've got it back in my room if you want to look at it."

"What kind of trouble?"

Smith took off his glasses and polished them with the end of his shirt.

"Ah, now we will have to be well and truly off the record, Delaney," he said.

"We're as far off the record as we can go," Delaney said.

"It said that they, or he, or whoever wrote it, would tell my wife back in London I was having an affair out here."

"Ah," Delaney said.

"Exactly," Smith said. "Ah."

"You know what I am going to ask you now, don't you, Jonah?" Delaney said.

"You'd make a very good prosecutor, Delaney," Smith said with a bitter smile.

"So I've been told," Delaney said.

"Look, OK, here it is. I have been seeing a woman from another DVI team. We spend a lot of time together. Yes, it's an affair. But it's nobody's business."

"A lot of Western men meet Thai women when they come out to places like this," Delaney said. "No big revelation there."

He thought of Nathan Kellner, a lifelong ladies' man before he was killed in Burma in 2001. He thought of Kellner's Thai girlfriend solemnly feeding cats and goldfish in their apartment in Bangkok while she waited for word from Delaney whether her man was alive or dead.

"She's not Thai," Smith said. "It's not like that. She's not a bar girl. She's with the police. From Spain."

"And if the people you have pissed off tell your wife about that, is that a problem for you?" Delaney asked.

Smith put his glasses back on.

"I don't know," he said. "I don't know anymore. Certainly it would be complicated. But maybe not such a bad thing. Not sure."

Delaney paused for minute to process that frank evaluation of a marriage and to allow Smith to do the same thing.

"You think whoever wrote you that note would be police?" Delaney asked.

"Or civilian," Smith said quickly. "It could be a civilian. There are lots of civilian staff working out here from all over the place. From Thailand too. It could be anyone."

"How many people did you talk to about your worries on this thing?" Delaney said.

"Quite a few," Smith said. "Too many, in retrospect."

"I would say."

"And the place is a gossip's heaven. Anybody I asked about the file could have told anybody else. Word flashes around here like wildfire about any little thing," Smith said. "Who's sleeping with whom, for example."

Delaney drank tea. Smith worked on his bottle of mineral water. They watched each other for a while in silence.

"What is it you want me to do exactly, Jonah?" Delaney said eventually.

"Find out what's happening. Ask senior people the right questions on the record and see what they say. Light a fire under some of these people. And if they don't fix things up, then damn it, tell the world about it."

"And you think the world cares about one lost file, in a situation like this?" Delaney asked.

"You sound exactly like Braithwaite now," Smith said.

"You think the world wants to know about this?" Delaney asked again.

"I think the families of the people who got killed out here on a Christmas holiday would want to know if someone is stealing files. I'm sure the world would want to know if someone is trying to prevent identifications out here."

"Who would want to do that, Jonah?"

"I have been asking myself that question for several weeks now, Delaney," Smith said.

"Who do you think would want to do that? Prevent an identification. Seriously."

"Pedophiles," Smith said. "That's one possibility."

"Pedophiles," Delaney said.

"Friends of pedophiles. Or family. People with something to lose if a body turns up here and someone like me comes across a fingerprint record and a conviction back in Europe. Maybe one that isn't too widely known. I don't know. It's a possibility. I've thought a lot about it."

"Pedophiles," Delaney said again.

"We've already identified a few of these guys out here," Smith said. "It was easy once we started getting antemortem prints from criminal records back in Germany or Belgium or Sweden or wherever. Any number of countries back in Europe."

Delaney pondered this.

"You know what we call the Lufthansa flight from Frankfurt to Bangkok?" Smith said. "What we call it at Interpol?"

"No. What?"

"The Pedophile Express. Service seven days a week."

"Police humour," Delaney said.

"It's a well-known fact," Smith said. "Those flights always full of fat, middle-aged German men heading out here to prey on kids."

"Deutschland," Delaney said.

Back at the Metropole that night, Delaney did up his notebook after the interview as he had done too many times before, in too many silent hotel rooms all around the world and back again. He drank Jameson's whisky from the room's minibar and munched overpriced peanuts as he added details and possible angles to his notes. He sat for a long time and emptied too many tiny bottles pondering angles and scenarios.

Eventually he closed his notebook and went onto his balcony and into the languid tropical air. Down and to his right, a TV crew on another balcony bantered at top volume in Portuguese and rattled beer bottles and ice buckets as they dissected the day's journalistic takings. In the parking lot, an aging Thai man in a white uniform with gold braid and epaulettes sat alone on a battered aluminum chair beside a boom gate, listening to a transistor radio. The night man saw Delaney on the balcony and raised a hand in greeting.

Delaney waved back; suddenly, once again, he felt the raw loneliness that now came too often while working alone in hotel rooms somewhere in the world. He thought of the obsessively neat, antiseptic apartment in a Montreal highrise where he cocooned himself between assignments. He thought of calling Kate in Montreal, alone in her own cocoon, and then quickly thought better of it. She was growing tired of impulsive late-night phone calls from assignment hotels, again. She had told him so. She was growing tired, again, of waiting for Delaney in Montreal and of waiting for him to decide, as she put it, who he wanted to be when he grew up, who they could be together when he grew up.

One day soon, when he finally decided who he wanted to be, he would quit the game forever, leave the field clear for Tim Bishop and a new wave of information gatherers. He could see that coming, had known it was coming ever since his first disastrous departure from straight information gathering into the not so straight world of spies. Tonight, however, with Jonah Smith's story developing in his notebook and his curiosity engaged, he was reasonably certain, reasonably hopeful, that this time he could remain in the relative clarity of the journalistic realm.

Chapter 4

Delaney was not sure how much more time even the long-suffering editors of *International Geographic* would give him to finish his tsunami DVI story. He was sure, however, that they would not immediately buy into his now chasing a missing file story and a possible blackmail angle involving one member of one country's DVI team. The editors would respectfully advise him to tip off newshound colleagues in the daily press or one of the wire services, leave it to them, and get on with the big general feature he had been assigned to produce.

So he knew he would have to finish up his interviews in Phuket soon and appear to be at the writing stage to keep his editors happy. Ruth Connolly had now confirmed he could interview Adrian Braithwaite on Wednesday, two days hence. Smith had said he would brief Delaney before that encounter, to prime him with the right questions. So, in an email to his editors in Washington Delaney wrote: *FYI, tsunami item coming along nicely. Good cooperation from officials, good interviews, good human interest angle/pathos. Bishop's pix exceptional. Suggest we have cover story material. About to start writing. Please stand by for 5,000-word draft ASAP. Regards, FD.*

As in all such situations, Delaney began chasing a new angle, even one his editors would not want, by reading in. It is the time-honoured way in which any good journalist gets the feel for a developing story, gets familiar with background, issues, related events, and ways forward. The process was far easier than when Delaney first started in the game. Then, it would have meant relying almost entirely on librarians at home base to cull stories from the newspaper morgue on his behalf and fax clippings to him in a hotel somewhere in the field. He would also have carried a bulky sheaf of paper clippings along with him as he travelled, a sheaf that would diminish in value as new angles and questions developed while on the road.

Now, with the Internet and global news databases open to him, he was no longer at the mercy of curmudgeonly newspaper librarians and the world was, literally, at his fingertips. So the day following Smith's revelations, Delaney spent a few hours after breakfast at the desk in his room, tapping away at his laptop screen and scanning news agency archives, newspaper websites, NGO and government websites—any online sources he found interesting. After that he would call some of his contacts in the media and elsewhere—another time-honoured reporters' tradition—to see what they might know. His objective: to find anything that would throw light on why someone might want to prevent proper identification of a body at the Phuket DVI site, and why a German body in particular.

Delaney was making a few assumptions in his initial inquiries. One, that someone was indeed trying to prevent an identification in Phuket. He accepted Jonah Smith's version of events, at least for the moment, and accepted that the *Deutschland* file had not simply been lost or mislaid. Two, he bought into the assumption that the body in question was that of a German national. The tattoo on the corpse made that fairly obvious he thought, although that was not certain, and the actions of at least one member of the German DVI team added to his suspicions. Three, he felt it worthwhile to pursue a pedophile connection of some sort.

It took Delaney some time before he began to find what he was looking for in the news databases. The basic story was easy enough. Yes, Thailand and other Southeast Asian nations, particularly Cambodia these days and increasingly Vietnam, were a magnet for European pedophiles, homosexual or otherwise. Police reaction depended very much on the country in question and the level of official corruption. Thailand certainly made all the right noises about combatting sex tourism, but it was, Delaney found, still rampant there despite some recent high-profile arrests and convictions.

The Factiva database yielded, eventually, some very useful material. The keywords *pedophile, Thailand, Germany* and *identity* had borne fruit. Delaney stumbled across a series of 2002 reports from Reuters and from European newspapers about one Karl-Heinz Stahlman, a prominent industrialist from Hamburg and his taste for travel and for young Asian boys. There had been, apparently, rumours for some time about Stahlman's predilections. Eventually he had been arrested in Thailand, not in Phuket but in Pattaya farther north, and charged with interfering with schoolkids.

Stahlman, as befitted a respected member of the German business elite, was married with three children of his own. His arrest led immediately to his downfall. He narrowly escaped a prison sentence in Thailand—rumours circulated at the time, according to the German press, of his having generously bribed senior Thai officials to avoid such a fate. Stahlman's wife left him within days of his return to Hamburg, deported from Thailand and in disgrace. And of course the board of the giant medical-equipment manufacturing firm he headed showed him the door. Stahlman claimed to have resigned. The company said he had been fired.

Then the German press reported Stahlman's suicide. Delaney could not remember anything at all of this story, lurid though it was. Perhaps it had not been widely played in the

Canadian media at the time or perhaps he had simply missed it. In 2002 Delaney had been somewhat distracted, trying hard to avoid getting blown up or shot in crossfire in Afghanistan and after that he had become busy again with new assignments for CSIS. His erstwhile CSIS handlers had held their noses, forgiven him for his transgressions in Burma and once again taken an active interest in how a journalist such as himself could be useful to them, post-9/11, post-Afghanistan, post-new world order.

On March 8, 2002, Stahlman, according to media reports at the time, drove his SLK class Mercedes to the Baltic Sea coast near Rostock, parked it legally, left a suicide note in an envelope on the driver's seat, locked the car, and drowned himself. He was 52 years old. Police dragged the salt marshes near the shore for days, police divers scoured the area for days, police helicopters hovered overhead for days, but Stahlman's body was never found. The photo of Stahlman's elegant black car parked near the water's edge had made the cover of *Der Spiegel* under the headline: "Pedophile Industrialist Drowns in Despair."

It was an angle with very strong possibilities, Delaney decided. It was a dream angle, he decided as he disconnected from the Internet and closed his laptop. But it was one that would require far more investigation than a couple of hours on news databases.

Delaney had not spoken with Gunter Ackermann for more than a year. But as always in the news game, relationships among reporters, particularly those forged in conflict zones, stand the test of time. In early 2002, Ackermann and Delaney had been in a group of foreign correspondents pinned down in Afghanistan near the medieval fortress at Mazar i Sharif while U.S. and British Special Forces tried to take it back from Northern Alliance *mujahadeen* prisoners who had wrested control from their guards.

It was chaos, and the media who watched it happen were

lucky not to be incinerated in the firefight and air strikes that lasted two days. Confusion reigned because many of the U.S. and British forces were dressed in civilian clothes. The prisoners were a mix of Arabs, Pakistanis and Chechens. The soldiers said it was difficult to tell who was who. Delaney thought they didn't try very hard. More than five hundred were killed.

The last Northern Alliance holdouts had taken cover in an underground tunnel. They stayed there despite having no food and repeated attempts to force them out. Coalition troops started fires in the tunnel and even tried gas. They finally forced out the last few fighters by pumping water down the entrance hole and filling it up.

Ackermann was filing to *Die Welt*, one of Germany's most-respected newspapers, where he was chief political editor. He had put his hand up for the Afghanistan assignment because, he said, he was bored with years of covering German domestic politics after reunification in 1990. He had held up well during the siege of Mazar i Sharif, despite weighing well over 100 kilograms and smoking 50 cigarettes a day, on days when he could get them. He had loaned Delaney the *Die Welt* satellite phone in the sand dunes a few times so his Canadian comrade could call his editors. They stayed in touch afterward and Delaney tried to see Ackermann whenever he passed through Europe.

"Francis, Francis," Ackermann bellowed out from Delaney's cell phone when he got through on Tuesday morning Berlin time. "What time do you think the most-respected German journalist of his generation gets out of bed in the morning? Especially when recovering from a most exhausting night out?"

"We're both a little too old for that, Gunter, surely."

"Speak for yourself, Francis. You Americans are too wholesome for me anyway, it makes me sick. What time is it anyway, for the love of God?"

"Canadian, Gunter," Delaney said. "Not American."

"How could I forget? But worse, even worse."

"Gunter, I need some help, I'm on the tsunami story out in Phuket."

Delaney heard the scratch of a match in Berlin and knew Ackermann was lighting his first smoke of the day, probably while still in bed. He imagined Ackermann would almost certainly be alone, despite his legendary escapades, as it was his policy never to bring women back to the extremely disreputable flat he owned in a rundown corner of the former Soviet sector of the city. That was what cheap hotels were invented for, Ackermann would say to anyone who asked about this aspect of the bachelor's life.

"Of course, of course," Ackermann said, "I am accustomed to this, yes, as always you fail to telephone for many months and then call again only when you need help, forgetting poor old fat Ackermann who saved your life many times in Afghanistan, who fed you and clothed you and wiped your nose as you cried for your mother when the fighting raged around us and you never call me now except to ask for favours. It makes me sick, Francis, sick in my heart that I will help you again as I always do."

Delaney heard him take a long drag on a cigarette 9,000 kilometres away. "You defame me horribly, Gunter," Delaney said.

"What is it this time, my friend?" Ackermann asked.

"Not sure, Gunter, exactly. Maybe a coverup of some kind out here. Not sure. Something to do with pedophiles maybe."

"And German, of course," Ackermann bellowed. "Am I right? This is why you call me? Phuket is like a little German schoolhouse playground for these animals. Bastards, bastards."

Delaney filled Ackermann in on all he had gathered so far. He told him also about what his research had gleaned about Herr Stahlman and his last solitary swim off the North German coast. Delaney had no fear that Ackermann would take the story for his own. It was part of an unwritten code that most, but far from all, seasoned journalists worked under. Ackermann was one of those who could be trusted with a possible scoop.

"Why would they bother, Francis?" Ackermann said finally. "Why? It's police out there with you, mostly, correct? The police love to identify these bastards, living or dead. If it is German police they would very much prefer pedophiles to be dead. Why cover anything up?"

"That's what I'm trying to figure out, Gunter," Delaney said.

"And Stahlman, no, Francis, no, the man killed himself, he was in disgrace, he was chewed up by whales in the Baltic Sea. I know the Stahlman story, I was on the desk at *Die Welt* when the scandal started and when it finished."

"They never found the body."

"The currents out in the Baltic Sea are famous, Francis. Come visit, we will drive up there, I will throw you in just because you wake me too early in the mornings and they will never find your body either."

"It all sounds too neat. Car parked, suicide note, then no sign ever of the body."

"We Germans are a very precise people, my dear Francis, even in death. I have my own funeral planned down to the last detail. Extra-large coffins need to be ordered weeks if not months in advance."

"Not worth a further check around, Gunter?"

"Unfortunately everything is worth a little further check around," Ackermann said. "We are too many years in the business not to know that, Francis. I will check for you and I will find nothing extra that we do not already know and it will be a ridiculous waste of my precious time and then you will owe me one more favour, to add to our list of hundreds you owe me already. A big dinner at Zur letzten Instanz next time you are through. Number 14 Waisenstrasse—put this in your notebook for reservations purposes. And a one-litre bottle of single malt whisky. At least that, for this favour."

"You're a friend, Gunter."

"Unfortunately," Ackermann said.

Delaney held off calling Rawson in Ottawa on the Stahlman angle, or any other angle, for the time being. CSIS would be there for him as a fallback for information on the *Deutschland* story probably, but he had been trying to limit the number of favours he asked his occasional spymasters. The more favours he asked for and the more assignments he took for them, the more they thought they owned him.

Since his near-death experience with Tim Bishop in Iraq in 2003, however, and since the long de-briefs he had given CSIS afterward about his captors and the questions they had asked himself and Bishop while they were detained, Delaney was very much back in the spy service good books. They accepted, as before however, that information gathering where Delaney was involved would have to be a two-way process.

Delaney had helped CSIS out with various assignments since Burma, some of which also yielded for public consumption good, if necessarily somewhat incomplete, news or feature stories. He had investigated for them the Canadian trucking industry and the incessant southward flow of vehicles, most never properly searched for contraband or for illegal migrants, crossing Canada's land borders into the United States. And he had helped them with some sting operations in Europe, posing as a reporter interviewing Canadian businessmen and scientists in bugged hotel rooms abroad to help CSIS find out who was behind the wave of industrial espionage that was increasingly part of the spy service brief.

They also took a keen interest in his book on the Vatican intelligence service, something he had sworn to write ever since his ill-fated Mazovia assignment in 1995. It had taken almost seven years to find the information he required and also to find the detachment he required to do the writing job. The book caused an initial stir and immediate fierce denials by the Vatican *curia* of any wrongdoing by their agents, rogue or otherwise. Then it sank with dismal sales and little lasting trace.

But the book had helped put an end to his obsession with Natalia. Kate Hunter had helped him end that obsession too—and his research proved helpful to CSIS. Or so they said. They, too, had had unanswered questions about a covert Vatican operation on Canadian soil—whether approved officially or not—that left a CSIS agent, as well as Delaney's then-lover, dead.

He was to meet Jonah Smith for a final briefing before the interview with Braithwaite, and only at that stage would he decide if he needed any information or insights from Rawson and CSIS in Ottawa to help him figure out what exactly was going on in Phuket. Delaney left the Metropole mid-morning the next day. The three desk girls at the hotel never seemed to have time off. They looked approximately 14 years of age, they were always impeccably dressed in beige Metropole skirts and vests, and they always broke into giggles when Delaney or any other *farang* visitor approached them for messages or information. Today was no different.

"No message, no message, Mr. D," said the desk girl with *Lek* inscribed on her name tag. Her colleagues thought this indescribably amusing.

"No message from your wife, Mr. D," Lek said. "Too sad. So sorry for you."

"No wife for Mr. D," Delaney said. "So no message no problem."

This sent the desk girls into further spasms of laughter.

"So sad, so sorry for you," they called out after him as he walked across the spotless white marble floor of the lobby and through the revolving doors to get a taxi. Smith's hotel was about ten minutes away. Delaney rolled the cab's passenger windows down to save himself from hypothermia in the air conditioning. The day was sultry, classically tropical. Out over the bay a thundercloud towered, already kilometres high. There would be a terrific downpour before nightfall, as usual at this time of the year.

Smith answered his door at the hotel almost immediately after Delaney knocked. He had taken the morning off to arm Delaney with questions for Braithwaite. Apparently, his superiors could do without Smith's services for a few hours. Apparently, Smith did not mind upsetting them if they could not.

A petite young woman in a UN shirt stood behind Smith as he greeted Delaney at the door.

"Delaney, this is Conchi," Smith said, moving aside.

"*Con mucho gusto*, Mr. Delaney," Conchi said as she shook his hand.

"Frank. Please," Delaney said. "You make me feel old."

"*Con mucho gusto*, Mr. Frank," Conchi said.

"She knows what we're doing today," Smith said.

Delaney looked sharply over at Smith. In his journalism and in his other less-well-known work Delaney valued discretion very highly.

"Don't worry," Smith said.

"Don't worry," Conchi said, with a very large smile. "I am to be trusted. I am almost police, no?"

"No problem," Delaney said, without much conviction.

"Good," Conchi said. "And my good friend Jonah is wrong about this file business anyway, Frank. So there is not much to worry about. That is my opinion."

"And that is why Señorita Concepción is going over to the management centre now to leave us two old worriers to worry together without interruption," Smith said.

"You are very rude to me, my love, in front of world famous journalist Frank Delaney," Conchi said, with another large smile and shrugging her small shoulders extravagantly. Delaney could

see why Smith would possibly risk a marriage for the fetching
Señorita Concepción. Conchi kissed her man extravagantly on
the lips, picked up a small leather knapsack and headed for the
door. Delaney noted that Smith's cheeks had reddened suddenly.

"Goodbye Mr. No Problem Frank Delaney," Conchi said.
"Maybe we will see you again when the worrying stops for the
day?"

"Yes, maybe," Delaney said.

He looked at Smith in silence when the door had closed.
Smith looked back.

"Yes, she is, isn't she," Smith said.

"Very," Delaney said.

"Too young for me really," Smith said.

"Apparently not."

"For now," Smith said.

"You seem to be telling a lot of people about this little problem of yours, Jonah," Delaney said.

"There's nothing to worry about with Conchi," Smith said.
"Don't worry."

Like Ackermann in Berlin, Smith did not buy into the Stahlman
angle at all. He felt it was too easy, too obvious, too neat.

"How would Stahlman have got out of Germany if he faked
his suicide?" Smith said. "How would he have got a passport and
a visa for Thailand in another name? How would he have got past
Customs at Frankfurt airport?"

"It's the European Union, Jonah," Delaney said. "He could
drive across a border, he could leave from any number of countries for Thailand. Inside the EU or out."

"His name would end up in a database somewhere if he left
the EU with his own passport. He'd have to have a plane ticket
in his name. How would a man like that get himself false identification? He was no criminal."

"Except that he liked to have sex with small boys."

"You know what I mean, Frank," Smith said. "And what would he live on? The minute he tried to access his bank accounts people would know he was still alive."

"If they were still looking. Or maybe he carried lots of cash with him."

"It would have to be lots and lots of cash to start a whole new life in Thailand like that."

"People can make that sort of arrangement if they want to disappear, Jonah."

"If they have time, maybe. And it all leaves traces these days. How soon after he got back to Germany from Thailand that year did he kill himself?"

"A couple of weeks or so," Delaney said. "Not that long afterward."

"There you go," Smith said.

"Maybe long enough."

"Maybe not."

"Why does it have to be complicated?" Delaney asked. "Why can't it be a simple explanation like this? A disgraced man fakes his own death, moves to Thailand, lives happily ever after until he drowns in a tidal wave."

"I just have this feeling there is more to it, Frank. Something really odd is going on around here. Why would Becker be involved?"

"We don't know that Becker is involved. He may well just be upset that you are questioning his integrity or his team's integrity. Why would a man like that get involved in some sort of coverup?"

"If that body actually is Stahlman's, if I accept that, why would a man like Becker feel he had to cover up the death? Of a convicted pedophile? What's the point?" Smith said.

"I don't say it's Becker. It could just be some friends of Stahlman, helping him out."

"After he has died?" Smith said. "Why would anyone

bother? If it is him, he's dead in a tsunami, what is there left to cover up? Who cares, once he's dead?"

"Family," Delaney said.

"Family infiltrating a massive international DVI operation, amateurs and civilians, tampering with police files under the noses of coppers from around the world?" Smith said. "How could they do that? Why would they even bother? The harm's done years previously anyway, the family's reputation is ruined, Stahlman's dead, whether it happened here or in Germany, so what is to be achieved in all of this if you accept that theory?"

Smith was relentless and, Delaney had to admit, began to make a good deal of sense. They left off their argument about Stahlman for a while, however, and turned their attention to the interview scheduled for that afternoon with Braithwaite. Their immediate problem was that if Delaney asked too pointedly about records procedures and missing files in the DVI operation, Braithwaite would know Smith was the source.

"I'll take that risk, Frank," Smith said eventually.

"Braithwaite sounds like a very tough guy," Delaney said. "He can make things pretty uncomfortable for you if he thinks you've been feeding lines of questioning to a reporter."

"What have I got to lose?"

"Twenty-one years at Scotland Yard."

"They can't run me out," Smith said.

"Oh yes they can. I've seen things like that happen before. Whistle-blowers often lose their jobs."

"So be it," Smith said.

"You think it's worth that sort of risk."

"When we find out what is actually going on, Braithwaite will thank us for it."

"That's in the movies, Jonah. Braithwaite may not look good at all in the end, no matter how it turns out. There are very few happy endings anymore."

"I want you to ask Braithwaite about this, on the record.

I want you to help me find out what is going on and I want you to tell the story as you find it. And I want you to quote Braithwaite in that story about what he tells you this afternoon."

Smith's face was reddening again, but no one was giving him a lover's kiss this time.

Braithwaite's reeking cigar glowed ruby red, and then the ash turned blue-grey again. He clearly did not enjoy having his picture taken nor did he enjoy being interviewed by a journalist. He was a man more accustomed to asking questions than answering them.

Tim Bishop took a final few photos of Braithwaite behind his battered desk and then began to stow his gear.

"All done," Bishop said. "I'll leave you guys to it. Thank you very much, Inspector."

"Can I see those shots before they go in the magazine, young man?" Braithwaite asked. He did not seem to like Bishop very much, had remarked sourly on the pony-tail when the photographer arrived. "And it's Chief Superintendent, not Inspector."

Bishop looked over at Delaney with a grin.

"Not my call, sir," he said. "Up to my boss Mr. Delaney over there."

"Not something we usually do," Delaney said.

The cigar glowed red again. It had done so periodically throughout the interview. Bishop's arrival to take pictures about 40 minutes in had provided a welcome interlude, despite the pony-tail.

"So, where were we?" Delaney said after Bishop had gone.

Braithwaite looked at his oversized diver's Rolex. "We were almost finished, I thought," he said.

Braithwaite had given Delaney some very good material for a magazine feature on the DVI effort, had Delaney still only been working on a magazine feature. Even discounting Braithwaite's heavy bias toward what the United Kingdom authorities were doing to assist, the extensive resources the UK authorities had committed to the disaster's aftermath, et cetera, et cetera, even discounting Braithwaite's obvious UK agenda in granting the interview in the first place, the Detective Chief Superintendent had given Delaney some good material.

Delaney had, as always, saved the most difficult questions for last. Any experienced journalist would have done the same. Get as much information as you can, routine or otherwise, before asking questions that may get you thrown out of the interview room, or worse, depending on what country you were in and who was across the table from you.

Braithwaite had responded in what Delaney thought was a reasonably forthright way to questions about the initial problems in Phuket and mistaken identifications and angry relatives of the dead. He had responded as well, and without too much stoking of his ever-present cigar, to questions about whether certain DVI teams were concentrating primarily on identifications of their own nationals, with a view to hasty exits once all of their citizens had been accounted for. Braithwaite had, naturally, denied this.

He had lavishly praised all members of all national police teams who were on the ground in Phuket, had assured Delaney that all aspects of the operation were now on track and under control, and that it was only a matter of time—still months to go admittedly, but with an end very much on the horizon—before almost all the bodies would be identified. Braithwaite did not deny, however, that some bodies, perhaps a significant number, would never be identified despite the best forensic work possible. This was simply an accepted outcome of any such postdisaster situation, especially in what he insisted on calling "the Third World."

"And security at the sites, the mortuary site or other places, has that proved to be a problem at all?" Delaney asked after Bishop had gone.

"What do you mean, security at the sites?" Braithwaite said, suddenly wary.

"Security as in preventing unauthorized people from entering," Delaney said.

"Why would unauthorized people want to enter a disaster victim mortuary site, Mr. Delaney?"

"Families, possibly."

"Families are welcome to ask for assistance at the management centre information desk," Braithwaite said. "We have teams there, as I mentioned earlier, to deal with queries and concerns from families. And trained grief counsellors."

"So security is not a problem?"

"I don't really understand your question," Braithwaite said. "You're talking about people wanting access to the mortuary site? Unauthorized access?"

"Or here at the management centre."

"I really don't understand what you are getting at."

Delaney, after conducting hundreds of interviews in his career, could see this one drawing rapidly to a close.

"So you're saying that the sites and their equipment and records and so forth are secure."

Braithwaite put his cigar down in a coffee mug on his desk. He looked intently at Delaney and said nothing for a while.

"This place, and the mortuary site, and all other sites related to this DVI operation are literally crawling with police officers," Braithwaite said. "I can tell you that much. However, I see no reason to have to say such a thing because I fail to understand why you would even ask such a question. Why would anyone want to gain access to such places in an unauthorized fashion?"

"Why indeed?" Delaney said, locking eyes with Braithwaite. "Can I quote you as saying then that you are having no problems with security at the sites, and with securing confidential police records and other data here in Phuket. Is that correct?"

"Your question makes no sense," Braithwaite said.

Delaney waited. It was an accepted law of journalistic dynamics that silences must always get filled.

"Who else have you interviewed for this story of yours, Mr. Delaney?" Braithwaite asked eventually.

"I have done a lot of interviewing. Your press officer has been very helpful."

"Interpol's press officer."

"I understood that she represents the DVI operation as a whole," Delaney said.

"Yes and no," Braithwaite said. "I take it she doesn't sit in with you when you interview members of the DVI teams?"

"She isn't sitting in with us today, Superintendent."

"I'm the joint commander of this damn operation," Braithwaite hissed. "I take full responsibility for what I tell journalists. I don't need a press officer to help me out with that."

"Well, the other people I have interviewed didn't appear to need that support either."

Delaney wondered if Braithwaite would actually mention Jonah Smith by name.

"I'd like to see the story you are working on before it goes to your editors, Mr. Delaney. If you wouldn't mind."

"I have never done that in more than twenty-five years in the field," Delaney said.

"Is that right," Braithwaite said. "In the field, as it were."

"Yes," Delaney said.

"Well, I may just have a word with your editors after you have submitted your story, Mr. Delaney," Braithwaite said.

"You're welcome to contact them. You have my *International Geographic* business card there on your desk. Phone and fax numbers. Email address. They will tell you the same thing I told you."

"Will they now?"

"I'm confident they will," Delaney said.

"Well, be confident about something else, will you Mr. Delaney? I don't like the tone of your last few questions. I don't like the tone at all. Be aware that I won't have some hack journalist attacking this operation in any way, do you hear me?"

"No one is attacking this operation, Superintendent," Delaney said.

"Not yet anyway. Not on my watch. I won't have it. And now you can consider this interview terminated. I will be calling Ruth Connolly immediately after you get out of my office and I will be looking at the list of people you interviewed for this story of yours. I will make up my mind then as to what, if anything, I decide to do next. I do intend, however, to call your editors in, where is it, Washington, to have a word with them about this story of yours and about you personally."

"You're welcome to do that. The magazine knows my work very well. I've filed to them from Afghanistan, Iraq, a number of places, over the years. They know how I operate."

"Do they now? Well, they will now also know how I operate and how the police operate in a situation like this. We don't deserve to be criticized in any way, is that clear? We have dedicated teams of very talented officers out here from more than twenty countries doing the best work they possible can. We do not deserve to be criticized. I won't have you going off half-cocked chasing wild rumours or loose talk about document security."

Delaney knew this spelled trouble for Jonah Smith.

"It's a natural thing to ask about, Superintendent. In a situation like this."

"Is it really?" Braithwaite said, getting up from his chair. "We'll see about that."

Delaney remained seated.

"This interview is over, Mr. Delaney. A highly experienced

journalist who has, goodness me, filed stories from exciting places like Afghanistan and Iraq can see that very clearly, I would imagine."

Delaney couldn't remember the last time he had been to a karaoke bar, in Asia or anywhere else. This may have been because one usually goes to such places in a drunken state or unavoidably ends up in such a state, and memory often fails in such circumstances.

The night after his interview with Braithwaite, this was very much the case. He was drunk, Jonah Smith was drunk, so too was the lovely Concepción and a young forensic dentist from Netherlands named Stefan Zalm. The only sober ones among them were Tim Bishop and Zalm's extremely young and extremely shy Thai girlfriend, whose name was Rattanasiri. She was known to all as Rat. Even she and Bishop, however, appeared to have been carried away by the spirit of karaoke.

The Whale Bar did not do karaoke. The group had ventured farther down the bar strip after their dinner together to an extremely crowded, extremely noisy and extremely hot place called Electric Light. The patrons were a mix of well-heeled locals and international police with far too much money to spend on booze and far too little time to do it.

"Who do you want to be tonight, Jonah?" Conchi shouted, her face flushed with the heat and the noise and cigarette smoke and the rum she was drinking in large quantities. "Who do you want to be tonight, Mr. No Problem Frank Delaney? Tom Jones? Be Tom Jones, yes please. Frank Sinatra? Yes, yes. No, no, maybe Julio, yes be Julio Iglesias for me please. I love Julio, very, very, very much."

Delaney could see again, all too well, why a man like Smith would risk all for this young woman. Conchi's olive skin glowed in the intense downlights of the bar—she glowed with warmth and vitality and possibility. Her purple T-shirt clung to her like an exhausted dance partner. A small silver crucifix sparkled incongruously on a chain round her neck.

Delaney ignored her pleas, having arrived at the still, small space where large amounts of alcohol, if taken at precisely the right dosage, could transport him. But Conchi continued to insist that he get up and sing.

Bishop grinned at Delaney across a table laden with glasses and large bottles of Singha beer, raising high his customary glass of lemonade. He knew the signs when Delaney was drunk.

"What song does a journalist sing, Frank?" Conchi shouted. "Who do you want to be tonight? Tim Bishop, Tim Bishop, Tim Bishop, make your boss sing."

Her question was uncannily like what Kate Hunter asked Delaney all too often these days, and what, in fact, Rawson and CSIS asked him too often as well: Who are you, really, Francis? Who do you want to be? Journalist or spy? Or, perhaps, neither anymore?

Jonah Smith was a quiet drunk, like Delaney. He sat contentedly beside his breathtaking Spanish girl, watching everything unfold and looking occasionally over at Delaney with a thin smile. He had been briefed earlier about the difficulties with Braithwaite. The news did not appear to be spoiling his evening.

Eventually, Zalm rose unsteadily to his feet.

"I will now sing," he announced with a slight bow from the waist.

"Hurray, hurray, hurray for the Dutchman!" Conchi shouted.

Other bar patrons applauded wildly as Zalm made his way with some difficulty through minefields of tables and chairs to a raised dais at the front. A revolving mirror ball mounted on the ceiling cast squares of light on his bony shoulders. The master of ceremonies, a small Thai individual of uncertain sexuality and heavily gelled hair, shouted into a portable microphone that sent waves of feedback and distortion through giant speakers mounted in every corner of the bar.

"What song, please? What song please?" the MC shouted. "Who will you be?"

Zalm picked up another portable mike and peered at the audience through the glare of smoke and spotlights. He held onto a small railing for support.

"I will sing a Tom Jones song for the girlfriend of my British friend, as she requests," Zalm said, slurring his words ever so slightly. "I will sing, I think, 'It's Not Unusual.'"

A tremendous roar went up from the bar patrons and the MC tapped buttons on an electronic console. Suddenly, a wave of overproduced rock and roll, with overblown orchestral backup, blasted through the room.

Zalm was transformed. He stood stock-still, as if electrocuted, and then raised his eyes to the ceiling, raised his microphone at an acute angle to the floor, and became, for a few minutes, an international singing celebrity. The audience, too, was transfixed. They gaped at this sudden, complete personality transformation they had been invited to witness.

Zalm belted out an extraordinarily energetic rendition of the Tom Jones hit, complete with outstretched arms and legs, and the occasional pirouette and pelvic thrust. The sound was deafening, the audience mesmerized. When he was done, the room erupted with applause, laughter, shouts, whistles, stamping. A star was born. Bishop stood near the stage, firing flashgun salvos with his camera, representing paparazzi everywhere.

When Zalm was finally allowed to regain his table by ecstatic fans, he was dangerously flushed.

"For you, my dear Concepción," he said gallantly as he sat down, panting in the heat and the accolades. "And of course for my little Rattanasiri."

Rat said nothing, content, as a bar girl, to have been invited anywhere at all. Conchi leapt up and planted a kiss on Zalm's sweating cheek.

"Thank you so much, Stefan, my friend," she said. "*Gracias, gracias, mi amigo.*"

She stood, hands on hips, and scolded Smith and Delaney for their failings.

"At least one of us, at least my good friend Stefan Zalm knows who he wants to be tonight, no?" she said. "Jonah Smith? Mr. Frank Delaney? No?"

Chapter 5

Just before word came that Smith had been badly beaten and rushed to hospital, Delaney was on the telephone with Brian O'Keefe in Montreal. Both of them were under the weather, though thousands of kilometres apart. Delaney was suffering grievously from the effects of the previous night's drunken karaoke expedition; O'Keefe was suffering the effects of a lifetime of heavy drinking, smoking, womanizing, journalism.

O'Keefe had become, whenever Delaney stopped to consider such matters, his closest friend. A man who had spent almost his entire journalistic career at the *Montreal Tribune*, originally a promising young hotshot and a fine writer, the archetypal newshound, with a flare for dramatic leads and an intense desire for front-page bylines. Standard stuff, for most talented young reporters early in their careers.

Delaney's career, however, took off and led him far from Montreal and from local stories. O'Keefe's career, whether because he was just a city reporter at heart, or because he married unwisely and became mired in domestic disharmony and professional bitterness, or because he was by then simply a lazy drunk, never really flourished as it should have.

Delaney was not sure whether O'Keefe's catastrophic career problems and marital problems were the cause, or the effect, of his legendary drinking. But now, as he and others of Delaney's generation of reporters began to age gracelessly, the effects of his lifestyle had well and truly caught up with him.

O'Keefe had been in and out of hospitals for much of the previous two years, stricken with everything from alcohol-induced pancreatitis to smoking-induced bronchitis and pneumonia to obesity-induced knee and ankle problems. He was recently out of hospital again and Delaney called him often, as O'Keefe always did when Delaney was in a bad way.

"I'm doomed, Francis," O'Keefe shouted down the phone line from his bedroom in the disreputable house on the small farm south of Montreal that he and his wife still shared with the greatest of unease. "The doctor says I have less than twenty-four hours to live."

"That's longer than a lot of us expected for you this time around," Delaney said. "Make the most of it."

"Yes, I will, there is something very good on the TV tonight, Karen tells me. We can watch that. A sixty-year-old black-and-white movie. A love story. Young Karen and I will watch it together on my sickbed. I will drink a couple of shots of hot milk, the aphrodisiac qualities of which are well known, and we will fall hungrily into each other's arms as the credits roll. All will end beautifully, in life as in celluloid art."

"Nice," Delaney said.

"Nice," O'Keefe said.

"When can you go back to work?"

"Doctor says two more weeks. Bed rest required, as he still so quaintly puts it. An older man, he is. Like myself, in fact. Nurse Karen agrees with the advice about bed rest. It is true that my gut is still really quite sore."

"So take his advice, take my advice, stay in bed and try not to die. I'm in the middle of something over here and can't fly back there to stand by your graveside just now."

"You are always in the middle of something somewhere. I

do not expect nor require your presence at my funeral, my friend."

"I'll come anyway."

"What is it you are in the middle of, anyway?" O'Keefe asked. "You in trouble yet?"

"Not yet," Delaney said. "I'm still in Thailand on the tsunami story for *International Geographic*. The disaster victim identification thing."

"Tell them to come to my house when they're done. It's a fucking disaster zone over here as you can imagine. Complete with my putrefying corpse."

"It's a good story over here too, Brian. Everybody's a bit tied up to do you."

"What hat you wearing this time, Francis? You still a reporter on this one?"

O'Keefe was one of the very few who knew something of Delaney's extracurricular activities outside journalism.

"Of course, always a reporter, a simple gatherer of facts," Delaney said.

"I've heard that before. Then you call me from Burma or somewhere and tell me you've been arrested and fucked up for consorting with spies. Wanting sympathy."

"So far, so good, Brian. There is a little bit of an angle developing here on some missing documents, however."

"Oh, oh . . . here it comes."

"Nothing earth-shattering so far."

"I'm sure you will leave no turn unstoned," O'Keefe said.

"Exactly."

"And your love life? Thailand's reputation being what it is?"

"I'm a one-woman man, Brian."

"That is not what young Kate Hunter of the RCMP tells me, my friend. Which woman are you referring to exactly? Kate called me last week, pretending to inquire after my pancreas but clumsily fishing for information about her missing loverboy. It seems you call your ailing pal O'Keefe more often than you call

Captain Hunter of the Mounted Police. She seems to think you're a bit of a no-woman man right now."

"Complicated," Delaney said.

"We know that. Are you guys on again or off again? She seems to want to know."

"Not sure."

"You never are."

"Correct," Delaney said.

"Are we on the record on this, or off? On again, off again with Kate, on or off the record."

"Off."

"The record, or Kate?"

"No comment."

Conchi was in a bad way, too, when she called Delaney later that morning in his room at the Metropole. She was very upset, almost in tears, losing her English in the agitation, her Spanish accent heavier than usual.

"Jonah's lying there with bruises, bruises, bruises, all over him, Frank. He is breaking my heart, my heart is gone in two. They gave him a bad, bad, bad beating, Frank. For what? For what?"

"What hospital, Conchi. Where?" Delaney asked.

"Phuket International. On the bypass road near the airport. They seem good there, Frank, they seem like they are smart. They say he will be OK. He is just sore, he says."

"He's conscious," Delaney said.

"Yes, yes. But he went unconscious right after. Someone found him near the Electric Light. Very late."

"You weren't with him?"

"He wanted to stay for more beer with the Dutchman and some others. I went home in a taxi."

"Who was with him?"

"Nobody, I think."

"Why? We were in a big group at the end."

"Frank, Frank, I don't know this, we were drunk, every-body's drunk, who knows? It is like this with drinking, no?"

"Who beat him up?"

"Frank, Frank, please, how can I know? Come to the hos-pital. You find out who beat Jonah, OK? You are a reporter. Find out who beat up Jonah and put it in your newspaper, OK? Bastards, bastards . . ."

"Is he badly hurt?"

"The doctor say no. Bruises, concussion probably. Cuts. Jonah says they used sticks."

"How many?"

"Sticks? Frank please, don't act stupid, OK?"

"How many people, how many guys beat him up?"

"I don't know this, Frank. Come to the hospital, OK?"

Delaney got there by midday. He was not sure the wheezing Mazda taxi he had climbed into outside the hotel would make it in the intense tropical heat. Conchi was waiting at the hospital entrance, wearing her UN shirt though Delaney doubted she had been to work that morning.

With her was an extremely disreputable-looking individual, unshaven and smelling distinctly unfresh, wearing a crumpled Interpol shirt. He was clutching a dented red Thermos flask, stained with coffee.

"Frank, good, good, you are here," Conchi said. She kissed him on both cheeks. "This is one of Jonah's Interpol people. He's just arrived too."

"I am Brajkovic, Janko, Interpol team leader on this opera-tion," Brajkovic said stiffly. "And you are?"

He offered Delaney his hand. Delaney took it, despite the filthy fingernails that came with the package.

"This is Jonah's friend," Conchi said. "Frank Delaney. A Canadian."

"His friend," Brajkovic said. "I do not know you from this operation. Which team?"

"I'm a journalist, actually. Covering this story. For *International Geographic*. Jonah has been helping me out."

"As a friend," Brajkovic said.

"I suppose so, yes. I've interviewed him a couple of times. We've had some drinks."

"Janko, Janko, stop playing policeman, OK, please," Conchi said. "Frank is OK. Jonah likes him."

"A journalist and a friend," Brajkovic said. "Not always an easy combination in my experience, in my country Croatia in any case."

Delaney had heard variations on this refrain throughout his career.

"Your country Croatia is a Fascist hole, Janko," Conchi said. "Please stop this now. Jonah wants to see Frank."

"I have not authorized press interviews, Conchi. Not now and not even before, in fact, though Jonah seems to have gone ahead anyway."

"I'm visiting him today as a friend," Delaney said.

"Possibly," Brajkovic said. "But it's a good little story, Mr. Delaney, you would agree? Police official getting beaten in Thailand while trying to do his work after the tsunami. An Interpol man?"

"I don't know if it's a story or not," Delaney said. "People get beaten up and robbed on resort islands all the time."

"Do they?" Brajkovic said.

"Was he robbed, Conchi?" Delaney said.

Conchi looked uneasy. She gave Delaney a steady look and then looked at Brajkovic. "I don't know," she said.

"Didn't Jonah say?" Brajkovic asked.

"No," Conchi said, with another look at Delaney. "He just said they gave him a bad beating up."

"Let's go see him now," Brajkovic said.

"He's tired, Janko, and sore all over," Conchi said.

"Too sore to see Mr. Delaney as well, then, too," Brajkovic said with a thin smile jammed with nicotine-stained teeth.

"Frank is a friend."

"I am his team leader. I will come too," Brajkovic said.

"Let him come, Conchi," Delaney said.

"Thank you so much, Mr. Delaney," Brajkovic said. "For your kind permission to see one of my men."

"Don't be Fascist, Janko, please OK?" Conchi said.

Hospitals in Thailand can be very good. This appeared to be one of the good ones. The surroundings were clean and ordered. An extremely young, white-uniformed Thai nurse was bustling around when they came into Smith's room—filling a water glass, straightening Smith's covers, adjusting the speed of a ceiling fan. There was another bed in the room, unoccupied. The nurse gave the visitors a brief wai, a quick smile, and retreated saying nothing at all.

Smith did in fact look very bad. He was propped up in his white metal bed, pale and bruised. What was left of his thinning hair was tousled. He needed a shave. He was not wearing his glasses, and one of his eyes was blackened and swollen almost shut. One side of his mouth was also swollen and cut, with stitches showing where doctors had patched him up. His sinewy forearms, protruding from a white hospital gown, were bruised and cut; wounds, Delaney knew, that were inflicted on those who have fended off police batons or civilian sticks in a beating.

"Well, you are a mess, Smith," Brajkovic said, placing his Thermos flask on the bedside table.

"And you've brought me some of your foul coffee as a gift, thank you for the gesture," Smith managed to say through his swollen lips. Spittle glistened at edges of his mouth as he tried to form the sounds. He winced. "It's a bit hard, talking."

"Don't talk, Jonah," Conchi said, sitting on the edge of his bed. "Rest. We will talk later."

"Who did this to you, Smith?" Brajkovic asked. "Robbers?"

"Yes, probably," Smith said, looking over at Delaney. "I would imagine so."

"Did they get your wallet?" Brajkovic asked, ever the steely Croatian police investigator.

"I think so. It's missing anyway," Smith said, dribbling slightly. Conchi dabbed the corners of his mouth with a tissue.

"I will have to make a report. To Braithwaite and Colonel Pridiyathorn, and to the Secretary-General in Lyon," Brajkovic said.

"OK," Smith said, putting his head back on the pillow.

"Why would anybody want to beat you up, Smith?" Brajkovic asked. "Have you been annoying people again with your questions, questions all the time? Is that it? This file business?"

Smith said nothing. He sighed in his bed.

"He's tired, Janko. Talk later," Conchi said.

"And our journalist friend?" Brajkovic asked.

"I'm not interviewing anyone today," Delaney said.

"Thank you very much," Brajkovic said. "I will be the source of comment on this incident, in any case. On behalf of Interpol."

"I'm not writing a story about this," Delaney said.

"That is good news," Brajkovic said. "I will therefore leave you nice friends all together."

He turned to Smith.

"We have told your wife in England about this, of course," he said. "You have been injured on assignment. She says she will come immediately to your side. As wives do."

Brajkovic looked from Jonah to Conchi and back again, flashing beige teeth, clearly enjoying his minor role in a major domestic drama.

"Thank you very much," Smith said.

After Brajkovic had gone, coffee flask in hand, Delaney tried to get more information from Smith, though it was hard for the battered fingerprint man to speak clearly through his swollen lips.

"They just came at me out of nowhere," Smith said slowly.

"Thai?" Delaney asked.

"Yes."

"How many?"

"Three."

"You see their faces? Anyone you'd recognize?"

"No. It was really dark, I was drunk, they came at me really fast and then it was all a blur of sticks and kicks. I went into a ball and tried to protect myself."

"They say anything?"

"They were sort of yelling at me or at each other in Thai, mostly."

"Nothing you could understand."

"I think one of them was saying in English, "Watch out, watch out." But he could have been talking to his mates for all I know. I hardly heard what they were saying in any language."

"How were they dressed?"

"What do you mean?"

"Not police?"

"No. Civilians," Smith said. "They wouldn't beat me up in police gear, Frank."

"I've seen it done, Jonah. In a lot of countries."

Conchi said: "Police wear civilian clothes too, Jonah."

"These were Thais, Conchi," he said.

"Not Germans," Delaney said.

"Definitely those men were not Germans," Smith said.

"And they robbed you," Delaney said.

"My wallet's gone. But whether they took it, or it fell out of my pocket, I don't know."

"It could be lying in the karaoke bar, Frank," Conchi said.

"Maybe. Or maybe they took the wallet to make it look like it was a robbery," Delaney said.

"Or maybe it was a just a robbery," Smith said.

"Maybe," Delaney said.

"There's the letter," Conchi said.

"They gave you another blackmail letter?" Delaney said, looking over at Smith.

"No, no, I just got the one."

"But that letter said you should back away," Conchi said. "They beat you up as warning number two, no? Frank?"

"We don't know that, Conchi," Smith said.

"I know that, Jonah," Conchi said. "In my heart I know they are warning you again about that file business you won't let go."

Smith put his head back on the pillow and closed his eyes.

"You sore?" Delaney said.

"Yes. The headache's a bit bad now."

"They said he should rest a lot and take care of himself, Frank," Conchi said. "Let's go now."

As if on cue, the Thai nurse came in and said quietly: "This patient must sleep now."

"We're leaving," Delaney said. "But Jonah, we'll need to talk about this some more."

"Tomorrow," Smith said wearily. "OK?"

"When does your wife come," Delaney asked.

"No idea. Whenever she wants. I've not spoken to her," Smith said.

"Good," Conchi said.

In the corridor Conchi looked worried.

"He's OK, no?" she said.

"Sure," Delaney said. "He's just been knocked around a bit. No permanent damage."

"Mister no problem journalist man. Now a medical man. You see people beaten every day, correct?"

"Every day, correct," Delaney said.

"He is crazy, that Jonah, about this file," Conchi said, lighting a cigarette as they exited the hospital into the brilliant midday sunlight. Delaney had never seen her smoke before. She stood flicking ash compulsively onto the shimmering parking lot asphalt.

"Someone is very angry with him now," she said.

"It could have been a robbery, Conchi."

"You do not believe that, Frank. Do you?"

"No, not really. No."

"There. So who? And what do we do?"

"We try to find out where the file went and why it went."

"And Jonah gets beaten up again, maybe worse next time."

"He'll be more careful now, Conchi."

"Who cares about a lost file, Frank? There are hundreds of people dead around here. Families with no kids anymore. Kids with no parents. From all over the world. Who cares about just one file here after the tsunami anyway."

"Jonah."

"He's crazy. He always wants to identify people. He even took my fingerprints too."

"He's a professional. He wants to do the right thing."

"He's crazy."

"We're all crazy sometimes, Conchi. Me too."

"Journalists and police, crazy, crazy," she said. "You always get into trouble."

"You're in trouble maybe now too," Delaney said.

"Me, no," she said.

"You're his girl, people know that."

"And now his wife will know, right? So maybe I am in trouble a little bit," she said, with a giant Mediterranean siren's smile. Coy, shy, experienced, sensual, all at the same time.

"That note they wrote him, have you seen it?" Delaney said. "Jonah never actually showed it to me."

"I have it right here," Conchi said. "Jonah wanted it out of his hotel room and I don't want it in mine." She rummaged in her leather knapsack. "Here."

It was on a single sheet of plain white paper, photocopier paper apparently, folded once. Inside, in neat printed script in black ballpoint pen, a very short message: "Mind your business, Smith. Mind your business or your wife will know your Spanish business."

Delaney wondered if a linguist would be able to tell him whether the writer was a native English speaker. The message was too short for such analysis, probably, even if he had access to the expertise required.

"Short and to the point," he said.

"His Spanish business," Conchi said. "Funny."

"Jonah's wife is coming quite soon," Delaney said. "Someone may tell her."

"I know that, Frank, I know that," she said. "I will be a good little mistress girl and stay back."

"That part's not really any of my business, Conchi," Delaney said.

"Oh? Good. You are the only one not interested in that, in this big gossip place," she said ruefully.

"The faster we find out what's going on with that file, the faster we can find out who's interested, who wrote the note, who gave Jonah the beating."

"And so, we find out, big deal. What do we do when we find out?"

"We'll decide that when the time comes," Delaney said.

"And until then?"

"We take care."

"And I stay away from British ladies for a while."

"Probably a good idea, in this case," Delaney said.

"The case of the British wife," Conchi said. "The big bad British wife."

They got a taxi from the rank outside the hotel. A good car this time, a gleaming Corolla with air conditioning and a properly functioning transmission and suspension, unlike so many of the Phuket cabs. The driver wore an oversized dress shirt with epaulettes, baggy shorts and rubber flip-flop thongs.

"So sorry you have illness in your family," he said before they set off, making a wai.

"Thank you," Conchi said, getting into the back seat beside Delaney. "I'm going to the International Management Centre. Frank, where do you go?"

"Me too, I suppose, the management centre," he said. "I'll check in with the press officer."

"Reporters?" the driver said as they pulled away from the hospital. "TV? Big-time TV?"

"Yes," Delaney said. "But not TV, not big time."

"Not me," Conchi said. "Police."

"Ah, police," the driver said, growing quiet. Then he said: "Too many dead now. Who is who, even all you police, nobody knows."

"We're trying," Conchi said.

"Too many bodies, everywhere. I saw right after the wave. On the beach, everywhere, everywhere, everywhere, too many bodies."

"Did you lose family?' Delaney asked.

"Yes, yes, my aunt, some of my cousins, some of my driver friends. Everyone loses someone in Phuket in the wave." He drove very slowly, looking often at them in his rearview mirror. "Too many."

"The bodies were found? The people you knew?" Conchi asked.

"Some," the driver said. "Some still in the sea. The spirits are still in the sea."

Their route took them past the airport. In the distance, Delaney could see activity in the place from where identified foreign bodies were sent home. It was where he had first met Jonah Smith. Today, three coffins with Australian flags on them were ranged under the canopy and a small crowd stood beside them while an official spoke.

"Can we stop here for a minute, please?" Delaney said.

Conchi did not look surprised. The driver pulled over onto the scorched grass near the airport perimeter fence and they watched through the wire links as the little send-off ceremony for the bodies proceeded. Like the one Delaney and Smith had watched together some days earlier, this ceremony did not last long before the coffins were unloaded from cars and carried to the waiting aircraft. Grieving relatives embraced. Consular officials in summer suits hovered. A uniformed Thai police guard saluted.

"Three more going home, hundreds and hundreds still to go," Conchi said.

"Important, important," the driver said. "Families want this very much, I know. Thank you for coming from your countries to help us in Thailand."

"In Bosnia," Conchi said to Delaney slowly, "after the war, families used to come down to the sites, the mass graves, and watch us as we worked. We had a sort of rope line around the sites and the families would stand there for hours, just watching us dig in the mud and brush dirt off things and put corpses and bones and clothing and wallets and eyeglasses into bags. The women would cry for hours. The men would just stare."

Delaney had seen his share of mass graves and knew the scene she was describing all too well.

"Everyone wanted to know what happened to the ones they loved," she said. "Take them home."

"Everybody, everybody wants this," the driver said.

Delaney wondered who might possibly have loved the man, the *Deutschland* man, now proving so hard to identify. He wondered also who might have hated him or feared him enough to now be trying to prevent his identification. Family? Almost certainly not. For families, identification is the goal. A little ceremony, some tears, a grieving process, and the file is closed. For the enemies of this particular man, however, or for those who feared him and what identifying him could mean, the goal, clearly now, was something far different.

At the management centre after their driver dropped them off, Delaney and Conchi were almost bowled over on the steps by a phalanx of BBC people—a sun-burnished reporter, various producers, a cameraman, sound man, script assistant, other hangers on. Braithwaite, in his Metropolitan Police uniform today, was with them. So too were a couple of British embassy types in expensive tropical-weight pastel suits.

The BBC wave poured down the steps toward a small convoy of waiting silver vans. Still getting carte blanche access for their documentary on the heroic efforts of the British DVI teams, and, presumably, the efforts of one Detective Chief Superintendent Adrian Braithwaite, to identify and repatriate all of the British dead.

Braithwaite spotted Delaney and pulled away from the TV crew briefly.

"I'll need to speak to you, Delaney," he said. "When I get a moment."

"Anytime, Inspector," Delaney said.

"Chief Superintendent," Braithwaite said.

"Sorry," Delaney said.

"Your man Smith has run into some trouble," Braithwaite said.

"I know that," Delaney said.

"I thought you might," Braithwaite said. "I'll need to speak to you."

"Anytime."

The policeman looked over at Conchi.

"And perhaps you too, Miss," he said.

"This is my place of work," Conchi said, indicating the building behind them. "I am here every day."

"I've had a word with our press officer, Delaney," Braithwaite said.

"That's exactly who I'm looking for right now," Delaney said.

"Well, she's in there waiting for you right now. I've got to get going but be assured we will speak later. Today, or tomorrow latest," Braithwaite said.

A British consular official rushed up.

"Pardon me, Detective Chief Superintendent, but I must ask you to join us in the cars as soon as possible," she said. "The crew says the light is perfect now for shooting at the mortuary site. Could you join us please?"

"Yes, I'm coming," Braithwaite said.

"Face away from the sun when they roll tape, Inspector. Don't squint into the camera," Delaney said.

Braithwaite said nothing as he hurried away for his fifteen minutes of BBC fame. Conchi laughed and lit a cigarette.

"Chief Superintendent," she said.

"I know," Delaney said.

"Crazy, crazy," Conchi said. "Journalists and police. Cats and dogs."

Then they watched as a somewhat dishevelled woman moved down the low steps from the entrance of the management centre, calling out as she went. Her accent was distinctly Scandinavian.

"Officer Braithwaite, please, a moment," Mrs. Stokke called out. "Please, is there any news?"

Braithwaite was climbing into a BBC vehicle, red-faced as usual in the heat.

"Not today, Mrs. Stokke," he said. "No news for you so far today."

Ruth Connolly was in what passed for her office. It was a little anteroom off the cavernous hall used for press conferences and media briefings. Her room was littered with folders, newspapers from a number of countries, books, pamphlets, rolled-up posters, yellow Post-It notes, cigarette packs, ashtrays, coffee mugs. On a whiteboard, someone, presumably Connolly herself, had shakily tried to design a planning calendar for the month of March and part of April with a green marker pen. This planning attempt was not going well, from all appearances.

Connolly sat in a battered stenographer's chair, smoking a Marlboro and fanning herself with a copy of *Crime and Justice International* magazine. She looked exhausted, or hung over or fed up, or all three. Her Interpol shirt needed a pressing and her tangled thicket of hair needed a good combing out.

"Just the man," she said when Delaney put his head in the door frame. "Sit. Good dog."

Delaney sat.

"Well, where shall we begin, Delaney? Maybe with your friend Braithwaite? Or your friend Jonah Smith? You seem to make friends everywhere you go."

"I saw Mr. Braithwaite briefly on the way in," Delaney said. "He was rushing out with friends of his own from the BBC."

"And you are still ambulatory. That's police talk. As in, he didn't break your legs and/or shoot you in the kneecaps."

"Not in front of a BBC TV crew. And I don't see why he is so upset anyway."

"Please. Please."

"Tell me."

"Smith. File. Hassle. Bashing. Injury. Hospital. Bad," Connolly said. "Just off the top of my head."

"Ah," Delaney said.

"Ah," Connolly said.

"Smith got beaten up outside a bar in a dark part of Phuket Town, Ruth. Tourists are regularly beaten up in places like that.

Right? This would be how you see it, right?"

"He's not a tourist, he's a fucking Interpol man," Connolly said. "He's not supposed to get beaten up outside a dumpy bar in Thailand. The Secretary-General was on the phone from Lyon with Braithwaite this morning, asking all sorts of questions. And now Smith's damn wife is coming out from London. She is said to be a harridan of the worst sort, that's what I'm hearing, and she doesn't like cops, or even her own husband, apparently. That's the scuttlebutt around here. And guess who Braithwaite has assigned to shepherd Mrs. Smith around . . ."

"I'm more interested in who you think gave Smith his beating," Delaney asked. "Who do you think it was?"

"Ah, very good. A trick question. You almost had me blurting out my theories. What a good journo you are, Frank."

"Seriously."

"Seriously? Off the record? Way off?"

"OK."

"I think Smith has pissed someone off with his incessant questions about that missing file, or alleged missing file. I have no doubt he has told you all about his crackpot theories about that. Braithwaite has no doubt about this either. So Smith has asked so many questions and hassled so many teams and Braithwaite himself about this that someone has arranged to give him a little beating."

"Police, you mean."

"Come off it, Delaney. You think cops don't punch each other out sometimes? After a dozen beers? We're forever thumping bad guys in the cellar of the station house, even while stone cold sober."

"They were Thais who beat him up."

"Don't be naïve, Delaney."

"Why would a few questions about a missing file upset anybody so much?"

"Because Smith is more or less accusing other people,

openly, of being incompetent or up to something strange or God knows what. He's making people look bad, Delaney. Police do not like that. Police definitely do not want to be made to look bad."

"Especially German police?"

"You're good, Delaney. You're very good. My, you almost had me there."

"But what if Smith is actually onto something?"

"Like what?"

"A file goes missing because someone doesn't want a particular body identified."

"Oh, I see. Does that really make sense to you, Delaney? Really? In a place like this, after a disaster like this?"

"What do you think, really?"

"Off the record?"

"Yes."

"I think some lazy, tired out, distracted, heat-stroked cop has lost the damn thing, or misplaced it somewhere. Or some Thai clerk has lost it. Or a cleaner has thrown it away. Or one of the super-sized Thai cockroaches has carried it off for his lunch."

"I see."

"Why would anybody want to steal a file like that anyway? Be serious. Why would anybody want to prevent us from identifying a body over here?"

"Why indeed?" Delaney said. "That's what Smith is asking."

"And now Delaney of the *Geographic* is asking too."

"Yes."

"For your magazine piece."

"Possibly."

"When I was a girl, *International Geographic* just did nice picture stories about rivers and rainforests and young black African girls with bare tits," Connolly said, lighting another cigarette off her previous one.

"That's still the magazine's bread and butter. Pretty much."

"Braithwaite will have your ass in a sling if you go with that angle anywhere in your piece, Delaney. And my ass. And Smith's."

"I'm not sure what I'm going to do with this angle, Ruth. Maybe nothing."

"Excellent idea."

"But if I do go with it, I'll need something on the record from your side. You. Or Braithwaite."

"Braithwaite is not going to tell you anything except to warn you to pull your head in. I'm not going to tell you anything on the record, except that, let's see, the international DVI teams have received the utmost cooperation from the Thai authorities in setting up a highly efficient forensic identification operation here, under very difficult conditions. We are all working steadily toward our common goal, which is the rapid identification and repatriation of all victims. Et cetera, et cetera. Blah, blah, blah, blah."

"Thank you, Officer Connolly. That's Connolly with two N's and two L's?"

"Yes. Ruth with an R."

"I would very much like to put a few new questions to Braithwaite about all this. Seriously I would."

"You can't be serious. You're joking, of course. You think Braithwaite will answer any of your questions, on any subject."

"Can you try to set something up for me, just to see?"

"How long do we have to have you around here, Delaney? Can't you just finish your piece fast and piss off home?"

"I've still got bits and pieces left to gather," Delaney said.

"Well, do me a favour, OK?" Connolly said. "Will you please interview one of the DNA guys for me before you go? Get those people off my back? They're upset that reporters are not interviewing them as much as the fingerprint guys and you know what they're like. Or do you? Perhaps you, like Smith and his crowd, are lost in the fingerprint era. Nowadays, in case you've missed it, it's always DNA this and DNA that and the DNA guys are sniping at the fingerprint guys day and night. Fingerprints not reliable anymore, comparison errors, examiner error, mistaken identifications. Or so the DNA boys say. I have someone good lined up for you already, from the DNA team. They want him to tell people how good they all are at what they do."

"All right, Ruth. That's actually one of the things I still need."

"It's a Canadian officer. RCMP. One of yours. He's very good, apparently. Young guy, terribly earnest, doesn't appear to have ever needed to shave. What is it with you Canadians anyway? Don't you ever get weathered and wrinkled?"

"It's the fresh air."

"Can you get his picture taken too? Even if it doesn't run in the mag? That will get his team off my back for a while."

"OK."

"And can you use that cute young Tim Bishop guy for your shooter? I will personally escort that particular young photographer anywhere. As in up to my room. He's a spunk, as we used to say at the Dublin convent school for wayward girls."

"Not your type, Ruth. Tim doesn't drink or smoke. He's vegetarian. Goes to bed early. Works out in the hotel gym."

"Disgusting. I shall bring him down into the gutter in no time at all. I have been flirting with him since the day you guys arrived in this tropical paradise."

"I thought you were flirting with me, Ruth, on the day I met you anyway. Am I wrong on this?"

"I thought it was the other way around."

"Ah."

"You look married, anyway, Frank. To my practised eye."

"Do I?"

"Yes, you do."

Delaney thought for a moment of Kate Hunter, and

Natalia. For some reason, the image of Natalia lying dead in the snow in the Quebec woods suddenly flashed up as well. He had not thought of Natalia for a long time. And certainly not of that particular winter's day, so long ago now. Connolly watched him with great interest.

"Something I said?" she asked.

When he got back to the Metropole, there was a voicemail message on his telephone from Conchi. She wanted to see him again that night, to talk about what to do next. Why she hadn't just sought him out at the management centre after his meeting with Connolly was not immediately clear.

Tim Bishop had also left a couple of messages. Bored, he said, with waiting around for whatever was next on the *International Geographic* assignment. Delaney was wondering about that too, though now clearly on a different sort of assignment than the one he and Bishop had embarked upon.

He checked emails and the news headlines using his laptop and the hotel room broadband link. He scanned the faintly glowing computer screen while drinking a Singha from the bar fridge. The usual journalistic emails, editors' emails, junk emails scrolled past him. One message from his sister in California. Her American husband, it seemed, was thinking about spending his vast tech-boom wealth on another helicopter. Such were the concerns of Delaney's only surviving blood relative.

No emails so far from Ackermann in Berlin. And no freelance spying assignments from Rawson. The Canadian Security Intelligence Service had been able to go about its work without Delaney's assistance for some time now, it seemed. But there was a somewhat ominous message from Kate Hunter in Montreal.

Hi Francis. Haven't heard from you for a bit, so just checking in. I'm fine, in case you are wondering. I assume you're doing OK over there or I would have heard something. Maybe. I hear from Brian O'Keefe, though, that you two have been in touch. He says you are over there trying to figure out what you want to be when you grow up. He's funny, Brian is. If he had said that about anyone else but you I'd think he was joking around. Bests, Kate.

He read Kate's message several times, seeking subtexts beyond the obvious. Her theme was always the same, of late. And O'Keefe was not helping the situation at all. Delaney tried several times to compose an appropriate reply. Perhaps this?

Dear Kate . . . I'm fine, thank you for asking. Weather in Thailand is lovely, hotel fine, food very good. Yes, I am in fact still trying to figure out who I want to be when I grow up. Or who I am right now. I am surrounded by experts here who can help me on this. I will let you know when the identification process is completed . . .

Delaney closed his laptop, no messages sent, and opened another beer instead. Sometimes, even after all his years as a journalist, words failed him.

Chapter 6

Perhaps because Delaney had spent so much time in recent years consorting with spies, or perhaps he was simply becoming reckless, but it was he who suggested breaking into one of the refrigerated storage containers to take fresh fingerprints off the *Deutschland* body.

He had expected to encounter strong resistance to this idea from Smith, after his release from hospital, because Smith was Scotland Yard—a by-the-book man, a correct procedures man. Instead, Smith simply sat in a chair on the balcony of his hotel room in the intense sunlight, a day after leaving the hospital, and stared at Delaney intently for a long time before saying, eventually: "Good idea."

Smith was looking better. They had kept him in the hospital for 48 hours, and now his black eye was fading and his mouth was far less swollen than it had been. But he still very much looked like a man who had been in a fight.

"I like it," Smith said. "We really have no other choice at this stage than to get a fresh set of prints. Who knows when the pathology teams will get around to that body again, or even if they'll get to that body again at all."

"You think we can get in there and get what you need?" Delaney asked.

"Yes, I think so," Smith said. "We can go in after the pathology people go home, after dark. From memory, there is only one man, a Thai policeman, at the gates to the compound late at night. In the mortuary buildings there may be people working late, doing paperwork, but all the bodies get returned to the containers at night. There are no postmortems done after about seven or so. We'll go in very late. Three, four o'clock in the morning."

"The containers are all locked, I would imagine," Delaney said.

"Yes, but just padlocked. The locks aren't heavy ones. They're just on there for form's sake, because police like to lock things up as a matter of procedure. They would never expect anyone to actually try to break in to one of those containers."

"The fence?" Delaney said.

"Easy to get over that."

"For guys like us."

Smith smiled broadly at Delaney.

"Easy," he said.

"Bolt cutters? For the lock," Delaney said.

"We'll need them, but I can find one of those. The lock won't be a problem."

"It might be a problem the next morning when they see the lock's broken, though."

"Yes. True. But I would imagine if we take it away with us the Thai policeman who opens the container doors in the morning will just think someone forgot to lock up properly the night before. From what I can see, those young constables just want to avoid getting shouted at by their superiors these days. I would imagine whoever opens up in the morning will just think someone forgot to lock up properly, and he'll go find another lock to use at the end of the day and say nothing."

"Let's hope so."

"They don't want problems, Frank. They've got enough

problems. No one is panicking about a missing file. Do you think they'll worry just because someone forgot one night to lock up a container full of unidentified dead bodies?"

"We'll see, I suppose. If they do, and if word gets back to Braithwaite, he will immediately think it's something to do with you."

"Braithwaite won't ever hear anything about it. You'll see."

"I hope you're right," Delaney said.

"I'll assemble what we need, Frank. Bolt cutters, flashlights, as you North Americans like to call them. My fingerprinting gear."

They grinned at each other—schoolboys planning pranks. They raised their beers.

"You will need a jumper, Frank. It is minus eighteen degrees Celsius in those containers at all times."

"Like Canada."

"Godforsaken place," Smith said, drinking beer. "So. When do we break in?"

"Soon, as soon as possible. After your wife leaves? You can't be sneaking out of the hotel in the middle of the night with her around."

"My dear Frank, I regret to report that Mrs. Smith has arranged for her own very comfortable room, on another floor. To allow dear husband to get the sleep he needs after his unfortunate accident."

"I see. It's like that, is it?"

"Yes, I'm afraid so. Here, in London, everywhere. It's like that. Marital bedrooms. Plural."

"I see."

Madame was in fact resting in her room as they spoke on the balcony. Delaney had not seen her since the first day she arrived. He had expected her to hover around her bruised husband, if only to keep up appearances. Smith told him not to be naïve.

Before they planned their break-in, Smith had told him a little more about the night he got beaten up. It was much as he had described it when Brajkovic was in his hospital room. Three Thai men, late twenties, early thirties. Standard shirts and light trousers and sandals, nothing to distinguish them from thousands of other youngish Thais around Phuket.

They had set upon him with sticks, but Smith said he really didn't think they were trying to hurt him badly. The blows rained down for a few minutes, there was some shouting at him and some kicks, but if they had wanted to really hurt him or kill him they would have done it differently, or so Smith thought.

He thought they had actually taken his wallet, but he couldn't be sure. Perhaps that had been lost in the attack. He thought they had raced off afterward on two motorbikes, but couldn't be sure. He thought it had happened around 1 a.m., perhaps 2 a.m., but couldn't be sure.

"It would be easier for us to figure this out if they were speaking German, Jonah," Delaney said eventually.

"Precisely," Smith said.

"What do you think? Becker, maybe? Hires a couple of local guys to give you a little beating."

"Maybe. Yes."

"Becker sounded very mad, the way you describe him that night he came up to your room. An upset cop who isn't above arranging a beating for someone who has pissed him off."

"He's not a copper, Frank. He's a pathologist. A good one apparently. Civilian. Very well respected, from a military hospital in Frankfurt or somewhere."

"Whatever. You have pissed someone off in this town, and you got a warning note. And then you got beaten up."

"I seem to have upset more than one person in this town. Becker's just one."

"Braithwaite would never have you beaten up, would he?"

Smith paused for a moment.

"No. Probably not. But the pressure's on out here, especially for the UK teams. The government back home is pushing them hard to get all the British bodies back home as soon as possible. There are families back home calling the Foreign Office hotline every day asking for updates. Braithwaite's under a lot of pressure. I suppose he could have just decided to send me a little message."

"Not very likely."

"No. Not really."

"Well, in any case, you'd better watch your back after this."

"I shall, Frank. Have no fear."

Delaney had been summoned to Braithwaite's office the day after they bumped into each other on the steps of the management centre.

"Jonah Smith is getting himself in a lot of trouble out here," Braithwaite said, blowing as much cigar smoke in Delaney's face as he could from across his battered desk.

"Apparently," Delaney said.

"I blame you," Braithwaite said.

"Do you?"

"Yes, I fucking do. You are looking for some kind of scoop like all hack journalists and you've got Smith thinking conspiracy theories and bullshit. It's clouding his judgment. He used to be a good fingerprint man, well liked, good at what he does. A civilian, but a good Scotland Yard man. Now, he's fouling up. I'm this close, this close, to sending him back to his little sinecure in Lyon with those Interpol types. And sending that little bit of Spanish crumpet back home too."

"I would imagine that will only draw more attention to this missing file business, Superintendent," Delaney said. "Won't it?"

Braithwaite glared at him and said nothing. He studied the end of his cigar the way Smith studied the ends of his fingertips while concentrating on a problem.

"I don't like it when one of my people gets hurt on the job, Delaney. Even if he has stepped out of line. I don't like it when people beat up my people."

"So you don't think it was a robbery?"

"I wouldn't tell you what I thought about it under any circumstances," Braithwaite said. "All I'm telling you is that you've got a good man off track over here, on a very important operation, and I want you out of it. I want you to leave all these officers alone to do their work. I'm this close to pulling your media accreditation and putting you on a plane for Bangkok."

Delaney waited a moment before replying, letting Braithwaite smoke for a little.

"Well, that would be unfortunate, Superintendent. But whether I have a press pass or not, you can't stop me from staying on in Phuket, unless you charge me with something and have me arrested and deported. I wouldn't be able to go to the press conferences without a press pass, maybe, and I wouldn't be able to interview anyone officially, but there is no way you can stop me from staying on here in Phuket. You know that and I know that."

Even as the sweating, sun-reddened policeman studied the glowing end of his cigar for a solution to this conundrum, Delaney knew he knew that.

"I won't authorize you to interview any more people around here, then. I want you to finish up your work and get the hell out of my hair. And if you write anything crazy about missing files, if you write one thing that is inaccurate or damaging to us or defamatory in any way, I'll have your ass."

"I'll send you a copy of the article as soon as it is published, Superintendent."

"I'm going to be in touch with your editors well before that."

"OK," Delaney said.

Braithwaite glared at him from his chair.

"I'm actually still due to interview someone from the DNA

team," Delaney said. "Your press officer has organized that for me. I take it you won't authorize that now? Officer Connolly seems to want that angle in my story for balance."

"For fuck's sake, Delaney, get out of my office, will you just get out of my office? You know what I'm saying to you. OK, interview the damn DNA man, fine, fine, and then do us all a favour and get on a plane after that. But I won't stand for any more bullshit about missing files, now or in your article, do you understand? And no more bullshit from Smith either. I'm going over to see him at the hospital and tell him personally. If he wasn't getting over a beating I'd send the bastard back to Lyon tonight. I would, I swear I would. And now his damn wife is over here to boot. I don't need any of this nonsense."

Mrs. Smith, as Ruth Connolly had warned, was a harridan indeed. Delaney had gone out to the airport, at Jonah Smith's request, to greet her when she came in to Phuket on a flight from Bangkok. Connolly was to be the official Interpol greeter. Delaney was to be the concerned friend.

"This is your classic shit assignment," Connolly said as they waited in the international arrivals area. She was ignoring the No Smoking signs. The Thai police driver with them did not attempt to enforce the rules in this regard. "They did nothing at all to prepare us for this sort of thing in the academy," she said, blowing a perfect smoke ring ceilingward.

When Mrs. Smith came through, pushing a luggage trolley, she looked very much like she would prefer to be pushing a shopping trolley through a tidy Tesco supermarket in southern England. She was a woman in her early forties, wearing a matching pastel blue skirt and blouse combination, and a yellow cardigan, and pearls. A wide-brimmed sunhat was perched atop her luggage. No hint of a smile escaped her lips as she surveyed the crowded terminal for what she clearly expected would be an appropriate reception committee.

"That's got to be her," Connolly said to Delaney. "A home counties lass, no doubt about it. Poster girl. Love the cardigan. Handy in the tropics."

Connolly went over, flashing a giant smile, offering her hand.

"Mrs. Smith? Ruth Connolly, from Interpol. Welcome to Phuket."

Mrs. Smith shook Connolly's hand weakly.

"How was the flight?" Connolly asked.

"Dreadful, Officer. It was dreadful. Interminably long, smelly, noisy, a trial."

"It is a very long haul, London to Bangkok."

"Via Dubai, for some reason. British Airways never told me there would be a stop in Dubai."

Smith had told Delaney that his wife was the only daughter of a Royal Air Force wing commander with a hyphenated name of some kind. She was, Smith said, a woman who had spent many years before marrying in the presence of ramrod straight military people and their wives and children. She liked order, hierarchy, politesse, doing the right thing. She disliked untidy homes, disobedient dogs, civilian rabble and, it seemed, most aspects of her life with Jonah Smith. Delaney wondered how long it would be before she inquired after her husband's health.

He went over as well and offered her his hand.

"I'm Francis Delaney, Mrs. Smith. A friend of Jonah's."

She looked him up and down.

"From London?" she asked. "We've not met. One of Jonah's Lyon friends perhaps."

She said the word *Lyon* as if it denoted some sort of bodily excretion.

"No, I'm from Canada. Jonah and I met here."

"He's a journalist, Mrs. Smith," Connolly said. "A famous one, or so they say."

"Oh, I see, well, I certainly hope you are not going to make too much of this unfortunate business of Jonah having been robbed out here," Mrs. Smith said. "One does always run the risk of robbery in countries like this."

"One does," Delaney said.

He hoped Mrs. Smith's next question would be about her husband's well-being, or, he thought, the marriage was truly over, with no hope of reconciliation whatsoever.

"Jonah is well?" she said.

"Yes, fine now," Connolly said. "A nasty thing, and he got some cuts and bruises, but he wasn't too badly hurt. They got his wallet . . ."

"I see," Mrs. Smith said. She placed her sun hat firmly on her perfectly waved hair. "Can we go to the hotel now? I would like to freshen up."

"Yes, of course," Connolly said, motioning to the Thai police driver, who took over pushing Mrs. Smith's luggage trolley. "We'll get you to the hotel and then over to the hospital. Jonah is due to be released tomorrow."

"I see," said Mrs. Smith.

Connolly very wisely sat in front with the driver on the way to the hotel, but turned around often to flash big smiles at Mrs. Smith, who sat beside Delaney in the back. Delaney started to wonder why Smith had asked him to come along to the airport at all, except, possibly, to see very early in the game what his wife was like.

At the Bay Hotel, Delaney stayed discreetly back as Mrs. Smith checked in to her room on the eighth floor. Jonah Smith's room was on six. Connolly bought Delaney lunch and several Singha beers in the hotel restaurant as they killed an hour before Mrs. Smith reappeared, apparently ready at last to shoulder her wifely burden and go to the hospital. She had changed her blouse. The cardigan now rested loosely on her shoulders, as a concession to the local weather.

"Not sure you'll need a sweater out there today," Delaney said.

"The air conditioning in these places and in all the cars is absolutely freezing, don't you think?" she said.

"True," Connolly said.

At the hospital, Mrs. Smith dutifully kissed her husband on his cheek.

"Goodness me, you do look a sight," she said, sitting in the sole visitor's chair, purse positioned in her lap. "And that mustache. I wouldn't have recognized you."

"I'm all right, Fiona," Smith said. "On the mend now."

"They got your wallet, I'm told. Dreadful story," she said.

"Yes," Smith said.

Delaney could already feel the silence starting to build. It billowed like a thundercloud on a sultry Thai afternoon. He did the right thing, and made his exit. Connolly was not far behind.

Delaney had found over the years that police officers and spies, or those who work closely with police officers and spies, are very good at break-ins and other extralegal activities. Smith had prepared everything, had prepared for every imaginable problem or eventuality. They met in a small street behind the Bay Hotel at precisely 3 a.m. on a hot moonlit night. Smith was driving a car borrowed from Zalm, whose DVI team, apparently, believed that all members should be assigned rental vehicles while in Thailand.

Delaney had taken a taxi from the Metropole. His driver seemed to think nothing of dropping off a foreigner in the middle of the night in a darkened back street, the Phuket brothel scene being what it is. Smith said the watchman in the parking lot of his hotel had been similarly nonchalant as he waved Zalm's car through the gate on the way out.

In the trunk of the car was a small rucksack that Smith had crammed with the tools of the trade. Flashlights for each of them, bolt cutters, a length of nylon rope, a notebook, camera, bottled water, and a smaller bag containing what he said was fingerprinting gear. In the back seat he had stowed a small folding stepladder he had liberated from a cleaner's cupboard at his hotel.

Smith wore an Interpol baseball cap, in navy blue, and darker blue crime-scene overalls, emblazoned on the back, unfortunately, with the words: Interpol Incident Response Team. Delaney also wore a ball cap, an ancient maroon Loyola College number that had outlasted all of his adult relationships put together, including his now long-defunct marriage. He had chosen a black T-shirt and jeans for his freelance break-in work and had tied a grey Montreal Amateur Athletic Association sweatshirt around his waist.

They drove slowly out to the mortuary compound. There was little traffic at that time of night. What there was consisted mainly of taxis ferrying tourists, and presumably visiting international police, back to hotels from the always crowded bars in Phuket Town. Occasionally they saw sleepy-looking Thai hotel workers in uniform, resolutely pedalling homeward or workward on battered bicycles.

Smith had done excellent preparatory work in all other regards as well. He had pulled from the DVI computer system the serial number of the container that held the *Deutschland* body and the approximate place in the compound where that container sat. He also had a printout of the body roster for that particular container. It showed five columns, corresponding to the five wooden racks that would be inside, and nine spaces per column, corresponding to the shelves in each rack that could hold bodies.

Container CRL0912863 would be sitting well toward the back of the compound, luckily for them, not far from the two-metre-high fence in prefabricated concrete sections that had been installed in the weeks after the tsunami disaster. It would hold, Smith's papers showed, 29 numbered bodies, so not all available shelves would be filled. Five bag numbers had been highlighted in pink, indicating that the bodies in those bags had been identified but not yet released for transport home. All the rest were so far unidentified.

The *Deutschland* body, the papers showed, was numbered PM68-TA0386 and would be on the top shelf of Rack 4, one rack from the back. If, as Delaney pointed out on the drive over, the body was actually still in there. Smith looked troubled by this prospect. The body being missing altogether was one of the very few eventualities he had apparently not considered.

They would have crossed over the fence at the back of the compound no matter where the container they sought was located. The narrow dirt road in that area was adjacent to a thick grove of very tall palms. Smith pulled their white Nissan well into the palms, off the road, and they got out immediately. Smith pulled on his rucksack. Delaney carried the ladder.

They walked a little away from the car in the brilliant moonlight. Smith took his length of rope from the rucksack and quickly tied one end to the top step of his ladder. He pulled the ladder's legs apart and placed it at the base of the wall. Delaney watched, impressed, as the fingerprint man climbed quickly up and hoisted himself up on top of the fence, clutching the other end of the rope. He jumped down to the other side and called out to Delaney: "Your turn. Hurry up."

Delaney climbed up and over, landing lightly in the weeds on the other side. Smith pulled the ladder up and over the fence using the rope, folded it, and stowed it in the weeds. They crouched there together, watching and listening. There was no sound at all except for the night breeze that whispered in the container corridors. No watchman's feet crunched on the compound's gravel pathways.

"You seem to be an expert burglar, Jonah," Delaney said.

"I am." Smith said. "Have to be, in police work."

"Really?" Delaney said. "There's a story in there somewhere."

"Many stories, Frank. Not for publication."

They waited and watched and listened some more.

"OK, let's go," Smith said.

Crouching slightly, they walked quickly along the back row, looking for CRL0912863.

"It'll be a Carlisle container," Smith said. "A lot of them are. They got a big load of the Carlisle ones when they were setting up."

Many of the containers did indeed carry the blue Carlisle Shipping logo. The one they sought was not in the back row. They turned up the next corridor and found what they were looking for, three containers into the row. It was battered, like most of the others, and had a plastic document holder taped to the door. Inside that plastic sleeve was the same body roster Smith carried. Smith peered closely at both documents, using his flashlight.

"This is it. Our man's in here," he said.

"Great stuff," Delaney said.

Smith pulled the bolt cutters from his pack and fitted them to a very flimsy padlock, better suited to garden sheds than to forensic evidence containers full of disaster victims. He pulled and strained with the cutters for a few minutes, and then the hasp of the lock fell away. He picked up the various pieces and stowed them in his pack before turning to Delaney again.

"Perhaps you'd better stand watch while I go in and do the deed," he said.

"I don't know, Jonah. Better if we both go in and shut the door, I'd say. If a watchman comes around, I don't want to be out here any longer than I have to."

"Are you squeamish?" Smith asked.

"No," Delaney said.

"Have you seen dead bodies before?"

"Yes, of course," Delaney said.

"Decomposed, weeks after death, postautopsy, that sort of thing?"

"Jonah, for Christ's sake. You'll need someone to hold the light anyway, won't you?"

"OK, all right. The smell's not too bad because it's so cold in there. But it smells. It will smell."

"I'll be fine."

"It will be really cold in there."

"Jonah . . ."

"All right."

Jonah pulled on a white V-neck tennis sweater. Delaney put on his sweatshirt.

"Let's go," Delaney said.

Smith pulled open the large corrugated steel door of the container. It squeaked loudly. Billows of frozen vapour poured out into the tropical night air. Smith trained his flashlight inside onto the rough wooden racks. Delaney had a sudden memory of the eerily similar wooden bunks he'd seen while visiting a former Nazi concentration camp in Poland, horror tourism, to see where exhausted Jews had been crammed in to sleep and await extermination.

Bodies lay silently in Container CRL0912863 in heavy white plastic bags. Delaney followed Smith inside, taking care not to slip on the treacherous flooring of sawdust, ice and steel. Body PM68-TA0386 was precisely where Smith's roster said it would be: Rack 4, Top.

Smith wasted no time. He put his pack on an empty rack below the *Deutschland* body and pulled out his smaller bag of fingerprinting gear. Delaney held a light. Smith opened the gear bag and arranged small bottles of ink and black powder on the rack, as well as an assortment of tape, gummed labels, index cards, small brushes, sticks, scalpels, tweezers, scrapers.

"Scotland Yard issue," Delaney said.

"The original and genuine. Purveyors of the finest fingerprints to Her Majesty the Queen."

The air inside the container was very cold, Canadian cold.

It smelled sharply, as Smith had warned, of putrefaction and chemicals and damp. It was a smell that lingered in nostrils and memory for many hours after being inhaled. Delaney had inhaled such morgue smells before.

Smith put on surgical gloves. He pulled the bag's heavy zipper open to about mid-body level. The face of the *Deutschland* man when it appeared in the flashlight beam was horrifically disfigured by seawater and sun damage and general decay. All that Delaney could really make out of the features in the narrow shaft of light was a balding head and what would have once been a prominent nose. The lips were stretched back over the teeth in the terribly familiar rictus of death. Some grey hairs glistened on the man's chest.

Smith pulled the stiff left arm out of the bag. It, too, had grey hairs still standing. The hand was in bad condition. The skin had tightened on the bones, looking for all the world like shrunken plastic now, in a dreadful blue, green and tan hue.

"Frank, can you give me a bit more light here?" Smith said. He held the corpse's hand up high, crouching slightly to look up at the palm and fingertips from below. The wrists of refrigerated corpses do not cooperate when fingerprint men try to twist them around.

"Fuck," Smith said. Delaney had very rarely heard him swear.

"What?" Delaney said.

"They're gone," Smith said.

"What's gone?"

"The prints, Frank. They're gone. Someone's taken them completely off the hand. Have a look."

Delaney crouched and looked up at the dead man's accusing fingers. He saw, with some difficulty, that each finger pad had been removed. On some fingers, he saw bone where fingerprints should be.

"Bastards," Smith said, as Delaney straightened up. "It's

been done by someone who knows the business, too. Excised, with a scalpel. Gone."

Smith rummaged around in the body bag.

"Nothing in there. Gone," he said.

He pried open the corpse's mouth and shone his own flashlight inside.

"Bastards," he said.

"What?"

"Molars gone too. Everything's gone from the back. Not a tooth left in there with any fillings. This body's all but useless now for dental ID too."

Smith seemed genuinely angry, not just perplexed. Delaney had not seen him so angry before. The fingerprint man reached into the pack and took out his digital camera.

"Hold up the arm, Frank. I want to get a shot of those fingers. You want to wear gloves?"

Delaney hesitated.

"Here, here, hold the wrist with this," Smith said, handing him a cloth from his bag. "It won't take long."

Delaney stood holding the *Deutschland* arm aloft while Smith, with forensic care, took a series of pictures of the hand. The flashes were very bright in the pitch dark container. The mouth of the corpse was open. Smith took closeup pictures of where the back teeth once had been. He also took two pictures of the body bag number—a closeup and one from a step or two back, bag open and *in situ*.

"Now I'm going to take prints of the damage," Smith said. "And a palm print."

"What use will that be?" Delaney asked.

"Probably no use whatsoever," Smith said, in no mood for queries about method.

Delaney watched as Smith worked swiftly, professionally. He dusted the mutilated fingertips with brush and slightly greasy black powder. Then he pressed a gummed label to the end of each finger, rolling the label around on the tips to produce a wide impression of as much surface as possible. He stuck the labels onto small index cards, one per card, and wrote brief notes on each with a felt tip pen.

Then he did the entire palm of the left hand and began to work on the right. This one was harder to get at, and he had to reach across the body and struggle with a stiff limb while Delaney held the light.

As he slid his index cards into a plastic sleeve and stowed his gear, Smith said: "I have never seen something like this before. Never, in all my years in the trade. Damaged fingers, yes, often. But finger pads excised with a blade, no. Never."

He still looked extremely angry.

"Interesting," Delaney said.

"It's more than bloody interesting, Frank. It's a crime, for one thing. And it totally eliminates the possibility that I will ever be able to check this man's prints again, against any database, anywhere."

"Let's get out of here and think things through."

"I'm going to go to Braithwaite."

"I don't think that's a very good idea, Jonah. Let's get out of here, and we'll just think things through a bit."

Delaney went to the front of the container and peered out. Smith zipped up the body bag and joined him.

"Still clear out there," Delaney said.

"Bastards," Smith said.

Delaney drove the car. Smith was still very angry indeed. He sat and fumed in silence as they headed back toward the Metropole. No watchman had accosted them at the mortuary site; no one had seen them as they clambered back over the compound fence.

Under the awning at the entrance to the hotel, Delaney climbed out and Smith slid over to the driver's seat. By Delaney's watch it was 4:50 a.m. The sun would be up soon. An extremely tired-looking night clerk, well past retirement age, came out to open the hotel door, securely locked against burglars such as themselves at this hour.

"Take it easy, Jonah," Delaney said. "We'll think this through later. We'll go to Plan B."

Smith said nothing, hands on the steering wheel but not driving off.

"Don't make any decisions yet on what to do next. OK?" Delaney said. "I think it's a mistake to tell Braithwaite anything about this right now. Jonah?"

Eventually, Smith said: "I want to identify that body, Frank. I want to know who that man is."

He put the car into gear.

"We'll do that, Jonah. I'm sure we'll do that eventually," Delaney said.

"I'm going to go get some sleep," Smith said.

He pulled away, saying nothing else. Delaney watched him drive off.

The night clerk said: "Your evening in Phuket was enjoyable, sir?"

When Delaney got up to his room, he did what all self-respecting journalists and burglars do. He opened a beer from the mini-bar and a tiny airline-sized bottle of whisky and drank them both in quick succession. Only as he munched peanuts and paced around his silent room, did he notice that an envelope had been pushed under his door. He had missed it in his initial haste to pour himself a drink.

It was on Bay Hotel stationery, not Metropole stock. The desk clerks must have held it at the front and then delivered it very late because he was sure he had not seen it when he left earlier to meet his break-in accomplice. He looked at the signature before anything else. Fiona Smith.

In perfect British private school calligraphy, the note said:

Mr. Delaney, I wonder if you would be so kind as to join me for breakfast tomorrow morning? I would be happy to come to your hotel. There is something extremely important I would like to discuss with you. I propose 8:00 a.m. so as not to interfere with your workday. I will wait for you in the restaurant. Please let me know if this is convenient.

Delaney read the note twice, seeking, as always, subtexts. None was apparent. He looked at his watch. Already 5:30 a.m— Mrs. Smith would have gone to bed expecting her breakfast meeting was on. She was not the sort of woman who expected such invitations to be refused.

For a moment, he considered calling Mr. Smith, to discuss the new development regarding his wife. Something made him decide against that. Smith was already angry enough and worried enough as it was.

Fiona Smith went nowhere at all without a cardigan, it seemed. She was sitting in a booth in the busy restaurant, surrounded by hotel hubbub. Thai waitresses in standard server-issue uniform rushed to and fro. International police and Thai policemen, some of them in another sort of uniform, helped themselves to the vast breakfast buffet. There were few, if any, tourists, in post-tsunami Phuket. In the far corner, Delaney saw the BBC TV crew, plotting and scheming.

Mrs. Smith had already nibbled on a plate of fresh fruit. A half-finished cup of tea was on the table and the British Airways in-flight magazine she had apparently brought with her to while away any idle moments.

Delaney shook her hand before sitting down. He had got perhaps an hour's sleep, and looked it. He had also decided to leave shaving for another day. The quartet of empty Jameson sample bottles in his room, with matching beer bottles, may have been a contributing factor to his overall appearance. Mrs. Smith looked like she did not approve at all of her breakfast companion but, as Delaney had already discovered, she approved of very little in this life.

"Thank you for coming, Mr. Delaney," she said.

"Frank, please," he said. "'It's Francis, actually, but most people call me Frank."

"Thank you for coming," she said again. She did not invite him to call her Fiona. "Will you eat something?"

She looked like she hoped the answer to this would be negative.

"I will, yes," Delaney said. He motioned to a waitress to bring coffee, and went to the buffet to get medicinal eggs, sausage, tomato, baked beans, croissants, butter, jam. He was unable to also carry back the glass of orange juice his aching body required and he doubted Mrs. Smith would stand for his making two trips.

She watched for a moment as he ate. Apparently, it was up to him to begin with small talk.

"Jonah seems like he is doing better," Delaney said.

"Yes, he does," she said. "Nasty business, that."

"Yes."

It seemed that uncomfortable silences accompanied Mrs. Smith wherever she went. Delaney ate. He drank coffee. He resisted commenting on the weather or the air-conditioning excesses.

Eventually, Mrs. Smith said, "I would like to be very forthright with you this morning, if I may, Mr. Delaney."

"Please," he said.

"I have been briefed by Detective Chief Superintendent Braithwaite on the situation out here," she said.

"The situation?"

"Yes."

Delaney waited.

"Superintendent Braithwaite tells me that my husband has got it into his head that something, Lord knows what exactly, is amiss with procedures out here and that he has been speaking to you about this for your magazine article. Superintendent Braithwaite is not at all happy with this situation."

"Superintendent Braithwaite has told me so himself," Delaney said.

"And did he tell you about the possible consequences for my husband's career?"

"Not directly. Not in so many words."

"Well, it's very clear to me, Mr. Delaney, that Jonah has upset the powers that be. I feel it is my responsibility to intervene. Jonah is clearly not himself. He has clearly forgotten himself out here. One can see that even in the way he dresses. That mustache . . ."

"None of that has anything to do with me, Mrs. Smith. This is something between Jonah and his superiors, and Jonah and yourself."

"No it is not, Mr. Delaney. Not if you are going to write nonsense in your article."

"I'm writing something for *International Geographic* magazine, Mrs. Smith. About the DVI effort here. It's not a scandal sheet, by any means."

"Not so far."

"What is it you want from me, Mrs. Smith?"

"I want to avoid scandal," she said. "Obviously."

"Is there a scandal?" Delaney asked.

"If you fabricate one," she said.

Delaney had been in the game long enough to ignore insults to his professionalism. Usually.

"Did Superintendent Braithwaite ask you to come see me?" he asked.

"Not directly. But he made it quite clear that he was concerned. I told him I would do what I could to prevent Jonah from putting his career at risk."

"That's Jonah's decision to make, wouldn't you say?"

"No. Not entirely his, no. His decisions affect me. And they affect his colleagues at Scotland Yard."

"Is it your job to defend Scotland Yard, Mrs. Smith? Is there something there that needs defending?"

"It's one of Britain's great institutions," she said.

"Mrs. Smith, I'm not sure where this conversation is going," Delaney said.

Jonah Smith's wife waited for a moment.

"My husband has confided in you," she said.

Delaney said nothing.

"I'm going to be absolutely forthright with you, Mr. Delaney," she said.

"Please," he said.

"I believe my husband has been out here far too long. And in Lyon too long. His behaviour has changed. His judgment is impaired, if you like. He doesn't know who he is anymore. I feel it is my responsibility to try to prevent him from harming his reputation and his career any more than he has already done by confiding in you and encouraging you to write stories about his work or the work that is going on generally out here and the way police officers are behaving far from their home environments."

"What does that mean, Mrs. Smith?" Delaney asked. "That last bit."

She hesitated.

"I want no scandals, Mr. Delaney."

"You've said that."

She waited.

"I have received a very disturbing telephone message that makes me think my family is at risk of becoming embroiled in a tawdry little scandal out here and I will not have it."

Delaney watched her, saying nothing.

"I have received on my hotel phone a voicemail message that suggests my husband has been unfaithful to me, Mr. Delaney. There you have it. With a Spanish woman of some sort.

The message suggested you would be aware of this as well."

"I'm a journalist, Mrs. Smith. I've never been interested in gossip. Never. I deal in facts. I don't write racy gossip stories for the women's magazines."

"That's not the impression I got from that phone message, Mr. Delaney."

"I can't control your impressions, Mrs. Smith. And you don't know anything about me anyway."

"I am asking you to behave professionally, Mr. Delaney. I am asking you to not print salacious trivia about my husband and I am asking you to not print wild allegations about the police operation he has been assigned to. That's what I'm asking you to do."

"Mrs. Smith, you can be sure I won't be writing about people's personal lives. Certainly not in *International Geographic* magazine. Does that help?"

"It does. Thank you very much. And this crazy conspiracy theory of Jonah's?"

"That's another matter altogether."

"I see."

They regarded each other over plates and cups and cutlery.

"May I ask you something now, Mrs. Smith?" Delaney said. "My turn."

"If you must," she said.

"This phone message. On your voicemail. Did you recognize the voice by any chance?"

"Don't be silly," she said.

"It was in English, obviously. Western accent? Or Asian? Thai?"

"You're playing detective now, Mr. Delaney?"

"Humour me, OK? Asian accent?"

"No."

"European?"

"Yes."

"British?"

"Great Britain is not Europe, Mr. Delaney," she said.

Delaney did not rise to the invitation for morning political debate, with a medium-level hangover and one hour's sleep.

"What part of Europe?" he asked. "What accent? In your view?"

"This is silly," she said.

"Humour me."

"Well, German," she said. "I would say German."

Chapter 7

The day Stefan Zalm made what Delaney and Smith would refer to afterward as his "confession" was the day Mrs. Smith headed back to the relative tranquility of England. It was also the day Mrs. Smith confronted her husband about what Delaney knew she would always refer to afterward as the "scandal." She waited until she had checked in at the airport for her flight, Smith told him. Smith had insisted on driving her there himself in Zalm's car, declining a police driver. This left the Smiths for too long in uncomfortable, unsupervised proximity.

At sundown on the day of Mrs. Smith's departure, Delaney and Smith were drinking beer on the balcony of Delaney's hotel room. Smith had come directly to the hotel from the airport, for there was much to discuss in addition to disintegrating marriages. They had not, for example, decided what to do next about the excised *Deutschland* fingerprints. Smith had not yet told Braithwaite about what they had found in the mortuary compound. He was far less angry and prone to impulsive acts than on the night of the break-in, but he was no less perplexed, no less determined to rectify the situation.

"Fiona knows about Conchi," Smith said to Delaney, squinting into the afternoon sun.

Delaney had not told Smith about the breakfast encounter with his wife a day earlier. He wasn't sure why.

"We knew there was a risk someone would tell her," Delaney said.

"I really thought they wouldn't bother," Smith said. "What does it achieve, when you think about it?"

"You have enemies now. They want you to lay off this thing and they're obviously willing to use anything they can to get at you."

"I know that," Smith said. "But it's not working."

"How bad was it, with Fiona?"

Delaney disliked Mrs. Smith enough to feel immediately after his question that there was something unpleasantly familiar about his using her given name.

"She was very civilized about it. Very English. We English are so . . . " Smith groped for words, ". . . English about these things."

"Meaning?"

"She clearly just wants to avoid a scandal. That's basically what she said, Frank. She didn't say anything about ending the marriage or what we should do next or ask whether I was going to come home, now or after my stint in Lyon is over. She just said she wanted to protect our family name. Her family name, more likely."

"That's pretty Victorian of her," Delaney said.

"Precisely," Smith said. "She has a hyphenated maiden name, after all."

"Quite," Delaney said. "My good man . . ."

"At least she didn't go down the path of somehow blaming me for the death of our baby. Not in that conversation at least. It used to come up somehow in just about every other argument we had, about anything. Before we stopped bothering to even argue anymore."

Delaney said nothing. This was a level of personal detail he could do without. Smith saw this, looked embarrassed at his very un-English display. They sipped beer.

"She ask you to break it off?" Delaney said eventually. "The Conchi thing?"

"Not in so many words. She did say she was confident I would do the right thing."

"I see."

"I told her we should both spend some time thinking about things for a little while."

"How very civilized."

"Do the right thing, my good man."

"She knows it's Conchi?"

"She knows it's Spanish."

"Who would have told her?"

Delaney felt uneasy about not having told Smith about the breakfast meeting with his wife, but things had gone a little too far in their conversation for him to raise it now. There was no strong reason to bother now in any case; there was no new information for Smith, really. In the realm of marital breakdowns, Delaney had been through a particularly nasty one himself, had been watching O'Keefe's marriage disintegrate at a glacial pace for years, had watched far too many media marriages hit the shoals to be overly troubled by the family secrets Smith was sharing with him in the fading tropical light over a beer.

"She said she didn't know who it was," Smith said. "Someone just left her a phone message. I'm guessing Becker, or someone on his team. That's what I think. And Braithwaite has basically warned her to warn me that I'm on decidedly shaky career ground if I keep on with this. So she said at the airport."

"We knew about that already as well."

"Quite," Smith said.

It took them a number of additional cold Singhas before they decided what it was they should do next. The beer helped, of course. But it was Zalm's rather theatrical arrival and subsequent confession that clinched it.

Before Zalm swept into the hotel room to bare his soul, Delaney told Smith about his telephone conversation that morning with Ackermann in Berlin. Ackermann had been in a rush. A woman was waiting for him in some seedy bar or other. But he had done his reporter's work very well, as always, and Delaney would owe him yet another favour and another expensive meal.

"No way that body over there is Stahlman's," Ackermann had said. "Not a chance, Francis Frank Delaney."

"You really sure, dead sure?" Delaney said. "No body was ever found."

"Dead sure Stahlman is long dead. I've triple-checked in my obsessional Germanic way and the man was dead, dead, dead long before any tsunami in Thailand became the biggest damn story of 2004. Every police contact who knew the case, every friend of his friends I managed to find, every government contact I used, even the vice-president of the damn company that took over Stahlman's firm after the suicide, everyone, everyone, everyone assures me that the man killed himself. There was never the slightest trace of him being alive after his little outing at the seashore. No money trail, no phone calls, no letters, no sightings, nothing, nothing, nothing. You are on the wrong track Francis Frank. Trust Ackermann on this."

Delaney himself had all but ruled out the possibility that the *Deutschland* body was disgraced pedophile Karl-Heinz Stahlman. Stahlman's reputation had already been ruined well before his last solitary swim in the Baltic Sea. Delaney could think of no reason for anyone—friend, family or police—to go to such lengths after the tsunami disaster had taken so many other lives to try to cover up a story about a German pedophile having faked his own death in order to start a new life on the beaches of southern Thailand. Even if body PM68-TA0386 had in fact been Stahlman's.

"So who?" Delaney said.

"I can't do all your work for you, Frank. You are the world famous investigative journalist, am I correct. Still? So go out and do some investigative journalism. Or perhaps use your good friends in cloak and dagger realms to help you out on this one."

Ackermann, like a very small circle of Delaney's closest media colleagues, had developed suspicions over the years that at least some of his investigative work was not actually done for newspapers and magazines. Delaney never bothered to deny this when the suggestion came from a man he trusted as well as Ackermann. Nor, however, did he ever actually confirm it.

"Have I now earned my supper?" Ackermann asked.

"I suppose," Delaney said. "I would have preferred a full name and a police fingerprint card for this body. Or a DNA match. But if this is the best a German newspaper man can do . . ."

"You are too much, Francis Frank. You are lucky I love you more than life itself. Now will you let me get along to meet the young woman who helps me to forget about you for a time and mend my broken heart?"

Smith had, very unwisely in Delaney's view, already told Conchi and Zalm separately about the break-in at the compound and what he and Delaney had found in the body bag. Or, more importantly, what they had not found.

Smith said Conchi had been angry that he and Delaney had taken such chances. Then she was angry about not being invited along to help them. Then she was angry the fingerprints had been removed from the body.

Conchi was wise enough, or, possibly experienced enough in such matters, to have kept a low profile while Mrs. Smith was in town. Delaney didn't see her for several days. He did not ask how, or when, or how often, Smith had managed to meet with her while his wife was doing the right thing in tropical climes.

Zalm, Smith said, had been surprisingly agitated by the news that the *Deutschland* body was now without finger pads or back teeth. The break-in story itself had alarmed the Dutchman, clearly. But the revelation that someone else had broken into the container before them and expertly removed potential evidence seemed to shake him up badly, Smith said.

Zalm wasn't angry like Conchi. Instead, Smith said, he was upset; one might even say frightened.

The reason for that became clear soon after Zalm hurried into Delaney's hotel room and joined them on the balcony. He refused offers of a beer. He refused offers of a chair. His face was flushed. He lit one of the fragrant Indonesian clove cigarettes he now liked to smoke. He was carrying a large, overstuffed brown envelope.

"What's wrong with you this evening, Stefan?" Smith asked. "Are you in love, or something?"

The beers appeared to have relaxed the Scotland Yard fingerprint man somewhat, despite the heavy problems that faced him. Or perhaps it was the departure from Thailand of his wife. Or both.

"What's in the envelope, Stefan?" Delaney asked.

The Dutchman looked as if he were about to burst into tears.

"What is it, Stefan? What's going on?" Smith said.

"I've done something terrible," Zalm said.

"Come off it," Smith said.

"I've done something very stupid, Jonah. I'm so sorry."

"What?" Smith said, looking over at Delaney. "What?"

"Jonah, please, just listen before you condemn me, please just listen first."

Zalm sat down at last on a chair facing them both. He placed his mysterious brown envelope on a low table beside him.

They waited. Delaney resisted the journalist's urge to reach for a notebook and pen.

"I'm so sorry," Zalm said, running his left hand through his hair, rubbing his head nervously. "This is my first big international DVI assignment. I wanted to do well. You know? They said I would be representing Holland and with all the Dutch victims out here they were expecting the whole Dutch team to do very good work, to work fast and get lots of positive IDs. They wanted all the Dutch bodies home fast."

"All the teams want that, Stefan," Smith said.

"Yes, yes, I know. But I felt I had to do particularly well, because I'm a civilian and I'm younger than a lot of the police and I just wanted to do well and make a lot of IDs. It's not always easy, with teeth. You know that, Jonah. Frank, you know how hard these DVI things can be. You do."

"It's hard with fingerprints, too, Stefan," Smith said.

Delaney could see that Smith was getting annoyed even before he knew what it was Zalm had actually done.

"What did you do, Stefan?" Delaney asked.

"I took things from files," Zalm said.

"You what!" Smith shouted.

"Not whole files, Jonah. Things from inside problem files. I took copies of some of the things in them. Some of them."

"You what!" Smith shouted again.

"Jonah, please. I'm sorry. I wanted to do well so I took copies of some of the things in the problem files so I could study them slowly and look at people's notes at night in my room and sort of get a sense of things so I could do better work. Some of you had good notes about possibles, things like where people might be from, which country, maybe which city. You, for example Jonah, left good notes when you were struggling with a hard fingerprint match or looking at palms. You would say whether the body was probably male or female, young or old, manual worker or office type. The other guys might say things about clothes found on the bodies or rings or tattoos and I wanted to study these things alone at night so I could make better guesses about where people might be from or if they were Dutch and where I might get people back in Amsterdam to go to try for good antemortem dental records. You see? So I could do well. I wanted to make a lot of matches. I thought it would help me to know where the matching process was going for some of the harder files. I thought the papers would help me in my own work."

"That's crazy, Stefan," Smith said. "You didn't need to do that. Anyone would have told you what they thought. I would have helped you anytime. You could have looked at any files anytime."

"I know, Jonah, I know. It's crazy. But I wanted to spend more time on the files at night without seeming like I was going around asking people for favours like a police cadet. It's crazy, I know. I just photocopied things instead and brought them to my room to study them alone at night."

"That's crazy."

"So what are you saying exactly, Stefan?" Delaney asked.

"Well," he said. "I have some papers from the *Deutschland* file. Here with me. Copies."

"You what?" Smith shouted, jumping up from his chair. "What? Are you crazy?"

Delaney wondered if Smith would actually go over and hit Zalm.

"Easy, Jonah. Easy," he said.

"I'm sorry, Jonah," Zalm said. "I couldn't tell you before now. I thought you would be so mad. You have a right to be mad. But how could I tell you I was acting like a fool? I thought the file would turn up anyway or that maybe it didn't matter very much anyway that one file went missing because eventually the pathology teams would get to the body again and have another look and take more fingerprints and you could work on those again, eventually. But then when you told me you and Frank had been out to the compound and that someone had been in the containers and that the prints were actually taken off the fingers altogether, I knew this was getting serious."

"It's always been serious, you bloody fool," Smith shouted.

"Easy," Delaney said.

"I'm sorry, Jonah," Zalm said.

Smith looked over at Delaney.

"This is unbelievable," he said. "Why would anyone do such a thing?"

"I wanted to make IDs," Zalm said again.

"You're a fool," Smith said. "I thought you were a friend."

"Please don't say that, Jonah. Please. I am your friend. Look. I can fix it now, look. I have the papers. Here."

Zalm picked up his envelope and pressed it into Smith's hands.

"This is the *Deutschland* file?" Smith said.

"Yes, yes. A lot of it. Copies. And most of the photocopies of papers in other files that I took. It's not all *Deutschland*. But we can fix it now, Jonah? Can't we?"

Smith looked over at Delaney again, incredulous and angry at the same time.

"Why didn't you tell me before this, long before this? You knew very well that I needed those papers badly, Stefan. You knew I was in trouble about them. I even went to Braithwaite. You let me go to Braithwaite about this."

"I couldn't tell you, Jonah. I couldn't tell you. I felt ashamed and stupid."

"Why are you telling us now?" Delaney asked.

"Because it's getting serious now," Zalm said.

"It's always been serious, Stefan, right from the beginning," Smith said. "You stupid man."

"I know, I know, Jonah. But if people are cutting prints off the fingers . . ."

"You foolish, foolish man," Smith said again.

He sat and stared at the battered envelope on his lap.

"What you need is in there, Jonah. I'm sure," Zalm said. "There's a copy of the *Deutschland* prints in there. I looked again. And some of your notes."

Smith just looked dejectedly at the envelope.

"I can't believe you would do this to me, Stefan," he said.

"We can fix it now," Zalm said. "Can't we?"

Smith said nothing.

"Have a look, Jonah. Maybe we can fix it," Delaney said.

Smith slowly opened the envelope and spread the contents out on the table. He took out some reading glasses and suddenly became very serious, professional. He sorted papers and studied some of them very closely. Delaney and Zalm said nothing, letting him work. Zalm chain-smoked clove cigarettes.

Eventually, Smith said: "These aren't the same prints. For the *Deutschland* body."

"How can that be?" Zalm shouted. "I got them right from the *Deutschland* file."

"How can you know that, Jonah?" Delaney said. "How could you remember something like that? Even you can't memorize people's fingerprints. Come on."

"I know these aren't the same," Smith said. "I told you both, remember I told you both, there were only three prints taken off that body that were of any use at all. The other seven were not usable; the quality was simply too bad. I told you both this, several times. Then those three possibly usable prints went missing from the file. Then the whole damn file itself went missing altogether. But these prints Stefan's brought today are not the same. They're all quite good quality. Not just three of them."

Smith peered at them again.

"That's not possible," Zalm said. "I took those from the file. I know I did."

They all stared at each other in silence. Smith's anger

seemed to be subsiding as his forensic imagination became engaged.

"Eventually, Delaney said: "Maybe someone substituted the prints. After Stefan made his copy."

"What do you mean?" Smith said.

"Well, maybe someone took the first set out and put a less good set in. After Stefan made his copy. Maybe from another body. No?"

Smith pondered this.

Zalm said excitedly: "Yes, yes, maybe. Jonah? What do you think?"

"Why would they do that?" Smith said.

"To confuse things, to confuse you. Because the original set was too good, maybe. I don't know. They went to a lot of trouble on other things. Why not this?"

Smith stared at the prints again.

"These are quite good," he said. "Classic whorls, most of them. Some composites. And a nice little scar on the middle finger, left."

"When did you make the photocopies, Stefan?" Delaney asked.

"Oh, Frank, I can't remember exactly," Zalm said. "Weeks ago."

"Before I told you about the trouble?" Smith asked him.

"Yes, Jonah. I can't remember exactly when, but it was before that."

"It's possible someone changed the prints, isn't it, Jonah?" Delaney asked. "To confuse things. Before you had a really good look at the file?"

"Anything is possible, Frank. I can see that now," Smith said. "But why would they then take the three not-too-bad-quality fingerprints away from the file after that?"

"To confuse things further?" Delaney said. "It's possible, no? Or maybe they were afraid you'd actually make another match of some kind with those three that would be so implausible for that body that you'd know something strange was really going on?"

"Yes, that could be it," Zalm said hopefully.

Smith stared at the Dutchman. Delaney was not sure what Smith would do next. He looked calmer, almost resigned to something now.

"You are a very foolish man, Stefan," Smith said.

"I know that, Jonah. I'm sorry."

"You behave like a stupid police cadet."

"I know."

"What you did was illegal."

"I know, Jonah."

"I can't believe you would do such a thing."

They all sat in silence. Smith stared at the *Deutschland* prints. Delaney watched Smith. Zalm smoked nervously, and watched them both.

"I'll run these through the DVI databases here in Phuket," Smith said eventually. "There may be some antemortem prints in there that match. If that doesn't come up with a match, I'll run them through the Interpol database back in Lyon."

"Won't people know if you do that, Jonah?" Delaney asked.

"No," Smith said. "I have access to the antemortem print database here, from all countries. Whenever a tsunami missing person's AM marks get sent from a country somewhere, they go in. To check prints against a national police records somewhere, I have to make a special request. But for the DVI databases here, no. And for Interpol, no. I have access. And one of my very good friends in Lyon is in charge of all the forensic databases there anyway. He can help me if I need extra help."

"And if all that doesn't give us a match?" Delaney asked.

"Then I'd have to request a records search in a national police database."

"Germany."

"Yes," Smith said. "That would be the one, I'd say."

"Tricky."

"Yes. But let's see what I can turn up before that. Let's cross that bridge when we come to it."

"We can fix this," Zalm said. "I know we can."

Delaney felt it was time he called in some markers from the Canadian spy service, providers of substantial freelance income and substantial useful information over the years. Much of the information CSIS deigned to provide him was incomplete, when it suited them or when they decided he didn't need complete information to do the jobs they occasionally asked him to do. He was accustomed to treating CSIS information cautiously, sometimes skeptically, but always with respect. They treated the information he provided to them in precisely the same way.

Jonathan Rawson was Delaney's CSIS handler and, in a way, after almost ten years, his friend. Rawson knew all about the Natalia story, had been heavily involved, and he knew about some of the angry, violent and illegal things Natalia's murder had subsequently inspired Delaney to do. Some, but not all.

Delaney dialed Rawson's private number in Ottawa immediately after Smith and Zalm left his hotel room. He was reasonably confident the Englishman and the Dutchman would not launch themselves into a fistfight in the elevator on the way down.

Rawson had, paradoxically, become a far happier man after the September 2001 terrorist attacks on New York and Washington. Suddenly, with the world irrevocably changed, and security and intelligence work around the world seen in a fresh light, Rawson's personal crusade to transform CSIS into what he always called a "real" spy service rather than a Canadian facsimile of a spy service had started to bear fruit.

Suddenly, Rawson and his like-minded colleagues no longer had to go cap in hand to their bureaucratic and judicial masters to beg permission for more resources, more staff, more latitude in operations outside Canada's borders. Suddenly, everyone who mattered in Rawson's world came onside and gave him and his colleagues virtual carte blanche. Suddenly, Rawson could work alongside American and British and French and other spies, could design and execute covert operations on foreign soil, and not feel so much like a country bumpkin anymore.

The same changes had in fact occurred in the RCMP. Delaney had watched as Kate Hunter's police work changed from standard financial crime investigation, the white-collar crime work she was so good at, into higher level, far more complex and far more consequential investigations into the financing of international terrorism, the illicit flows of money around the globe that financed deadly operations aimed at maximum carnage for civilians and maximum martyrdom for perpetrators. Kate's RCMP world, too, had in its way also been transformed by the September 11 attacks.

Rawson was as Delaney expected, in his office in Ottawa, just back at that time of the Canadian morning, from his customary jogging excursion around what many believed was one of the most boring capital cities in the world. Delaney had always argued that only Canberra, Australia, was worse.

"Jonathan Rawson, good morning," Delaney's spymaster said in his customary mellifluous tones. Delaney could imagine him in his office overlooking the Rideau Canal, jogging gear hanging on a peg behind his door, freshly shaved and showered, not a strand of salt-and-pepper hair out of place—ready and willing to fight terrorism and intelligence service budget cuts on all fronts.

"Francis Delaney, good evening," Delaney said.

"Ah, Francis, good to hear your voice," Rawson said. "Where are you, in evening time zones?"

"Thailand," Delaney said.

"On no," Rawson said. "Please. Not another catastrophe I have to bail you out of."

Rawson had done excellent work in early 2001 negotiating Delaney's release from Insein Prison in Rangoon after he had badly upset the Burmese authorities, and a number of other extremely unpleasant people, while on assignment for CSIS. Delaney had been deported eventually to Bangkok and had proceeded to upset Rawson and CSIS even further.

"Not so far, Jon. Playing reporter this time."

"So you were last time. Or that was the original plan."

"The real thing this time. I'm doing up an *International Geographic* piece on the tsunami. Disaster victim identification."

"You are the right man for that job," Rawson said. "Disasters."

"I'm staying out of trouble."

"I doubt that very much," Rawson said. "Not if you are calling me from overseas."

"Can you talk?" Delaney asked.

"The new CSIS has the latest toys, Francis. I'm in my nice new office on my nice new secure phone, if that's what you mean. Go."

"OK, Jon, I need a favour."

"Oh no."

"Can you check out a couple of names for me? And a third one if I get it? Police types, the first two. One from Germany and one from the Netherlands."

"Police," Rawson said. "This doesn't sound good."

"Police types. Civilian guys, working for the police on the DVI operation over here."

"That's slightly better," Rawson said. "Not much better."

"Horst Becker is the German's name. He's a pathologist attached to the German team here. Works usually at some military hospital in Frankfurt, apparently. And Stefan Zalm, who's a dental guy, a forensic dentist, working with the Dutch police over here."

Delaney had been in the information and disinformation game long enough to be asking himself if he should be suspicious of Zalm having suddenly produced ten good-quality fingerprints for the *Deutschland* body. Sometimes in the information-gathering game it paid to be skeptical of good news when it came your way.

"What's up, Francis?" Rawson asked.

"Here's the question. Why would anyone want to prevent the body of a tsunami victim from being identified?"

"Hmm," Rawson said. "Interesting. Not necessarily a CSIS matter, of course."

"Probably not," Delaney said. "Very unlikely. But something CSIS can help me with maybe."

"This doesn't sound like your basic *International Geographic* hippos in the waterhole kind of story to me, Francis."

"No, it doesn't to me either," Delaney said.

"So who's your client for this? Editor or spook?"

"You know I report to only one spook, Jon."

"I've never been too sure about that, Francis. As you get better and better at what you do. As word of your talent spreads."

"I'm a one-spook kind of guy, Mr. Rawson."

"Do I owe you any favours at this point?"

"Dozens, according to my calculations."

"I see. And who's the third guy?"

"He's a dead guy. With his fingerprints surgically removed. Probably German. I thought for a while he might be a fat old pedophile type who made himself disappear. I don't know about that anymore. Doubtful now. I'd tell you his name but I don't have it. That's the problem at the moment. Or one of the problems. If I get a name I'll give that one to you as well."

"I see," Rawson said again. "Interesting. Not really an *International Geographic* sort of story at all."

"Nope."

"Disaster victim identification."

"Yup."

"What do you get out of this? Besides a story maybe?"

As usual at this stage of his journalistic and extrajournalistic career, Delaney was not at all sure what use he would, or should, make of any information he set out to gather. That was his biggest problem, as Rawson, Kate, O'Keefe and any number of other freelance career counsellors never tired of telling him.

"Not sure yet," Delaney said.

"What do I get out of this?" Rawson asked.

"Is that the kind of relationship we have? I thought you guys loved me for my brains and good looks."

"Besides that."

"I doubt you guys will get anything out of this, Jon. You'd be doing it for love. And future considerations."

"It's the future considerations part that gets me, Francis. Every time you run into a little jam."

"I'm not in a jam this time, Jon. I told you that."

"Not so far."

Tim Bishop called him from the house phone in the lobby. It was quite late in the evening for Bishop to be up and about. He usually retired to his room early, after a vegetarian dinner without wine, to work on his computer or watch TV.

"Can I come up?" Bishop said.

"Sure," Delaney said. "Troubles?"

"Not really," Bishop said.

It turned out that Bishop was bored. He was in a bad mood. He wanted more picture assignments or he would go back to Paris. He felt Delaney had been spinning his wheels on the DVI story and it had all become too boring. What, if anything, did Delaney want him to do next?

"Well, we've got the interview with the Canadian DNA man tomorrow, right?" Delaney said.

"Big deal," Bishop said grumpily. "Head shots. If they make it into the magazine at all."

"Tim, we can't always be jumping in and out of helicopters," Delaney said.

"That's a shame."

"Can't you go out and get pissed and find a promiscuous Thai girl like photographers are supposed to? Kick back a little in a tropical setting?"

"I think I'll head back to Paris the day after tomorrow, Frank. Unless you need me for something else."

Delaney thought a request for pictures of a corpse's mutilated finger pads might cheer Bishop up, but did not make such a request. Jonah Smith's little digital camera had done that job already, though almost certainly with far less panache than Bishop would have brought to it.

"Stand by for a bit, OK Tim? This might get more interesting soon," Delaney said. "And maybe the magazine will send us to the Maldives to finish up. I hear Thai tsunami bodies are washing up on beaches way over there. That's thousands of kilometres away. Bodies in the water for weeks, bloated way beyond recognition."

"That sounds better," Bishop said hopefully.

Delaney had only a few unshakeable rules at this stage of his professional and personal life. One of them was to never argue with wives or ex-wives or lovers on the telephone from an overseas location. He completely abandoned that rule in his phone call to Kate after Tim Bishop left.

Without understanding why, he dialed Kate's number in Montreal. In his heart, if he had looked there as required, he might have been trying to do a little relationship maintenance work, even if he knew, also deep in his heart, that this relationship was going nowhere and could go nowhere until he decided if he wanted this or any relationship at all. Or perhaps observing the Mr. and Mrs. Smith saga had simply stirred his unconscious somehow.

Natalia had been a psychologist. He had never felt closer to any woman anywhere, anytime in his life. Not long before she was murdered, when he had been getting all too comfortable with that closeness, she had pronounced him impossible to understand. How could he, therefore, a rank amateur in the introspection business, be expected to fully understand his actions and his motivations?

Kate, like Rawson, was all business when she answered telephones.

"Financial crime, Hunter," she said.

"Kate, it's me, Frank," Delaney said.

"Who?" she said. "I don't know anyone by that name. I once had a loverboy by that name but he has gone away and disappeared. He never calls, he never writes."

"Does he at least email?"

"No," she said. "Not a word."

"Not a nice man. You're better off without a guy like that, maybe."

"I've been thinking along those lines," she said.

"Can you talk?"

"I can take a moment away from fighting terrorism, yes," she said. "Can you talk? That's more to the point."

The signs were not good for this call. Delaney began to very much regret that he had telephoned the Mounted Police.

"I'm sorry I'm so bad at staying in touch, Kate."

"When you are away or when you are in Montreal, Francis?"

"Both," he said.

"So go and sin no more. Or whatever," she said. "Whatever the priests are supposed to say in confession. Or was that Jesus who said that?"

"I'm on a story."

"You are always on a story. Always. How is this new?"

"Come on, Kate," he said lamely. "Don't be in a bad mood."

"OK, I'll cheer up. I'm a single woman cop, never married. I've just clicked over forty on life's little odometer. I've been in love with this nice journalist guy since quite some time after the real love of his life got killed and we've had some very nice times together. For a while it seemed really, really good, in fact. But now he's on the road all the time and he's busy even when he's in Montreal and he doesn't seem to know what he wants anymore. It's all a bit classic, really."

"Come on, Kate."

"You still on that disaster victim identification story? Where are you, Thailand still?"

"Yes."

"Well, do something for me, OK Francis. While you're over there, try to find out who you are too. Make a firm identification. Will the real Francis Delaney please stand up."

Delaney said nothing. Kate filled in the blanks.

"How many years have you been trying to figure out who you are, Francis? Approximately. Hotshot journalist? Maybe a spy guy? No, hang on, part-time spy. No, that's right, no comment on that one. Right? Maybe it's Kate Hunter's loverboy. No, that was last week, last month, I forget. No, I remember, you're the guy who's not sure he wants to get really and truly involved. The guy who can never get over Natalia."

"I'm over her, Kate. For God's sake. That's a very old story. That's a long, long time ago now."

"I suppose you must be over her, yes. Your sailboat isn't named after her anymore."

"I'm over her, Kate. Really."

"Are you over me, too?"

Delaney knew that in such conversations a millisecond of hesitation after a question like that was too long, far too long.

"No," he said.

"Was that a slight hesitation I heard just then, Francis?"

"Kate, this is starting to piss me off."

"Good," Kate said.

"Look, seeing we're talking about it, who are you these

days?" Delaney said. His adrenaline was rising, more than he subsequently thought justified. "Any idea?"

"What are you talking about?"

"You're a Mountie, right? RCMP financial crime fighter? Foot soldier in the war on terror, so called. Tough girl. Or, no, maybe a career woman, going places in the RCMP. First woman commissioner one day, maybe. No, wait. That's not right. You're a jealous girlfriend. You're jealous of a dead woman you never met. No, wait, this is it, you're the marrying kind, is that it? You want more. Police work is not enough. Delaney the boyfriend is not enough. You're not the girlfriend type, is that it? You're the marrying kind. Is that who you are now?"

"Fuck you, Francis," Officer Hunter said.

Delaney had never seen Smith so excited. They were in Delaney's hotel room again, the next afternoon. Zalm was with them again too. Smith and Zalm had rushed in to the Metropole lobby just as Delaney was getting back from his interview with the DNA man. Tim Bishop's fears had proved justified; it was a boring interview indeed. But Smith's news was anything but boring.

Delaney watched, and marvelled at, the enthusiasm with which this underweight, bespectacled Scotland Yard fingerprint man with an incongruously large and reportedly very new mustache approached his identification work. Delaney had observed that in their first meetings, and again in the formal interview he had conducted with Smith about the post-tsunami DVI challenges. He had observed that when they broke into the mortuary compound together. And he saw it clearly again now.

As Smith himself once told him, the time that any good fingerprint man likes best is the short period after a definite match has been made. For that very short time, he believes he is the only person in the world to know a suspect's true identity.

Smith insisted on telling Delaney and Zalm in great detail how he made the *Deutschland* match. Delaney was willing to acknowledge that Smith was surely allowed these few moments of delight, before the even harder work began.

Smith had worked for hours at his desk in the management centre, he told them, using the AFIS system to check for hits against the steadily growing database of antemortem missing persons' prints taken in countries across the globe and sent by police to Phuket. There was nothing of any interest. Not even any possibles.

Delaney could imagine Smith at work, an island of intense concentration in a sea of DVI movement, quietly hunched over fingerprint cards and then peering up at his twin computer screens, flicking back and forth through possible matches the system had thrown up for examination. Oblivious to police and civilians rushing around him as he worked, oblivious to the telephones ringing, fax machines humming, keyboards clacking, two-way radios crackling.

The Phuket databases having yielded nothing, Smith said, he then interrogated the Interpol database, using the I-24/7 police communications system the new Secretary-General had hurriedly put in place, at great cost and amidst great commotion after the September 11 attacks. It was aimed at bringing Interpol urgently into the 21st century and, for fingerprint examiners like Jonah Smith, it meant now being able to transmit to Lyon heavily encrypted emails with high-resolution fingerprint images attached for checking from the field.

The Interpol fingerprint databases were relatively small, Smith said, tiny when compared to the FBI's collection, for example, or even the New York Police Department's. But the collection at Interpol contained a fascinating mix of international criminals, members of organized crime gangs, major fraudsters, big-time car thieves, convicted and suspected pedophiles, and other particularly nasty ne'er-do-wells. And now there was of course an ever-growing file of terrorist suspects.

Not all the Interpol files, fingerprints or otherwise, contained extensive detail. Sometimes a fingerprint match would yield up a complete history, criminal and personal, of a person of interest. Or sometimes, a fingerprint set would be sent to Interpol by a national police force or an antiterrorism squad along with little detail at all, sent simply to set off an alarm if it cross-matched with prints taken from a crime scene somewhere or from a suspect traveller crossing a border point somewhere that had been set up to check fingerprints from afar.

In such cases, Interpol was merely being asked to act as a go-between, letting Country A know that a person of interest had left prints at a crime scene in Country B, or had been arrested in Country C, or had crossed a border into Country D. Sometimes, setting off such international alarm bells was all that a national police force or intelligence service might want Interpol to do. Sometimes, for very good investigative or judicial or other reasons, it was enough for a country just to know where someone was, without sharing too much detail with authorities in other countries or with Interpol in Lyon.

Sometimes, a good fingerprint examiner like Jonah Smith, would interrogate the Interpol database from a place like Phuket, Thailand, and would see on his screen thousands of kilometres away from Lyon that, yes, there was a possible match. Sometimes, in such cases, the file would tell a good fingerprint examiner a subject's name, nationality, date of birth and little else. But sometimes even that was enough. Sometimes even that little morsel of information was enough to break the logjam in an investigation, to open up new realms of investigative possibility, to yield new questions that needed to be asked and new people who might be able to answer them.

This, Smith announced proudly in Delaney's hotel room, was precisely what had happened in the *Deutschland* matter. The good-quality prints that Zalm had given back had thrown up about a dozen possible matches. Smith had downloaded these from the I-24/7 system into his computer in Phuket and then used the AFIS matching software to look at them more closely.

He eventually narrowed the field down to two possibles, using minutiae in the fingerprint ridges and other details in the print to get closer and closer to a genuine match. For a good fingerprint examiner like Jonah Smith, 12 points of similarity was the minimum standard required for certainty. Sometimes, he insisted on explaining to Delaney and Zalm, these days, FBI men or others were happy with 10 or even just 8 points of similarity. This Smith insisted on telling them, was simply not good enough. Not for certainty.

In the *Deutschland* matter, Smith told them proudly, he had found no fewer than 14 points of similarity between the fingerprints taken off the body in Phuket and a set in the Interpol database. This, Smith said, was more than enough for him. Alarm bells rang. He was sure he had found a match.

With a flourish, and a grin like a show-off police cadet, Smith spread a computer printout on the table before them, pushing bottles of Singha beer aside. Delaney and Zalm peered at it over his shoulder. The document contained few details, but, in Smith's professional opinion, it was cause for celebration. The document said:

> **Subject known to Interpol.**
>
> **National Police Contact:**
> Bundeskriminalamt, Weisbaden, Germany.
>
> **Klaus Wolfgang Heinrich.** Male. German National.
>
> **Date of Birth:** Dresden, former German Democratic Republic—18 May 1940.
>
> **Deceased:** Bonn, Germany—8 October 2001.

Chapter 8

The possibility that the body of a tsunami victim lying in a mortuary container in Phuket, Thailand, in March 2005 was that of one Klaus Wolfgang Heinrich, born 18 May 1940 in Dresden, in the former East Germany, and who died, supposedly, on 8 October 2001 in Bonn, West Germany, was enough to set off a series of alarm bells.

The alarm bells were in Gunter Ackermann's head. First when his telephone rang unbearably loud and unconscionably early in the morning, Berlin time. Then they started ringing again, loudly, when Delaney told him what he had discovered.

Delaney had thought he would first check out the Klaus Heinrich name in news databases, before calling Ackermann. But then he decided he would ask Ackermann about the name right away.

"Gunter, I'm sorry, I know it's really early over there," Delaney said when Ackermann eventually answered his phone with an incomprehensible oath. Delaney had tried a home number first and then, when that wasn't answered, Ackermann's cell phone.

"Francis, for God's sake, what can you possibly want?" Ackermann growled.

Delaney heard a muffled woman's voice saying: "*Wer ruft denn um diese Zeit noch an, Schatz?*"

"If you called me any earlier, Francis, you would have caught me in the physical act of love," Ackermann said.

The woman's offstage voice said: "*Schatz, steh jetzt nicht auf, sag denen sie sollen verschwinden.*" Ackermann said: "*Tut mir leid, Liebling. Gunter kuemmert sich darum.*"

To Delaney, Ackermann's language was not so charming: "Francis, call me back later, for God's sake. I will kill you for this," he said.

"Gunter, no, don't hang up. I have something quite interesting on this *Deutschland* body over here," Delaney said. "Don't hang up."

"Can't this wait for a civilized hour?"

"No, Gunter. This is good. Listen to me. The body I've been talking about. I have a name now. German."

"You had a German name before, Stahlman, and it was bullshit," Ackermann said. Delaney heard the click of a lighter and the faint breeze of a cigarette being lit and smoke inhaled in Berlin. And one last plea from Ackermann's very sleepy lady friend.

"You ever heard of a guy named Klaus Wolfgang Heinrich?" Delaney asked.

"Klaus Heinrich? It's a common name where I come from, Francis. And I have just woken up."

"Born 1940 in Dresden. Died 2001, Bonn."

"Bonn," Ackermann said. "2001."

"Or Phuket, Boxing Day 2004. Depending on your point of view."

"How old is this guy?"

"Come on Gunter—1940, 2004. He'd be sixty-four. If he hadn't drowned in Thailand three months ago."

Delaney could hear Ackermann smoke as he pondered this.

"German, around sixty, Klaus Heinrich. Dead in 2001 in Bonn," Ackerman said eventually.

"2004, in Phuket, Gunter."

"I think I know who that could be, Frank," Ackermann said. "If it was Bonn. This could be good."

"Who could it be?" Delaney said.

"Klaus Heinrich. Germany's super spy. Dead 2001 in Bonn. Exactly. I'm waking up now."

"What? What do you mean, super spy?"

"Klaus Heinrich. For God's sake. Where were you in October 2001? Do you never read the newspapers?"

"I was getting ready to go to Afghanistan in October 2001, Gunter. And you were too. Everybody was heading to Afghanistan to watch the Americans bomb terrorist training camps."

"Well, that didn't stop me from reading the bloody papers before I went, Francis. Klaus Heinrich. The spy who came in from the extreme cold. Literally. You must remember, for God's sake. He was our big spy man, West Germany's most famous spy, some would say. He spent years of his life working undercover in East Germany for our side. Then after the Wall came down in 1989 and everything collapsed over there, he came back in and was a big bloody hero. One of the few guys our side had ever managed to place over there as a mole. Stasi had hundreds of spies over on the West side and we couldn't ever manage to place more than a few over in the East. Klaus Heinrich was a very, very big hero after the Wall came down."

"I don't remember that story at all, Gunter," Delaney said.

"For God's sake, you Americans are ignorant. Parochial, pathetic fucking . . ."

"I can't remember every news story from 1989, Gunter. And I'm Canadian."

"You are an asshole, Francis Frank," Ackermann said. "Especially in the morning. I don't care what nationality you are."

"What happened to this guy?"

"Oh, they gave him a bloody big reception and pinned a medal or two on him and put him in a nice, high-paying little job in the Foreign Ministry or something, over in Bonn. Nice town.

They set him up for life. He was an academic by trade, if I remember now. On paper anyway. I think he gave some lectures in the West, after, too."

"But what happened to him?"

"Well, he died, Frank. Don't tell me you don't remember this. If it's the same man you're talking about. It was a bloody big story over here. He worked in Bonn from about 1990 or so, had a very nice little life, big hero, nice life, and then he died. October 2001. I remember it very well. Everybody was working like bastards, after the 9/11 thing in New York, for weeks after. There was no news story in the world except 9/11, 9/11, al-Qaeda. Then this silly bastard gets himself killed and finally we had a nice German story to put on Page One for a change. Heinrich died in a big nasty fire out in the woods somewhere. A cottage or a cabin he had outside of Bonn somewhere. I would have to check where. It was very big story at the time."

"In 2001."

"Yes, Frank, yes."

"They find the body? They never found Stahlman's body."

"Of course they found the body. He was fucking famous. The police were all over it. It was front page."

"A house fire."

"Yes, Frank, yes. Some of us thought for a while that some hard-core former Stasi spy, or two, or ten, might have killed him for playing around with them for so many years in the East. But there was a big investigation. The fire marshals said a heating stove had blown up. They didn't see anything criminal about it. Everybody wanted to know and they did a very careful investigation. There was an arson investigation, a murder investigation, an autopsy, everything. He just died when his damn heating stove blew up."

"So who's this over here in Phuket then?"

"It can't be the same Klaus Heinrich, Frank. I don't see how. Not possible."

"We've got fingerprints off his body. We've got a match on the Interpol database."

Ackermann paused, in his bed in Berlin. Delaney could hear him smoking his cigarette as he pondered the situation.

"Then you may be onto a very good little story, Francis Frank. If that's really Klaus Heinrich in a body bag over there."

Ackermann, as usual, was absolutely correct in matters of history and current affairs. Delaney got online immediately after hanging up the telephone and checked databases for the Klaus Heinrich story. Ackermann had said he would stand by to help out. As any good German journalist would be more than happy to do in such matters.

There were in fact lots of news stories in the databases about master spy Klaus Heinrich coming in from the cold after 1989. A simple Google search of his name and the keyword *spy* was all that was needed. There were far fewer stories about his death in a house fire in the autumn of 2001, however, if only because the world media machine was locked in on, fixated on, the 9/11 attacks and the subsequent U.S. invasion of Afghanistan. But the Heinrich stories were there in 2001 as well, for those who took the time to look.

Heinrich had come in after a long and brilliant spying career deep undercover in East Berlin. A couple of profiles published in late 1989 and after German reunification in 1990 noted, as the all too brief Interpol file had also noted, that he had been born in Dresden, German Democratic Republic. But the media had much more detail, apparently, than Interpol. Heinrich had moved to the West alone, as a university student, in 1959, just before the Wall went up a year later and everything in German politics and world politics profoundly changed. Many thousands of East Germans had made the same move, prior to 1960. Such migration westward was one of the reasons for the wall being built in the first place.

In 1990 interviews, Heinrich said he had left the GDR because he found it "stifling," as so many were finding it at that time and afterward. He finished his PhD in political economy at the Free University of Berlin and then, it appeared, he had been recruited sometime in the early sixties by the Bundesnach-richtendienst, West Germany's intelligence service, like a lot of bright young people at the time.

The difference, in his case, as Heinrich appeared only too happy to tell Associated Press and *Die Welt* and the BBC and anyone else who interviewed him, post-1990, was that he eventually managed to insinuate himself back into East Germany as a BND mole.

He had been a radical, a far left university student, in West Germany. Or so it appeared. He had marched in the 1968 student protests that shook Europe, had got himself arrested, even though somewhat past prime student age by then, and had been active in student Communist groups and other far left groups of various descriptions. Then, at the height of the Cold War and the East-West tensions, he defected to the East, with much fanfare and blazing front-page stories in the GDR and Soviet press.

Heinrich, it seemed, was a young man who could not bear being stifled, anywhere. West German capitalism, he had now decided, was stifling him unbearably. He had made a mistake in 1959, he said. He could no longer in good conscience live in West Germany and he wanted to go home to the GDR where he could feel truly at home and make his contribution to the socialist paradise. And perhaps visit his ancient mother in Dresden. Or so he said at the time.

Heinrich left West Germany just months before the spectacular story broke of a Stasi spy, Gunter Guillaume, having made it to the very top echelons of Willy Brandt's Social Democrat government. Guillaume had managed to have himself appointed a top aide to Brandt himself. That scandal brought Brandt down as Chancellor in 1974, and brought Stasi and its enormous, Byzantine network of spies inside and outside East Germany, into very sharp focus. Everywhere it was said that Stasi had completely outmanned and outclassed the BND in the spying game.

But one Klaus Wolfgang Heinrich was providing a success story at the time that no one in West German intelligence wanted to put on any front page—not yet. In fact, said the post-1990 news and feature stories, Heinrich was never anything other than a loyal member of the BND, despite his high-profile defection back to the GDR, and for years this deep undercover super spy sent back a constant stream of excellent-quality intelligence to the West.

East Germany had, very unwisely as it later turned out, embraced their brilliant high-profile defector with great enthusiasm and given him a political science lectureship at Humboldt University in East Berlin, where everyone was ideologically sound indeed. Heinrich moved from there into very powerful circles, acting as a sort of informal government adviser on all things West German, rubbing shoulders with senior bureaucrats and politicians and like-minded academics and intellectuals. His sources in the GDR were excellent, he had access to high-level discussions and reports and files, and no one, it seemed, ever suspected that this Dresden native was anything other than what he appeared.

In those first chaotic days and weeks after the Wall came down in 1989 and thousands of Stasi files were seized that showed in detail the breathtaking level of infiltration of West Germany by East German spies, the Klaus Heinrich story, about the man who had duped the best Stasi minds for more than a dozen years, was a welcome counterweight to the impression that Stasi had outmaneuvered the West at every Cold War turn.

Heinrich was the kind of hero West German intelligence sorely needed at the time and they used him for all he was worth. Until, of course, a defective heating stove blew up in Heinrich's little cabin in the Siebengebirge hills and his brilliant career finally, spectacularly, ended.

As Ackermann had said, there were the inevitable suggestions at the time that Heinrich had been assassinated by Stasi stalwarts in retaliation for his betrayal. But those stories soon faded away, partly because from every possible level in West Germany there came assurances that the house fire had been no more than what it appeared. That Heinrich had died accidentally at the age of 61 from smoke inhalation and horrific burns, leaving a charred corpse in the ashes for all investigators to examine for suspicious bullet wounds or knife wounds or poisons or whatever other signs of displeasure a Stasi assassin might have left behind.

The stories faded away after the very thorough official investigation. They faded also because the world's attention was understandably elsewhere at the time. In October 2001, the death in the Rhine countryside of a former West German Cold War super spy in a house fire was news from another era. It was not a story to hold media interest for very long. The media, post-9/11, had far too many new preoccupations to spend very much time writing feature stories and analysis pieces about the death of one Klaus Wolfgang Heinrich.

Delaney himself was feeling stifled after such a long online research session in his room. It was a sultry Phuket evening and from his open balcony door he could see giant thunderclouds building over Chalong Bay. A heavy overnight rain might break the oppressive humidity but any downpour was some hours away yet. His air conditioner was off, as usual. After years of life spent in hotel rooms, he had developed a strong preference for sleeping under fans.

He headed down to the lobby bar, laptop in hand. The night-desk girls, like the day shift, were aware, apparently, of his preference for solitude, possibly celibacy. Unlike so many of the male hotel residents, he had not found himself a local Thai "friend," whether male or female, to bring back to his room each night. The night-desk girls found this worthy of an intense round of giggles every time he returned to the hotel alone and asked for his room key. As he passed them on the way to the bar, the giggles followed him until he was well inside.

The Metropole bar, like thousand of bars in upmarket hotels around the world, was dark, heavily carpeted, tinkling faintly with piano sounds, clinking with ice in glasses, and humming faintly with conversations in many languages. He sat at the long wooden bar along with the usual suspects. Journalists on assignment, stir-crazy European sales representatives, and, in this case, a good sampling of off-duty police, European and Thai. The hotel management frowned on prostitutes actually sitting in the bar, so Delaney did not have to fend off offers of company here.

He had developed the habit, again from too many years alone on the road, of repairing to such dim oases to think things through; when on assignment he needed some time to reflect carefully on information gathered and information still required. He ordered a double Jameson's and a beer, and pondered the situation he had encountered.

Rawson was absolutely correct. This was not at all the usual *International Geographic* hippos in the waterhole kind of story that he was starting to cover, or uncover. But, as usual for him, exactly where a story might lead and whether a story would ever make it into print was actually beside the point. At this stage he was simply seeking information.

Eventually, having read through and amplified his many pages of notes on the story so far, from the day he had first met Jonah Smith at the victims' funeral service at Phuket airport until logging off the news databases only a short while ago, having given the developing saga his undivided attention over a series of overpriced whiskies, Delaney made up his mind that his next destination must be Berlin.

He opened his laptop and composed two email messages. The first was for Rawson in Ottawa:

Jonathan, I have the third name for you. It is Klaus Wolfgang Heinrich. D.O.B. 18/05/40. Deceased possibly 08/10/01, possibly 24/12/04. Apparently a West German spook. What have you got? Bests, FD.

For Ackermann, there was this:

Dear Gunter. So sorry to have caught you, as it were, so early this morning. Far too early, I know. Sorry, sorry, sorry. But pressing affairs of state made it unavoidable, et cetera. Some good news for you, my friend. You will be delighted to know I'm coming to Berlin ASAP. Fun times ahead. Stand by. Regards, Delaney.

Delaney decided to approach Horst Becker directly. He didn't ask Smith for an opinion on this move, because he suspected that Smith would advise against it. He didn't ask press officer Ruth Connolly for permission to interview this particular member of the DVI teams; first, because he was absolutely sure she would forbid it, and second, because she seemed to be drowning in a sea of other troubles in her unenviable assignment of managing the world's media in Phuket while simultaneously managing a giant sampling of the world's police.

He had seen Connolly squabbling again a day previously with the Kendall man, about some public relations misdemeanour or other. And he had seen her locked in conversation, or possibly debate, with Braithwaite on the steps of the IMC as he arrived a day before that. As he passed them, Connolly and Braithwaite stopped their conversation and watched in silence. Perhaps, Delaney thought, as they would watch a condemned man walking to the gallows. Wishful thinking on their part. Or perhaps he was just becoming paranoid.

Delaney called Becker quite late, after he had got back to his room from the hotel bar. His decision to take the step of calling the German pathologist was assisted somewhat by the rapid series of whiskies and beers he had consumed that evening. Smith had told him Becker was staying in a villa somewhere well out of town with a number of other German colleagues. His phone number was on a neatly typed list of DVI team contacts Smith had been given by the Thai police when he arrived in Phuket, a copy of which Smith had very kindly donated to *International Geographic.*

"*Ja,*" Becker said after just one ring on his mobile phone.

"Mr. Becker, this is Frank Delaney. I'm a journalist doing a story here for a magazine. I'm sorry to call you after hours."

There was only a slight pause at the other end.

"I know about you, Delaney," Becker said.

"I was wondering if I could perhaps come to see you, to do an interview."

Another pause, again only very slight.

"I see you have abandoned altogether the proper channels for such requests," Becker said.

Now the slight hesitation came from Delaney's end.

"I suppose I have," he said.

"I am not surprised by your request, Delaney," Becker said.

"I see," Delaney said.

Another slight hesitation from the German side. Then Becker said: "Tomorrow, yes?"

"That's fine. When and where?"

"It is for you to choose. The prerogative of the journalist?"

Delaney hadn't thought this would be so easy. He had not expected to also be able to choose the venue. He thought the management centre would be too public a place, in case discussion got heated.

"Your villa?" he said.

"You are already aware of my accommodation details," Becker said. "Very good."

"Will that be all right?"

"Yes."

"Ten o'clock?"

"Yes. I will be alone here then."

"If you prefer," Delaney said.

"I do," Becker said.

Delaney called Bishop in his room. It was well after 11 p.m.

"You sober, Tim?"

"Always, Frank. Are you?"

"Sort of. Not really."

"What's up?"

"You want to take some wildlife pictures tomorrow?" Delaney said. "A possibly dangerous beast?"

"Sure. What time?"

Delaney rented a car the next morning for the drive out to the German team's villa. In his experience, it was always better to have return transportation arranged, if an interview was expected to be hostile and it was to take place away from major thoroughfares where taxis ply their trade.

Bishop was happy to be on a shoot of any sort. Delaney explained on the way that Horst Becker, however, would not be happy with the sort of questions he was going to be asked about a missing DVI file and that they both might get ejected from the house. He did not tell Bishop that he badly wanted a photograph of Becker to show Ackermann, and possibly others in Berlin and Ottawa, if required.

Becker's bald head looked for all the world like a glistening, partially excavated flesh-toned cannonball. The archeological impression was reinforced by the grey beard that covered the bottom half of the aging sphere.

A Thai houseboy had come to the door of the villa, but Becker was standing right behind. The German pathologist wasn't wearing a DVI team shirt. Instead he had on a khaki expedition shirt, with button pockets on the chest, and epaulettes.

Khaki trousers matched the safari look. All was immaculate, military-style, precisely pressed. Only the leather sandals betrayed a certain informality.

"And who is this with you, Delaney?" Becker said as they all stood at the doorway. He did not offer a handshake.

"This is my photographer, Tim Bishop," Delaney said.

"You said nothing about bringing a photographer."

"It's standard procedure for my magazine to have pictures of people I interview."

Bishop was fitting a wide-angle lens to one of his cameras while he waited.

"There is no need to prepare your equipment, young man. There will be no photographs taken here today." Becker said.

"Why is that, Mr. Becker?" Delaney said.

Bishop looked over at Delaney, as he had looked often in previous assignments in many places around the world, often rather unpleasant and dangerous places, waiting for a cue as to whether to try to take a few quick shots before being sent away by an uncooperative subject.

"No photos," Becker said. "If you raise that camera, young man, I can assure you your career will be over."

Bishop enjoyed such situations very much. He was no longer bored. Becker locked eyes with Delaney.

"Let's not play journalist games this morning, if you please, Delaney. Send your young man away. You and I will go inside."

"I'll go have a juice somewhere, Frank," Bishop said. "There's a place down the road I saw coming in. Call me on my cell when you're done."

Delaney was sure Bishop would take lots of shots of the exterior of the house as he left, as well as the car in the driveway, the mailbox, the houseboy if possible, the neighbours' houses and anything else of any remote possible interest.

"OK, Tim. Maybe Mr. Becker will change his mind after we've had the interview."

"This will not happen," Becker said.

They sat at a wicker dining table in an alcove near sliding doors to a long back courtyard filled with fragrant flowering jasmine and bougainvillea. The houseboy brought them iced tea. Delaney wondered if the boy might be Becker's bit of local R&R. Becker looked like any number of aging German sex tourists who got off planes in Thailand on any given day. Except that Becker had other reasons for coming to Thailand, possibly even legitimate ones.

"I am not a man who likes to waste time, Delaney," Becker said.

"I see," Delaney said. "Well, then, thank you for agreeing to meet me today."

"Let us not waste time then pretending you are here as a journalist today," Becker said.

"I am a journalist," Delaney said.

"Please," Becker said. "You insult my intelligence. My only problem has been trying to find out who you actually work for."

"Why do you think I'm here?"

"The file," Becker said without hesitation. "Jonah Smith."

Delaney had not expected to get down to basics so quickly that morning.

"That's something that would interest a journalist, wouldn't it? A missing file?"

"Or someone else."

"Like who?"

"That is what I would like to find out. Who you are and why you are here in Phuket."

"So you will be interviewing me today?" Delaney said.

"In a sense, yes," Becker said.

"Look, Mr. Becker, as you don't like to waste time, I'll just get straight to the point. I'm a journalist, despite what other theories you might have developed. I'm doing a story for

International Geographic about the DVI work here and in other places like Sri Lanka and the Maldives. I've interviewed a lot of people. Along the way, I've been told about a file that's gone missing here. . . ."

"By Smith," Becker said.

". . . It sounds to me like a breach of procedure or security and it may be that a body that could have been identified may now not get identified. That's something that would interest a journalist, surely."

"Or someone else."

"Can you help me with this angle, Mr. Becker?"

"Why do you think I would have information on such matters, Delaney?"

"The body was a German national."

"Was it?" Becker said.

"I believe so."

"Someone has told you this, or you have proof?"

"There was a tattoo, for example. It said *Deutschland*, apparently."

"You have seen this body? You have seen such an identifying mark? You have seen the missing file? Some papers? Who tells you such things? These are confidential matters. You are confident about these facts?"

"Can you confirm any of these facts for me, Mr. Becker?"

"Why would you think I am able to do that, Delaney? And why do you think I would assist you in police matters even if I had such an ability?"

Delaney said: "Why did you go to Jonah Smith's hotel last week and warn him to stop asking about the file, Mr. Becker? As we're not wasting any time here today . . ."

Becker got to his feet and stood over Delaney, as short men often do. His face had been reddening. Beads of sweat glistened on the top of his smooth head.

"Smith is an extremely indiscreet man. He is also a fool,"

Becker said very quietly.

"But is he correct?" Delaney said.

"About what?"

"Has the file been stolen?"

Becker remained on his feet. The Thai houseboy hovered in the doorway to the main house.

"Back inside," Becker snarled at him. The boy retreated. Delaney waited.

"Who do you work for, Mr. Delaney? Becker said.

"*International Geographic* magazine. On this assignment. I'm a freelance journalist. I work for a number of clients."

"Not all of them media," Becker said.

"You're confident about these facts? You've seen my personal file? Some papers?" Delaney said, knowing Becker would not have much patience for sarcasm. He was correct.

"You insult my intelligence, Delaney," Becker said. "I will find out more about you easily."

"Why would you agree to see me if you don't think I'm who I say I am, Mr. Becker?"

"I had something I wanted to tell you," Becker said.

"I'm listening," Delaney said.

"It is the same thing I told Smith when I saw him in his hotel. I will not have you or anyone else jeopardizing this operation. I will not have you spreading lies about me and my team and that file. You will stop this immediately."

"Or someone will get beaten up?" Delaney said.

Becker was trembling slightly. Delaney had seen the telltale signs of adrenaline coursing through the body of an adversary many times before.

"Have you had much to do with police in your work, Delaney? In whatever work you actually do?"

"Quite a bit, yes."

"Then you will be familiar with the reactions of police who think they have been unfairly accused."

"No one likes to be unfairly accused, Mr. Becker. Not just police."

"Police do not like to have their reputations damaged, Delaney."

"No one does. Journalists don't. And I thought you were a civilian anyway. Are you a policeman? Or maybe you're a military man."

There was a pause.

"So now a warning comes, is that next?" Delaney said eventually.

"What is your feeling on that, Delaney? Do you think a warning is likely in such situations?"

"Maybe not an explicit one," Delaney said.

"Ah," Becker said. "Perhaps you have had some real experience of dealing with police after all."

On the way back, Bishop was as cheery as Delaney had seen him in days.

"I took a few frames of the house and the car and the licence plate," Bishop said. "I went around the back to try to get a shot of you guys inside with a long lens but no dice. The wall was too high and I couldn't see you at all."

"That's OK, Tim. He's got a pretty unforgettable face."

"Bulldog boy. Seems like a nasty little guy."

"Yup."

"A bit shy around cameras."

"Yup."

"I'll try to get a shot of him when he goes in to work at the IMC tomorrow maybe," Bishop said happily.

"Careful, buddy."

"Always."

"Wildlife photography."

"Love it. Savage beast shots."

There was a telephone message slip pushed under Delaney's door when he got back to the hotel. And the message light was flashing on his phone. Jonathan Rawson had been trying to call, very late, it seemed, Ottawa time. Delaney had taken to switching off his cell phone when editors were getting anxious.

The CSIS man answered his phone on the first ring.

"It's Francis, Jon. What's up?" Delaney said.

"Well, my friend, you seem to have a talent for digging up interesting stuff. That's why we love you over here at Canada's finest and only security intelligence service."

"What you got?"

"A little bit of CSIS freelance money for you, I would think. From right now."

"I've got an assignment already here, Jon. Magazine piece, with nice pictures to go with it. You'll read it in your dentist's office sometime in the next month or so if I ever sit down to write it. I don't need any extra CSIS dough."

"We think it's a story for CSIS too now, probably. If not for some other spook outfit somewhere."

"What have you got?"

Delaney heard Rawson shuffling papers in Ottawa.

"Well, for that young dental guy from Netherlands, nothing much. Sounds like he's who he says he is. A dentist with forensic tendencies. No big deal. A bit of trouble at university with pot smoking, maybe more than usual, but then everybody in Holland is stoned all the time anyway. Nobody cares over there. He's a nice normal young Dutchman, it seems. Helping identify tsunami victims for his country."

"And Becker?"

"Ah, well, Becker is slightly more interesting. An Army doctor, German."

"Army?"

"Retired actually. He works still at the big military hospital in Frankfurt. Pathology. Cuts up soldiers who get killed. That sort of thing. High security clearance, or so my good friends in Germany tell us over here in Canada. Nothing strange on his file that they were willing to share with us anyway, but he smells high level to me. Strange guy to be sent out to do routine cadaver stuff at a disaster scene."

"There were a lot of German tourists drowned out here, Jon."

"And there's lots of German pathologists who aren't senior ex-Army to go out to Thailand to do their bit."

Already, Delaney was getting the impression that Rawson knew more about Becker than he was willing to share with a free-lancer. Whether it was a freelance journalist or freelance CSIS operative. It was always like this, with Rawson & Company. Sometimes Delaney had patience for it, sometimes not. Tonight, he was patient.

"And Heinrich?"

"Ah, Heinrich," Rawson said. "Now this Mr. Heinrich could be very interesting, if it's actually him over there. This could be big, Frank. This is why we figure you're in for a little CSIS expense money about now."

"What you got?"

"Who wants to know? *International Geographic*?"

"Spare me, Jon."

"Seriously, Francis. Who's your client going to be now, on this one? Who are you going to be this time, reporter or spy?"

"Do we always have to do this, Jon?"

Rawson and CSIS valued Delaney highly, for his skills and his contacts and his performance in the field on past spook assignments for them. They often told him so. But he had also upset his CSIS clients a couple of times, by failing to follow instructions, or publishing more on a story than they had expected, or simply going off, as they would put it, half cocked.

"Can you just give me what you've got on Heinrich? Then we'll worry about my career?" Delaney said.

Rawson hesitated, and then said: "It's my career I worry about, Francis, whenever I work with you."

"Be brave, Jon."

"Well, look, anybody who reads the papers could have told you that Heinrich was a heavy duty Cold War spook working for the West Germans for many years. But actually inside the GDR. One of very, very few."

"Yes? And?"

"You know this stuff already, you must, by now," Rawson said.

"What else have you got that I don't know?" Delaney said.

"It's what you've got that's the thing, Francis. If that is actually Klaus Heinrich's body you've got over there, this could be very big."

"For who?"

"Any number of people. Or just us, even, because we like to know about such things. Little Canada and the little intelligence service that could . . ."

"You make sure the Germans and God knows who else knows that CSIS is out there doing serious work."

"Sure, of course. It never hurts. It's a mutual back-scratching sort of world now, Francis, more than ever before. You know that. Post-9/11, blah, blah, blah."

"So basically, this is a little tidbit of information you can throw to the Germans, or the Americans, or whoever, for, what, future considerations?"

"Maybe. Not sure yet. It's just nice to have interesting information in the satchel. I like that feeling. So if that actually is Klaus Heinrich you have over there, and if he didn't die in 2001 like we all thought he did, well, you've got an interesting story on the go, my friend. We like that. That's why we all love you so much."

"Why would anybody want to make it seem like Heinrich died in 2001 and then, what would it have been, shift him over here to live?"

"Why indeed? That is the question. But I can think of a number of very interesting scenarios for something like that, Francis. Can't you? Cloak and dagger stuff."

Delaney had already been pondering cloak and dagger scenarios for several days.

"If it's actually Heinrich over here," Delaney said.

"You seemed pretty sure in your email to me, Francis. You're not going to get coy with your Uncle Jonathan now are you?"

Delaney had been a journalist for more years than he cared to remember. He had been on assignment in more places than he cared to remember and he had been in danger more times than he cared to remember. People in war zones had pointed guns at him. People had beaten him up. Airplanes he had flown on had often seemed like they were going to crash and burn.

He had always, however, thought that if he was going to die on assignment somewhere, a car would be the most likely cause of death. He had hurtled down very bad highways in Nigeria in overloaded, rickety, trembling Peugeot 504 station wagons, the deathtrap taxi of choice in West Africa. He had sat sweating in fear beside apparently suicidal local drivers on hairpin roads in Haiti. He had ridden notorious intercity buses in the mountains of Peru and Mexico, with drivers and passengers crossing themselves and kissing rosaries throughout the journey. He had even had people try to run him down with cars.

Despite, therefore, his recurring fear that a car would be the end of him one day, Delaney did not at all expect someone to try to kill him with a car in the big parking lot behind the Metropole Hotel early on the morning after he spoke to Rawson by phone. He was walking to where he had parked his rented Toyota under some shade trees on the far side, on his way to a Phuket Town travel agency to buy a plane ticket to Germany. He was lost in thought, pondering scenarios, with no reason, yet, to think anyone was upset enough to try to crush him under the wheels of an automobile.

The windows of the white van moving through the hotel parking lot that morning were tinted very dark, as with so many vehicles in Thailand. Delaney could not see the driver at all. But there was nothing immediately alarming about a large passenger van with tinted glass moving through the parking lot in the distance as he went to his car.

What was definitely alarming was that the van suddenly accelerated with a mighty roar and a burst of blue-black diesel smoke. It careened left around a line of parked cars to Delaney's right, and came swaying and skidding into his lane. He could not see the driver clearly through the dark glass but he could see, all too clearly, that the driver was trying to kill him.

Delaney dove with all his strength between parked cars to his left. He landed painfully on his forearms, then stomach, then thighs on the hot pavement, ripping his clothes, scraping his skin. He smelled diesel and rubber and hot asphalt and fear, white hot fear.

The van sideswiped the line of parked cars with a terrific crash of metal and plastic and glass. Lying in the shade between two cars, panting and bleeding, Delaney heard the van shift gears and roar mightily again, this time as it sped away. He heard the squeal of tires as the driver made another wild turn, and then he heard a rumble in the distance and the shout from a guard as the driver apparently raced off through the parking lot gate.

All went suddenly silent. Delaney rested where he lay. He breathed deeply, calmed himself, listened and waited for a while in the rubber-scented, fuel-scented shade. For the moment, and for some time afterward, his thoughts were no longer on Berlin.

PART 2
Phuket, Berlin and Bonn — March 2005

Chapter 9

Jonah Smith was a fingerprint man. But he hardly knew himself in Thailand. He knew full well he had been transformed. However the transformation had now gone far beyond an unaccustomed suntan and a new mustache or his growing collection of floral shirts and the Chinese-made bicycle he rode to work.

He sat, alone, fully dressed, on his bed at the Bay Hotel, pondering who he had become. The identification was proving difficult.

Delaney was in Berlin. Conchi was at her own hotel, sleeping alone tonight. Zalm was likely drinking far too much in a bar somewhere in Phuket Town, doing penance for his sins over the *Deutschland* file. Mrs. Jonah Smith was in England where she belonged, surely untroubled by questions of who she was or how to do the right thing.

Jonah Smith, for his part, was alone at the Bay Hotel, pondering who he had become.

Frank Delaney, Smith thought as he sat propped up on his immaculate hotel bed, did not appear to have any trouble knowing who he was or what needed to be done. Delaney had simply decided he would go to Berlin to pursue the story wherever it might lead, had bought a plane ticket and gone.

The new Jonah Smith, on the other hand, enjoyed no such certainty. Doing the right thing was no longer easy, the way no longer clear. He could no longer distinguish good guys from bad.

In the past it had been easy. He would work alone at his small desk at Scotland Yard or at Interpol, matching fingerprints, following crime scene stories wherever they might lead. In the past, like any good fingerprint man, he simply made the match, informed his police superiors, and went on to the next case, the next match, the next story, wherever it might lead.

This time it was different. The rules of the game had been breached; victims and villains were no longer easy to tell apart. His Phuket police colleagues and superiors were either angry, or not to be trusted, or both. He no longer had anyone he could trust on this, except perhaps a Canadian journalist he had known for just days, and a Spanish woman he had loved for just weeks.

Smith was a man who had always sought—in his professional as well as his personal life—certainty, confirmation, clarity. He had found none of these things in Thailand, nor, he thought ruefully, could he find them any longer in London or Lyon, either professionally or personally.

He got up from the bed and went to examine himself in the bathroom mirror. The new Jonah Smith looked tired tonight, a little bit worse for the wear. The scrapes from his beating had faded but not disappeared. A deep shadow remained under his left eye socket but the bruise was no longer quite so black. A thin linear scab had formed at the corner of his mouth where the stitches had been. His hair, though now sun-bleached, looked thinner than ever. It was the hair of a tired middle-aged man; at least that much of the identification was certain.

Before leaving Lyon for Thailand, Smith had consulted the classic fingerprint literature for certainty, guidance, inspiration, as he always did before any important forensic assignment. He carried with him to Phuket, as always, a few of his favourite texts. Smith went over to the shelf where he kept his books and consulted them again for assistance.

In Phuket, Thailand, in the Bay Hotel, in late March 2005, a passage by Sir Francis Galton once again provided him with wise counsel, despite the words having been written in 1892. Smith smiled as he imagined the father of fingerprint science writing quietly, with Victorian-era certainty, at his old desk at the Royal Society in London all those years ago:

Whenever honest persons travel to distant countries, the need for a means of recognition is more keenly felt, Galton wrote. *The risk of death through accident or crime is increased and the probability of subsequent identification diminished . . .*

Frank Delaney was clearly not a man who would spend his time reading classic texts by Sir Francis Galton. Smith understood that perfectly well. But Delaney did know a lot about the risk of death through accident or crime in distant countries. Before leaving for Berlin, he had told Smith, and Conchi, about his near-death experience in the parking lot of the Metropole Hotel.

Smith thought Delaney was remarkably sanguine about someone having tried to kill him with a car. Conchi, on the other hand, thought Delaney was remarkably foolish, and she told him so, angrily, as the three of them sat around an outdoor table at the Whale Bar on the very humid Phuket afternoon before Delaney left. She was angry because Delaney had approached Horst Becker about the *Deutschland* file, she was angry that someone had subsequently tried to kill him, and she was angry that someone might now try to do the same thing to Smith.

"You are stupid, Frank Delaney," she said. "Stupid, stupid. Do you think now that this German will leave us all alone?"

"We're not absolutely sure it has anything to do with Becker," Delaney had said.

"Oh really?" Smith said.

"Of course it is Becker," Conchi said. Smith could see that Delaney almost certainly thought so too.

"Well, our only choice now is to find out what's really going on and sort these people out," Delaney said. "That's why I'm going to Berlin."

"Someone will try to kill you there, you watch," Conchi said. "And someone will try to kill Jonah here too. And me too now, no? In Spain we know how Germans are when they get mad."

"You'll be all right, Conchi," Smith had said. He touched her arm. She looked over at him and touched his arm. He could see Delaney filing this little scene away in his journalist's memory.

"This is all stupid," Conchi said. "Men, you're all stupid. You get mad, you get so violent, you make me mad, all of you stupid men. Jonah gets a beating, his face gets scratched up. Stupid Frank almost gets killed by a car. For what?"

"We want to know who that dead man really is," Smith said. "You don't really have any trouble understanding that, Conchi. I know you don't."

"Yes, I do, yes I do have trouble understanding that."

"It's not worth it if they kill you."

"Why do you work so hard in Bosnia to identify bodies in those mass graves, Conchi. Hmm?" Smith said.

"That's different, Jonah. There are families over there who need to know. No one tries to kill me for it."

"This *Deutschland* guy may have a family who wonders about him too," Delaney said, somewhat lamely, Smith thought. Delaney had not told Conchi about who he, and others, now thought the *Deutschland* man had actually been. He had asked Smith not to tell her either.

"Bullshit, Frank, bullshit," Conchi said. "You want to know who the guy is and what happened to the file because you get a big story maybe for your bullshit newspaper."

Delaney suddenly looked very uneasy. Smith thought that Conchi had struck some sort of chord that Delaney clearly preferred to leave alone.

"Conchi . . ." Smith said.

"And you, Jonah, you want to know because you are stupid too, just stupid for fingerprints," Conchi said.

"You sound a little like Fiona now, Conchi," Smith said with a thin smile.

Conchi had flounced away from the table in high Spanish displeasure. She had to get back to the management centre to identify dead people for her own set of reasons—better reasons, or so she would have them believe, than theirs. Smith still had a couple of days left before he was to return to work after his hospital stay. He sat with Delaney for a while longer.

"This is all getting more dangerous by the day, Frank," Smith said after Conchi had gone.

"It is," Delaney said.

"You think they will go after Conchi now too?"

"It's possible, Jonah," Delaney said. "You'll both have to watch yourselves while I'm away."

"I'm not sure it was a wise idea to confront Becker so directly on this, Frank. I don't," Smith said.

"Maybe not. I'm not so sure. But he didn't seem at all surprised by it. It's too late now anyway. But there's no doubt he's angry. I'm just not sure if he's angry because he's worried he'll take the blame for this missing file or if he's the guy who's actually responsible for it going missing in the first place. I'm not sure if it's actually just because he doesn't like the idea of his team being accused of things if this all blows up."

"It's all blowing up already, Frank."

"You got that right," Delaney said. "He got you beaten up and maybe he's got someone to try to run me down. He got someone to tell your wife about Conchi."

"You think it's Becker who did all those things, Frank? Really?"

"Who else could it be?" Delaney said.

Smith had pondered this for a while. He drank some tea. He noticed that Delaney ordered beer now, or something even stronger, no matter what time of the day they met to ponder situations together.

"I feel we should have a clearer plan of some sort," Smith said.

"The plan is, I go to Berlin, and try to find out what's really going on. If that body really is Klaus Heinrich, we're onto something big. As in big enough for a guy like Becker to play hardball with us."

Delaney had told him what he found out from what he called "good sources" in Germany and Canada. Smith had no choice but to assume that Delaney's information was solid, that his sources were as good as he claimed.

"Why would an ex-Army man like Becker, if that's who he actually is, and a pathologist, why would he be over here trying to prevent people like me from identifying a man like Klaus Heinrich?" Smith said. "All right, maybe it will turn out that Heinrich was a spy who didn't die when people said he died or maybe he faked his own death, or whatever. People do that sort of thing sometimes. We thought Stahlman did that. Fine, all right. But what's in it for a man like Becker? Heinrich's already dead, one way or the other. So what are people trying to hide in this thing?"

"Jonah, congratulations, you are now asking exactly the right questions," Delaney said. "That's what I'm going to Berlin to find out. When I find out, you'll be the first to know."

For reasons he could not quite understand, the new Jonah Smith had some doubts about whether this was how things would actually work.

Smith went back to work at the IMC on a Wednesday, after the period of rest ordered by Thai doctors, by Braithwaite, and by Interpol team leader Janko Brajkovic. Delaney had already been gone for two days when Smith returned to work.

Brajkovic took the fingerprint man aside on the day Smith returned for what the Croatian policeman called "some friendly career advice."

"You have done badly, my friend," Brajkovic said. "Everyone is pissed off. I myself am pissed off."

"About what, Janko?" Smith asked.

Brajkovic was seated in his usual place, with his usual flask of coffee on hand to fight the morning-after effects of alcohol and other excesses. Smith waited beside Brajkovic's extremely untidy desk to hear how the Croatian would describe the present situation.

"Your ridiculous search for that missing file has made everybody mad here, Smith. Braithwaite, Colonel P, I can never pronounce those damn Thai names, the entire German DVI team, me. You make it seem like everybody's either a criminal or a fool around here, Smith. No wonder you get yourself beaten up."

"I got robbed, Janko," Smith said.

"You are too smart to really think that, aren't you, Smith?"

"Why would someone beat me up just because I am trying to locate a lost file?"

"Because, fool, I told you, because you make everybody look like fucking criminals around here."

"No, I do not," Smith said.

"Braithwaite is so close to sending you back to Lyon you better have your bag packed and ready. I hear he has been talking to our illustrious Secretary-General. I hear the Secretary-General is not a happy man."

"I'm not interested in police gossip, Janko," Smith said.

"You better be," Brajkovic said. "If they ship you back to

Lyon like a bad boy, our illustrious Secretary-General may very well then ship you back to London like a very bad boy. Your wife won't like that much will she, Smith? Or the lovely Concepción."

Brajkovic had a remarkably irritating grin. His bared his nicotine-stained teeth to leer at what he assumed would be Smith's extreme discomfort.

Smith, in fact, had considered the possibility that he could be sent back to London for his actions over the *Deutschland* file. The prospect of exchanging the Thailand disaster zone for the disaster zone of his marriage did in fact fill him with discomfort, if not quite dread. He did not want Brajkovic to see this, however, if only to prevent more fuel being tossed on management centre gossip fires that were now burning bright.

"Braithwaite wants to see you," Brajkovic said, baring his yellow teeth once again. "He said you should report to him the moment you came back to work."

"What on earth for?" Smith said.

"Maybe you are not so smart, Smith, if you don't know why Braithwaite wants to see you. Maybe I am wrong about you," Brajkovic said.

On the way to Braithwaite's office Smith passed by the German DVI area. This, he thought as he approached it, was perhaps not so smart.

Horst Becker was not there. He would normally be working at the mortuary compound if he was on duty today at all. Hamel was there, however, and Krupp. Both policemen stopped what they were doing at their computer screens and stared coldly at Smith as he passed by.

Hamel called out: "You have balls, at least we can say that, Smith. To come back in here."

"Why on earth should I not come back in here, Hamel?" Smith said.

"Why on earth should I not come back in here? Krupp, do you hear what this idiot is saying? Idiot," Hamel said.

"The knocks on his head have left him damaged in his brain," Krupp said.

"Precisely," Hamel said. "Idiot."

Smith felt an unaccustomed wave of rage beginning to build in his system. Before his various transformations in Thailand, he was not a man prone to extremes of emotion, least of all rage.

"You have balls too, Hamel," Smith shouted. "To speak to me like that."

"Oh, my God, the fingerprint man is upset," Krupp said. "Too many blows to the head."

"You both have a nerve to joke like this. You're police officers. You think it's funny that someone beat me up? You wouldn't have had anything to do that, would you, Krupp? Or you, Hamel?" Smith shouted. His face was reddening.

"Steady now," Hamel said. "Watch your mouth, Smith. Don't shout at Landeskriminalamt policemen, that's never a good idea."

"Steady, Smith," Krupp said, standing up behind his desk.

Brajkovic had heard the raised voices and came running into the section. Some other DVI officers and some Thai clerical staff started to gather round.

"Smith, Smith, just go," Brajkovic shouted. "No more trouble from you. No more."

"There's no trouble here that we cannot handle, Janko," Hamel said from behind his desk. "We have the situation under control. There's nothing here that a German police baton cannot handle."

Krupp laughed extravagantly and sat back down behind his desk. Hamel continued to stare at Smith, inviting another outburst.

"Just go, Jonah. Go," Brajkovic said.

Braithwaite looked like he had been beaten up as well. But his face bore the signs of strain and fatigue, not batons.

He sat very still for a time, simply looking quietly across his desk after Smith had sat down. A cigar lay extinguished in the coffee mug he used for an ashtray.

"You puzzle me, Smith," Braithwaite said eventually.

"Why is that, sir?" Smith said.

"You seem to be a good man, good at what you do, dedicated. Smart. They think highly of you back in London. You're a good Scotland Yard man."

"Thank you."

"They thought highly enough to send you over to Interpol for a few years on a nice little secondment in the south of France," Braithwaite said.

Smith said nothing.

"The Interpol people then thought highly enough of you to send you over here on this very important operation."

Smith still said nothing.

"What has got into you, exactly, Smith? Can you tell me? Why would you risk all of that, and jeopardize this operation and risk harming the reputation of Scotland Yard and Interpol and the German police, one of the finest police forces in the world, with this nonsense. Can you explain that to me, please?"

Smith was about to try, but Braithwaite spoke again. He really did look very tired, Smith thought.

"You exhaust me, do you know that?" Braithwaite said. "I'm tired."

"It's a very hard assignment for you, sir."

"They gave you a pretty good beating, didn't they," Braithwaite said.

"Yes, they did."

"It wasn't actually a robbery was it, Smith?"

"No, sir, I don't think it was."

Braithwaite suddenly looked even more tired. He rubbed

his eyes with both fists. He stared at his unlit cigar.

"I don't like it when a Scotland Yard man gets beaten up, Smith," he said. "That would be rather an obvious position for someone like me to take, correct?"

Smith said nothing. Braithwaite rubbed his eyes some more.

"That reporter has left Phuket, I'm told," Braithwaite said suddenly.

"He has," Smith said.

"Is he coming back?"

"He might," Smith said. "You never know with reporters."

"No," Braithwaite said. "That's what gets my goat."

Smith waited for whatever it was the Detective Chief Superintendent actually wanted to communicate.

"Here's a suggestion, OK, Smith?" Braithwaite said. "From a Scotland Yard colleague. You go back over to your desk and start working again on those fingerprint IDs. We need you on this operation. I want you to keep your head down from here on and get us as many damn matches as you can get and I want you to stay out of the way of trouble of any sort. I don't want you to upset people anymore about that damn missing file and I don't want people beating up my people anymore about that damn missing file. Is that clear? I want all of the people on this operation to just get back to work and identify all those bodies in those bloody containers and then we can all go home and leave this godforsaken place behind us. Do you follow me, Smith? I don't want any more trouble here. It's enough. You forget about that file, someone will do another postmortem on that body at some point when they get around to it, we'll get some more prints off it and you can have another look and in the meantime we can all just get on with our work. Do you follow?"

Smith thought that Braithwaite was far too tired to want to hear about break-ins at the mortuary site or fingerprints having been surgically removed. Braithwaite appeared to be under enough strain as it was.

"Thank you, sir."

"I don't like it when a Scotland Yard man gets beaten up," Braithwaite said. "OK? I've told the German team leader that. No more drunken brawling on my watch."

Smith did not inquire as to what the German team leader might have said in response.

"Thank you, sir."

"No more trouble. Do you follow?"

"I do."

"Out," Braithwaite said.

Smith and Conchi slept that night in his giant hotel bed for the first time in a long while. With his wife back in England, and Delaney in Germany taking whatever next steps that had to be taken, and a reprieve, apparently, having been granted by Braithwaite, things were somehow back to whatever could now pass for normal for Smith and Conchi in Phuket.

"You can love me for now, again," Smith said as they lay together under his sheets.

"Maybe for a little, little time extra after that too," Conchi said. "Maybe."

The new Jonah Smith had found himself becoming prone to strong emotions, like rage and pleasure and sometimes something almost like joy. The old Jonah Smith had felt nothing much of anything for a very long time.

"I like the sound of that, Conchi," he said.

"It doesn't mean I don't think you are very stupid, Jonah, about things like little file folders that have gone missing."

"I understand that," he said.

Conchi paused, and then said: "Frank Delaney says we should watch ourselves now, while he is away. Shall we be scared maybe?"

"No," Smith said.

"They tried to kill Frank Delaney with a car," she said.

"We'll be all right," Smith said. "When Frank finds out what's going on, we'll tell the right people and it will all be over."

"Do you think so, Jonah Smith fingerprint man?" Conchi said, tracing a fingertip down his face from forehead to chin. "We identify the bad guys."

"We shall identify the bad guys," he said.

"File stealers. We throw them in jail, maybe, no?" Conchi said."

"Maybe," Smith said.

Once in a while in Phuket, Thailand, in the spring of 2005, in the months after the tsunami disaster, there was some good news. Some of that good news came on the day after Smith returned to work.

The body of Mrs. Stokke's daughter had finally been identified. While Smith was in hospital and then recuperating on the orders of his superiors, a Thai search team had found the body of a European child deep in a storm water culvert more than 10 kilometres from the beach where she had been swept out to sea on Boxing Day. Search teams were still, more than three months after the tsunami, occasionally finding bodies in obscure places far from the tourist beaches.

Very few DVI people had any doubt that this horribly disfigured and deteriorating body brought to the mortuary compound in a child-sized body bag was that of young Charlotte Stokke. Then, while Smith was on sick leave, Werner Eberharter, Interpol's Austrian deputy team leader and, Smith was willing to admit, a reasonably good fingerprint examiner, had made a tentative match against antemortem marks taken from Christmas wrapping paper on the gifts Charlotte Stokke had opened before her family flew to Phuket for their ill-fated holiday.

Norwegian policeman Magne Vollebaek had brought a

variety of AM prints to Phuket personally. He had done as much as any policeman could in the months after the tsunami to help identify Mrs. Stokke's daughter. Charlotte's fingers had, as would be expected, deteriorated badly after weeks in tepid brackish water, but Eberharter was as sure as he could be that prints from two of the girl's least-ruined fingers matched some of those that a Norwegian technician had found on a torn piece of metallic red and green Christmas paper.

Vollebaek had also brought X-rays from Charlotte's Oslo dentist. The little girl had had no fillings; at eight years of age, she was too young for that. Forensic dentists like dental fillings. They stand out clearly on postmortem X-rays and they can be matched easily with antemortem images. Charlotte had no fillings, but her parents had apparently been worried about how some of their little girl's teeth were aligned. They had asked for X-rays to be done, and these X-rays, of a slightly crooked line of children's teeth, were also carried to Phuket by missing persons detective Magne Vollebaek.

With the acceptable fingerprint match and the very good dental match, the Identification Board had formally ruled that the body in the filthy drain culvert was that of one Charlotte Margaret Birgitte Stokke, born 21 July 1996, Oslo, Norway, died 24 December 2004, Phuket, Thailand. No one, it seemed, had any interest in preventing identification of this particular disaster victim. No files had gone missing, no one was under any threat whatsoever for trying to identify Mrs. Stokke's daughter.

Vollebaek had hurried to Phuket from Oslo as soon as he received word that a little girl's body had been found in a drain culvert. For his troubles, Vollebaek had been given the task of informing Mrs. Stokke when the identification was officially declared valid.

Vollebaek stood on a chair in the management centre when he told a small group of DVI officers from a variety of countries how it had been. They gathered quietly in a cramped corner of their maze-like partitioned workspace to hear about it. They looked quietly at the ground and at each other as Vollebaek described Mrs. Stokke's shriek—the shriek, Vollebaek said, almost like that of an animal—when he had told her that the body in the child-sized body bag had been identified. Conchi and Smith stood at the back of the small crowd as the Norwegian policeman spoke.

Vollebaek told them how Mrs. Stokke had shrieked and shrieked and shrieked, and then how she had collapsed in his arms, sobbing as if she would never be able to stop. When, eventually, the tears stopped coming, for a short time, he had driven her back to her hotel and arranged for a Thai nurse and a Thai policewoman to help her undress and get into her hotel bed. A day later, Vollebaek said, Mrs. Stokke was still, apparently, in that bed, with the same Thai nurse sitting by her side.

"My commissioner in Oslo has asked me to congratulate all of you on behalf of the National Police Directorate and the Police Minister," Vollebaek said.

Smith thought Vollebaek looked even more worn out than Braithwaite looked. The Norwegian detective was probably only a very few years away from retirement. He was a policeman of the old school; he would not give up on a case until it had been definitively solved, no matter how many hours of casework it took, no matter what the toll on his personal life and his health. Vollebaek was the only person in the sweltering IMC that day wearing a dark suit and tie, downtown detective-style. Sweat poured from his ruddy Scandinavian face.

"You are all heroes, all of you on the teams here," Vollebaek said, allowing himself, as Smith and Conchi decided afterward, to get somewhat carried away.

"It's our job, Magne, it's what we're all here for," an Austrian DVI man called out.

"Here, here," Smith called out from the back.

Conchi squeezed his arm.

"Don't, Jonah," she said.

Hamel and Krupp looked around to glare at him from where they stood. Horst Becker, it seemed, had decided not to attend today's little celebration of identifications made, of files closed.

Smith wondered if Klaus Wolfgang Heinrich—assuming that body number PM68-TA0386 in mortuary container CRL0912863 was indeed that of Klaus Wolfgang Heinrich— had a family somewhere who would mourn his death. Perhaps a family had already mourned for Heinrich, mistakenly, in October 2001. Smith wondered if any tears were likely to be shed when he and Delaney and others, confirmed, if they ever managed to do so, that body of tsunami victim PM68-TA0386 was indeed that of one Klaus Wolfgang Heinrich, West German spy.

That night, Jonah Smith dreamed of his own dead daughter. It was a recurring dream, always the same in every detail, but he had had to endure it only occasionally in recent years. In the years immediately after his baby had died in his wife's womb, Smith had the dream far too often for his own good or for the good of his marriage:

In the dream he is in London on a busy street. Hundreds, thousands, of pedestrians block his path as he tries to hurry along on his appointed duties. Cars and black taxis and red double-decker buses block streets and intersections on all sides. He carries a Scotland Yard evidence card, clutches it tightly in his right hand. On the card are the tiny perfect fingerprints of his unborn daughter. It is his job to match these prints to the beautiful young girl he is certain she would have one day become. He pushes and shoves and elbows his way desperately through the crowded London streets, peering into the face of every little girl child he sees, urgently trying to identify his daughter. He grasps at the hands of bewildered, frightened children, trying to peer at their fingertips to make the all-important match that only he is qualified to make. Angry parents push him away, shout warnings at him, call out for the police to come and take this bespectacled madman into custody. Little girls he has frightened run away from him, crying for their fathers and mothers. Then his wife glides slowly past, standing up in the back of an elegant open car. She points an accusing finger at him from the big black car as she passes by. Everyone in the heaving crowd of parents and wailing children now points accusing fingers at him. The evidence card with the crucial fingerprint evidence slips from his grasp. His only hope of a positive identification is about to be lost forever . . .

Stefan Zalm had been keeping his distance ever since the day he confessed to his sins. He nodded to Smith in the morning when they crossed each other's paths at work, but he had not proposed drinks at the Whale Bar for days. Smith thought the young Dutchman was looking distinctly unhealthy and certainly unhappy.

Smith did not share Delaney's lingering suspicions about Zalm. In fact, Smith doubted whether Delaney himself was truly suspicious of Zalm at all anymore, or simply keeping what the Canadian reporter would call "all options open." Smith thought Zalm had just made a mistake, had been too eager to succeed in Phuket, had let ambition or dedication or immaturity or inexperience get the better of him. Smith did not believe that Zalm was part of what one might call the conspiracy to prevent the identification of the *Deutschland* body.

He decided to defuse the situation and put Zalm at ease.

"I'm not mad at you anymore, Stefan," Smith said late one afternoon as he stood beside the Dutchman's desk. "I was, but I'm not now."

Zalm looked up from the dental X-ray he was examining with a magnifying glass. He looked like he was going to burst with relief and delight.

"I'm so glad, Jonah," he said, putting down his work. "I never meant to cause this trouble."

"Someone else caused this trouble, Stefan."

"I'm sorry they beat you up, Jonah."

"It's all right, Stefan."

"Thanks, Jonah."

The Dutchman paused.

"But that Frank Delaney still thinks I'm no good," he said. "He asked me a lot of questions before he went to Berlin. He thinks I'm involved somehow in all of this mess."

"He's a reporter. They always ask a lot of questions."

"I want to find out who that German guy really is too, Jonah."

Smith, despite trusting that Zalm wasn't part of any conspiracy, had not told him what Delaney had already found out about Klaus Heinrich. Perhaps this was the real test of whether he did trust Zalm one hundred percent. Or perhaps he was simply spending too much time with a rather jaded Canadian journalist these days.

"We'll find out about him, Stefan."

"I think we will, too, Jonah," Zalm said.

He did not, however, look entirely convinced. He hesitated, and then said hopefully. "Pedophile?"

"Maybe. I'm not so sure about that," Smith said.

"There's so many of them out here, Jonah. From Germany, from everywhere in Europe."

"Frank is in Berlin working on this right now."

"He's a reporter, Jonah. He's not even police."

"Yes? And?"

"He wants a story."

"So. He gets a story and we find out who our man really was."

Zalm looked uneasy.

"I suppose it's none of my business anymore after what I did, maybe it never was my business, this," Zalm said. "But you can't tell with reporters what they're going to do with information when they get it, Jonah."

"You can't tell what police are going to do with information, Stefan. You can't predict what anyone's going to do with information when they get it."

"You should be the one who decides on this, not Frank," Zalm said. "Don't you think? We don't really know very much about him, what kind of person he is, who he really is. But I suppose it's none of my business anymore."

"He's a well-known journalist. He's a foreign correspondent. People know about him. I saw the stuff he wrote about Burma a few years ago. He's written books about the Vatican, Cuba, Quebec. He's who he says he is, Stefan."

Zalm still looked unconvinced.

"Frank isn't going to do anything without talking to me about it first, Stefan," Smith said.

As he spoke, Smith realized, in his heart, how naïve that sounded. However, Zalm, on his best postconfession behaviour, appeared willing to let naïve remarks pass unchallenged. "I'm not going to fingerprint the guy and check him out with Interpol before I let him help me, Stefan. Am I now?"

Zalm still looked glum.

"Drinks?" Smith said. "At the Whale?"

"Always, Jonah."

Chapter 10

I t seemed that the new Jonah Smith was becoming prone to anger. He got very angry indeed when Conchi told him a day later that Horst Becker had come to her room at the Royal Phuket Hotel, where the Spanish DVI team was billetted in luxurious surroundings. Becker she said, was drunk again, or feigning drunkenness again, and exuding menace. Conchi was, she told Smith during their walk through Phuket Town on their lunch break, just out of the shower with a towel around her head and wearing a hotel bathrobe. Becker had pushed his way into the room when she opened the door.

"Why did you open the damn door?" Smith shouted at her. "Don't you know that's dangerous, to open a hotel room door to just anybody? Didn't you look through the peephole first, for goodness' sake?"

"I thought it was the night maid bringing me the little chocolate they always bring at bedtime, Jonah," she said. "They turn down the beds at the Royal at night."

"And Becker pushed his way in?" Smith said, stopping amid the traffic and crowds of Krung Thep Road to look directly at Conchi as she described what happened.

"He didn't push exactly. He just came right inside without waiting, before I said it was OK."

"It is certainly not OK. It's not OK at all," Smith shouted.

A passing Thai driver slowed down and called out to them: "Taxi, taxi? Airport?"

Becker, Conchi said, had stopped short of threatening her directly. But there was no doubt in her mind that the visit was another warning. Becker had said as much.

"He said it was the last time he was going to warn us to stop making a fuss about the file," Conchi said.

Passersby stared at the two foreigners having such a heated conversation in the middle of a busy noontime sidewalk.

"What does 'the last time' mean? What on earth does he mean by that?" Smith shouted again.

"Jonah, Jonah, stop your shouting in the street," Conchi said.

"I'm going to go find that bastard right now,' Smith shouted.

"Jonah, please, take it easy. We know what that Becker is like," she said.

"Precisely. Precisely. That's why I've had enough."

Becker had not stayed long in Conchi's room. As he had done the time he arrived unannounced and exuding menace at Smith's hotel, Becker railed at Conchi for a few minutes about German reputations being at stake, about unfounded allegations being tossed around, about unspecified consequences for Conchi and for Smith and for Frank Delaney if they did not stop stirring things up about the lost file.

"I was scared a little, Jonah," Conchi said. "Just a little. But I knew he wouldn't hurt me."

"Of course you were scared. The bastard meant for you to be scared. He meant for me to be scared when he got some goons to beat me up and he meant for Frank to be really, really scared when someone tried to run him over with a car."

Conchi started walking again down Krung Thep Road.

"I'm going to bloody Braithwaite about this, Conchi. This is getting out of hand," Smith said.

"What good will it do, Jonah? What is Braithwaite going to do? He wants you off this thing about the file too."

"Well, if Becker is also threatening you now . . ."

"He wasn't exactly threatening me, Jonah. He was just mad."

"Well, I'm bloody well mad now too."

"He was mad, too, he said about his ID card."

"His what?"

"His ID card. He said we stole it from him."

"He what?"

Smith stopped again in the street.

"He said his ID badge was missing. He thinks we took it."

"Why would we take his damn ID badge?" Smith said. "He's a damn fool. What's wrong with that man?"

All members of the international DVI teams were issued photo identification passes by the Thai police when they arrived in the disaster zone. Everyone—police, civilian forensic experts, local clerical staff—wore the passes around their necks whenever they were on duty. Smith and Conchi were wearing theirs now as they walked through Phuket Town at lunchtime.

"He said he knew we stole his ID card and he wanted it back," Conchi said.

"He's crazy," Smith said. "Why would we do that? Why would anyone want to do that?"

"He just said he wanted it back."

"He's lost it, the fool. Why doesn't he just go get another one? What use is a photo ID card to anybody else?"

"He said there would be big trouble for us if we didn't stop bothering about this file thing and if we didn't give him his ID card back."

"Big trouble," Smith said. "Was that the phrase he used?"

"Yes, Jonah."

"The bastard," Smith said.

Conchi had eventually persuaded him not to confront Becker about the hotel visit. Smith had not seen Becker for days in any case. Conchi also persuaded Smith not to go to Adrian Braithwaite about Becker either.

They were sitting at the Circle Café in Rasada Street where they often ate lunch. Smith had calmed down a little. He started to see that Conchi was probably right, that there was not much they could do now except watch out for themselves and hope Delaney would be able to gather information that would defuse the situation somehow.

"We're right in the middle of this thing now, Conchi," Smith said as he watched her eat *kuaytiaw* noodles and drink tea. "We're just going to have to ride this out, I'm afraid. But Becker has really gone too bloody far this time."

"No, Jonah," she said. "This time it's OK, really. But he got you beaten up. And he got Frank into bad trouble with a car. That's what's going far, Jonah."

They agreed Smith would tell Delaney what had happened and do nothing else for the moment. Except watch their backs, and hope that Becker wouldn't decide to go further than he already had.

"Don't be scared, Conchi," Jonah said.

"I'm not that scared," she said. "I've been to Bosnia. I like to dig up bones from graves. I'm a tough Spanish girl from Madrid."

"I love you, Conchi," the new Jonah Smith suddenly deemed it entirely appropriate to say.

"For now?" Conchi said with one of her brilliant Spanish smiles. "Or for a little longer maybe?"

Smith also now deemed it appropriate to tell Conchi what Delaney had found out about Klaus Heinrich. He told her as they walked back to the IMC after lunch. She listened carefully, saying nothing at first. Then it was her turn to stop in the middle of a busy Phuket street.

"A spy," she said.

"Apparently," Smith said.

"A West German spy ends up dead in the tidal wave here."

"Apparently."

"Why? Why was he hiding in Thailand?"

"Congratulations, Conchi. That's exactly the question I asked Frank when he told me about it."

"How does Frank Delaney know these things?"

"Sources," Smith said. "Or so Frank tells me. Doesn't that sound exciting? Media sources or goodness knows what kind of sources."

"Sources," Conchi said.

"Precisely."

"Maybe not so precise. Not always. A German spy. Jonah, come on."

"It's possible. Anything's possible."

"But why hide? After the Wall, everything changed in Germany. There was no East–West stuff over there anymore, so who cares about spies anymore?"

"Spies make enemies, right? Maybe that's it."

"So this Klaus Heinrich, he hides, OK, maybe. Then he dies in a tidal wave on the beach. OK. So who cares then? People find out. But he's dead."

"That's what Frank is trying to find out in Berlin as we speak."

"Maybe Frank better hurry up."

Conchi stayed with him that night in his hotel bed where she now belonged. She slept, as always and despite their situation, deeply, easily, happily, letting out ever so slight, almost imperceptible, snuffles and wheezes as she slept.

Smith liked to watch her sleep. He liked to listen to the snuffles as she slept. He lay beside her, happy despite the present difficulties, and pondered scenarios.

He imagined Delaney playing reporter in Berlin, getting in and out of taxis, going into homes and offices, asking hard questions of everyone he met, writing things down in little notebooks as reporters do. He imagined German officials and police and media sources being helpful to Delaney; being forthcoming, knowledgeable, generous with their time. He imagined Delaney finding out everything they needed to know about Klaus Heinrich and why he had ended up dead in a tidal wave in Phuket instead of in a house fire in Bonn.

He imagined Delaney returning to Phuket with the real story. He imagined Delaney writing that story and it appearing on newsstands everywhere, and it bringing people to justice if justice needed to be done, confirming suspicions of various sorts, clearing up mysteries, uncertainties, moral ambiguities.

He imagined the *Deutschland* story coming to a happy end, with all loose ends tied up, all players, good guys and bad, getting exactly what they deserved. He imagined himself and Conchi celebrating after the *Deutschland* story had ended, and again after the entire disaster victim identification operation had ended, after the international teams all started at long last to go home.

But here the imagined scenarios began to get murky. Smith stared at the ceiling, as his lover slept deeply at his side, and tried to imagine how the Jonah Smith–Concepción Garcia Ramirez story might eventually end.

Delaney had congratulated him once for being able to ask the right questions. But regarding the Jonah Smith–Concepción Garcia Ramirez story and how it would eventually end, perhaps, for the moment, it was better not to ask the hard questions at all.

The next day, Smith came back to his hotel alone at about 6 p.m. Conchi was working late, with some of the other bone people because a big file of DNA profiles had arrived from the lab in Sarajevo and there was matching to be done.

He was pleased, in fact, to have some time alone, in order

to continue pondering scenarios and to rest. He was becoming, like Conchi, a little frightened by the situation, even a little paranoid. He imagined as he cycled home from the management centre that he was perhaps being followed by persons unknown. He imagined that people in Phuket and possibly elsewhere were plotting against him, and against Conchi and Delaney and possibly others. He let his imagination go.

He opened a beer and wandered aimlessly around his little apartment, absent-mindedly gazing at his books and his files and the pictures on the walls and the telephone and the bar fridge and the television and desk. He was in a deeply contemplative mood. An intuition of some sort was building, but he could not quite capture it.

He went onto the balcony and looked out over Chalong Bay. There was still plenty of light left. The air was still hot and humid. Cars moved in and out of the hotel parking lot. Their windshields mirrored the intense sunlight, flashing mystery signals up to him as he watched. Thai workmen in big straw hats dug listlessly with shovels at the base of a massive palm tree. Their portable radio played tinny Thai songs. Cyclists glided by.

Smith went back into his room. He stood gazing at what now passed for his home, holding his bottle of beer, waiting for the intuition, whatever it might be, to resolve itself in his mind. He thought it might have something to do with his wife. Or Conchi. Or both. Or perhaps neither. He stood quietly examining the tips of his fingers for clues, inspiration, answers. No inspiration came.

In the stillness of his room and in the stillness of his mood his eyes wandered to an electrical socket in the baseboard on the wall of the main room. The cleaner had apparently left a floor lamp unplugged. For reasons he was never able to fully explain afterward, he became interested in some dark finger marks on the wall around the socket. He walked over to the offending socket, replaced the lamp plug and stood absent-mindedly sipping beer, pondering fingermarks left by Thai chambermaids.

But then he suddenly put his beer down on a table and looked more closely at the finger marks and at the light socket. He pulled his eyeglasses down the bridge of his nose and knelt to have a closer look.

A tiny semicircle of back metal could be seen just at the edge of the white plastic socket cover. Only the idle, or the paranoid, or those who had spent too much time with police, would ever have noticed anything unusual at all. Smith peered at the tiny bit of black metal, sitting flush with the plaster wall, then stood back and picked up his beer again to take a very long and thoughtful drink.

He went to the kitchen area to get a small knife. He returned to the main room immediately and unscrewed the socket plate with some difficulty. He placed the plastic plate on the table and stood pondering the fruits of his paranoia.

At the edge of the rectangular patch of wall previously covered by the plate was a small round microphone device. Someone had punched a small hole in the plaster board exactly at the right-hand line of the socket cover and pushed the microphone inside, taking care to leave only a very small bit of microphone exposed when the plate was replaced. Two short lengths of fine wire ran from the microphone to the heavier electrical cables that disappeared into the wall. The microphone wires had been crimped securely into the main cables. The bug was neatly, expertly placed and the implications were profound.

Smith had seen listening devices before at Scotland Yard and elsewhere when he was called out to sweep crime scenes for fingerprints. This one was of very good quality. Not all of them were. They came in all shapes and sizes. Some were cheap, amateur affairs, easily obtained at stores for electronics enthusiasts on Tottenham Court Road or elsewhere if one were in London and wanting to plant bugs in hotel rooms. Such things could be purchased in almost any big city in the world.

This one, very compact and very effective, was something that professionals would use. It was called an AC sender. Smith knew from his experience at Scotland Yard that a device like this would take a small amount of power from the main electrical wiring of a room and use the same wiring to send a sound signal out. Usually, a listener would tap into a wire on the same electrical circuit somewhere else on the target's floor or somewhere else in the building, and listen from there. Or the listener could install a transmitter on the circuit somewhere, so conversations could be heard on a receiver outside, in a car or in another building close by.

For the next hour, the old Jonah Smith, fuelled by beer and anger and an increasingly justified paranoia, proceeded to methodically and completely examine every electrical socket, light switch, lamp and fixture, every electrical device or telephone or radio or TV or other appliance in his rooms and among his personal possessions. He lacked the tools for a proper police sweep, but he knew what he was looking for and he was a very thorough man. As thorough as he had always been at crime scenes.

He found just one other bugging device. It was in his bedroom, similarly placed behind a wall socket. It was the same model AC sender as the one in the main room. He did not remove the bugs. He simply, for the moment, revealed them. And when he thought he was done with his sweep he sat down on the sofa, very still, very thoughtful. He pondered paranoid scenarios for a very long time.

Smith cast his mind back over all the possible conversations he had had in these rooms since the beginning of the *Deutschland* file affair. He tried to imagine at what point someone would have deemed it necessary to plant listening devices behind wall sockets in his room. He tried to imagine what important conversations with Delaney or Zalm or with Conchi the listeners might have heard in his hotel room in recent days. He also imagined, with the intense embarrassment of a good Englishman, what sounds of lovemaking and intimacy those listeners might also have heard in recent days.

Smith, usually, was not a man who drank to excess. But in this case, as he sat for hours alone in his room, pondering scenarios and watching the light fade slowly over the Chalong Bay, he drank to excess. The entire situation—from the time he had first noticed irregularities with the *Deutschland* file, to his conflicts with colleagues over the file having gone missing, to the warnings he had started to receive, to the beating he had endured, to the attempt on Delaney's life, to the most recent threatening behaviour by Horst Becker in Conchi's room—was, he thought as he drank too much bar fridge whisky and beer and fought paranoia, getting completely out of hand.

Smith had not uttered a word since he first noticed the telltale smudges near the wall socket. Silence, now, was crucial.

He decided he would not follow his first impulse, which was to simply rip the listening devices from where they had been placed. He decided that he would not alert his listeners by doing this just yet, though he feared the very act of unscrewing switch plates and rummaging around for other devices in his room may have alerted them in any case.

Instead, he decided, he would carry on as before, but extremely careful now about what he said to anyone in his room or on the telephone. At least until he decided on a better strategy or until the entire situation was resolved. He hoped that Conchi would not call him on the telephone to say goodnight.

He got up from his sofa as night fell and somewhat unsteadily, given his unaccustomed overindulgence in alcohol, replaced switchplates and arranged appliances and restored order to his room. He did so as quietly as possible, in the uncomfortable awareness now that someone was likely listening to every move he made, every scrape of a knife blade on a screw, every click of a lamp or closing of a door.

When a semblance of order was restored and in the evening silence of his room, oddly oppressive now, Smith sat before his laptop computer and got online. Delaney had given him his email address and Smith now had important information to convey.

Frank, Smith wrote, *there's trouble here. I'm drunk and in my hotel room and what do you think I've found in here tonight? A bloody bug, two of them, good quality too. They were planted in some electrical wall sockets. Some bastard has been listening to my conversations in here, can you imagine? It must be Becker, who else could it be, the bastard. I'm not sure what to do and I can't call you from here anymore. I'm not sure where I should call you from actually. I've just left the damn things where they are for now. Also, Becker went over to see Conchi at her hotel the other night and basically told her there would be trouble if we all didn't back off. The fool also accused her or us or someone of stealing his bloody DVI identification pass, can you imagine? Who on earth would want to steal the man's ID badge? He's lost it, the bloody fool. He scared her, Frank, and I'm getting madder by the minute. I'm also drunk and it's getting late and I've got to go back in there tomorrow and match fingerbloodyprints all day as if nothing's happened. Mrs. Stokke leaves tomorrow. What are your thoughts? Have you found out anything good in Berlin? I haven't seen Becker myself. Best regards, Jonah.*

Smith hit "Send" and shipped the message to Delaney in Europe. The drinking had started to make him morose and somewhat reckless. He felt another message coming on. He decided this was entirely the right moment to write a letter to his wife. Not via email, but on proper Bay Hotel stationery, a formal document, a confession, duly signed.

He drunkenly pawed through various items in the slim drawer of the hotel desk, eventually coming up with writing paper and an envelope. He laid the paper out on the desk, raised his pen and contemplated ice cubes melting slowly in the glass of whisky before him.

My dear Fiona, he wrote eventually. *I have something extremely important I need to tell you. I'm drunk and in my hotel room and I'm writing this letter to you at long last because it's time for us to be honest about a number of extremely important things. You really need to know some things about the sort of man I've become over here. I'm not at all who you think I am . . .*

Smith's letter to his wife—long, maudlin, extremely jumbled in syntax and structure—was never mailed. As the fingerprint man regained consciousness the next morning, almost sober, alone in his hotel bed, he saw the letter on his desk, sealed and ready to go. It went, instead, directly into the wastebin.

He showered listlessly, hangover symptoms sapping his energy. He was scheduled to go out to the mortuary compound that morning with a larger than usual group of DVI people to see off Mrs. Stokke and her dead daughter. Something about that prospect, and about dead daughters generally, had in all probability contributed to his reckless mood the night before.

There were no email messages yet from Delaney on the laptop. Smith looked at his watch. It was after midnight in Berlin. Perhaps, he thought, Delaney was at that very moment alone in a silent hotel room somewhere, drinking too much and composing reckless emails, letters, confessions to wives, lovers, enemies, friends.

The intense sunlight outside the hotel made his hangover worse. Smith was not a man taken to wearing sunglasses. He squinted painfully against the sun as he hailed a taxi from the rank in the parking lot. The doorman who usually hailed cabs for guests was nowhere to be seen this morning. The taxi driver was too friendly, far too cheery, for a man in Smith's condition.

"The container compound, thanks," Smith said. All the Phuket drivers knew all the DVI operation venues; it was their new bread and butter. Tourism had collapsed and disaster victim identification was now a going concern.

"Everybody go there this morning, thank you, thank you very much," the driver said. "Is big day there, yes?"

"Yes. Big day," Smith said.

The fact that the sendoff was for a child, and a child that everyone had worked so hard to identify, and the fact that it was Mrs. Stokke, whom the DVI teams had gotten to know all too well, were strong drawing cards. Several dozen people crowded under the sun canopy in the open gravel area near the mortuary buildings. Smith had not been in the compound since the night he and Delaney broke in on their fingerprint expedition.

The Norwegian ambassador had flown in from Bangkok with his wife and some officials for the ceremony. Magne Vollebaek, of course, was there. He and the ambassador wore old-fashioned dark, European-weight suits. They were black blots in the intense tropical sunlight. The rest of the embassy delegation wore stylish summer clothes in light colours. The DVI teams were in a mixture of team shirts and T-shirts and standard pathologist-issue smocks.

Delaney's American photographer was there, too, with his prematurely grey pony-tail very neatly tied back with a black ribbon for the occasion. A BBC cameraman was there, too, and a couple of reporters carrying standard reporter-issue notebooks.

Conchi was there. Smith went to stand by her side. He wondered how many such ceremonies she would have attended marking significant junctures as part of her United Nations DVI work in the mass graves of Bosnia. She looked tired this morning and smiled wanly at him when he came up. Smith doubted that her sleepless nights had anything to do with solitary bouts of excessive drinking.

As with all significant sendoffs in Phuket, the authorities had somehow managed to find a man of religion from the home country in question to share a few words of wisdom. The Norwegian priest they had found wore no clerical robes. He was young, not yet 40, Smith thought, and looked quite unpriestlike in a short-sleeved white shirt and casual slacks.

There was a silver crucifix hanging from his neck, however, and he did carry a large black Bible. He read some passages from it in Norwegian and he said a few prayers and made a few signs of the cross over the small flag-draped coffin and over Mrs. Stokke and over anyone else he seemed to think needed a blessing of some sort. The ambassador spoke in Norwegian and in English, expressing official condolences, thanking all concerned, wishing Mrs. Stokke a safe trip home to Oslo.

Mrs. Stokke looked better than Smith had seen her in weeks. She no longer had the haunted look the DVI teams had come to dread encountering as they left the management centre most days during her vigil. She looked calmer than Smith had seen her in weeks. Just before her daughter's coffin was loaded into the back of a station wagon, she, too, thanked everyone for their efforts. Her voice was faint, but did not falter.

"My family came here together at Christmas time to enjoy ourselves and to be happy," Mrs. Stokke said. "That is not what happened to us. Nor did it happen to the other families who came here from around the world for Christmas. And now I'm going home to Oslo after Christmas with my daughter. At least my little Charlotte and I are going home together. Thanks to all of you. And especially, you, Magne."

Vollebaek began to cry. He brushed his tears away roughly with the backs of both hands at once. Detectives very rarely cry in public, though Smith knew several who cried, when required, in private or with trusted friends or colleagues in certain dimly lit drinking establishments in London.

Mrs. Stokke began to cry. The ambassador's wife began to cry. Conchi began to cry. Some of the international police rubbed their eyes. Smith refused, however, to cry. If he allowed himself to cry about this dead Norwegian daughter, the ghosts of other dead daughters, and particularly a dead British daughter he had never met, might completely overwhelm him. This was not allowed.

The young priest asked Vollebaek if he had anything to say. The detective shook his head. No one else took up the priest's invitation to speak, so the coffin was loaded into the car, Mrs. Stokke and some of the embassy officials got into other cars and the ragged little procession pulled away for the short drive to the airport.

None of the spectators moved for a moment. Two Thai policemen folded up the Norwegian flag. The BBC and Tim Bishop stopped taking pictures. Then Vollebaek, still roughly rubbing his eyes with his fists, strode purposefully into the closest mortuary building. This was a welcome signal to everyone that public displays of emotion were no longer allowed.

Smith stayed where he was with Conchi until everyone had dispersed. A gravel parking area in a sweltering mortuary compound on the outskirts of town was not at all likely to be bugged.

He told her about the eavesdropping device he had found. Her eyes widened. He had expected her to be angry, as she had often been in all of this to date. Instead, Conchi simply looked afraid. She actually looked more frightened then she had looked after his beating or Frank's narrow escape from under the wheels of a car.

"You can't be serious, Jonah," she said. "This is too much. It's too much now."

They stood face to face in the mid-morning heat and light. Smith said nothing.

"They could have heard all sorts of secret things," Conchi said. "How can we remember what we said? Frank Delaney was in your room to talk. And Stefan Zalm, and me, a lot. They can know everything we're thinking, Jonah."

"I know that, Conchi. It's not a good situation at all."

"And us," she said. "In the bed."

"I know," Smith said.

"It's horrible to think of. Someone listening like that."

"Yes. It is."

"It's too much."

"Yes."

They stood together in silence. Conchi seemed to be waiting for a cue from him as to how to proceed. He had no cues to give her.

"I've left their equipment in my room so they don't know that I know," he said.

"Is that the best thing to do?"

"I don't know what the best thing is anymore, Conchi. We're just in the middle of this thing now."

"That's all you always say now, Jonah," she said.

"It's all I can say now, Conchi," he said.

"Have you told Frank Delaney?"

"Yes I have. I sent him an email last night."

"Maybe they read our emails too."

"No, Conchi. I don't think so."

"We have to fix all this somehow, Jonah," Conchi said.

"I know that."

"What should we do?"

"I think we have to wait for news from Frank."

This prospect seemed to give her no comfort.

They went back to the Bay Hotel together. Smith thought it appropriate to show Conchi one of the listening devices he had found. She stood silently as he carefully unscrewed one of the plates over the wall socket. He stood aside to let her look. She stared at the listening device for a long time. The silence in his room was heavy as she looked.

Then he carefully screwed the plate back into position, and, finger over his lips to call for more silence, motioned for Conchi to sit down while he opened up his laptop and looked for news from Frank Delaney.

Delaney's email was timed well after midnight Berlin time. The message gave no indication of whether the author was drunk or sober, in a hotel room or elsewhere, alone or with a companion:

Jonah, Frank wrote, *this bug thing is not good at all. We're had too many talks in that room of yours for this to be any good at all. Luckily, we talked a lot on your balcony if I remember. And at the Whale Bar. That may help us a bit. And we don't know how long those things have been in there. I agree that you should leave the bugs where they are. We don't want to alert people that we know. And, maybe we could use them for some disinformation if we figure out what we want them to think we're thinking. Let them hear what we want them to hear. Let me think that one over for a bit. But we both have to try to figure out if we can what we're pretty certain they know that we know now. They probably know I'm in Berlin, I'd say, and they may even know we know the body out there is Heinrich. That would be very bad at this stage of the game. At least we were in my room when we looked at Stefan's papers that day and you told us in my room what you got from Interpol that other time. I just can't remember whether we used his name much in your room or on the balcony or God knows where now. We will just have to assume they know a lot about what we know, that's for sure.*

You'll have to just keep on being careful and obviously now you can't say anything you want in your room. But I don't need to tell you that, really. We've just got to be careful until I find out what's going on. I'm working on that. I may have found a guy over here who can let me have a look at the original autopsy report that was done for the body they found in that house in Bonn. That would be a good break and probably give us a steer in this. I'm hoping to get that stuff today or tomorrow, Jonah, so sit tight and who knows, we may get this thing sorted out fast. OK? Don't panic just yet.

Smith motioned for Conchi to come over and read Delaney's email over his shoulder. She read, grim-faced at first. She pointed to the words "Don't panic just yet" and then twirled her index finger at her temple. Smith smiled. Conchi almost smiled.

The thing is, Delaney wrote, *it's really hard to figure out who might be doing what at this stage. There are actually a few people who might want to bug your room when you think about it. Becker, obviously. Probably it's him. But then maybe Braithwaite could have ordered it up, to see what you're telling people. Maybe. Or maybe the Thais. Colonel Pridiyathorn could have got wind of this and be worried enough to bug your room. He certainly wouldn't want a scandal of any sort. It's probably Becker's people, I'd say, whoever they are, but it could be others. Zalm? You won't buy that, though, I'm sure.*

The thing is, Jonah, in my line of work, I find that the longer your list of potential enemies is, the more interesting the story actually becomes. Right? We're starting to develop a good little list of possible enemies now.

Smith imagined Delaney, probably in his Berlin hotel, smiling as he wrote those last few words. He pointed at the lines for Conchi. She again made the sign with forefinger twirling at temple.

About the ID card thing, Delaney wrote, *that was me. I thought it might be useful to have an official document of some kind with me here in Germany to show people who this Becker is and what he looks like. I stole it from his villa when I was there that day. It was on a table near the door. Tim couldn't get a shot of him and I thought the ID card would be good for us to have anyway. Something official with his name and signature on it. And I figured it would piss Becker off something terrible to lose his ID card and I liked that idea too.*

Even Conchi smiled broadly at the last line as she read it. Smith smiled too. He almost, for the first time that day, laughed out loud. He started to wonder if there wasn't a lot more he should know about this bearded, middle-aged Canadian journalist who liked to steal official items from people's houses. He wondered if there wasn't a lot more about Frank Delaney—foreign correspondent, investigative journalist, book writer, thief—than met the eye.

Chapter 11

Delaney had taken the Pedophile Express to Germany—
Lufthansa Flight 9715, nonstop Bangkok to Frankfurt.
True, not all passengers on that flight were late middle-
aged German males travelling alone and displaying clear signs of
alcohol abuse, nicotine addiction, severe sunburn and a predilec-
tion for illicit sex with Asian children. Some of the late
middle-aged German males on board were not travelling alone
and were, in fact, travelling with young Thai women of barely
legal age, or with extremely young Thai men.

And, yes, in fact, a good number of passengers on board
Flight 9715 did not fit the sex-tourist profile at all. Delaney
acknowledged as he found his seat that he had perhaps been in
the information business too long, had become far too cynical
and suspicious, had been rubbing shoulders with cynical and suspicious police officers for far too long. Some of the passengers on
board were in fact regular tourists—backpackers from any
number of European nations, nice little families heading home
after impeccably wholesome vacations, impossibly young couples
on possibly impeccable honeymoons. Not everyone heading to
Frankfurt from Bangkok was a pedophile or a potential
pedophile.

Still, any good demographer would find the population

sample on board somewhat heavily weighted toward late middle-aged German males travelling alone. Middle-aged Canadian journalists travelling alone were no statistical anomaly, however, and were of course above suspicion.

The overnight flight left Bangkok airport at 23:40, precisely on time. Delaney had flown up to Bangkok on a tourist shuttle turboprop a few hours previously, after dropping off his rental car at Phuket airport and, understandably, taking extra care not to be murdered by drivers of speeding vans as he made his way from the parking area to the terminal building. The incident in the parking lot of the Metropole had left him wary, as well as bruised and scraped.

The flight to Frankfurt would take just over 14 hours. There would be a short wait in Frankfurt and then about an hour more in the air would bring him to Berlin. But Delaney was looking at the long journey to Europe as useful thinking time, analysis time, worrying time. There was much to consider, in the hours he would be confined to his dim Lufthansa cocoon.

Delaney was travelling in Economy Class, not an ideal place to spread out notebooks and documents for a long session of thinking and worrying. But, as he was far from sure that *International Geographic* would pay for a Business Class ticket for him to travel to a city 9,000 kilometres away from where he was supposed to be on assignment, on a journey that would almost certainly yield nothing the editors either expected or required him to publish, he had bought an Economy ticket.

The Canadian Security and Intelligence Service, of course, always made sure that he travelled Business Class. But, as was so often the case, Delaney had not quite decided who he was working for on this assignment. Rawson, as always, would make the rash assumption that Delaney was back on the CSIS freelance payroll. Delaney, as always, would delay making decisions about assigners and expense payers until the situation became clear.

And there was much that was still far from clear. He was

counting on Gunter Ackermann, and the German journalist's array of contacts, to help rectify that.

Like Ackermann, and despite the passenger demographics on Lufthansa Flight 9715, Delaney had ruled out a pedophile connection in this story. The Karl-Heinz Stahlman pedophile angle had simply not panned out. Delaney trusted Ackermann's judgment and contacts and journalistic skills enough to accept that.

He also trusted Jonah Smith's judgment and contacts and fingerprinting skills enough to accept that the body of the tsunami victim who apparently interested so many people so much was that of Klaus Wolfgang Heinrich. Delaney accepted that and he accepted that Heinrich had been a highly effective West German spy working in East Berlin for many years.

But beyond this, Delaney could be sure of nothing much at all. Why Heinrich had ended up dead in Phuket in 2004, and not in a cabin outside Bonn in 2001 as the world was meant to believe, was just one of many unanswered questions. Why would Heinrich want to fake his own death, if indeed that is what had gone on? Why might someone else want to fake Heinrich's death in this way? Why would anyone then go to great lengths to prevent true identification of his body in Thailand? Why would anyone beat up and then threaten with blackmail a Scotland Yard man who started asking questions? Why would anyone try to run down a journalist who came across the story? And what, more importantly, might these people try to do next?

Nor could Delaney shake off his worries about young Stefan Zalm, apparently a dedicated young forensic dentist who also stole confidential files from friends and colleagues and then miraculously brought them to light once again just when needed. With Zalm's help, the trail had suddenly pointed almost too easily to Heinrich. Was this just a lucky break or were there people who now wanted to make sure that Smith, and Delaney, or both, clearly saw the Heinrich connection?

Delaney found it quite easy to worry about such matters as he reclined in his grey faux-leather airplane seat en route to Frankfurt. He also worried a little about the health of his relationship with Kate Hunter, about the health of his old friend Brian O'Keefe, and about his various failings, misdeeds and misdemeanours, past and current. Such worries came naturally to him on a long overnight flight alone.

At one point somewhere over India, after too many hours of enforced introspection, he even began to worry that he had failed to renew his driver's licence before leaving Canada. But eventually the drone of the engines soothed him, and the small airline blanket on his knees gave him a certain comfort. A series of very small airline whiskies played their part as well.

As always, Delaney had tried his very best to avoid eye contact, or any other contact, with his seat mate on an airplane. In this case, the strategy proved successful until the plane was making its final approach in to Frankfurt. But as people began gathering up the debris of a 14-hour journey, folding blankets and stowing magazines and jockeying for position outside lavatories, an extremely dishevelled woman of about 30, driven, it appeared, to the brink of madness by the long flight and unaccustomed solitude, looked over at Delaney and pleaded with her eyes for conversation.

Delaney broke one of his most important rules of a lifetime of travel and smiled weakly in the woman's direction. This opened the floodgates.

"First trip to Germany?" she said, combing knotted ash-blonde hair with her fingers. "I'm from south London. I've been on a volunteer project in Laos. I'm doing international studies at City University. I went back to school late. For my Masters."

"Interesting," Delaney said, watching her struggle to put on a pair of extremely grubby hiking boots.

"What do you do?" the woman asked. "You a salesman?

You're wearing a suit jacket. Or was it a holiday? Wasn't it just the most terribly long flight? How do you find it, travelling alone? I don't like it much at all, really. Especially on a long flight. It gets me crazy."

She began applying bright red lipstick without the aid of a mirror. The result was not good.

"You getting off here?" the woman said.

"I'm going on to Berlin," Delaney said.

"What for?" she asked.

"It's a bit of a long story," Delaney said.

"The mysterious type," she said. "Well, Berlin's the place for you. Used to be, anyway."

"So I'm told," Delaney said.

"Stay out of trouble."

"I'll try."

Berlin Tegel airport is a throwback, like so much in the city, to the 1960s, to the Cold War, to a Europe that is fading fast. It's an airport that could still be used, without too much work by set decorators, as a backdrop for a B-grade movie about glamorous people rushing along to some intriguing appointment with modernity—handsome spies in narrow-lapels and willowy women in haute couture in the afternoon, throwing expensive leather luggage into the back of throaty silver roadsters.

Delaney had always marvelled at the odd hexagonal design of the Berlin terminal, with its corridors and departure gates arranged around a yawning core. Even when the airport was far from capacity, the design produced the impression of congestion, confusion, urgency.

The flight from Frankfurt arrived at 7:55 a.m., once again precisely on time. Far too early, however, for Delaney to even dream of asking Ackermann to meet him even if his old friend had been able to get away from the newspaper that morning. Ackermann was *Die Welt*'s chief political editor, which, as he had reminded Delaney on the telephone, was a position of extremely heavy responsibility entrusted only to the very best minds that German journalism could produce.

Ackermann had said he would meet Delaney late that afternoon. This meant, Delaney knew all too well, that the night's drinking and eating would begin early and still end extremely late.

A row of cream-coloured Mercedes taxis waited in an orderly line outside the terminal building. Delaney slid into the back of one driven by a broad-shouldered woman with hair the colour and texture of brass wire.

"The InterContinental, please," Delaney said. "Budapester Strasse."

Berliners, and those who know Berlin well, refer to the hotel as the InterConti. Like Tegel airport, it is a throwback, a medium-rise sixties structure with a checkerboard front and a glass pyramid lobby that dominates the local streetscape. Delaney liked it for the same reasons he liked the airport. It was also walking distance from Cold War landmarks such as the Reichstag, Potsdamer Platz and the Berlin Zoo, backdrops to cloak and dagger plotlines almost since movies began to be made.

The taxi driver immediately launched into a heavily accented diatribe against Turkish guest workers, railing against them in particular and the decline of Germany's gene pool in general.

"Scandal, scandal, do you follow?" she shouted over the seatback, watching in the mirror for any sign of inattention from Delaney. "These bastard Social Democrats are fucking this country with their immigration stupidities, do you follow? This Schroeder bastard must be thrown out, do you see?"

"Maybe in the election this year," Delaney said wearily.

"Yes, yes, of course. No question. It is necessary, yes," the driver shouted.

The dark marble and wood of the hotel lobby was a

sanctuary after the cab ride. However, the young desk clerk—beautiful, elegant in her navy blue InterConti pantsuit, but, as the taxi driver would surely point out, suspiciously Turkish in appearance—first needed to be persuaded that it would not be a serious breach of her duties to allow Delaney to check in at approximately 9 a.m. when the rules clearly stated that check-in was to be carried out, always, at 3 p.m.

"Is there a room available now?" Delaney asked, his weariness increasing.

"Yes," the clerk said without a smile.

"Well then I don't see the problem."

"Check-in is at 3 p.m., sir," she said. "That is the hotel policy and it is indicated on your reservation slip. See, it is written just there."

"You know it would be silly for me to wait for six hours to check in to my room if it's vacant now," he said.

"Those are the rules, sir."

"You're not going to make me call for the manager after my long flight from Asia, are you?" Delaney asked.

"Perhaps you should have scheduled yourself on a later flight?" the clerk said.

The manager proved extremely helpful and a model of flexible hospitality. But the clerk had stood her ground until given official dispensation to do otherwise. Problem solved, Delaney went immediately to his room for a long day's sleep in the giant, 1960s-style InterConti bed.

Gunter Ackermann had always demonstrated a limitless capacity for drink, cigarettes and conversation. None of this had changed when Delaney met him that afternoon in a run-down workingman's bar in what was once known as East Berlin.

Ackermann had just finished his day at *Die Welt*, which consisted, as he put it, of explaining the political situation of the country and the wider world to the German industrialist classes and bourgeoisie. He refused, however, to fraternize with his newspaper colleagues after work and he generally chose his drinking establishments in the comforting surrounds of the former German Democratic Republic.

As agreed, Delaney had brought with him a one-litre bottle of single malt whisky, an installment payment for Ackermann's assistance and advice. He had also made a reservation for dinner that evening at Zur letzten Instanz, a move that he knew would cost him no less than 200 euros, minimum. He very much doubted that either *International Geographic* or Canada's security agency would pay expenses for the night that was to come.

"The reservation tonight will of course have to be for three persons, Francis, for I am once again in love," Ackermann said after he had embraced Delaney in a huge exhalation of cigarette smoke and beer fumes. Ackermann was getting fatter and redder by the year, it seemed. Two large bottles of Krombacher Pils beer sat at his place on the table, both empty. His tiny smudged drinking glass was in need of a refill and his ashtray badly needed emptying.

"Three people?" Delaney said. "That wasn't our deal. Impossible. I'm a simple reporter from Montreal and I can't afford to take three people to Zur letzten Instanz."

"You most certainly can. And you shall. The prices are modest. And she is very, very beautiful," Ackermann said. "Young, as well. Far too young for someone like me."

"What's she doing with someone like you, Gunter?"

"It is of course my reputation as a sexual athlete."

"Of course."

Delaney knew he would have to pace his drinking carefully that afternoon and evening if he was to get any work done at all. There was much to discuss with Ackermann but, as always, such discussion could not take place without vast quantities of alcohol. And as a young woman was now to join them for dinner, most of the work would have to be done before her arrival.

No meeting with Ackermann could begin without a detailed joint recollection of their experience together in the sand dunes of Mazar i Sharif. Delaney ordered two more Krombachers, and the reminiscences began. Ackermann always asked Delaney to repeat the parts about any of his, Ackermann's, particularly heroic and selfless efforts to aid and protect journalistic colleagues in general and Delaney in particular from U.S. friendly fire and the Taliban.

"And tell me Francis once again how I lent you my precious satellite phone," Ackermann said. "At great personal cost and putting my own career with *Die Welt* in grave danger. Satellite telephone charges being what they are."

"You were a hero, Gunter," Delaney said. "Even the *Time* magazine guy didn't do as much."

"Precisely. Exactly so," Ackermann said. He shook Delaney's hand gravely.

"Under fire," Ackermann said. "You and me together."

"Exactly," Delaney said.

"And now you want Ackermann's help again. As always. You cannot live without Ackermann, is this not factual?"

"I can't live without you, Gunter. Impossible."

"You are it seems to me onto another very nice little story, Francis my friend."

"I would say."

"It has, as we reporter types so much like to say, all of the elements, am I correct Francis?"

"It does."

"But what you do with it, that is the question, as always. Am I correct in this, Francis?"

"Correct. As always."

"Well, I can tell you that anything to do with Klaus Heinrich, anything that has not been reported one million times before, is of course front-page news, surely. Here in Germany and quite possibly around the world."

"Quite possibly."

"If it has not been reported before."

"I don't think this has been, Gunter. Really I don't. Heinrich not dying in Bonn in 2001 but in Phuket, Thailand in 2004? I don't see that anywhere."

"Nor do I, my friend. Nor do I."

"So," Delaney said. "The question is why. Why fake the death?"

"It's a very Cold War sort of question, in my view," Ackermann said.

"Meaning? We're talking about 2001 or 2004. Not 1961 or '64."

"You have to remember, Francis, what it was like after the Wall came down. It was the most amazing thing; they were the most amazing times imaginable. Suddenly, or it seemed so sudden even though we all in retrospect could claim to have seen it coming, a regime that controlled every aspect of every person's life, simply collapsed. Suddenly a wall that people regularly died trying to cross was broken open and a whole country seemed to pour over into the West, and with them came all of their stories and tragedies. And all of the Stasi stories, all the stuff about surveillance and informants and spies and counter spies and moles and tapped telephones and people thrown in jail just for saying the wrong thing on the street. Suddenly all of that came flooding over the Wall into West Germany like a tsunami in 1989 and into 1990 and beyond that into reunification. We are all in a way still trying to digest all of those stories and make them a part of Germany, not just of East Germany. Do you see what I mean, Francis? So there are very probably still bits and pieces left to, how to say in English, integrate. You seem to have picked up one of those pieces, with this Heinrich story. Possibly."

"In Thailand."

"Why not? Do these stories always have to end in Berlin or Moscow or Washington?"

"All right, but I've thought this through a hundred times and I still don't understand it. Heinrich was what you've called a super spy. He was a big success story for the West. He worked for years undercover in East Berlin and he sent back a lot of good information. OK. Then the Wall comes down and his cover is blown . . ."

"No, Francis, not really blown. It's just that he didn't need his cover anymore. The game was over. No cover needed."

"Are you sure? I'm thinking the Stasi guys would have been very, very pissed off with Heinrich after 1989. They would have wanted to take him out."

"Why? Too late. And Stasi, essentially, dissolved along with the Wall."

"What about the true believers? Revenge. People want revenge long after big things have happened, Gunter."

"Maybe. Maybe. But the West, on this side, they would have been aware of that. They would have given Heinrich good security along with his nice little retirement job and his cabin in the hills outside Bonn. And in any case, Francis, nobody murdered Heinrich. He apparently died in a house fire. In his pajamas, probably."

"No he didn't. He died in the tsunami in Thailand."

"What I'm saying is, nobody tried to murder him in Germany. I don't think so. Either he died in the fire, which we now see quite possibly didn't happen at all, or he died in the big wave in Thailand last Christmas. Even the Stasi true believers can't manufacture a tsunami wave, Francis. They were good at putting listening devices inside transistor radios, but not natural disasters."

They sat silently together for a moment, drinking beer. Ackermann lit another cigarette.

"So a faked death," Delaney said eventually.

"Quite possibly."

"What else could it be?"

"That is not the essential question for me, Francis. The question for me in this story is the following: who benefits from such a faked death?"

"Exactly."

"Heinrich? Not so much. He has his little life arranged in the new Germany. People come to interview him occasionally. He gets his picture taken. He probably gets laid any time he wants, like a rock star. Why fake your death and move to smelly Thailand."

"So not his idea."

"Thank you."

"Whose idea?"

"Ah, now you want me to do everything. For only one litre of somewhat inferior-quality single malt whisky. But then, in a crucial election year for Germany, with the government in trouble, the chief political editor of *Die Welt* has nothing but time to while away the hours helping old friends after a long day's work."

They drank beer. Ackermann smoked. In the far back corner of the bar, a group of six drunken British boys noisily sang football songs and clinked glasses. The bartender and a couple of burly bar patrons glared at them and muttered darkly, but the visitors took no notice whatsoever.

"Those fucking no-frills airlines are bringing hundreds of such scoundrels into my city every day, Francis," Ackermann said. "It is a tragedy. I will soon have nowhere cheap and quiet left to drink."

They drank, pondering this small tragedy together.

"So whose idea, Gunter?" Delaney said eventually.

"You are relentless, my friend. The night is young. It is not even night time yet, officially."

"Stasi fakes the Heinrich death, kidnaps him, to interrogate him?"

"Brings him to Thailand, sets him up nicely there and lets

him live happily ever after? No. And what would Stasi want to know from him anyway? Even if Stasi was still operating at that point in history, which it was not."

"Any number of things."

"Such as?"

"Names of other agents, maybe? Other moles working in the East?"

"So what? They get some names, who cares? The Cold War is over."

"Revenge."

"We've tried that theory."

"Money?"

"What money?"

"Bank accounts? Secret stashes of money Heinrich knows about?"

"This is not a spy novel, Francis. We do not do secret bank accounts anymore. The Swiss have been co-opted by the money-laundering investigators. There is a war on terror going on, apparently."

"What were the theories at the time, then, Gunter?"

"Oh, like you, some people thought Stasi, revenge, assassination, spy novel stuff. But our man died in a fire. It is there in the official, detailed, stamped, notarized and framed autopsy report, everything the careful Germans are famous for. I was on the news desk when the story was going on in 2001. I knew it well. Everybody covered it. Press conferences every day for weeks, it seemed. Case closed."

"Did no one even think at the time Stasi could have started the fire?"

"Yes, of course. But the fire marshals said accident. And Stasi was *kaput*. I keep telling you this."

"I thought Stasi were good at that sort of thing. Clever little murders, for example."

"Before. Before. But yes, OK, Francis. OK. Let's imagine

Stasi did start the fire. Then we come around again to the fact that the man died in Thailand, not Germany."

"Nothing at all seemed strange at the time?"

"No. Eventually not. But we were all more interested in the 9/11 attacks anyway at that point. Heinrich, or Stasi, or whoever you are suspicious of, chose the wrong time to light his little stove if he wanted to go out in a blaze of glory. Those planes smashing into the World Trade Center were competing with him for the front page. It was tough to get any German story on the front page of the paper in those weeks. I remember. Even when the Bundeskriminalamt chief resigned it was still a struggle in that period."

"The BKA chief?"

"Oh, that was another local story people were excited about when al-Qaeda was acting up. The president of the federal police resigned suddenly a couple of weeks after the 9/11 unpleasantness, and after the Heinrich fire thing, and even then it was a battle to get anyone to take notice. Ulrich Mueller. The BKA's big man. Nice career. Suddenly *kaput*. Good story."

"Why did he resign?" Delaney asked.

"Oh, at first some of the more paranoid among us thought it might have to do with the Heinrich fire, maybe. Before everyone ruled out assassination, we thought he had to resign maybe because of a lapse in security at Heinrich's house. Or something. But it was not that. Trust me. I was on the news desk at the time."

"So what happened with Mueller?"

"Never clear. We think maybe he just ran afoul of the Interior Minister, or something like this. He fell from grace. Police politics. There was talk about moving BKA headquarters from Weisbaden to Berlin, for example, at that point. The rank and file BKA officers over there didn't like that at all; there was some very bad press. Maybe it was that. Maybe Mueller just got tired of being a policeman. His wife committed suicide, of course."

"Gunter, for God's sake."

"What? So what? Wives commit suicide all the time. Some of mine certainly threatened to do so over the years. What's this got to do with Heinrich anyway?"

"The head of the BKA police suddenly resigns at the same time as Heinrich dies or is supposed to have died. The man's wife commits suicide."

"What's the connection?" Ackermann said.

"Exactly," Delaney said. "What is the connection?"

"No connection."

"How do you know?"

"I was on the news desk at the time."

"Yeah, yeah."

"Your psychotherapy is not going well at all, Francis. You are aggressive, paranoid. It is sad."

"Humour me."

"There was a big car accident on the *autobahn* around then, too, Francis. Trucks and cars, dozens of vehicles involved, horrible, many killed. A famous German road accident. Perhaps this had something to do with Heinrich's house fire. We must investigate this together. Maybe the BKA chief was driving the lead car; maybe it was all his fault. In his anger and confusion he sets fire to Heinrich's cabin. This is good. Because, let's see, Mueller's wife is Heinrich's secret lover. That's it. Yes. So she kills herself. Mueller suddenly resigns after an illustrious police career. That could be it. So sad. There is the connection we need."

They agreed to disagree for the moment. And Delaney knew he had better get something to eat before he drank anymore. He knew it was time to contemplate and analyze and imagine a little, before absorbing any further information and coming to any conclusions as to ways forward. Ackermann was already looking a little the worse for wear, and Delaney wanted him to be able to function for some time yet.

Ackermann's girlfriend was indeed very young and very beautiful. Of Turkish extraction, as it turned out. Delaney didn't even try to guess how young she was, lest mid-life male jealously overcame him. Her name was Zynep. She was a clothing designer. She was also Muslim and didn't drink alcohol, which made her a very strange partner for Ackermann indeed.

Ackermann liked to eat at Zur letzten Instanz because it was said to be the oldest restaurant in Berlin and because, he said, he was reputedly the oldest political editor in the city. It was located on two floors of a baroque building just outside the crumbling brick wall that once ringed medieval Berlin. Everyone from Napoleon to Beethoven to the illustrious Ackermann himself had eaten there, many times.

"Prisoners used to stop off here for a final beer before going to jail, my friends," Ackermann said as they climbed a difficult circular staircase to a series of small rooms on the second floor. "I myself did so before both of my wedding days."

The place was crammed with locals and tourists, extremely noisy but therefore a place where conversations could not be overheard. Zynep was a woman of few words, it turned out, although her English was quite good. She seemed content for the most part to watch the two old friends trade information and barbs throughout the evening.

She did say at the outset, however: "Gunter thinks you are an excellent journalist, Frank. He told me some very interesting stories about you. And about you and him together."

Gunter had gone for what would be an increasingly frequent series of visits to the toilet.

"He is an excellent journalist himself," Delaney said.

"Are you working on an important story here in Berlin?" she asked.

"I'm never sure," he said.

Delaney and Ackermann were able to talk at length as the

evening progressed about Germany, Stasi, the Cold War, house fires, dead chiefs of police and next steps, without having to fill Zynep in. Much of what they discussed was general; when things became more specific they told the young designer that Delaney was planning an investigative piece.

"She's simply not interested in politics or journalism," Ackermann told Delaney when Zynep herself had left the table. "That is a perfect situation. She likes design and clothes and making money with her little shop. She will not report us to aging Stasi stalwarts possibly lurking on the first floor of this very restaurant. Have no fear."

Delaney found Ackermann's musings and reminiscences and outrage about the changes in Germany to be most useful. His knowledge of the country was encyclopedic and, as a card-carrying Marxist, he had taken a special interest in the Cold War era.

He seemed genuinely delighted at the fact that for many years, always, Stasi spies had completely outfoxed and outclassed West Germany's. The legendary East German spymaster Marcus Wolf had scattered his spies throughout West Germany, right into the highest echelons—in the 1970s, right into President Willy Brandt's inner circle. Inside East Germany, informants and listening devices and hidden cameras were everywhere. There were reportedly far more informants and intelligence officers per capita in East Germany than anywhere else in the Communist world, including Russia, Poland and Czechoslovakia.

So the fact that West Germany had had such a success with Klaus Heinrich, the fact that he had been able to insinuate himself deep into the East German intelligentsia and bureaucracy, was a much-needed success story for those on the Western side of the Wall. The eventual propaganda value, not to mention the preceding years of intelligence value, provided by Heinrich could not be overstated.

"It was a fucking triumph for the Westies, Francis. Don't

you see that? Can't you see how important a figure Herr Heinrich actually was?" Ackermann shouted as he attacked his giant plate of *schnitzel* and *spaetzle* and pork shank and red cabbage.

When the Wall came down and the GDR regime with it, and when the files began to be opened—those that Stasi, in those final chaotic days had not managed to burn or bury or shred—it became even more abundantly clear just how outclassed the West Germans had been in the spying game. The files that survived showed the extraordinary extent of the infiltration of West Germany by Marcus Wolf's spies.

For more than ten years after reunification, as the "puzzle women" in an office in Nuremburg painstakingly put back together files from the bags of shredded paper found in GDR offices, and as other, unshredded, files came to light, the names of more spies and moles and informants surfaced as well. There were subsequent denunciations, resignations, even some high-profile espionage prosecutions. But always there was the possibility of even more embarrassment for the West.

In 1992, the surviving Stasi files had been declassified by a reunited Germany. In 2000, Washington returned another swathe of such files seized in 1989 by their own delighted operatives in the East as the Wall came down. That the CIA had carefully perused and copied these before their return was in no doubt. Postreunification, there were also persistent rumours that the infamous Rosewood file, said to contain even more high-level names of GDR spies, informants and sympathizers and even more potential embarrassment for the former West Germany, would be returned by the Americans at any time.

So Klaus Heinrich was a godsend for the West. If Klaus Heinrich did not exist, Ackermann said, he would have had to be invented.

Delaney, despite his increasing intoxication and the huge plates of old-fashioned Germanic peasant fare littering the tables, had managed to take notes for most of the evening. Zynep watched in amusement as this process became more and more laboured, and Delaney's notebook more and more stained with wine and *sauerbraten* sauce and beer.

"Shall I act as stenographer for a while, Frank?" she said.

"Never!" Ackermann roared. "A good journalist is always able to see to his own precious notebook. Never!"

As midnight approached, and the crowds in the restaurant began to thin, logic and memory were in short supply at Delaney's table. Only Zynep appeared to be thinking clearly and her interest in proceedings was peripheral.

"The autopsy report, Gunter," Delaney said eventually. "We must have it."

"Yours? You don't look so good."

"Heinrich's, of course."

They didn't bother to explain any of this to Zynep. Ackermann looked suddenly alert, every so slightly sobered.

"An intriguing proposition, my dear Francis," he said.

"Easily done, for a man of your skills and experience."

"Exactly so. Obtaining such confidential medical and police documents is my specialty. As you know."

"Thank goodness for that."

"I shall have it for you within hours or days, my friend. We shall peruse it together. You may then call your editors on my satellite phone as we dodge bullets."

"Exactly."

"And your job, my friend Francis Delaney, I have decided, is to now follow up your foolish theory about former BKA President Ulrich Mueller. Your incessant, how shall I say, your incessant references to this matter have piqued, if this is the correct English word, my interest."

"I'm so pleased you see the wisdom of this," Delaney said drunkenly.

"This prospect is also of interest to me because it would

243

involve a visit by yourself to Mareike Fischer, a lovely young undercover drugs officer employed by Berlin's esteemed Landeskriminalamt police. The lovely Mareike is Herr Mueller's niece, perhaps his only surviving relative, or so they say. His poor departed sister's little girl. Now a member of the Berlin drugs squad. Police work runs in that family, clearly. However, the police niece in question is, if I may say, one of the loveliest under-cover drugs officers in the LKA or even in all of Germandom. She is also said to be a nymphomaniac. My apologies for this characterization, Zynep. I know this only from secondary sources, of course. I know her only slightly and professionally. I know her by reputation, one might say."

Zynep was still able to smile after a long evening of watch-ing two journalists get drunk.

"This sounds intriguing," Delaney said. "It has taken you all night to tell me about this part of the plan."

"It has taken you all night to convince me it is an angle worth pursuing."

"It's the beer. It must be."

"As Chief Political Editor of *Die Welt*, I hereby assign you to meet with this young police officer and ask her straight out why her Uncle Ulrich resigned just before retirement, minutes before retirement. The fact that you have intrigued me with such questions tonight, Francis, does not mean however that I think Mareike Fischer's answer will lead us anywhere in the Klaus Heinrich matter. It will, perhaps however, stop you from harass-ing me about this angle any further. And it may well get you laid. Something I highly recommend to visitors while in Berlin. Where is my mobile phone? I shall call her immediately to set up an appointment with the world-famous Delaney. She is probably out consorting with biker gangs and drug dealers as we speak. She loves her work. She loves it so much she forgets who she really is sometimes, or so I am told."

"An excellent plan, Gunter."

"Which part of it exactly?"

Delaney smiled at Zynep, instead of answering. Ackermann's chin had suddenly sagged toward his chest. A barely audible snore escaped his lips.

"Time to move the *Die Welt* political desk out of here, Zynep," Delaney said. "Some heavy lifting involved. I'll help you."

"Thank you, Frank," Zynep said, still, apparently, neither bored nor angry.

By the end of a very long evening, therefore, they all had their assignments. Ackermann, among other things, to obtain the Heinrich autopsy report—no easy task. Delaney to seek out Mueller's niece, a task that Ackermann apparently still dismissed as a useless waste of time except for the possibility of gratuitous sex. Zynep to get the very large and unwieldy *Die Welt* editor into a taxi and safely home in his extremely intoxicated state.

Another cream-coloured Mercedes taxi let Delaney off at the entrance to the InterContinental. He had had to endure no anti-Turkish diatribes on the way back from the restaurant, however. His driver this time was content simply to drive silently through the rain-slicked streets of Berlin and listen to waltzes on the car radio.

A hotel doorman in a black raincoat came out from under the glass pyramid, proffering a large umbrella. Delaney suddenly decided that he was too drunk and too full of conspiracy theories to go immediately up to his room. He took the umbrella and told the doorman he would walk for a while instead.

"Take great care," the doorman said, clearly disapproving of such a plan. "It is night. Avoid walking by the zoo."

Delaney walked the other way down Budapester Strasse, in the direction of the Reichstag. He hoped the walking time would allow him to begin to sort out what he had gathered from a night full of talk. The cold spring rain might also sober him up.

He could understand why Germans, and Europeans in general—whether pedophiles or not—flocked to the sunny beaches of Thailand in their thousands. In March, Berlin was damp, chilly, grey. The contrast with the bougainvillea-scented humidity and the blue-yellow heat of Thailand could not be more complete. Delaney thought of the scene 9,000 kilometres away at the Metropole Hotel in Phuket, where the night-time doormen would be dressed in short-sleeved shirts and sandals, wiping sweat from their brows, not cold northern rain.

Eventually, more or less consciously, Delaney came into Potsdamer Platz, the very centre of the new Berlin and, some would say, the heart of the new Europe. Delaney had been there many times, before and after Berlin was a divided city, and it was as emblematic now as it was then.

Before 1989, Potsdamer Platz was a Cold War wasteland, bisected by the Wall, doomed to a heavy political fate. Abandoned tramlines wound across it to abruptly meet the cold graffiti-covered concrete that split Berlin. Weeds grew from cracks in what was one of the last undeveloped major open spaces in a major European city. Bombed-out buildings from the Second World War had been bulldozed so as to give East German border guards a clear line of fire in case anyone was foolish enough to choose this desolate point from which to make a bid for freedom.

The Cold War symbolism continued deep underground. The S-Bahn trainline remained open, briefly passing under East German territory on the way from one part of West Berlin to another. Potsdamer Platz became the best known of the so-called S-Bahn "ghost stations," sealed off from the outside world and patrolled by armed guards. Trains raced straight through, never stopping.

Now, all was transformed. From a symbol of Cold War nothingness, Potsdamer Platz had become a boom city's beating heart. The real estate, now breathtakingly valuable, had been divvied up fast in the years post-1989. The world's corporate and industrial titans had competed for attention with grandiose building projects. Delaney stood, as he always did on such visits, marvelling at and dwarfed by the excesses of the Sony Center and the towering Daimler-Benz headquarters. Rock music thumped in a dozen stylish bars. Tourists and locals jostled in and out of shops and cineplexes.

It was a very good place, in fact, to think about Klaus Heinrich and Stasi and Cold War and Thailand and sudden tsunami waves and disaster victims and identities hidden, lost or found. Everything in a place like, on a night like this, was a good story, a front-page story, all at the same time.

Delaney closed his InterContinetal hotel umbrella and let the cold spring rain wash over his face. Alcohol and confusion coursed through his brain. Under the lurid lime green and violet lights of the new Berlin, he tried, without success, to gather his spinning thoughts.

Chapter 12

Delaney, of course, slept very late the next morning in his giant hotel bed. The window shades were models of German efficiency and right until he slowly parted them just before noon the room remained tomb-black. He peered out, monstrously hung over, though the pale grey square of European light into the courtyard below and bitterly regretted, as always, the excesses of the night before.

He shuffled around for a time, sipping water, watching CNN, deciding against a restorative mini-bar beer. The message light on his telephone was flashing. Amazingly, it was a voicemail from Ackermann, older and far drunker the night before than Delaney, but already behind his desk at the newspaper.

"Ah, Francis, of course you are asleep, still," Ackermann's voice thundered from the depths of the hotel messaging system. "Of course, of course, my delicate flower. I, on the other hand, was able to spring into action as usual at the very edge of dawn, the crack, perhaps you say in English. Newspapers do not get produced by those who remain late in bed, in case you have forgotten. Nor do criminals get arrested. The lovely Mareike has already been made aware of your request to discuss something important with her. I used my world-famous powers of persuasion to good effect. She can see you this evening at her flat in the fashionably seedy Friedrichshain neighbourhood. I will email you the address and telephone number because I would suppose you are too ill to use pen and paper just at the moment as you stand there in your pajamas feeling sorry for yourself and trying not to vomit. Am I correct? But she will see you; I have done what I promised. I will now, as I have nothing else to do here at the newspaper in an election year, attempt to persuade someone to let us look at the Heinrich autopsy report. We shall speak later, my friend. And bring Viagra for your meeting with Inspector Mareike Fischer. That is my advice."

Delaney called Ackermann right back. "You amaze me, Gunter," he said.

"That is what young Zynep said to me late last night as well, after the adventures that followed our return to her flat," Ackermann said.

"So Mareike is willing to see me . . ."

"Of course."

"She an ex-girlfriend or something?"

"She is everybody's ex-girlfriend, Francis. Most of LKA Berlin, a good random sample of media stars, others. She is that type."

"Does she know what I want to talk about?"

"No. Do you?"

"Yes. Sort of."

"Pull yourself together, my friend. This may break the case, as they say in the TV shows. Or it may show you are simply a hopeless paranoid."

Delaney ordered room-service coffee. Food would have to wait until after his recovery. His email inbox was brimming with news, none terribly good, some very bad indeed.

From Rawson, the following:

Francis, it always really worries me when you go to ground like this. It worries all of us here. It's not really fair of you to share bits of information about something like the Klaus Heinrich thing and then go to ground, is it? Please get in contact as soon as possible to discuss. And how is Germany by the way? Our Thai friends have always been very helpful to us here at CSIS when we have some questions for them about people's movements. We note your departure from Bangkok airport a couple of nights ago. Presumably you have some pressing reason now to be in Germany? Can you let me know what hotel you are at to save us all a lot of further fussing around? Thanks and bests.

Delaney would reply to that later.

From Jonah Smith in Phuket, some quite bad news about bugging devices in his room at the Bay Hotel. Smith, too, it seemed, had been drinking to excess. His email sounded angry, somewhat desperate. There was also an element of fear in the text. Delaney replied to that one right away, using various phrases intended to soothe:

. . . You'll have to just keep on being careful, Delaney wrote *. . . Don't panic just yet. . . . The longer your list of potential enemies is, the more interesting the story actually becomes. Right? We're starting to develop a good little list of possible enemies now . . .*

From Tim Bishop, a workmanlike colleague's note:

Hey Frank, just FYI, back home in Paris now. Thought I couldn't justify hanging around out in Phuket any longer. Got some good shots of little Charlotte Stokke's funeral ceremony before I left. Standing by here if you need me for anything.

And from Kate Hunter of the RCMP, this message, workmanlike in a different way:

Dear Francis. I've been thinking a lot about a lot of things since our last phone conversation, or phone argument or whatever you want to call it. I think it would be good for us to stop all this now. It's already gone on far too long as it is, this situation, don't you think? It's not good for either of us anymore. Bye. Kate. Sorry to do this in an email.

Delaney was not sure there would be much use replying to that one at all.

Investigative journalist Francis Delaney was, therefore, in a somewhat end-of-the-world mood when he rang Mareike Fischer's doorbell that evening. He had sobered up, cleaned himself up, but a dark mood hung over him like a stubborn North Europe rain cloud. It was an appropriate mood in which to meet the most undercover member of Berlin's Landeskriminalamt undercover drug squad.

Inspector Fischer had worked so far undercover for so long that she now forgot, as Ackermann suggested, who she really was. Her apartment was in a rundown third-storey walk-up right on Simon-Dach-Strasse, the cacophonous main drag in a hodge-podge area of bars, restaurants, makeshift galleries, punk squatters and Turks. It was a place where police did not generally make themselves known.

The first thing any drug dealer or anybody else would notice about Mareike Fischer was her fantastical fairy-tale mane of flaming red hair. If she had been wearing it loose, it would surely have cascaded to the middle of her back. When Delaney arrived, it had been gathered into a giant pony-tail that was struggling to break its bonds.

She was almost exactly Delaney's height, and buxom, broad-shouldered, fit, tanned, alert. She was wearing a grey NYPD T-shirt and black jeans, both items clearly meant for someone far, far smaller. A diamond stud glittered in her right nostril. She locked eyes on Delaney's eyes after opening the door and did not let go. Her apartment smelled of incense.

"Gunter's favourite Canadian," she said.

"Frank Delaney."

"A solid Canadian name. Good and solid. Come in good, solid Gunter Canadian."

The apartment was crammed, utterly, with big old pieces of wooden furniture and overstuffed upholstered sofas and arm-chairs. Books were piled on shelves and on the floor. Magazines, rolled-up posters, potted plants, flowers in various vases. A collection of masks hung on a wall—from Africa, Southeast Asia, the Venice carnival.

A small, expensive Teac stereo was playing Miles Davis very low. And a holstered Sig Sauer 9-millimetre pistol sat on a sideboard.

Mareike saw him looking at it.

"You like guns? That is standard LKA issue, the Sig nine millimetre."

"Not very undercover," he said.

"I usually put it away when I have guests. Certain ones. Or I wear it under my shirt."

She waited for Delaney to comment on how hard that would be to accomplish, at least today.

"You didn't put it away for me," he said.

"Gunter tells me you are a man of the world. To be trusted. Calm when around guns or under fire in Afghanistan and other places. Why put the gun away for you? I am a cop lady. You know this. Bang, bang, shoot, shoot. Another bad guy gone to heaven."

They sat side by side in a very sixties red velour sofa. She pushed aside some magazines and placed a bottle of Stolichnaya vodka and two small glasses on the heavy wooden coffee table. Delaney noted a small mirror with white dust and a single-edged razor blade on it among the debris on the table. She saw him looking at that too.

"Props. For my druggie act," she said. "Yes?"

"Realistic," he said.

"You're a user? Coke?" she said.

"No comment," he said.

"Reporter man," she said.

"And you? A user?"

"Only professionally," she said. Her smile, when it broke open, completely illuminated her face.

The vodka helped extinguish the last of Delaney's hangover. It lubricated, as it was invented to do, any potentially tricky conversation between strangers. Delaney wanted to get right to the point, to pump Mareike for information and then get out of the apartment without getting drunk on vodka or stoned on cocaine or into some kind of complicated sexual snarl. But he circled the issues for a while, for form's sake. And because vodka in the early evening in an end-of-the-world Berlin apartment with a pretty red-haired woman actually suited his mood.

She told neighbourhood stories and some police stories. He told reporter stories and Gunter Ackermann stories. They drank and told stories and eventually Mareike signalled that smalltalk was to end—a policewoman after all.

"So now, we have a little vodka buzz, and we are friends, we have not been impolite to each other and now you will tell me why you need to talk to me. I will not be offended. I will not feel used and abused. You have done the right thing. We have waited the decent amount of time. I love Canadians. They are so polite."

She touched him briefly on the side of his face.

"Go," she said. "Tell me now."

Delaney put down his vodka glass.

"Your uncle," he said.

"Ah," she said.

"Ah," Delaney said.

The vodka had increased his blood pressure as it was invented to do. His face burned slightly and he felt a pleasant pulse in his head.

"You are doing a story about my Uncle Ulrich."

"No story. Not yet."

"It's a very sad story, my Uncle Ulrich's story," she said.

She had not put her vodka glass down. She drank another large shot, poured herself a refill. He eyes locked in again on Delaney's.

"I need to know why he resigned his job so suddenly,"

Delaney said. "Gunter said you might be able to help me understand that."

"You need to know, or you want to know?" she said.

"Both," he said.

"I see," she said. "For a story."

"Not necessarily."

"If not a story, then what?"

Despite Ackermann's suggestion, Delaney had really not prepared very well for this interview, if that is what it could be called. He had not decided beforehand how much of the tsunami story he would share with Mareike Fischer, how much she would need to know before deciding whether to help him. He hesitated. Mareike did not.

"My uncle was treated very badly by the BKA at the end, Frank Delaney," she said. "The police eat you up when you make a mistake. They will eat me up one day. I am making lots of mistakes. I enjoy making such mistakes. But they will eat me up eventually when I make one mistake too many."

The giant smile again illuminated her face.

"Why should I tell you secrets about my uncle?" she asked.

"Because I'm someone who can tell his story, maybe. Would that be enough? I can help you tell people that he was treated unfairly."

"Why would you want to do that?"

"It's what I do, when I can," Delaney said. "And in this case, it would help me understand something even bigger, maybe."

The vodka, or the end-of-the-world mood, or any number of other things, loosened his tongue and he, quite unwisely perhaps, told her a little—far from everything, but a little—about the tsunami file, and the Klaus Heinrich connection.

"Now I need to know if there is a connection between your uncle, or your uncle's resigning, and Klaus Heinrich," Delaney said.

"An intriguing question," Mareike said.

"But do you know the answer?" Delaney said.

The giant smile.

"Some of it," she said. "But maybe not enough of it. No one has asked me about this for a long time. And no one has actually asked it in quite this way. There was never a tsunami in the background."

"So was there a connection?"

"Why do people always think there has to be a special connection between things?" she asked. "Police, journalists. Why can't things just happen here and there, just like that?"

"There's just too much of a coincidence between the big Heinrich story—he dies suddenly in a fire—and your uncle's story. The head of the German federal police resigns suddenly, just like that, at almost the same time. I just have this strong feeling there must be some kind of connection."

Delaney then for some reason thought it appropriate that evening to say: "I was in love with a psychologist in Montreal once who really believed there were significant connections a lot of the time between seemingly unrelated events. She thought you just had to look at things properly to see this. Synchronicity. The so-called acausal connecting principle. She was a Jungian."

Natalia had also frequently said that the connections people start to see could tell you just as much about a person's psychological state as about the situation itself. Delaney didn't at all know what she might have said that night about his current psychological state.

Mareike looked at him closely.

"You know, Frank Delaney, you are starting to seem a little bit like a relatively interesting man," she said.

The smile again. She sipped vodka and slipped deeper down into her overstuffed old sofa.

"He's very sick, you know," she said eventually.

"Your uncle?"

"Yes."

"Is he here in Berlin?"

"No. He is in France. In disgrace, in France."

She lit a cigarette.

"Smoke?" she said.

"No," he said.

"Pot? Nice with vodka in the evening. Let's smoke some confiscated police pot together."

Delaney had not smoked marijuana for a long time. The suggestion brought back a sudden intense memory of smoking with Nathan Kellner's Thai girlfriend on the balcony of the missing journalist's Bangkok apartment on a sultry evening when there was still hope that Kellner had not been killed in Burma.

"Not right away," Delaney for some reason thought it appropriate to say.

"We are working," Mareike said.

"Yes," he said.

"After," she said.

"Perhaps," he said.

Mareike seemed willing to tell him some of what he needed to know. But she claimed she did not know everything. She also seemed to think it was her uncle who needed to tell the rest, whatever that was. If her uncle wished to do so.

"He was a really excellent police officer, Frank Delaney. The best. Not like me. Always everything by the rules. He joined the BKA when he was a young man, it would have had to be in the 1960s. He worked hard and he had his little wife in the suburbs of Weisbaden. Never children—he was too busy fighting the bad guys to have children. That is what he would say. But I was like his daughter, I suppose. He loved me. I know that. But he would not approve of the police work I do these days, not very much. Not the way I do undercover."

Delaney let her reminisce and muse. Musings and reminiscence can be a deep and productive gold mine for journalists, and for spies, depending on the assignment in question.

"He shocked everyone when he said he was going to leave the police. It was all sudden, sudden, sudden you know, like a big storm. He would have been able to retire in a year or two years, maybe. He didn't retire. He just quit. He stopped. After all those years on the police. He said he had had enough of the BKA. My aunt couldn't believe what was happening. She said he changed. He got sad and quiet, she said. She then got sad and quiet too. Then he left her. Can you imagine? A good German of that age, the head of the BKA. He just left his wife and moved to France. Then she killed herself. Like that. Poof. It was like in a play by Shakespeare. They found her dead in their nice little house in Weisbaden. It was pills. My uncle didn't even come back to Germany for the funeral. He must have had good reasons, no?"

Delaney began to see some possible reasons for Mareike Fischer's deep undercover lifestyle. She was working undercover in a place where memories like this didn't often intrude. But she seemed willing for some reason to come partway out of her hiding place to look at them tonight.

"What do you think his reasons were, Mareike?" he asked.

She paused, drank, smoked.

"He said he had been betrayed, Frank Delaney."

"How? Who by?"

"He never told me. I call him on the telephone in France sometimes or write him letters. He would just say he had been betrayed when I still bothered to ask about it. The newspaper stories about him said all sorts of crazy things at the time. He said all of the stories were wrong."

"A man like that would normally just retire, even if his career fell apart."

"The BKA didn't seem to think he deserved his pension."

"What income did he have, then?"

"I don't know. They were savers, my auntie and he. I don't know. They had some money."

"How does he live in France?"

"He bought a big old ruined chateau house. Not big like a chateau castle. A big house like they used to call a chateau in the old days. It was beautiful but ruined and cheap. I saw it once or twice. I visited. He fixed it up slowly, and it wouldn't cost much to live down there now. It is in nowhere, in the Ardeche. Not in Provence, not like that. In the Ardeche hills south of Lyon. It's hard even to find his house it's so nowhere."

She sat silently for a time—musing, reminiscing, and probably, like Delaney, very much enjoying the secret warmth that superior-quality vodka can bring.

"He is very sick, Frank," Mareike said again, eventually. "He will die soon. I'm sure of this. But maybe you are what he actually needs right at this moment. Maybe it's the moment in his life for him to tell his story. Maybe yes."

Delaney felt the short, sharp jolt that any good reporter feels when he believes he is onto a story that is about to break.

"I could go to speak to him," he said.

"You would go down to France?"

"Of course."

"A man of action."

"Ask Gunter."

This time they both smiled at the same time.

"OK, Frank Delaney, I will do you and my old friend Gunter Ackermann this favour. I will ask my uncle if he maybe wants to talk to someone who can help him tell his story. OK? Before he dies. I will tell him that I personally think this may be the right moment to do this. Because I do think that this might truly be the right moment. Is that OK for you?"

"Very OK," Delaney said.

"Drink? Smoke?" Mareike said. "A toast?"

"Of course. Drinks."

She poured two more vodkas for them, the latest in what had been a long series that evening.

"To the Bundeskriminalamt," she said, raising her brimming shot glass. "That we may one day teach them a lesson."

"To the BKA," Delaney said.

"And to Ulrich Mueller. Policeman and BKA chief, now retired."

"And to disaster victims everywhere," Delaney said.

When Delaney smoked marijuana on the balcony of Nathan Kellner's Bangkok apartment months and years before, the smoke and Asia's humid night air and a lonely Thai girl had wafted him into an extremely comfortable bed. In Berlin, in a dimly lit and overstuffed apartment, the smoke and the rain-soaked European air and the extremely pretty woman beside him also wafted him eventually towards the bedroom.

Mareike's ancient bed was piled high with brocade cushions, velour cushions, satin cushions. The dim lamp beside it shone with a welcoming yellow light. They floated to her bed at the end of the night on streams of potent smoke and the vodka that still ran warm in their veins. Delaney's end-of-the-world mood and the smoke and the vodka wafted him gently, ever so gently, into the smiling policewoman's bed. He hardly thought of policewoman Kate Hunter or of psychologist Natalia Janovski at all.

Rawson seemed genuinely delighted to hear Delaney's voice when the call from Berlin came through. Delaney called him early Berlin time the next morning, Wednesday. It was very late Tuesday night Ottawa time.

"Ah, Francis, the prodigal spook," Rawson said. "So good of you to call."

"Were you sleeping?" Delaney asked.

He had come back to the InterContinental from Friedrichshain in a taxi a few minutes before. He could not identify his condition as hung over. Delaney could not accurately identify his condition that morning at all.

"No, no," Rawson said. "Working at home. Worrying. It's a dangerous world out there."

"Not with guys like us on the watch, Jonathan."

"Maybe. Where are you?"

"Still in Germany."

"Berlin still?"

"What do your Thai intelligence pals tell you?"

"BND pals at this stage, Francis. The Germans love me too. They tell me Berlin."

"Hotel?"

"InterContinental."

"Very good."

"Thank you so much."

"And who have I been seeing?"

"Ah, well, special surveillance, that's another story. Even my German friends balk at such BND overtime expense on behalf of CSIS. Unless the matter is very important indeed."

"Is it?"

"You tell me, Francis."

"You guys seem a little overexcited that I'm looking at the Klaus Heinrich story. Or you did a couple days ago."

"Oh, we're still excited, Francis. And glad to have you on the case, as it were."

"I'm not sure where this is headed at the moment, Jonathan."

"We aren't either."

"So why the excitement?"

"Because Heinrich is a big name in certain circles. Or was. Before he went and died on us."

"Big name for the Germans. Not for the Canadians, surely."

"Oh, I wouldn't jump to that conclusion, Francis."

"Why would Canada's little spy service give a shit what happened to a guy like Heinrich?"

"Because, as you yourself pointed out a couple of emails ago or a couple of phone calls ago, we are in the information business over here in Ottawa. We like to be ahead of the game once in a while, so as to have things to trade. Always useful to have little trinkets in your satchel when at the world information bazaar."

"This is not new, Jonathan."

"Well, Francis, how's this then? I'll tell you something to capture your attention and then you'll see why we want you working with us on this one. OK? I'll let you peek inside my information satchel for a bit, and then I get to look inside yours, OK?"

"As always."

"We pay top rates, as you know."

"What have you got, Jonathan?"

"How about the Germans were shopping this guy around to a few nice Western democracies a while back, seeing if anybody wanted to take him in and make him a new person somewhere comfortable and quiet."

"Who, Heinrich?"

"Yes."

"What, a new identity? In Canada?"

"Yes. Or New Zealand or Australia. Or somewhere similar. So we gathered. They asked around a fair bit at the time, apparently."

"When?"

"Around 2000 or so. Maybe late 2000, early 2001."

"Why would they do that? Heinrich had a nice little setup in Bonn. Why would they want to move him?"

"They didn't say."

"Why do you think?"

"Not sure."

Delaney had worked with Rawson & Company long enough to not immediately accept that this was factual.

"You must have a theory Jonathan. CSIS always has theories."

"Well, it could be any number of things. They could have detected a threat against him, for example. Stasi might have decided to take him out. Payback."

"Stasi was washed up by then."

"Not entirely, Francis. There were still some guys out there, there still are, who did good work for Stasi for years and years and saw the Wall coming down as just a minor inconvenience on the road to democratic socialism. They'd meet for drinks, talk all night, that sort of thing. Like the old Nazis used to do. Sing songs, have a beer or two, plot and scheme."

"I don't know, Jonathan."

"Or try this. Stasi files being reassembled. CIA working very hard on this. Others in Germany working hard. Files, files, coming to light all the time. You ever hear of the Rosewood file, Francis?"

"Yeah. Once. Lately."

"Thought you might have. Full of interesting stuff apparently. Decrypted version was due out any day, around then, apparently, or so it was said. That's why we want you on this. You hear things earlier than most people. So, all right, what if something big was coming out about Heinrich or about his service? I don't know what. But wouldn't you maybe ask the nice Canadians or the Aussies or someone where there's fresh air and sunshine to set your man up somewhere new, just in case?"

"But for what? What might have been coming out?"

"Maybe nothing. I don't know. We don't know. You find out for us. You want to go back on the freelancers' payroll right now? We pay expenses."

"Why wouldn't your guys have agreed to set him up somewhere new in Canada?"

"We're nice, Francis, but not that nice. I wasn't right in on that one, but they tell me people here felt they weren't getting the full story from the German side. Apparently no one over here was ever sure the idea had an official German government stamp on it. The Social Democrats were in government in 2000. Schroeder. But Heinrich was being run all through the eighties when the Christian Democrats were in power. Helmut Kohl's people. They were the ones who set him up in Bonn after the Wall came down. So we weren't sure who actually needed the favour—Kohl's CDU guys, or Schroeder's SPD, or maybe just some nervous old West German spooks. The numbers didn't all add up, so we didn't buy in."

"Cloak and dagger," Delaney said.

"That's my game," Rawson said.

"Interesting."

"So what have you got for us that's interesting?"

"Well, Heinrich surely didn't go to Australia, Jonathan. He ended up in a body bag in Phuket, Thailand."

"Imagine our surprise when you told us that, Francis. But that's old news by now, right? You've told us that already. What have you got that's new?"

On Wednesday, Delaney found himself once again on a crowded Lufthansa aircraft, this time an early-morning flight from Berlin to Bonn. He had toyed with the idea of taking the earliest flight possible, 6:45 a.m., but Ackermann warned him that this one would be too full of "industrialists and class enemies." As well, Delaney was still nursing the effects of too much alcohol and illicit plant material so he treated himself to an extra hour's sleep and took Lufthansa Flight 268 at the relatively civilized hour of 8:15 a.m.

The later plane was still heavily laden with industrialists and other highly suspect individuals, or so Ackermann would have said. It was not the Pedophile Express but almost all the passengers were German middle-aged men. They wore dark suits, not Thailand tropical wear, and their assignations in Berlin or Bonn would, with very few exceptions, have been for business, not pleasures illicit or legal.

Bonn does not have an airport of its own. Bonn-Cologne airport serves two cities, so Delaney faced a one-hour flight and then a one-hour train ride to get where he needed to go. Ackermann said that Hans Schneller would meet him at lunch hour not far from the state prosecutors' office where he worked.

"He will be very nervous, Francis, be patient with him," Ackermann had said. "He is doing this under protest. I don't know him and he owes me no favours directly. He is the son of a friend of a very close friend and he has been persuaded with great difficulty to do this and he is afraid he will lose his job and his pension and maybe even his nice wife."

Ackermann had refused to take time off work to go with Delaney to Bonn to look at the Heinrich autopsy report.

"Schneller speaks English," Ackermann said. "You will be there for fifteen minutes maximum. There will be nothing of interest in the report. He will tell you what it says and he will explain how these things work in Germany and you will get back on a plane and come back to Berlin. Why should I go down there with you?"

The Bonn prosecutors' offices were in Konigswinterer Strasse, not far from the *polizepraesidium* building. Delaney very much doubted the nervous Schneller would have agreed to meet him at all if he had actually been a junior clerk trying to take a file out of the police headquarters building. But taking a confidential file out of storage in the nearby prosecutors' building was, apparently, less of a risk.

Schneller had insisted the meeting be in the Hofgarten, a sprawling open area of green lawns behind the Bonn Palace. Of course it was raining and cold when Delaney arrived at the park in a taxi. Serious Germans with serious umbrellas made their way along tidy walkways. Only a small group of university students playing energetic soccer despite the rain lifted the scene somewhat.

Schneller was a very tall, very nervous lad of about 21. Acne still plagued him, despite his having exited the teenage years. He was using a red tartan umbrella when standard German issue in this park was normally, it seemed, basic black. One of the spines of his umbrella had broken, and stuck out at an angle from the soaked red and yellow fabric.

It was all very Cold War, Delaney told Ackermann afterward—all very cloak and dagger.

Schneller had a leather shoulder bag. After he gravely shook Delaney's hand he looked furtively around and then reached inside for a tan government-issue envelope with a string tie securing the flap. They did not sit Cold War–style on a park bench because these were all soaking wet. They stood together under their two umbrellas, fumbling with bags and papers as they simultaneously held up their protection against the rain.

"You cannot take this away," Schneller said. "I'm very sorry. It must stay here."

"That's fine, that's fine," Delaney said. "I just need to look at it for a few minutes."

Even that seemed too long for Schneller. He handed Delaney the envelope.

"You don't speak German at all?" he said.

"I'm afraid not. I'm told you'll help me with translation."

"Yes," Schneller said, unhappier by the moment.

The file contained surprisingly few papers. What was there was densely typed German text, with a variety of stamps and seals and signatures. There were also photos of a very badly charred corpse, in various shades of black and grey. The remains barely looked human at all. A disaster victim.

Delaney scanned the first sheet of paper in the file. It was dated 27 October 2001.

"That is the pathologist's summary. That is probably all you will need," Schneller said.

"Can you tell me what it says?"

Schneller took the paper back.

"Basically it says the victim died in a house fire in the Bonn area on or about 8 October 2001. The pathologist sees no bullet wounds or, how do you say, head smashes or body smashes. It says the body of this victim shows no elevated levels of alcohol or other drugs except for acetylsalicylic acid, the analgesic, in perhaps unusual quantities. It is aspirin in English, yes?"

"Yes, aspirin," Delaney said. Perhaps Heinrich had suffered from arthritis or headache or gout.

"This document says the victim died of smoke inhalation. The pathologist gives the exact concentration of smoke particles detected in the man's lungs and gullet. He includes a scale and the concentration is shown to be very high. The pathologist says the cause of death was, in English you say, what, acute, very high smoke inhalation."

"How did they identify the body?" Delaney asked.

Schneller looked through some other papers in the file, balancing umbrella on shoulder. Rain dripped dangerously near the confidential papers he would have to bring back to his office archives in a few minutes.

"It says here that the man had no living relatives apparently, or none that could be found. It said that colleagues from the man's professional life identified the body visually."

"That would be hard, judging from the photos," Delaney said.

"That is what it says here. Visual identification was arranged with colleagues. Also, he was found in a cabin belonging to Klaus Heinrich and a logical deduction was made this must be the victim."

"Ah, logic," Delaney said.

"Say again?" Schneller said.

"Nothing."

"It also says here that fingerprint identification was carried out. Positive matching to Klaus Heinrich. Fourteen points of similarity in the compared prints," Schneller said.

That would have satisfied even Jonah Smith, Delaney thought.

Schneller said: "Who anyway was this man you so badly need to know about?"

"You're too young to know this story, Hans," Delaney said. "It's a long story."

Schneller looked relieved that no answer was actually given to his question. He clearly regretted having asked.

"Would this autopsy have been carried out by a police pathologist, Hans?" Delaney asked.

"No, we do not have police pathologists here," Schneller said, apparently happy to share such general information in detail. It sounded like he had memorized a lot of material for examinations he had taken or was about to take.

"A coroner system like in the Anglo-Saxon legal zones does not actually exist here. Autopsies are not mandatory in Germany. The police generally request an autopsy if the case officer comes to the conclusion that the cause of a death is suspicious or the result of an accident. The state attorney, so to say, initiates an autopsy which is then executed by a pathologist at a hospital in the vicinity perhaps or at a medical university. It is not a police pathologist, just a doctor who is specialized in autopsies."

"Always the same people?" Delaney asked.

"Normally in large districts like Bonn you have three or four who regularly do this for the police, next to their normal jobs," Schneller said.

Delaney took the file back from Schneller and flipped through it again despite the German words being unintelligible. He looked closely at names and signatures on various pages. One name immediately stood out: Horst Becker.

It was the kind of break in a story that every journalist dreams of. When a missing link falls into place like this on a big story, journalists reach for the champagne. Delaney reached instead into his shoulder bag for Horst Becker's security pass from Thailand. He left nothing important behind in hotel rooms on such assignments. Schneller watched in amazement as Delaney then clumsily balanced his umbrella on his shoulder and held the card up against the signature on the pathologist's summary report. The signatures were a perfect match.

Becker's bulldog face stared stonily out at them from the plastic Thai Tsunami Victim Identification badge. The card on a bright blue cord inscribed with the white letters TTVI belonged to the pathologist who had worked on Klaus Heinrich's body in Phuket, Thailand, and also, supposedly, in Bonn, Germany, more than three years previously. This, as the Germans would undoubtedly say, was not logical.

Schneller looked more closely at the ID card and the name and signature on the file document.

"This is amazing," Schneller said. "What is the meaning?"

"It means we're looking at something that is not logical," Delaney said.

"Who is this Horst Becker?"

"A German pathologist I've met," Delaney said. "He's in Thailand at the moment. Usually he works at the military hospital in Frankfurt."

"That is two hundred kilometres away from here. Normally, this would not happen. A pathologist would not travel so far to do work for police in Bonn in such matters. That would be unusual."

"Not logical."

"Not at all logical."

"Thank you very much," Delaney said.

PART 3
Saint Lager Bressac, France
— March 2005

Chapter 13

Delaney liked it when a story started to break very fast. At Lyon airport's curvaceous ultramodern terminal after his early-morning flight from Berlin via Frankfurt, he rented a car, a sports model Peugeot 307 to suit his upbeat mood and to help speed him through southern France to Saint Lager Bressac, where Ulrich Mueller lived in disgrace and isolation.

Delaney had told only Ackermann what he and young Schneller discovered in the autopsy documents in Bonn. He did not tell Mareike Fischer, he did not tell Jonah Smith and he did not tell Jonathan Rawson. When a story starts to break, Delaney knew from experience that for a time the fewer people who were aware, the better.

Mareike, of course, was aware he would travel to France. She had arranged the meeting with her uncle as promised. Actually finding Mueller's Chateau de Bressac deep in the Ardeche hills would be Delaney's immediate problem.

It was a fine early spring day in a splendid part of France. Light streamed through the sunroof of the car as Delaney headed away from Lyon, negotiating his way carefully among the dozens of oversized Dutch- and German-registered holiday trailers thundering southward on the highway along with him. Even at this early stage of the warm season, the annual invasion of the French countryside by sun-starved northern Europeans had begun.

As he neared Montelimar on the Autoroute de Soleil, his phone rang. He had been ignoring the cell as much as possible through much of his tsunami assignment in Thailand and again now in Europe. This time, however, the little Nokia screen indicated a call from a German number. He answered it, with difficulty behind the wheel at 140 kilometres per hour, and heard Mareike's voice.

"I was expecting you last night, Frank Delaney," she said. "As you are still relatively interesting to me."

Delaney felt a too-familiar tug of unease in his guts, as he realized he had perhaps started something with a highly unpredictable woman that could now go somewhere he did not at all want to go. Ackermann had questioned him closely about his encounter with Mareike, and then given him a variety of dire warnings and cautionary tales about her.

"Tied up, Mareike, sorry," Delaney said. "I was getting ready for the France trip."

"I called you," she said.

"I had my phone turned off."

"On the hotel line."

"Missed it. Sorry."

"You will come to see me when you get back, however," she said.

"Of course," Delaney said. "I'll have to head straight back out to Thailand, though. Finish up my assignment."

There was a too-long pause at the Berlin end of the call.

"You know where I am," she said. "If you can spare a moment."

Ackermann had been most impressed when Delaney told him what he and Schneller had discovered.

"Fuck me dead, Francis, please pardon my French," Ackermann had said. He came to the InterContinental for drinks with Delaney the night he got back to Berlin from Bonn. "This is starting to look very interesting, even for an old drunken hack like myself."

"I told you, Gunter," Delaney said.

"Don't gloat, please," Ackermann said.

"I told you this was going to get big," Delaney said again.

"Big? Yes, yes, it's big. A respected pathologist from Frankfurt's big army hospital is either falsifying an autopsy report in Bonn or he is falsifying things in Thailand. With signatures that match nicely and all. That is big enough. But it also involves Klaus Heinrich, only the biggest fucking spy West Germany ever ran in the East. This is much more than just big, Francis. You amaze me, sometimes, my friend. The things you get yourself into. You will need my expert guidance on how to handle this matter from here."

Ackermann now also had more time for Delaney's intuitions and theories about disgraced former chiefs of the BKA.

"Of course, of course, yes, go to France, my friend, go," he said. "Find out all you can about Herr Mueller. This also is a good story, possibly. If he gives you something fresh about why he left the BKA, well and good. But if you can also link him somehow to the Heinrich story and now to this Horst Becker angle, well Francis, Francis, you can be a German media superstar."

"If that's what I decide to do," Delaney said.

"For the sake of Jesus, Francis, what else would you do? Publish, publish, publish."

"Maybe. Let's see what I turn up."

"Please, Francis, do not punish me like this. I'm sorry I mocked your theories. I'm sorry. I will buy you another drink. Please don't be coy. Of course you must publish all of this. It is an election year in Germany. The people of Germany have a right to know about these fools and charlatans and thieves who run this country or who ran the country back then. Or the actions of their police lackeys. If we are very, very fortunate, we will bring down the whole stinking capitalist edifice together, yes, in Germany first and then we start on the ordained path to world socialism. The workers' paradise."

"Does *Die Welt* know they have a rabid revolutionary editing their political section, Gunter?" Delaney asked.

"From each according to his ability, to each according to his need," Ackermann shouted. "We're on to something very big, Francis. It is the beginning of something very big."

He raised his beer glass and began to sing the "Internationale" at top volume. Ackermann was getting overexcited. Drink and seditious talk always had that effect on him. The waiter looked distinctly uneasy about these two suspicious characters sitting at his bar in extremely heated conversation.

"Gunter, calm yourself," Delaney said. "First I need to gather all the information, and then I need to decide what to do with it. First I'll go visit Mueller. Then we'll see."

"Always, always the same thing with you, Francis," Ackermann said. "Don't be coy. You find information, you report it. It's simple. That is who you are."

Mareike's instructions on how to reach Mueller's house had been precise, obsessively detailed. Nonetheless, somewhere south of Valence and west of the Rhone River, Delaney got hopelessly turned around. He missed the tiny turnoff on a small road that led to the village of Saint Lager Bressac and ended up climbing a switchback to the little hillside town of Privas, well past where he wanted to be.

By the time he had asked various locals in his Quebecois French for directions and had circled back to find the turnoff and then the village and then the truly obscure track through lavender fields and hayfields that led up to other hills and onward to the chateau itself, it was almost 1 p.m. Finally, with the Peugeot bouncing and sliding on gravel ruts and the fallen branches of trees, Delaney saw a high stone wall and a stout wooden carriage gate looming in the distance.

A tiny sign said: *Chateau de Bressac. U.Mueller/ P.Rochemaure.* An aging Renault van was parked by the wall, beside a big silver BMW with Paris-area licence plates. Delaney pulled his car off the track and under some trees. He got out looking for a bell or a knocker to announce that he had arrived.

Mareike had told him only a little about Pierre Rochemaure, the Parisian architect who had helped Mueller renovate the wrecked chateau and who now spent much of his time there, finishing up the last of the renovation project and, apparently, helping to look after the ailing policeman. Mareike had not told him much else about Rochemaure, but Delaney was surprised to see the architect's name inscribed alongside Mueller's on the proprietor's sign.

"My uncle has agreed to see you, that is the principal thing," Mareike had said. "You're the reporter man, so you will go, you will see what you will see, and you will make your conclusions. Yes? You will make up your own mind about what you find there."

Somewhere far on the other side of the stone wall, a bell clanged when Delaney pressed an old brass button. Eventually, he heard the crunch of gravel. The heavy door opened. A very tall, fit, handsome man of about 45 stood on the other side. He did not offer Delaney his hand.

"Monsieur Delaney?" he said in English.

"Yes," Delaney said. "I'm here to see Ulrich Mueller. His niece in Berlin arranged a meeting for me."

"I know. I am Rochemaure, Pierre. Come inside."

The Chateau de Bressac was one of those old, elegant, absolutely inviting French places that people dream of finding, renovating and living in happily ever after. On the other side of the wall there was a small courtyard of gravel and some formal garden squares and hedges. A few round metal tables and some park chairs were set out, stylishly rustic. The house itself, two imposing stories with an old black slate roof, was covered in vines and other signs of graceful aging.

Rochemaure led him in silence across the gravel and through a set of thick oak double doors into the cool, echoing stone vestibule of the house itself. Worn stairs to the second floor led up and away to the rear. To the left of the vestibule, Delaney could see into a large restaurant-style kitchen, with a stainless steel chef's stove and copper-bottomed pots and pans hung in careful disarray above a large central counter island. To the right through an archway was a long sitting room, painted in intense shades of Provençal blue and yellow. Expensive sofas in deep reds and off-white faced each other before a shoulder-high fireplace. Framed modern oils and charcoal sketches of walking and reclining figures lined the walls.

All was stylish, superior quality, perfect. It was a house that could very well have been featured in *Architectural Digest* or another glossy decorating magazine. Not at all the humble retreat Delaney would have imagined for a disgraced German policeman in hiding from his past.

Rochemaure brushed a hand over his unruly mane of wavy black hair. A few flecks of grey had been allowed to develop, Delaney noted, but they appeared, like everything else in the scene, to be part of a master visual plan. Rochemaure's deep tan and bright floral shirt did their part in the overall set design as well.

"Ulrich is resting," Rochemaure said. "He rests in the afternoon. Mareike has told you he is not well."

It was not a question.

"I know he's ill, yes," Delaney said.

"I believe the telephone call from Berlin upset him," Rochemaure said. He seemed to expect an apology of some sort.

"Why would that be, do you think?" Delaney said.

They regarded each other in silence for a moment.

Then Rochemaure said: "Your room is upstairs."

Delaney hadn't been sure whether he would be invited to stay or even if he would need to stay overnight. He began to realize he had very little idea how any of this was actually going to unfold, now that he had arrived.

"Ulrich says he will see you at dinner, tonight," Rochemaure said.

A pause.

"You will need lunch?"

"I ate on the plane to Lyon," Delaney said.

"The housekeeper comes back later in the afternoon. I can offer you for the moment some cheese and bread and wine. Perhaps some fruit also."

"That would be lovely."

Rochemaure brought him to his room upstairs. It was just above the main entrance door, overlooking the courtyard, and it, too, was perfect—a magazine spread waiting to be photographed. Elegantly worn stone floors, a painted metal bed, a small washbasin near the window, an antique writing desk, more framed oils and charcoals. The bathroom with requisite clawfoot tub and brass towel rack was not far down the ochre-tiled hallway.

When Delaney came back downstairs, he could see that Rochemaure had set a place at one of the outdoor tables, with sliced bread in a basket, a small selection of cheeses on a platter, and butter, apples, grapes, nuts. A dark bottle of wine with no label stood at the ready, beside a small glass.

"I hope this will be sufficient for you, Monsieur Delaney," Rochemaure said.

"It's perfect. Thanks very much."

"I have some work I must do. *Bon appetit.*"

Rochemaure then disappeared into the house. Delaney sat alone in the warm spring afternoon, munching fruit, slicing excellent cheeses, sipping local wine. Butterflies and bees flitted around. The only thing missing in this scene from the pages of *Chateau Living* magazine was a warm welcome from the host.

Delaney wandered around the grounds after he had eaten, marvelling at the grand view down the valley toward Privas and at the horizon pool perfectly placed to make the most of that view. A small stucco outbuilding near the pool contained a bar fridge, a microwave and a sink. There was a tennis court about 25 metres farther away, all but hidden by trees.

As he lay resting on his bed a short while later, Delaney wondered how even a man on a generous German police pension could afford such surroundings, let alone an officer who had left the Bundeskriminalamt without collecting any pension at all. Rochemaure's high-end BMW 735i parked outside provided a clue, Delaney thought. There was more than a hint of old Paris money about Rochemaure and about the supremely comfortable house he had helped renovate. And, Delaney thought as he waited that afternoon to finally meet Ulrich Mueller, life at the Chateau de Bressac also gave off more than a hint of discreet homosexual domesticity.

Delaney woke from his siesta to the sound of gravel crunching outside. He went to the window and saw an older woman with a kerchief on her head crossing the courtyard. She was carrying a string bag of groceries. The housekeeper, apparently, returning to work after her own afternoon break. It was almost 6 p.m. He heard the big door open and close below his window and then the clatter of things domestic being done in the chateau kitchen.

He went downstairs and put his head into the kitchen.

"*Bonjour, madame,*" he said.

The housekeeper looked startled, and then smiled grimly. She had beefy, reddened forearms and hands, and what appeared to be a gold tooth.

"*Bonjour, monsieur. Bonjour*," she said. She did not ask who he was nor did she introduce herself. Like Rochemaure, she had very few words to say to houseguests.

Delaney wandered to the living room and sat down. Rochemaure did not immediately appear. But a voice came from behind a closed door at the far end of the room, between the start of a long corridor that headed left to another wing of the house and a side exit door to the terrace and the pathway downhill to the pool. Rochemaure was on the telephone.

Eventually, he emerged from what looked like a small office. Delaney saw a photocopier and a computer inside. Rochemaure's mood had not improved.

"We eat quite early in the evening here, Monsieur Delaney, so as to give Ulrich an early night."

"That's fine," Delaney said.

"I will get him for you now," Rochemaure said.

He went immediately down the corridor to the left. Delaney flipped through magazines and resisted opening what was surely a liquor cabinet near the fireplace. Eventually, he heard voices speaking in French.

Rochemaure maneuvered Mueller into the living room in a wheelchair. The old policeman was fully dressed—no pajamas for this invalid. He wore brown corduroy trousers and a beige, vaguely military, short-sleeved shirt, immaculately pressed. His hair was grey but still thick and carefully combed. His grey mustache was perfectly trimmed.

He wore round spectacles set low on his large nose and these drew attention to his silver blue eyes.

But Mueller's shoulders were round with age and illness. His chest looked sunken and his legs were thin. His hands did not shake but they were covered with brown spots. It was the collection of faint red and purple lesions on his face and neck, however, that told Delaney the story. There could be no mistaking the telltale signs of AIDS, in an advanced state.

"Monsieur Delaney, this is Ulrich Mueller," Rochemaure said in English.

Delaney went forward to clasp the old man's hand. The skin felt papery and dry. There was not much power left in what Delaney was certain would have been, in another time and place, a solid policeman's handshake.

"Thank you for agreeing to see me, Herr Mueller. I know you're not well," Delaney said.

"It is at the suggestion of my niece," Mueller said in a slightly hoarse voice. His English was very good, almost without accent.

Mueller and Rochemaure watched Delaney trying to assess the old man's health.

"What is your guess, Mr. Delaney?" Mueller said with a bitter smile. "Can you guess what it is that's killing me?"

This was a test of some kind. Delaney waited a moment before answering.

"Go ahead," Mueller said. "Let's not wait. Tell us your theory."

"AIDS," Delaney said. "I would say AIDS."

"Well done," Mueller said. "Mareike told me you were an excellent reporter. Very well done."

Rochemaure looked furious.

"This is a stupid game you play, Ulrich," he said.

"Why should we wait, Pierre?" Mueller said. "Hmm? Let us get the preliminaries over and done with. Shall we, Mr. Delaney? So we can then have our little civilized French aperitif?"

"An aperitif sounds like a very civilized idea to me, Herr Mueller," Delaney said.

Mueller started to cough dryly behind his spotted hand.

"Pierre, Pierre, a handkerchief, if you please," he said. "A handkerchief and then a pastis with ice. If you please."

The brief coughing spell did not seem severe enough, Delaney thought, to warrant a request for handkerchiefs. Mueller just seemed to want his partner to fetch and carry. Rochemaure pulled a neatly folded square from his pocket, as if accustomed to such ritual, gave the handkerchief to Mueller and then stomped out in the direction of the kitchen.

Rochemaure apparently thought it appropriate to demonstrate to the houseguest that serving duties were actually for the hired help. The housekeeper emerged from the kitchen after a few minutes, glumly carrying a clinking tray on which were positioned a bottle of Ricard pastis, glasses, a water jug, an ice bucket, tongs and a small bowl of pistachio nuts.

"Thank you very much, Madame Chagny," Mueller said.

The housekeeper said nothing and returned with no enthusiasm to her dinner preparations. Rochemaure reappeared from the kitchen immediately afterward, his little demonstration that he was no fetch-and-carry boy duly completed.

The evening was all very civilized, very south of France. They drank pastis in the stylish living room in the fading light as Mueller and Delaney circled each other—Mueller clearly trying to size up this journalist with a sudden interest in his life story, and Delaney trying to decide how explicit his questions could be and how soon he should ask them.

"Pierre is of course the mastermind of all of the changes made to this house, Mr. Delaney," Mueller said.

He was looking slightly less tired as the conversation and the aperitif revived him.

"I came down here from Germany alone a number of years ago after I left the police. I heard that the Chateau de Bressac was for sale," he said. "But it was a ruin. There were holes in the roof; pigeons were nesting in the attic. I was living only in the section of the house on this side, here on the ground floor, like a hermit. Then I was fortunate to get a recommendation about Pierre's work. I called him in Paris and used my policeman's power of persuasion to get him to come for a weekend to see what I had found."

He looked over at Rochemaure.

"And you fell in love with the place, didn't you, Pierre?" Mueller said.

"I did, yes," Pierre said joylessly. "It was a challenge I could not resist."

"And now you see the fruit of Pierre's exceptional talents all around you," Mueller said. "Those are even Pierre's paintings on the wall, most of them."

"Congratulations, Pierre," Delaney said. Rochemaure ignored him, drank pastis.

"It is not clear, you understand, what would have become of this place if an old German police chief had been responsible for the changes," Mueller said. "Of that I can assure you. I would have made it into a replica of some Bavarian chalet, I would guess. Pierre saved me from that."

"It's a grand house," Delaney said. He wondered how much detail he would also be given about the domestic living arrangements.

"Of course we went through the usual trials of finding reliable local tradesmen to help us," Mueller said. "I was not well and there was very little I could do by myself. Thankfully, there are now Polish plumbers even here in the Ardeche, Mr. Delaney. Estonian carpenters, stonemasons from Bulgaria. We no longer need the French at all for such jobs. It is a good thing, the new Europe."

"It's a very big job, fixing up an old place like this," Delaney said.

"Yes. But Pierre began spending more and more of his time here," Mueller said. "He was the one who looked after things, and, in fact, after me as well, as my health got worse. I would say that we have almost become locals here now, as much as anyone can become locals in *la France profounde*."

"Not such a bad fate," Delaney said.

Rochemaure's expression darkened even further.

"There could be worse fates," Rochemaure said.

Dinner at a small table set off to one side of the stone vestibule was also a stylish, civilized affair. And it gave Mueller more of the time he clearly still needed to size Delaney up.

Madame Chagny was an excellent cook, despite her attitude problem. Perhaps she was a drop-out from the same hospitality school as Rochemaure. She had prepared an appetizer of zucchini flowers stuffed with salt cod. Then lamb with caraway seeds and rosemary and eggplant. The no-name local wine was the same red that Delaney had drunk at lunch and just as good at night.

"Mareike tells me you want to write an article about the last days of the disgraced head of the BKA," Mueller said eventually, as they ate little *rondelles* of the Saint Marcellin cheese that preceded dessert. Madame Chagny was banging pots and plates as loudly as she could in the kitchen. Rochemaure silently smoked another in his evening series of Marlboros. He had also been drinking large quantities of wine.

"Not quite," Delaney said. "I think it may be part of a bigger story, possibly. I'm also looking for connections to another big story. Did Mareike tell you about that too?"

"A little," Mueller said. He looked somewhat warily over at Rochemaure. Delaney wondered how much, or how little, Rochemaure had been allowed to know about Mueller's life before France.

"Who would be reading such an article?" Mueller asked Delaney.

"I haven't really decided yet what publication I would do it for," Delaney said.

"That is a little unusual, is it not?" Mueller said. "In my not always happy experience of how journalists work."

"I'm not even sure I'll write anything at all, Herr Mueller," Delaney said. "I'm really here just to gather information and see what I come up with. I'll decide afterward what to do with the information. That's how I usually operate."

"And why would I want to help you with something like that?" Mueller said. "Just tell you my little story, like that, with no clarity about how the information might be used."

"Mareike seemed to think you might."

"And why?"

"She thought the time might be right for you to have your say."

"Because I am dying?"

Delaney and Mueller looked steadily at each other. Rochemaure stubbed out his cigarette.

"*Merde*," Rochemaure said. "*C'est de la merde.*"

"Are you dying, Herr Mueller?" Delaney said.

"*Merde*," Rochemaure said again. "Why this crazy game?"

"Yes, I'm dying, Mr. Delaney," Mueller said. "You are an experienced journalist, this Mareike tells me. Do I not look like a man who is slowly dying?"

"I'm more accustomed to seeing the results of sudden deaths," Delaney said.

"As I was, in my work as a policeman," Mueller said. "Slow deaths were for old people, or so we thought. We always thought policemen should make their exits in a blaze of glory."

"Maybe that's still possible," Delaney said.

"The power of the press."

"Something like that."

"This is shit," Rochemaure said, pouring himself a very large glass of red. "*C'est de la merde.*"

Dessert was Madame Chagny's excellent cherries *clafouti* and small coffees and Armagnac. Mueller played policeman for a while, quizzing Delaney about his life and his career and his publications and his credentials generally. Rochemaure played stricken lover; his mood darkened as the evening passed, his social skills all but disappearing along with the supply of wine and cigarettes. Delaney still held off playing journalist, or spy.

Talk turned to Mareike Fischer and her unorthodox policing methods. Mueller knew more about how his niece operated than she apparently realized.

"She sails very close to the wind," Mueller said. "In drug squad work this is perhaps necessary. In the LKA in any case."

"Undercover work is tough," Delaney said.

"It is risky, always," Mueller said. "For one's health and one's career."

"I would say," Delaney said.

"Mareike's career in many ways is just starting. Her judgment is not always exact, but she is smart and has the hardness required for such work."

Delaney wondered if the veteran BKA man would approve of certain details of how his niece actually operated in the rough and tumble of local police work. The BKA was more concerned with national security and intelligence and analysis than it was with biker gangs dealing amphetamine in rundown city houses.

"Mareike's judgment about you, Mr. Delaney, is that you could be trusted to do the right thing."

"I'm glad she feels that way."

"She formed this judgment very fast, in my view," Mueller said. "Do you always have this sort of effect on people, Mr. Delaney?"

"I wouldn't be able to say. That's something other people would have to decide, I would think."

"She has urged me to cooperate with you," Mueller said. "Perhaps 'urged' is too strong a word. But I find this unusual. So quickly."

"Maybe that has more to do with what she thinks of you than what she thinks of me, Herr Mueller."

"Poor dying Uncle Ulrich. The man needs a storyteller before he leaves this earth for heaven, or somewhere else."

"Do you have a good story to tell, Herr Mueller?'

"Of course. Every policeman does."

"Your story seems better than most, as far as I can gather," Delaney said.

"It has drama. This I can say."

"Yes, apparently. At the end of your career."

"And before, Mr. Delaney."

"I'd love to hear about it."

"It has, what do the playwrights call it? Pathos. Perhaps it has pathos too."

"Does it?"

Mueller paused. Suddenly he was looking extremely tired. His eyes displayed what soldiers and journalists call the thousand-mile-stare, the gaze of those who see the end of their lives on the horizon. Delaney looked at his watch. It was 11:20 p.m.

"Ulrich should rest now," Rochemaure said, getting up from his place at the end of the table. "Enough talk."

"Pierre looks after me," Mueller said. "But he likes to order me around. It is I who used to give the orders, to hundreds of police officers, before everything changed for me. Now I am ordered around by my architect and my housekeeper and my niece in Berlin."

"Enough," Rochemaure said.

"We shall speak again tomorrow of these matters, Mr. Delaney," Mueller said. "Allow me to sleep and to consider, and we will sit together again tomorrow."

"That's fine," Delaney said. "I'd appreciate that."

Rochemaure, however, showed no appreciation for the prospect. He turned Mueller around in his wheelchair and then pushed it quickly out of the room. Delaney did not see either of them again that night. Madame Chagny had long since gone home. He sat alone, drinking excellent Armagnac until very late, listening to silences and ticking clocks.

As Delaney lay hours later in bed in his picture postcard room in a chateau in deepest rural France, he heard through his open window the muffled sounds of an argument. Voices he could not quite distinguish shouted hard words in French. He thought it could only be Mueller and Rochemaure, somewhere deep in the old house down in the back ground-floor wing, having some sort of lovers' quarrel. There were no other occupants in the Chateau de Bressac that Delaney knew of.

The arguing went on intermittently for some minutes. Then Delaney heard a series of thumps and then the sound of breaking glass. More muffled argument followed. Eventually the big old house went silent again.

Perhaps it was the absolute silence that followed, or perhaps the utter isolation of the place—far from all things urban, far from any neighbours, where no telephones rang, where all was far out of range of the familiar—that plunged Delaney into a heavy, introspective mood. Perhaps it was the wine. For what seemed like hours he lay in his little bed, evaluating information gathered and scenarios possible, pondering lives lived, pondering disaster victims alive and dead.

Eventually, his quest for clarity still not complete, he slept.

He dreams he is with Jonah Smith on an urgent quest to find Smith's missing daughter. They are stumbling around in the moonlight of deepest rural France, trying their best to find the missing girl. They hold flaming torches above their heads to light the way. Delaney is searching for something or someone precious of his own as well, but he isn't sure who or what that might turn out to be. Suddenly he is alone; Smith has disappeared. Suddenly Delaney is alone in the container compound in Phuket, Thailand, in moonlight, knowing that hundreds of disaster victims await him in body bags inside. He opens a container door, then unzips bag after bag, looking for someone and everyone at the same time. The bags contain the lifeless bodies of everyone he has ever known or worked with or loved. Former teachers and colleagues and editors he has not thought of for 20 years or more lie silently on the stark wooden racks. Friends and former lovers lie there, and his sister and his ex-wife, and Natalia, Kate Hunter, Mareike, everyone. Brian O'Keefe is there, and Jonathan Rawson, Tim Bishop, Ackermann, Rochemaure, Mueller. All lie lifeless in the disaster victims' compound in Phuket. Then Delaney slowly opens a last container, this one sitting well off to one side away from all the others. In the cold and dark of this last container, inside every body bag, he finds the lifeless body of Francis Delaney, disaster victim. Frantically he unzips each and every bag. He is lying lifeless inside each one. He cries out to himself, over and over: Who are you? Who are you? Who are you?

Chapter 14

Mueller and Rochemaure were still arguing the next morning when Delaney came down to the kitchen. They stopped immediately when he came in. Rochemaure was stony-faced, as usual. Mueller, in his wheelchair, looked flushed, unwell, tired already, even though it was still early in the day.

"I'll come back," Delaney said. "I'm disturbing you."

"No, no. No need," Mueller said. "Come in. You will eat breakfast. We have no secrets here in our little French hideaway."

Mueller clearly still had enough energy left to try to rattle Rochemaure's cage. It worked very well. Rochemaure's face darkened. He glared at the intruding houseguest with such intensity that Delaney thought he must be drunk or on drugs of some kind. It was a face full of anger and hatred.

"Pierre is not happy when things upset our little routine here, Mr. Delaney," Mueller said, still trying, it seemed, to provoke Rochemaure. "I must constantly remind him to mind his manners. He is getting badly on my nerves, these days. And vice versa, it seems."

That was enough for Rochemaure. He flung his cigarette at Mueller. It hit the old man in the chest, with a tiny shower of sparks. He rushed out of the kitchen past Delaney and they heard the rhythmic crunches of his footsteps in the courtyard gravel. The heavy carriageway door slammed shut and a car engine was brutally fired up. There was a fainter crunch and scramble of gravel outside the chateau walls and then Rochemaure was gone.

"He will now drive far too fast all around the Ardeche countryside in his very powerful automobile," Mueller said. "He will then go to the Café des Marchands in Privas and drink bad wine with our lazy local tradesmen far too early in the day. He is a creature of habit, my Pierre. My apologies for this little scene, Mr. Delaney."

"No need to apologize," Delaney said.

"He is always afraid someone like you will disrupt our little situation."

"Someone like me?"

"A questioner."

"So he knows your story?"

"A bit of it, yes he does. Not all of it. But enough, I would say, for him to worry about people who might one day want to ask me questions."

Madame Chagny appeared from the direction of the living room, as if she had been waiting for the domestic drama to be over before seeing to her appointed duties. She, too, was stony-faced this morning. She nodded briefly at Delaney and headed through the kitchen and out a side door to a small exterior area where she started, or perhaps resumed, hanging sheets from a wicker washing basket.

"She does not approve of men having sex together in this house, or anywhere else for that matter," Mueller said. "And she like all the French peasants in the Ardeche is petrified of AIDS. They think it is something like the black plague. But she needs the work we provide for her here, so she accepts to share this space with two homosexuals. She washes our sheets as if they come from beds in a leper colony. Not that there would have been much forensic evidence of sexual activity to disgust her, these past months."

Mueller's frankness surprised Delaney. The old man had clearly decided to confide some, but not necessarily all, aspects of his private life.

Mueller studied Delaney for a moment, and then said: "I spoke last night to Mareike in Berlin."

Delaney said nothing.

"She is my confidante, in a way," Mueller said. "My only one, now. And she worries about me here. She calls it 'nowhere.' And she worries about me with Pierre because she knows what he is like. She calls him my bit of rough trade, Mr. Delaney. You are familiar with the expression perhaps? In Berlin they have bars where angry violent gays like Pierre would go. If he were a German gay. In Paris too, they have them. He knows those Paris bars, my Pierre. I used to know them a little as well, when we would visit Paris, just after we began to disgust Madame Chagny. But I'm too ill now for any rough trade."

Delaney let Mueller go on. It would be a day of confessions, or so he hoped.

"Does homosexuality disgust you as it does Madame Chagny, Mr. Delaney?" Mueller asked.

"No," Delaney said. "It doesn't."

"Mareike told me that in your case there would in general be no hasty, narrow-minded judgments," Mueller said.

Mareike, it seemed, was still very much on Delaney's side in his quest for answers about Mueller, and other matters.

"That's not my style, Herr Mueller. I'm a reporter, not a judge."

Mueller studied him again.

"Mareike thinks the time is right for me to talk to someone like you, Mr. Delaney," he said.

"Do you think so too?" Delaney asked.

Mueller paused.

"Yes, I now think so, too. Yes, perhaps."

"Excellent," Delaney said.

"But first breakfast, yes?"

Mueller surprised Delaney by getting slowly up out of his wheelchair and going over to the stove to light a flame under the kettle. Apparently he did not think it the right moment to ask the housekeeper for much. He saw Delaney watching him.

"I'm not a complete invalid yet. That wheelchair helps me when I am tired but I can still get around without it when necessary."

He watched Delaney watching him.

"They can't tell me when I will die, Mr. Delaney. I take pharmacy loads of tablets and they prolong life very effectively these days for old homosexuals who have AIDS. Not very long ago, before all these new drugs, I would probably have died already. But the prognosis for me is still not good. Does this answer the question you have so far been polite enough not to ask?"

They ate at one of the outside tables in the courtyard. There was some sort of unspoken agreement between Mueller and Madame Chagny that morning and she did not offer to help. Delaney carried a tray of bread and butter and coffee outside, and then helped Mueller outside too, as he had by then lowered himself back into the wheelchair. Making coffee was enough for him for one morning it seemed.

They enjoyed the sunshine and the birdsong and the small breakfast. The questions came only afterward, and they came first from Mueller.

"What is your theory, Mr. Delaney?"

"About what exactly?"

"About all of this. About me and my little story and about whatever connection it might have to what you are really trying to find out. I like to hear people's theories in an investigation. It is a habit I developed as a policeman. Then I do not waste time with a lot of facts that are not actually needed."

Delaney decided to hold nothing back. He told Mueller what he had found out in Thailand, about the tsunami file and the attempts to hide a dead man's true identity. He told him about containers of disaster victims and about surgically removed fingerprints. He told them about Jonah Smith's beating and about having almost been run over in the parking lot of the Metropole Hotel.

"And so at first you thought pedophiles," Mueller said at last.

"At first."

"That was a good theory. Any policeman who knows that part of the world, especially a German or a Dutch policeman, would have thought pedophiles too. Thailand is a good place for such people to find children and a good place for them to disappear once they are not welcome in Europe."

"So we thought. And the police over there were apparently closing a few good pedophile cases when they started matching bodies with fingerprints. People who had disappeared."

Mueller laughed bitterly.

"Thank God for the tsunami," he said. "That is what my police friends would have been saying. We can close some good pedophile cases with no real investigative effort at all, thanks to the big wave."

He laughed again, genuinely delighted with the thought.

"But with Heinrich, that wasn't what was going on," Delaney said.

"So? Your theory?"

"That's where it began to get tough," Delaney said. "That's why I'm here."

"What is it you really need to know from me, Mr. Delaney?"

"I need to know about the connection between Klaus Heinrich disappearing and your resignation. If there is a connection."

Mueller studied Delaney closely, as he had been doing all morning.

"A very good investigative question," he said. "And your theories?"

"I have none, really. It's a dead end, possibly. I know a fair bit about the Heinrich story and I know a bit about your story, but I need to know how your stories come together. If they do."

"Whether the road to Saint Lager Bressac is a dead end," Mueller said.

"Yes."

"And if you make this connection, Mr. Delaney, you think you will be able to really understand why Klaus Heinrich disappeared."

"Yes."

"You are convinced the body in that burned-out little house in the Seibengebirge hills was not Heinrich."

"Very convinced."

"It must be wonderful to be sure of things in this world, Mr. Delaney, and of who people really are."

"It can happen sometimes."

"Fingerprints, DNA, forensic dentistry, expert testimony, police testimony, visual identification, blood type, distinguishing marks. This tells you who people really are?"

"You're moving into the philosophical realm, Herr Mueller."

"And so? I'm dying. This is allowed."

Delaney waited.

"The body in Phuket," Mueller said. "It had distinguishing marks?"

"Yes. A tattoo. On the right forearm."

"Appearance? What did it look like? What did it say?"

"*Deutschland*," Delaney said.

Mueller began to laugh. He laughed and ran both of his aging hands through what was left of his hair. He stared down at the gravel of the courtyard, hands still on his head.

"Oh, my dear, dear Klaus," he said eventually, looking up. He smiled at Delaney, and shook his head. "I always told him it made him look like a common thief, that stupid tattoo. My dear old Klaus . . ."

Madame Chagny was staying well away from them for the remainder of the morning, it seemed. And Rochemaure had still not reappeared. There was coffee and sunshine and comfortable chairs. Mueller began to talk; words flooded out of him. Delaney simply allowed himself to be submerged.

"You have to try to imagine the very worst thing that could happen when you are running a spy somewhere," Mueller said. "Not that the spy you are running gets killed or even gets thrown in jail by your enemies. That is too easy and simple. That used to happen all the time when the Cold War was on. No, not that. You have to imagine something worse than that."

Mueller sipped at his coffee.

"You have to imagine Klaus Heinrich working for years, perhaps fifteen years—I can't remember the exact number—over on the eastern side. He was our star. He had duped the East Germans into thinking he wanted to come home after his big life mistake in the West and that he would tell them everything he had learned and help them with their analysis and anything else they needed. But he was, remember this, our man was a West German spy, one of very, very few we ever managed to set up on the other side of the Wall. So, fine, it's fine. He works; he sends apparently very good information, interesting information, over to us in the West for many years. Then, boom, the Wall comes down. Suddenly, the Cold War is over. People are streaming across the border again, Heinrich's services are no longer needed, he comes home to the West, gets his nice reward and his little apartment in Bonn and his job and the cabin in Seibengebirge. OK. It's nice. His picture is in the magazines, he is a hero, no one from Stasi tries to kill him, everything excellent."

Coffee. Birdsong.

"Then, there are the files. The ones Stasi did not destroy are being evaluated, steadily, year after year, by the Germans and the Americans. There are also the shredded files. These too are being examined and put back together by patient people in little offices somewhere. Eventually, they also start to use computers to try to put the shredded and torn pieces of paper back together again. This is in the 1990s, after reunification. The new Germany. More information begins to be available every year about Stasi and its methods and its network which, Mr. Delaney, was everywhere, everywhere. On the East side and on the West side, in every department and university and on both sides of the Wall, Stasi had agents. So you imagine, one day, that someone notices a name in a Stasi file that is being examined or that has been put back together by a nice little German clerk somewhere in an office where she is doing good work all day for the new Germany. So try now to imagine what is the worst thing that could happen, for the German side that is running a spy. Let us say a spy like Klaus Heinrich. You have a theory now about the worst thing that could happen?"

Delaney could see, a little now, where this was going.

"He's a double agent."

"Very good," Mueller said. "Very, very good. For years, for let us say fifteen years, he works in East Berlin and the West side is happy. They think he is doing good work for them, he sends information back, but suddenly it now appears that this, some of it or all of it, could have been bad information, information the East side wanted us to have. Or, maybe, probably, Stasi found it useful for fifteen years to just know what things interested us on the West side. Which people interested us, which questions we wanted answered. You know, Mr. Delaney, in a war, a cold one or a hot one, it is very useful to simply know what your enemy would like to know. And my friend Klaus Heinrich did an excellent job for his masters in the East in this way for many years. He had come over to the West in, I don't remember, 1959 or 1960. He is a young man of about nineteen, twenty, he goes to university, he fools everyone, and then, suddenly, he defects back to the East. He is fed up with the West he says. It was all a big mistake. But, he is a BND spy, correct? No, not correct. In fact, he was always an East German spy, a mole first in the West and then a double agent in the East. The Stasi were smart people, very smart. And they were patient. They were willing to wait for years to set up a scenario like that. Let someone go to university, take his time, make friends, win trust. Wait, wait, you wait. Then, eventually, someone becomes useful. Maybe five, maybe six, maybe seven years into the game, he becomes useful. That is how the Stasi used to operate. That is why they beat us so badly at the spying game for so many years. They were patient people. And dedicated. They had a cause. World democratic socialism. Worth waiting for, yes?"

Delaney said: "Great story."

"Not finished, not finished," Mueller said. "So, we have this great story, as you put it. It is bad news for the West, very bad news. A file comes to light, certain people become aware in, I think it was 1997—'96 or '97—that Klaus Heinrich is not who he appeared to be at all. He was someone else. He was a double agent, not a hero to the West, but a double agent. Imagine this, then. The CDU government, Helmut Kohl's people, are in the shit, there will be an election soon, in 1998, and they do not want such a scandal. So what do they do? They, those very few who know, decide to say nothing at all. The BND people, those few who know, are instructed to say nothing at all. They decide to let our Klaus carry on as before in Bonn, so as not to make them look like the fools they are, in believing that he was always a good Western spy. Kohl's fools and his BND fools. Let us not even speak about Willy Brandt and the East German mole who climbed right into his own office, the chancellor's office and made a nest there before they found him way back in 1974. We do not need to even talk about that disaster that made everyone look like fools and brought down Brandt himself. But another such disaster, years later? Stasi wins, makes fools of everyone again? What has been learned since Willy Brandt's disaster? Nothing. Correct?

"But, maybe, no," Mueller went on. "Wait. Is there perhaps also another reason they allow Klaus Heinrich to stay on as before, hush hush, no one makes trouble, he is allowed to carry on as before a retired hero of the West. Is this really likely? No, it is not, actually. So why? Because there is something else. They are afraid not only of how much they will all look like fools before the 1998 election, having been duped again by a Stasi man. There is another reason, Mr. Delaney. Can it get worse? Yes, it can. It can get much worse."

"You've captured my attention," Delaney said.

"Theories?"

"No," Delaney said. "You go."

"Here is how it gets worse, Mr. Delaney. Listen to this now. What if, in addition to being a double agent, Klaus Heinrich with the cheap *Deutschland* tattoo on his arm, had some very, very interesting information he could use against those few people who knew the real story about him? OK, they don't want to be embarrassed by the first disaster and look like fools who were duped by a double agent for too many years. But what if Heinrich also has some important information he can use even if they decide to tell the story and take the chance and make it public and try to throw him into jail instead of leaving him alone to live quietly in Bonn? What could it be that he knew that was so dangerous they would leave him alone even if they really did not want to leave him alone?"

"No theory," Delaney said.

"Think," Mueller said.

"Sorry," Delaney said.

"You disappoint me, Mr. Delaney. But I will tell you. How does this situation get worse? Well, imagine if Klaus Heinrich, in addition to being a dirty double agent, was also a disgusting homosexual, the kind Madame Chagny hates so much. And imagine something else. Imagine that for some years after he came back to the West, after 1990, he was having a homosexual affair with a very senior official, very senior, someone who if this were to be revealed, would bring even more scandal down on the government and the spy service and everyone he had come into contact with. Imagine the scandal, Mr. Delaney, if the person Klaus Heinrich had taken on as his secret lover had access to very sensitive secret information. Even if there was no more Stasi, this would not be a good thing, you can imagine this, yes? It shows how lax everyone was at the time, to miss this double agent and then to later find he is also, after all of this, he is also having sex with a very senior, important man?"

"Amazing," Delaney said.

"Yes, precisely. And here is the next question. Who do you think this senior, very important man was, who was having sex with this dirty double agent Heinrich with the cheap tattoo?"

Mueller sat back in his wheelchair. There was no more coffee left, no more distraction possible. There was just a little metal table in the southern France morning at which a dying man was telling very secret stories to a gatherer of information.

"You," Delaney said. "It was you."

"Congratulations," Mueller said.

They sat in silence for a while, listening to birdsong and pondering disasters, victims, identities.

Mueller said eventually: "I loved him of course."

He paused.

"You are not one of these men, are you Mr. Delaney, who thinks it is impossible for men to love each other like this? And for big tough police officers to love other men like this? And a senior, important policeman such as myself?"

Delaney said: "It happens. I know."

"I was seduced, of course," Mueller laughed. "That is always the excuse, yes? But in my case it was true. Klaus seduced me. He sought me out. I was gay, yes, for many years. I was married; surely a senior respected BKA man must have a wife. But this happens, too. I was not chief at the time Klaus and I began our little affair. He had come back to the West, it was 1990, I had not been made chief yet but we met a couple of years later and we began our little affair. Gays sense it easily when they find another man who is still, what do you say in English, there's a nice expression. In the closet. Our famous spy Klaus Heinrich told me he knew right away that this important BKA man, not yet the chief of BKA, but this senior BKA man, wanted to have sex with other men, sometimes had sex with other men. He was not the first man I had such sex with, of course."

Delaney said: "But why would you take such a risk? If you were senior enough to even be in the running one day for the top job?"

"Because there is always an element of risk for gays, Mr. Delaney. In Germany at that time, in certain circles, and before that, and always. For some of us, the risk itself adds to the, what, the pleasure. No, that is not the word. It adds to the whole business, the whole life, the whole disaster of it. It's part of it, for some of us. The risk. And Klaus pretended that he loved me. I knew at the end that he did not, but he pretended very well for several years. So love is also worth a little risk, would you agree? And sex with a policeman, Mr. Delaney, it is a gay fantasy, yes? Policemen, spies, double agents, fear of discovery, rough trade, a gun and some cigarettes on the table. It is all too, what shall I say, too classic, yes?"

Heinrich, according to Mueller, did not have AIDS and was

unlikely even to have been HIV-positive when their paths diverged. But there was very little time for discussion of such things at the end, Mueller said, when their paths began to diverge in 2001. Mueller himself only became aware of his illness after he had left Germany for France.

"We were very careful homosexuals, Klaus and I," he said. "And in any case, he is now dead. He died before me in any case. AIDS did not get him. It was a tsunami wave. How strange life is."

Mueller knew every detail of recent German history and could recite it. In 1998, Helmut Kohl's Christian Democrats lost power. Gerhard Schroeder's SPD took over. As always in such changes of government, attitudes change in important agencies, senior personnel change, situations change. As well, Mueller said, the CIA began releasing a series of important Stasi files in 2000, handing them back to Germany after they had been copied, examined, analyzed and otherwise thoroughly poked and prodded. If the CIA had become aware of Heinrich's true status as a double agent, then it would only be a matter of time before the German side would have to act.

"I don't know if the information was in the files the CIA started to hand back in 2000 or so," Mueller said. "The German side knew about Klaus well before that, as I've said, but perhaps the truth was also in the files the CIA gave back at that point. That would have changed the scenario, of course. Or maybe it was in the Rosewood file. Everyone was waiting for that file to be released as well. Or maybe people simply decided that they could not hide Heinrich's identity any longer."

"So it was the SPD government that eventually fixed it up to look like Heinrich died," Delaney asked.

"No, not exactly. Spy services act, when they need to, independently, of governments. Sometimes governments look the other way, or maybe people with talent from a previous government help make certain things happen, or maybe spy services do what they want despite the government's knowledge or wishes. In this case, only a very few people knew about Heinrich's real identity. The ones who stood to lose the most were some of the Kohl people, who had stupidly made such a hero out of him when he came back from East Berlin. But the SPD was in power for three years before 2001. They had access to files, the new ones being revealed and released. They would not have looked good either."

"So some people just made it look like Heinrich died in a fire and set him up in a new life in Thailand," Delaney said.

"Yes. It's not so hard. And then I never saw him again."

"Why would he go? Why would he not use the blackmail idea he had? Why wouldn't he just say he would reveal everything about you and him?"

Mueller paused.

"At that point, what would be the use? If they were willing to sacrifice me, and take the consequences, Klaus had no blackmail power left at all. And he would not have wanted to go to jail. Even a man who liked rough trade."

"And you. What did they say to you?"

"Me, they simply washed their hands of. Again, not so hard for them. Some people came to see me. BND. They had one proposal only. Out, exile—forty years in the police and out. For me it was hard, but not for them. It almost killed me, in fact. It killed my wife. I came here. I met Pierre. Now we have a little life. Not an easy one anymore. But the house is the thing. Not Pierre. Not anymore."

"And the body in the cabin in Bonn?"

"Who knows? Some poor derelict, possibly. Cadavers are not hard to find. People die without identities all the time, police find bodies all the time. Interpol has hundreds of Black Notices for unidentified bodies around the world on any given day. And of course, they had some sympathetic pathologists in this thing, didn't they? This Horst Becker, you told me about, for example."

"And you don't know him?"

"I never met him. I don't think so," Mueller said. "But I have met his type, many times. He would be a man willing to do all that was required. Just as he is apparently now doing in Thailand."

Madame Chagny had quietly left while they had talked like conspirators at the little outdoor table. There was still no sign of Rochemaure—probably a good thing. The telephone had rung inside the house a couple of times as they spoke. Mueller seemed content to let it ring.

"It's a terrific story," Delaney said.

"That depends on your point of view," Mueller said. "But now you have the story."

"All of it?"

"What else would you need?"

"Who is trying to prevent it from coming out? About Heinrich. Possibly about you and Heinrich. Who attacked my friend Jonah Smith from Scotland Yard? Who is bugging his room in Phuket? Who tried to kill me outside my hotel?"

"Horst Becker. In my view that is obvious."

"And who else? Why?"

"This story will do no one any good when it comes out, Mr. Delaney. The present government in Germany, the previous CDU government. The spy service. The police, the BKA. No one looks good. There will be an election this year in Germany, almost certainly. No one will look good."

"Is that what you want?" Delaney asked. "To make everyone look bad?"

"Some people, yes. Some people deserve to look bad."

"Like who?"

"Well, allow me to pick my number one target. Let's see. Well, well. The Interior Minister? Yes? The man in charge of the world famous BKA police when I was made to give up my career?

He would be at the top of my list. There are others."

"What do you really want me to do with this information now, Herr Mueller?"

"That is up to you, my friend. You are a journalist. I am a policeman. You know your job. But the information will now get out, I have no doubt about this. And, in my experience, from what you have told me today, it is going to get out no matter what you do anyway. Have no illusions. Things are changing in the situation, Mr. Delaney. Your involvement, and quite possibly other factors, have now set things in motion. There are people already taking risks in Thailand, there are people very interested in what you are doing. Much is at stake. This makes people take risks and make mistakes and then things break open. I saw it many times when I was in the police. Things will break open, whatever you yourself now decide to do. But you can shape this, maybe. We can control this just a little, you and me."

"What will they do to you, when it comes out?"

"I don't care. I'm dying already. But do you think they will send someone to Saint Lager Bressac to shoot me? I doubt this very much. And it would be very hard to get a car in my little courtyard here to run me down. What can they do? If I cared."

Delaney sat in silence. Then he said: "Depending on how I handle things, this story could make waves in the German election."

"And so?" Mueller said. "Why not? Let us make a big wave. Let us see what happens then. Let us sit back and watch the wave come in. I would love, for example, to watch the Interior Minister drown."

They heard a car labouring up the steep rutted track toward the house. It was almost noon. They had been talking for more than three hours. They sat looking at each other in silence as a car door slammed outside the wall. Then the carriage gate opened and

Rochemaure came into the courtyard. He stood just inside the wall, glaring at them both.

Mueller, despite looking very fatigued from the long morning of talk, took the offensive. In his prime, Delaney thought, he would have been a formidable police officer and boss.

"Pierre, before you take one step further into this place, I warn you not to act like a fool," he called out. "Of course you are drunk. This is boring to me. So be very, very careful not to act a fool, my Pierre."

"This bastard is still here?" Rochemaure shouted.

"You have been warned, Pierre," Mueller said calmly. "There will be none of this."

Delaney wondered how Mueller intended to make good on his policeman's warnings, in his present condition and given Rochemaure's size and demeanour.

"You bastards," Rochemaure said, swaying very slightly.

"Go in and have a sleep. Do not embarrass me anymore," Mueller said. "Go. Your drunkenness disgusts me."

To Delaney's surprise, Rochemaure stood swaying where he was for a moment, then flung away his cigarette—clearly his nonverbal communication method of choice—and simply stalked on past both of them into the house. The heavy door slammed, and a moment later another door slammed inside.

"I'm sorry," Mueller said.

"It's fine, it's fine," Delaney said.

"It is like this now, I'm afraid."

"It's no problem. But maybe I should be going."

"Yes, perhaps. I would say."

"OK."

"And your plan now?"

"First, I need to go up to my room and write in my notebook. Before I do anything else. I want to make sure I'm clear on all of this and get some notes together. Then I think I'll head back up to Lyon and get a plane to Berlin."

"And then?"

"Then I'm not sure. I need to think. Thailand, probably. I'll absolutely need to speak to some people there. Then I can decide."

"As you wish," Mueller said. "You go to your notes. I will rest. You come to find me before you go."

"I will."

For some reason Mueller thought it appropriate to offer Delaney his hand. Delaney took it. The handshake was a pact of some kind. But neither of them, it seemed, was clear on what the pact actually entailed.

"You listen well," Mueller said.

"Years of practice," Delaney said. "It's what I do."

Delaney rested too for a while, then sat at the little writing desk near the window of his big old room, doing up his notebook. He stopped often to gaze out at the lovely French scene below—ordered squares of gravel and plants, well-trained vines, an ancient door in an ancient wall. Everything in its place. But there was no such order in his notes or in his thoughts. Not yet.

The house was quiet. Madame Chagny had so far not returned for her afternoon and evening duties. Cicadas hummed in the trees in the late spring heat. They almost masked the sound of footsteps coming up the stairs and down the tiled hallway to his room.

There could be no missing the very loud knocking on his door, however. His visitor didn't wait for Delaney to open it. There was more knocking, then the door flew open and Rochemaure strode in, still red in the face and still clearly not a happy man.

He was carrying an old long-barrelled revolver. It was blue-black. He waved it with theatrical flourish at Delaney as he came into the room.

"You must leave this house immediately, you bastard, you leave now," Rochemaure shouted.

Drunk. Angry. Delaney knew it was best in such situations to agree to everything.

"All right, that's fine. I'm going, I was about to leave anyway," he said quietly.

He wondered if Rochemaure was drunk enough or had seen enough bad movies to demand that opponents put hands up over their heads. Delaney very much doubted Rochemaure would use the gun, even if it were loaded. But with angry drunks and guns, accidents can happen.

"Go now," Rochemaure shouted. He went over to the bed and took Delaney's small travel bag and threw it onto the floor. He kicked over a wooden chair for theatrical good measure. "You go now."

Delaney slowly picked up the bag and began to toss his few things inside. He tossed his notebook inside.

"What is in that notebook?" Rochemaure shouted. "Give that to me."

"It's nothing, Pierre. Relax. It's my notebook for work."

"Give that to me," Rochemaure shouted again.

Delaney knew it was always best to surrender notebooks to angry people brandishing guns. He threw it onto the bed. Rochemaure picked it up and flipped through pages.

"What is in here, you bastard?" he shouted. "You are trying to ruin us."

Rochemaure, when Mueller appeared in the doorway, was attempting with mixed results to read Delaney's notes and look menacing with his gun at the same time. Mueller looked extremely flushed and worn out from the short climb up the stairs. He leaned heavily on a stout cane.

"What is this shouting, Pierre? I will not have such shouting in my house," Mueller said. He looked furious. A furious police officer confronting an unruly drunk.

"My house, my house. This is my house," Rochemaure shouted.

"Calm yourself, Pierre. Put that gun down immediately."

Rochemaure amazed Mueller and Delaney, and quite possibly himself, by firing a random shot into the ceiling. This was enough for Mueller. He stepped forward to smash his cane down very heavily on Rochemaure's skull. Rochemaure went to his knees immediately and dropped the gun. Mueller hit him savagely with the stick three more times, about the head and neck. They were extremely heavy blows. Delaney thought Mueller might add a few kicks after Rochemaure collapsed, unconscious and bleeding, to the floor.

Mueller sat down on Delaney's bed. He was panting heavily. He leaned with both hands on the cane.

"Jesus Christ," Delaney said.

"Now the fool is injured," Mueller said.

"I would think so," Delaney said.

He went over to have a look.

"Is he dead?" Mueller asked, far less worried than Delaney thought he had reason to be. Delaney put two fingers against an artery in Rochemaure's neck. There was still a pulse.

"He's not dead. But you could have fractured his skull, the way you hit him."

Delaney was kneeling beside Rochemaure now. He loosened the unconscious man's shirt and belt, and tilted his head back so he wouldn't choke.

"We'll have to get a doctor or an ambulance, I think," Delaney said. "I'd better not move his head and neck too much. He could be badly hurt."

"Good," Mueller said. "Very good. He deserves to be hurt, the fool. He has started to bore me with his nonsense. It is what he deserves."

Delaney tried as best he could to tend to Mueller's injured lover. Mueller watched calmly. He made no move to call for help. Delaney could see clearly that it was still far more dangerous to be this old policeman's enemy than his friend.

PART 4

Frankfurt and Phuket
— April 2005

Chapter 15

At Mueller's urging, Delaney left the house as quickly as possible. Madame Chagny had still not returned. Mueller thought it best if Delaney were elsewhere when she got there, and when the ambulance arrived and possibly the police.

Rochemaure was definitely in need of an ambulance. He had still not come to. His colour and breathing were not good. Delaney didn't like the look of him at all while he collected a few belongings before exiting the house. Mueller, however, was completely unperturbed.

"Just go," Mueller said. "I will take care of this."

"How will you explain what happened?"

"Leave it to me, Mr. Delaney. If you please. Just go and do what you now need to do in this matter."

"The police will have to consider this an assault," Delaney said.

"It was indeed an assault," Mueller said. "I'm familiar with such crimes after a long law enforcement career. I'm also a very good friend of the local Prefect of Police. He comes up here to drink my Armagnac from time to time. It was a crime of passion. He will understand this. Alcohol plays its part, emotions are allowed to get out of control. I am an old invalid, under stress, worried about my condition. Such things happen. This is France, and he is a very experienced police officer. Please do not worry."

Delaney found it hard to believe the situation would be resolved as easily as that, but he left the house nonetheless. He had no wish to be embroiled in a French police investigation just as his story was breaking wide open.

It was just after 1 p.m. He drove too fast down the winding track to Saint Lager Bressac and then onto the better D22 road that would take him toward La Neuve, then Le Pouzin and the bridge over the Rhone to the autoroute. As soon as the car bounced out of the trees and onto the paved road, he was back in cellular signal range and his phone rang immediately. The screen said: "Seven missed calls."

He pulled over near the modest Saint Lager church and listened to his voicemail. Two messages from Rawson, three from Mareike, one from Ackermann and one from his *International Geographic* editor asking for a firm delivery date on the tsunami article. Nothing from Jonah Smith. Delaney wasn't sure whether this was good news or bad news.

He had nothing but bad news about progress on his original assignment for the magazine, so he did not call *International Geographic* in Washington. Rawson didn't get a callback either. His message was the usual mix of quiet resignation and understated outrage at Delaney having gone to ground once again.

"Not good, Francis, not good," the second of Rawson's messages said. "Time for you to check in, very much so. This thing's getting more complicated by the day."

Mareike's outrage was less understated than Rawson's.

"I don't like this, Frank Delaney," she said in her final message. "Don't ignore me, I don't like this. No one answers the land line at the chateau. You don't answer your mobile phone. I want to know about your time with my uncle."

Ackermann was the only one whose call Delaney returned.

"So?" Ackermann said. "Are you smarter than me or am I smarter than you?"

"I'm smarter than you," Delaney said.

"*Sheise*," Ackermann said. "They're connected? Mueller and Heinrich?"

"Yes, absolutely. A very clear connection. Mueller admits to it. He's told me the whole story. Or as much of it as he wants to tell, and as much as I need to go to the next step."

"Which is?"

"I'll come back up to Berlin to see you and we'll talk things over. I may need some more facts checked out at your end. Then I'll have to get back to Phuket to see Jonah Smith and tie up some loose ends. A few more questions need to be answered over there. And Horst Becker is still in Thailand, I would think."

"And then? Then what?"

"Then we'll see what's the best way to play this thing."

"You torture me, Francis. You torture and you punish me. It is not right, how you treat me."

"I'll see you tonight. I'm just heading back to the highway from Mueller's place. I'll get the late-afternoon flight out of Lyon for Frankfurt and then catch something over to Berlin. Stand by until tonight."

As he was pulling back onto the road, Delaney noticed a dark blue Renault Espace van in the church parking lot. It had been there as he spoke on the telephone. It had Paris registration plates. Two men in windbreakers and baseball caps sat watching him through their windshield.

Delaney looked in his rearview mirror as he pulled away. After a few moments, the van also pulled out onto the road and rolled along with him toward La Neuve. It was close enough so that in the mirror he could see the van's passenger talking on a cell phone. The driver lit a cigarette and kept it between his lips as he drove.

There was little traffic on the backroads of deepest Ardeche even on a Saturday afternoon. Delaney put his phone where he could reach it easily on the seat next to him and drove fast, keeping an eye on the rearview. The van speeded up too. He slowed down suddenly. The van did not pull out to pass. If they were following him, the two men behind him made no attempt to disguise it.

The D22 ends at the Rhone. The long, low, narrow bridge over the river leads to the N304 approach road for the Autoroute de Soleil. The surface of the bridge was made of steel grates that hummed loudly as Delaney's wheels rolled onto it. The wheels of the van behind him hummed too, then suddenly far louder than his as the driver speeded up.

The danger came suddenly. The van rammed the back of his Peugeot with a terrific jolt and the impact threw Delaney's neck back hard against the headrest. Immediately the van driver powered forward again, engine racing as he shifted gears and hit the accelerator.

The second impact threw Delaney's car toward the bridge railings. The right front wheel of the Peugeot went up onto the narrow cement sidewalk and Delaney fought hard to control the steering. His right front headlight smashed as it grazed the steel rail, but he managed to wrestle the car back onto the road. He stamped on the accelerator and raced away from his pursuers.

The Peugeot he had rented was very fast. He saw the two men behind him gesticulating at each other as he sped away. They, too, were driving fast but it was clear he was going to be able to leave them behind. Delaney hoped they were not determined enough to stop him, or kill him, to begin firing guns from behind.

There were no guns. By the time Delaney had raced down the few kilometres of good straight road to the autoroute entrance ramp, he was at least 500 metres ahead of the van. He did not stop at the toll plaza to get a card from the automatic dispenser. There was no boom gate, so he just raced through. An attendant shouted in French and ran from his kiosk, but Delaney was already gone. Explaining at the autoroute exit near Lyon why he did not have a toll payment card was something he would address when the time came.

The driver of the van had to brake and swerve in order to avoid hitting the autoroute man. Delaney pushed the Peugeot as hard as it would go and the tachometer quivered into the red zone. Then there was heavy traffic on the highway, a mix of cars and big semitrailers from all over Europe. Signs warned immediately of speed cameras, radar, unmarked police cars. He doubted very much that the van driver would chance anything here, even if he had been able to clear the plaza and even if his vehicle could now catch Delaney's.

Delaney's heart was beating fast. He dried his palms, one after the other, on the thighs of his jeans. Far behind him, in the mix of cars that now streamed northward, he thought he could see a dark blue van. But the immediate danger appeared to have passed. Delaney ignored all the dire speed warnings and drove as fast as the car would go, thinking that being stopped by a radar cop might be one good solution to his immediate problem. Better still if the Espace van got stopped by the highway police instead.

He thought also that this might be the right moment to call one Jonathan Rawson in Ottawa. Suddenly, checking in with a spymaster, even a Canadian one, even one an ocean away, seemed like the wisest course of action.

Delaney knew Rawson's personal number by heart after the years they had worked together and sometimes refused to work together. It was almost 8 a.m. in Ottawa. As usual, Rawson understated his displeasure at Delaney's long silences.

"Ah, Francis," he said. "Where are you?"

"On the Autoroute de Soleil in France, somewhere just

north of a place called Loriol, Jonathan, to be very exact. I'll be passing Valance pretty soon."

"How lovely for you," Rawson said. "And all this time we thought you were working on the Heinrich thing in Germany. Silly us."

"Someone has just tried to run me off the road over here, Jonathan. They've followed me and they've tried to put me into the Rhone."

Whenever Rawson took a moment longer than usual with a comeback, Delaney knew he had well and truly captured the CSIS man's attention.

"You OK?" Rawson asked.

"Yeah. I can't see the guys anymore. Renault Espace van, dark blue. Paris plates."

"We can get the French police on this if you want. It wouldn't take long from here."

"Not sure, Jonathan. Seems OK for the moment. I just wanted to tell someone what was up in case it gets bad."

"That's what I'm here for, my friend."

It was true that Rawson had bailed him out of a number of bad scrapes in the past. A nasty few weeks in Burma's Insein Prison came immediately to mind.

"I'm in a black Peugeot 307 rental," Delaney said. "French plates. Heading to Lyon airport. Just in case there are any flaming wrecks reported later today."

Delaney knew that Rawson would be carefully writing down place-names and makes and models of cars on a sheet of paper in Ottawa.

"I don't suppose you will think it out of line, then, for me to ask you what you are actually doing in the south of France?" Rawson said.

Delaney was in one of those situations where he wasn't sure how much or how little CSIS knew, or how much they would insist on knowing before becoming useful to him again. He held his phone with his left hand and the wheel of the speeding car with his right. Even at highly illegal speeds, it would be at least two more hours to Lyon airport, depending on traffic.

"You said in your voicemail that this thing was getting more complicated by the day," Delaney said.

"My turn to ask questions, isn't it?" Rawson said.

"Jon, for fuck's sake. Someone's just tried to take me out down here. Who's so interested in what I'm doing that they would try to do that?"

"We don't even know exactly what you're doing, Francis. That's always the problem. It's always the same problem."

"What have you got, Jon? Seriously. Let's get serious, OK?"

"I would like that too in this thing."

Delaney drove in France. Rawson waited in Ottawa. Eventually, Rawson said: "Well, for one thing, the Americans are very keen to know more about what's happening over there, Francis. In Thailand in particular."

"The Americans. How did they get wind of this?"

"One thing leads to another in this sort of thing, Francis, you know that perfectly well. We make an inquiry here and there about a person or a file, and people prick up their ears. The Americans are all ears these days. You know that."

"For fuck's sake, Jon," Delaney said. "Did you have to start asking them about this stuff?"

"Everything's got everything to do with everything for the American spooks, Francis. Always. In this case, it's Stasi files they find interesting, some of which they themselves, or the CIA anyway, may have picked up off office floors in various places around East Germany when things went pear-shaped in 1989. They've been giving papers back to the Germans a fair bit in the last few years. They're very keen to know who's trying to use the information and who's trying to stop it from getting out. That sort of thing. They want to know what you know."

"Why don't they just concentrate on their crazy war on terror? Aren't they busy enough as it is finding terrorists under the bed?"

"Apparently not, Francis."

Delaney waited, and then asked: "Did the German side ask the Yanks to help them when they were looking for a place to stow Heinrich a few years back?"

"I don't know the answer to that question, Francis," Rawson said.

Delaney doubted this very much.

"Come on, Jonathan. They asked you guys, they asked the Australians and the New Zealanders, you said. Why not ask the Americans?"

"I don't think they did."

"So why do the Americans care now about Heinrich?"

"Well, here's a possible, Francis. Try this on. It's an election year in Germany. Gerhard Schroeder's government has not been too helpful at all about the war in Iraq. But it looks like the CDU could get back into power if all goes well, and then things wouldn't be as tricky for the Americans anymore with Schroeder out and like-minded people at the helm in Berlin. Angela Merkel is not as squeamish as Schroeder about helping out the Americans in Iraq, even if it's just airspace access over Germany, or back-room diplomatic support, nice comments in the media, that kind of thing. It's not going to look good to all those skittish German voters over there if the CDU now gets caught up in some crazy Cold War scandal about maybe faking a spy's death, giving a big-name spy a new identity for some reason, generally messing up. Germans want to think their governments are not doing that sort of thing. This could very much affect the outcome of the election, Francis. You must see that."

"The SPD is in power, Jon. Not CDU. It's the SPD that would have to take the heat for a faked death and a new identity for Heinrich, surely. We're talking 2001 when that happened."

Delaney wanted to know how much Rawson actually knew about the situation.

"It was the CDU guys who set Heinrich up in Bonn in 1990, Francis," Rawson said. "Christian Democrats, not SPD. They're the ones who ran him when he was spying over in the East."

"And what if both sides have messed up on this, Jon?"

"Both sides probably have. And nobody wants to carry the can. Happens all the time. I love politics, don't you?"

"So are you saying the Americans are chasing me down?"

"No, no, I don't think so. Not in cars, anyway."

"They've got their Canadian pals to find me for them instead, right?"

"Don't play naïve, Francis. Don't pretend you don't know how the world works."

"So who's trying to force me off the road and into rivers?"

"Germans?" Rawson said.

"Government? Or the German spy service? I don't think so. They don't work like that over here, Jon."

"Not officially," Rawson said. "But freelancers, maybe. Or old guard, or people who messed up in 1990 or in 2001. Who knows? Could be any number of people. You seem to be stirring the pot over there, Francis. So I hear. We're getting all kinds of echoes now."

"Please don't pretend you hear everything, OK Jon? Not CSIS," Delaney said.

"The Germans very much want to talk to you, too."

"Christ," Delaney said. "Were you indiscreet with the Germans too?"

"Francis, get serious. To get information you have to give information. Now the Germans want a little information from us. And so I need some information from you."

Delaney drove. He considered which morsel of information to now toss over to CSIS.

"You remember that Horst Becker name I asked you to check out for me a while back? The pathologist from the army hospital in Frankfurt?" he said.

"Yeah, I do," Rawson said.

"Phuket is a bit of an odd assignment for a guy like that; that's what we both figured, right? Well, he's still over in Phuket as we speak, still working with the disaster victim identification teams over there. And I have really, really pissed him off, Jon. Now I'm probably going to piss him off even worse."

"How do you plan to do that, Francis?"

"His signature is on Klaus Wolfgang Heinrich's autopsy report from 2001. Cause of death, smoke inhalation. Official, duly signed."

"Interesting."

"He's been saying very dire things to me and to a source of mine on the Interpol DVI team over in Phuket about our not so discreet inquiries into a missing tsunami file that had a set of Heinrich's fingerprints in it. This Becker guy says he doesn't like wild accusations, meddlers, journalists, pains in the ass generally. He's a very grumpy sort."

"This is getting good," Rawson said. "I like this."

"I thought you'd think that," Delaney said.

"I'll check him out a little more."

"Fine. Maybe try putting his name out among your pals in Berlin and Washington. Put the cat among the pigeons for me, will you? I'd like to see what happens when Herr Becker's name comes up in certain circles around now."

"You have the autopsy report?"

"I know where it is. It wasn't too hard to get at."

"Stand by, my friend."

"Thanks."

"I notice though that you haven't told me why this story gets you down to the south of France."

"No. I haven't yet, that's right."

"Any particular reason you can't share this with CSIS, Francis?"

"Things are still not quite clear yet, Jon."

"I can help you with that, probably."

Delaney was genuinely unsure how much to tell Rawson about Ulrich Mueller at this point. He decided not to throw Mueller's name into the mix. He would talk to Ackermann, and to Jonah Smith and others, first.

"Give me a little while more on that angle, Jon. OK?"

"I hate it when you say that, Francis. You know I hate that."

"I know, Jon, I know."

"I get called up in the middle of the night when you start saying things like that and when you start to piss people off. My wife hates it when the phone goes in the middle of the night."

"I'll try not to wake her."

"I'm thinking other people may start to call."

"I'll see if we can avoid that this time too, OK?"

"I'll have someone meet you in Germany."

"Not necessary at this stage, Jon."

"I think it is. The Germans will think it is. A little de-brief for them at this stage would mend a few fences for us, Francis."

"No way, Jon."

"You going to be on a Lyon-Berlin flight?"

"Via Frankfurt. But I have to get to the airport in one piece first, Jon. People are trying to run me off the road over here."

After his conversation with Rawson, Delaney still had a long drive to Lyon. He had been checking his rearview mirror all through the phone call. He saw no sign of the blue Espace. He slowed down a little, not wanting to be needlessly delayed now by traffic policemen.

The drive gave him some clear thinking time and worrying time. He tried as he drove to think of all the people he might have upset so far, or that Jonah Smith had upset so far, or that may have heard what Rawson liked to call echoes. It was a rather long list.

He very much doubted anyone officially representing the German government would be beating up Scotland Yard finger-print men in Phuket or trying to run down Canadian journalists on assignment there, or trying to run them off the road on assignment in France. Nor did he think the German spy service, officially at least, would feel any great need to do that sort of thing.

But, again as Rawson had said, freelancers and old guard might well be upset enough to resort to rough stuff. The question was: who had enough to lose in this thing to play rough?

Delaney wasn't sure he bought into the notion that any CDU power brokers would think it wise to play this way, even with an election on the horizon. That also went for the SPD, even though both sides had a lot to lose in the pre-election period if scandals were to hit them.

Delaney was more partial to the idea that some BND spy service types, freelancers, people who perhaps needed and wanted no authorization from on high, might be a better bet. People from the period just after the Wall went down, and who had been badly burned by Stasi in the Heinrich double-agent debacle. People who looked very foolish indeed when Stasi files started to reappear and who would now look even worse if they were shown to have faked a death to cover up their ineptitude. People not unlike Horst Becker, for example.

As Ulrich Mueller himself had said back in the chateau, spy services quite often do what they want despite a government's knowledge or wishes. Or rogue operators inside spy services. Delaney was all too familiar with that sort of scenario. Or maybe heavy political operators in an election, freelancers of another sort, will do whatever they want despite their party's official knowledge or wishes.

The problem with people like that, in such a scenario, is

that they wouldn't feel at all constrained at this stage. They would feel they had a lot at stake, they would be highly unpredictable, and, it appeared, getting angrier and more dangerous by the day.

The attendant at the toll plaza where Delaney had to get off the highway a few kilometres from Lyon airport was a man without empathy or humour. A career spent in a dark autoroute kiosk taking money from passing motorists had made him hard. He took no interest at all in Delaney's attempt to explain why he had no validated payment card. The only solution possible, the attendant insisted, was for the driver in such a highly irregular situation to pay as if he had started his journey in Marseille and travelled the whole length of road.

Delaney, under the circumstances, simply paid and then drove under the barrier which the attendant eventually raised. Despite the fact that no Renault Espace now loomed in his rearview mirror, he saw no good reason to waste valuable time arguing over a few euros and small points of procedure with French *fonctionnaires*.

He had missed the afternoon Lufthansa flight to Frankfurt by the time he returned his car, much worse for wear, and had another *fonctionnaire* moment with a distressed Hertz rental agent. The young woman had apparently had no experience whatsoever filling in the masses of forms required when a vehicle is returned in a damaged state. Delaney then had a restorative lunch at the Lyon terminal, along with three restorative glasses of wine, and managed to get himself in to Frankfurt just after 7 p.m.

Rawson was very good at ignoring Delaney's wishes and requests at such times. The reverse was true, of course. So Delaney was not terribly surprised as he exited the flight from Lyon to see two earnest young men in charcoal grey Hugo Boss suits standing to the side and scrutinizing all arriving passengers at that gate.

Young Man Number One identified himself as Richard Pearson. Rawson had assigned him to meet Delaney at the airport. His CSIS duty station was Berlin. Young Man Number Two was Karl Bauer, the BND's pick for the little international welcoming committee. Both took their work very seriously indeed.

Pearson was extremely tall and thin, all arms and legs and acute angles. His sideburns had been allowed to descend fashionably low on his cheeks, and were carefully shaped into flawless sloping wedges. Delaney imagined the young CSIS man patiently labouring over these each morning, with the shaving mirror and nice designer razor his girlfriend would have given him for Christmas.

Bauer's head was shaved clean. Most probably a style reaction to premature balding. He, too, would be spending a fair bit of time each morning with quality shaving gear and a mirror. The air around Bauer was heavy with men's cologne. The BND, like CSIS, was changing with the times.

"Anybody following you?" Pearson asked after he had gravely shaken Delaney's hand.

"I told Rawson I really didn't need an escort," Delaney said. "Thanks all the same. Everything's under control now."

"Mr. Rawson didn't think so," Pearson said. "He thought things were actually getting out of control."

"He's a worrier. Has been for a long time."

"We'd like a word with you, Mr. Delaney. And Karl's guys would."

Bauer knew a cue when he heard one.

"Exactly so," the German said. "Your inquiries are of interest to my service, Mr. Delaney."

"My inquiries for which story?"

"Story?" Bauer said.

"I'm a journalist. On assignment."

"Great cover," Pearson said.

324

"Shall we perhaps go to a quieter place to talk?" Bauer said. "The police have some interview rooms here at the airport which I'm sure they will let us use."

"There's nothing to interview me about, Karl," Delaney said. "I told Rawson everything's under control. No escort needed."

"It is not an escort I refer to, Mr. Delaney," Bauer said. "We would like some information from you, please."

The young German's face was reddening.

"Everybody wants information all the time, Karl. Sometimes they get it, sometimes they don't. Sometimes the time is not right for sharing."

"We like to cooperate with our BND colleagues whenever possible, Mr. Delaney," Pearson said.

"I'm sure you do, Richard," Delaney said. "It's the Canadian way."

He stood looking at the two young spies in silence. He wanted to see how they would fill such silences, at this stage of their careers. They looked distinctly uneasy. If there was a field manual available, perhaps they would have consulted it. Delaney was enjoying this more than he should.

"Are you refusing to come with us?" Bauer said eventually.

"Are you arresting me?"

"I am not a police officer, Mr. Delaney," Bauer said.

"Exactly," Delaney said.

"Come off it," Pearson said. "No need to get huffy."

Delaney smiled. "I am a bit huffy sometimes, Richard. It's true. It's sort of who I am. Rawson will attest to that."

"What's the harm in helping out our German friends in this?" Pearson said.

"What will our German friends do with information I give them, Richard?"

"I don't know. They'll decide later. What to do, how to play things."

"Exactly. Thank you. Information is a very tricky thing. Everything depends on how you use it. Personally, I like to know how information is going to be used before I share it. Or, actually, I just prefer to use it myself."

"That is not how these things work, Mr. Delaney," Bauer said.

"It's how they work with me," Delaney said.

"Hang on, hang on, let's not get huffy," Pearson said. "Give me a second."

Bauer tried to look menacing. Pearson pulled out his cell phone and dialed a number.

"Calling in air support, Richard?" Delaney said.

"Mr. Rawson?" Pearson said into the phone, a little too loud. "Richard Pearson here. I'm at Frankfurt airport with Frank Delaney and Karl Bauer, the BND guy on this detail. Mr. Delaney is, well, not happy with the idea of sitting down with us to have a little chat."

Pearson listened intently as Rawson spoke at the other end.

"So why do you use him?" Pearson asked eventually, looking over at Delaney, then at Bauer. He listened again for a while.

"I see. I see, I get it," Pearson said when Rawson had finished talking. He looked at Bauer again. "I see."

He listened again as Rawson spoke in Ottawa. Then he handed the phone to Delaney.

"Mr. Rawson would like to have a word with you," he said.

"Berlin your first overseas posting, Richard?" Delaney asked as he took the phone. "They can get tricky sometimes."

Rawson heard that.

"Francis, will you please stop hassling my guy over there?" he said. "Give the kid a break."

"He's doing a good job, Jon. He'll go far."

"For God's sake, man, just sit down with Bauer for a few minutes and bring him up to speed. He can probably help you."

"I doubt that, Jon." Delaney said. "Not yet anyway."

"The BND say they're worried about your safety when you go back to Berlin," Rawson said. "I've told them what happened to you on the highway down in France."

"That's nice of them to worry about my welfare, Jon."

"Let's not fool around, OK Francis? Please? For once? Just give them what you've got, let them look after you when you're in Berlin and then we can all decide what to do next."

"I'll decide."

"No, Francis."

"Yes, Jonathan."

"Christ," Rawson said.

"The Germans will want to do one thing. The CIA or whoever will want to do another thing. You guys will have your ideas. For all I know the damn Stasi will have a few thoughts on this too if there are any of them still around. Then there's the players out in Phuket, we've got a collection of good guys and bad guys over there. It's a free-for-all, always in a situation like this, Jon, you know that. So, I'll decide."

"That's not how it works, Francis. I have to tell you this over and over again. You never listen."

"I do, Jon. Sometimes."

"When it suits you."

"Yes."

Rawson said nothing for a moment. Delaney decided to help fill the silence.

"Look, Jon, you know me. I gather up little bits of stuff here and there. I pile it up and look at it. I'm a bit of a hoarder, you know that. I pile things up on my little wagon for a while and I look at it for a long time. But you know me, Jon. An ammunition wagon is not interesting in itself. I'm a rifle, not an ammunition wagon. I like to use what I've gathered. Bang, bang. Even just for target practice."

"We like to use ammunition too, Francis. We do too. We don't like to let information just sit there on the wagon either."

"No one does. The BND clearly don't, the CIA don't, the Yanks in general. Police certainly don't. RCMP, the BKA, who knows who else. It goes on and on. Stasi. There's a good example. Stasi were masters at gathering information, for years, right? But they really knew how to use it and when to use it. They had fairly strong ideas on how to use information. They really used it very, very well."

"I don't need a history lesson today, Francis."

"OK, I'll stop. I'll put your guy back on."

Delaney handed the telephone back to Pearson.

"Here you go, Richard," he said. "Your boss is a little pissed off."

He heard Rawson's faint metallic voice coming out of the phone before Pearson could put it to his ear.

Under the circumstances, Delaney changed his travel plans. He decided it would be unwise now to go to Berlin at all. Too many people there were interested in his movements. Bad guys and, supposedly, good guys. He was standing in one of the world's busiest airports, with a credit card in his pocket. There were any number of ways to get to Thailand from Frankfurt that night. The big flights to Asia left Germany very late, and he could be on one of them with no trouble.

Pearson and Bauer both looked stricken when he told them he had decided to head to Bangkok right away.

"This is a mistake, Mr. Delaney," Bauer said. "This is not good."

"I think it's good, Karl. That's what counts," he said.

Delaney managed to buy a very expensive one-way ticket to Bangkok on a Thai Airways flight leaving just before midnight. Flight 7663 would be in Thailand by mid-afternoon the next day, and he could be in Phuket by dinnertime Sunday. Pearson and Bauer accompanied him to various airport desks as he made his arrangements. Both of them also spent a bit of time on their phones.

"I could buy you each a beer before I take off," Delaney said eventually. "Cheer you both up."

Pearson looked interested. Bauer did not.

"Your lack of cooperation has now been noted in senior circles, Mr. Delaney," Bauer said frostily. "You should expect no help from my service now."

"That's OK, Karl. I understand."

"I'm not sure my guys are onside anymore either, Mr. Delaney," Pearson said.

"I'm used to that," Delaney said. "We have a bit of a love-hate relationship going on. Sometimes it works, sometimes it doesn't work. It's like a marriage. Don't worry. Tell Rawson I love him all the same."

Pearson seemed to be trying hard not to smile. Bauer would not stand for any smiling at this stage.

Ackermann, too, was disappointed about Delaney's change of plans.

"Come to Berlin just for tonight, Francis. We need to talk about this," he said when Delaney called from an airport bar.

"We can talk again on the phone later, Gunter. I'll call you when I get back to Phuket and I'll let you know how things are looking at that end. Or maybe an email's better. I'll tell you all about Heinrich and our French connection from there. It's all coming together now, this story. OK? Don't worry."

"This could be very big, Francis. It's big."

"I know that," Delaney said.

"Tell me a bit of what you've got," Ackermann said.

"I'm a little worried about this phone now, Gunter. I'll be in touch from Phuket."

"Give me some kind of indication of what you've got, Francis."

Delaney hesitated.

"Gay," he said.

"Gay?" Ackermann said.

"Yup."

"What, the two of them? Together?"

"You got it."

"Great story," Ackermann said.

"You got it."

Chapter 16

Delaney returned to Phuket at what the Thais would describe as a particularly auspicious moment. It was Sunday, April 3rd. Monday would be exactly one hundred days since the tsunami disaster killed thousands of people. Thai Buddhists believe that the hundred-day mark after a death—or after many thousands of deaths in this case—is precisely the moment when the souls of the dead can be put at rest and when those still living can move on.

Elaborate ceremonies were planned for each of the major disaster sites around Phuket province. On Patong Beach, 14 kilometres outside of Phuket town, there was to be an international sunrise ceremony with prayers by Buddhist monks and by priests from a variety of religions, as well as speeches and thanksgiving and candle lightings and banners and the launching of wreaths and little model boats in memory of the dead. Families of the foreign victims were arriving in Phuket to join the observances, as were politicians and diplomats and police and media from dozens of countries.

The airport was teeming with people when Delaney got off the shuttle from Bangkok. At first he was bewildered by the intense activity on a Sunday afternoon. The Phuket terminal had been busy ever since the tsunami, with identification teams arriving from all over the globe and aid workers coming and going, and with the relatives of the dead. But the throng when Delaney arrived was unusual.

His taxi driver, wearing a bright red baseball cap with a CNN logo, told him what was going on, apparently shocked that anyone would not be aware.

"One hundred days, one hundred days," the driver sang out from the front seat. "Tomorrow big ceremony, very big. All ghosts will rest. Is very good. Tourists start to come back maybe. Fishermen go back out to the sea."

Delaney was, therefore, lucky to find accommodation of any sort at the Metropole Hotel. He had no reservation and was only able to get a room because of a last-minute cancellation. When he eventually got to his room and put down his bag, he went out on the balcony into the early-evening air and breathed deeply of the tropics. The heat and the humidity and the fragrant flowering plants could not have been more different from the cold spring rain and diesel fumes of Germany.

He called Jonah Smith's room at the Bay Hotel. No answer. He called Conchi's room at the Royal. She was out too. Neither Smith nor Conchi carried cell phones. And, Delaney acknowledged as he took a first drink from the mini-bar, he had arrived unannounced. There was no reason for anyone to be waiting anxiously by their telephones for his return.

Delaney woke fully clothed on his bed just after 10 p.m. A post-flight session of whiskies and a nap had gone on too long. He called Smith's room again. This time the fingerprint man was in.

"It's me," Delaney said.

"Oh, Frank, good, I'm glad you're back," Smith said.

"Careful what you say in that room of yours, Jonah," Delaney said.

He was glad that the room he himself had been randomly

given at the Metropole could not have been wired up as Smith's was. Not yet, in any case.

"Sorry, sorry, yes, of course," Smith said. "Silly of me."

"We've got a lot to talk over, Jonah. But let's pick a proper spot to do that."

"Good, good," Smith said. "When?"

"Soon, as soon as possible."

"Tonight?"

"Maybe. I'm thinking, though, that I might come over there and say a few choice words into your microphones first. Put up a little smokescreen. Then maybe we can have a real talk tomorrow. Something like that."

"Tomorrow's the big ceremony at Patong, Frank. I've got to go to that. It's really early in the morning. All the DVI teams have to go. Everybody's going to go."

"Friend and foe alike."

"I would say," Smith said.

"I think I'd better come along," Delaney said.

He got to Smith's hotel around 11 p.m. for a bit of preventative play acting. He hoped Smith's acting skills were up to the challenge, for they would have no agreed script and a very attentive audience. Smith had a half-finished beer on the go and a fresh one already opened for his guest.

"Great to have you back, Frank," Smith said, pointing to a wall socket in the living room where they were standing.

"Great to be back, Jonah," Delaney said as he knelt to peer at the wallplate. Smith came closer, crouched down, and pointed at a tiny black semicircle that was just visible where the right side of the plate met the wall.

They both stood up and moved over to a sofa facing the hidden microphone.

"So, Frank, tell me. What did you come up with over there?" Smith said.

"Nothing. Not a damn thing," Delaney said. "A complete waste of time and money."

"Bad luck," Smith said. "Heinrich, all of that? No go?"

"We're no further ahead. The guy who was helping me out came up with nothing we can use. It's all a bit of a dead end. I'm stumped."

"Bad luck," Smith said again.

They drank beer.

"And Horst Becker?" Smith said.

Delaney thought Smith was showing a strong talent for disinformation. Becker himself might well be listening to their late-night performance,

"No connection that I can see," Delaney said. "I don't see where he fits in at all."

"Bugger," Smith said.

"Yeah," Delaney said. "Maybe after all this he's actually just pissed off that we were unfairly accusing the German team of something. Like he says."

They tried not to make it all sound too lame and they did not go on for too long. They were amateur actors, after all. But they did what they could over their beers to make it as clear as possible to their listeners that the tsunami file story was not coming together as Delaney had hoped.

"So who is it in that body bag then?" Smith asked.

"I don't see anymore how it could be Heinrich," Delaney said.

"It's got to be," Smith said. "The fingerprints matched."

"It can't be him, Jonah. You only had a few decent prints off that body in the end. And people make mistakes."

"I don't make mistakes like that," Smith said sharply.

Delaney hoped Smith's professional pride and his absolute faith in the reliability of fingerprints would not make him protest too much. He appeared to be forgetting who he was supposed to be in their little morality play.

"I don't think I buy it anymore," Delaney said. "I really don't."

Smith's expression turned glum. Delaney was suddenly having trouble seeing what was in character for the fingerprint man and what was not. He decided to end the performance and let their audience go home to bed.

"Don't let it worry you, Jonah," he said. "Sometimes things like this happen. I've had it happen a hundred times. In my line of work you sometimes think you're on to a big story and it simply doesn't pan out."

They finished their beers, chatted for a few minutes longer, agreed to meet before sunrise on Patong Beach, and said their goodbyes. They heard no applause coming out from the wall-mounted listening device, but they very much hoped the performance had been a success.

The world's media like nothing better than well-organized public displays of grief, particularly in exotic locales. The hordes of TV crews and radio recordists and reporters jostling for position on Patong Beach the next morning got precisely what they were looking for.

Diplomats and politicians and potentates also appreciate a good bit of pomp, pathos and ceremony. One hundred days after the Asian tsunami, on 4 April 2005, on Patong Beach at sunrise, they, too, got what they desired. Hundreds of people had gathered at the water's edge before the sun came up. Almost all, locals and foreigners alike, were wearing white as requested by the organizers. In the slowly fading darkness, a sea of candles flickered and yellow mourners' lanterns swayed. Dozens of bamboo poles, with multicoloured banners flying, had been driven into the soft sand.

Delaney stood well back, with Smith and Conchi. He had found them with difficulty in the crowd, not quite where Smith had said they would be standing. Conchi, as usual, gave Delaney a kiss on both cheeks but even in the dim glow of lantern light he could see she was not entirely pleased that he was back. She saw him, Delaney thought, as an inauspicious arrival on what was supposed to be an auspicious day.

A long column of Buddhist monks filed silently onto the sand wearing their burnt orange robes. Prayers were to begin the proceedings and then there would be speeches and testimonials and a minute's silence. Delaney watched mourners weeping and holding tightly to each other. Conchi held tightly to Smith's arm. She had apparently decided that on this occasion her sky blue UN shirt would not do. She wore a simple, locally made silk blouse, the brilliant white setting off her dark tan. Delaney could very much see what Smith saw in this young Spanish seeker of lost identities.

He scanned the crowd for friend and foe. Not far from where he stood with Smith and Conchi he saw Stefan Zalm in amongst a crowd of Dutch police and forensics officers. They had not worn white; all wore their navy blue Dutch DVI team shirts instead. Delaney had long since decided that Zalm was not in the enemy camp.

Far off, near the dignitaries' stand, Delaney saw the German team. They too had decided against wearing white. Even in the lantern light and the faint glow of the coming sunrise, he could see that Horst Becker was there. There could be no mistaking his bald pate and short bulldog's body. Delaney tapped Smith on the shoulder and pointed. Smith spotted Becker too. They said nothing.

Becker was also scanning the crowd. As mourners let go of flimsy paper lanterns that then wafted gently skywards on warm air currents from the tiny candles burning inside, Becker also tapped a colleague's shoulder and pointed to where Delaney and Smith were standing.

Becker's teammate leaned over and Becker said something

into his ear. That man, too, scanned the crowd. He nodded gravely.

After the Thai governor and other VIPs had spoken, a sombre Detective Chief Superintendent Adrian Braithwaite and an equally sombre Colonel Pridiyathorn, in full-dress police uniforms, then rose from their seats on the dignitaries' stand and went together to the podium. First Pridiyathorn, speaking in Thai, then Braithwaite in English said the requisite words of grief and of thanks to all who were working in the disaster victim identification effort. Ruth Connolly trudged through the sand as they spoke, distributing press releases to assembled scribes seeking post-tsunami morsels to feed the insatiable media beast.

It was Braithwaite and Pridiyathorn who led the ceremony into the minute of silence. As he stood with his head slightly bowed, Delaney again looked over toward Becker. Becker, too, was not properly concentrating on the officially designated sixty seconds of commemoration. The German pathologist glanced discreetly over at his foes, bullet-head not bowed at all. Like Delaney, his thoughts apparently focused on present difficulties, not on soothing the souls of the dead and the spirits of those bereft.

With the brilliant tropical sun fully up and the ceremony over, people began to slowly drift away from the beach. Many remained, however, for further private mourning or perhaps because it was simply a beautiful place to be.

Conchi said she had to head to work. Smith said he could take more time off.

"Let's talk here then," Delaney said. "Just the right place for a confidential chat."

Becker & Company appeared to have left along with the departing throng.

"I can't stay," Conchi said. "But I should stay, to stop you two mischief boys from making up some crazy plan."

"Don't worry, Conchi. I'm just going to fill Jonah in on a few things. We're not going to start an international incident right here on the beach," Delaney said.

"Not yet maybe," Conchi said. "After you get off the beach maybe."

"Don't worry, Conchi," Smith said.

"Don't worry, don't worry," Conchi said. "Every time Frank Delaney is in Phuket that is all you can ever say."

Smith laughed. "Don't worry," he said.

He kissed her on the forehead. Delaney duly noted Smith's increased capacity for public displays of affection and the way in which such displays were received. Conchi touched Smith's face and then turned and walked off toward the road, sandals in hand as she made her way though the golden sand.

Smith watched her go.

"She is. Very," Delaney said.

"Yes, isn't she," Smith said. "Very."

"Complicated for you," Delaney said.

"No so much, Frank. Maybe not."

"Oh?"

"Later, later," Smith said. "First tell me what you've got."

They walked to the water's edge and then strolled along the strip of firmer moist sand as they talked. The mourners and the journalists and the local officials who had stayed gave them the anonymity they required.

Delaney filled Smith in on the details of what he had discovered in Berlin, then in Bonn and then in France. He held nothing back. This was to be a day for important decisions and careful strategy. Smith deserved to be fully briefed. He listened with the concentration of a man who has worked a long time with the police.

"Incredible," Smith said eventually.

"That's how I would describe it," Delaney said.

"Imagine a man with that kind of life story—East Berlin, West Berlin, Cold War, spying, constantly dissembling, all that kind of very, what, very mysterious, politicized European kind of life—ending up killed on a beach way out here in Thailand by a freak wave."

"Ends up in a body bag in an old shipping container, ends up getting identified by a fingerprint man from Scotland Yard via Interpol."

"Ends up getting identified by a reporter from Montreal," Smith said.

"I got some more details that we needed. You made the identification."

"You got his life story."

"Some of it. You never get it all."

"You got the Mueller story. This business of a gay affair between a major spy and the head of the BKA. Unimaginable. No one knows about that. It's an incredible story and you got that for us."

"Some people know about that, Jonah."

"Not many. It's never been public."

"No. That's true."

"You're very good at what you do, Frank," Smith said. "Truly."

"So are you, Jonah. Truly."

"So here we find ourselves."

"Yup."

"And the next step?"

"Information is not valuable unless it's used, Jonah. Right?" Smith looked at him for a long time.

"I'm a man who makes identifications and hands them over to my police brethren," Smith said eventually. "All my life. Making the identification was the thing. Someone else decided what to do next."

"We don't have that luxury, Jonah. It's a big bad complicated world out there."

"So it is."

"I'm surprised I need to remind a Scotland Yard man about
that."

Smith said nothing.

"So?" Delaney said. "Next step?"

"We tell someone," Smith said.

"Yeah? Like who? How? What for?"

"Come on, Frank, for goodness' sake," Smith said.

"You're the ID man. We've got the ID now. What do you
want to do with it?"

Smith looked genuinely perplexed. He studied the tips of
his fingers as he pondered the situation.

"We'll go to Braithwaite," he said eventually.

"OK," Delaney said. "Then what? What happens to the
information then? What's the result?"

Smith was starting to look extremely uneasy.

"Come on, Frank. He'll act on it."

"You sure?"

"He's a career policeman."

"So was Mueller."

"Come off it, man. What else is there for us?"

"Well, as I told you, I've got some very good friends in the
Canadian spy service. They have friends in a lot of other spy services. We can tell them, for example. Tell them the whole story
and see what happens then."

"What would happen?"

"Up to them. Just like with police. It would be up to them
how they used the information."

"That's no good."

"Why not?"

"Well, what if they use it, I don't know, some way that's not
good?"

"Not good? Interesting concept. What does that mean?"

"Not the way we think it should be used."

"Which is?"

"Frank . . ."

"What outcome do you want, Jonah?"

"I just want people to know about this," Smith said.

"Who? How many? Where? To achieve what?"

"That's the sort of question you journalists have to ask," Smith said.

"Yes."

"Well?"

"OK, Jonah, fine, so we'll be journalists in this one. Is that what you want? We won't be spy guys or friends of spies. Not cops or friends of cops."

"Well, we certainly can't find out about a story like this and just let it go."

"Tell your cop brethren who the man was, and how Ulrich Mueller was connected to him, and tell them about the coverup and let it go. Make the identification and let it go. Isn't that what you used to do?"

"This is different," Smith said.

"It's a big bad old complicated world out there, Jonah."

They agreed to let the big questions ride for a little while longer. But Smith seemed in no hurry to go back to the IMC and Delaney wanted a briefing of his own.

"Becker?" Delaney said. "How's he been this past while? He certainly saw me today at the ceremony. He may think it's his move now. Or maybe he's the kind who'll wait for opponents to make another move."

"He hasn't said a word for quite a while," Smith said. "Since that time he went to see Conchi at her hotel just after you left; he hasn't come near us again."

"He scare her bad?"

"Yes, she was scared. But she's pretty tough. She didn't give anything away."

"He doesn't need much from her anyway if he's listening to your conversations with his little microphones. I hope he heard our little playlet last night."

"You think that's him with the microphones?"

"Quite possibly," Delaney said.

"Who else?"

"Police, maybe, from a couple of countries. Your own people, maybe. Braithwaite, for example. He's got a big stake in this. The Thais, maybe."

"No," Smith said. "Not Braithwaite. Not my people."

"German police. German intelligence. BND. The Americans."

"The Americans?"

"No, probably not. Not yet, in your case anyway. They're interested in what I do now, as I told you. Not you. Not yet. That bug was planted when the Yanks didn't even know your name. If they even know it now."

"The Americans can't be that interested in this in any case, surely."

"The Americans have a long history of taking a great interest in things that might influence elections. Anywhere. Things that might put like-minded administrations in power somewhere, or recalcitrants out of power."

Smith looked dubious.

"What about your people?" he said. "Your friends at CSIS."

"No, I don't think so. Canadian spooks play things a little different. They've got different priorities. They're still not in the big leagues. And they'd figure they don't need to plant microphones on this one anyway. They think they've got me for that sort of thing."

"Do they?"

"Not always."

They walked some more. A man and a woman dressed in white stood at the edge of the sand and looked forlornly out. The woman threw a small bouquet of flowers onto the water and started to cry. Her partner rubbed infinity patterns on her back with his left hand. Their child, a sunburned blonde girl also dressed in white, built sand castles not far away and talked happily to herself as she worked.

Delaney and Smith stopped to watch from a distance.

"I'm leaving Fiona," Smith said suddenly. "I thought you should know that, for some reason. Not sure why."

"Well, well, well. There's the lead story, as we say in the trade," Delaney said.

"Yeah. It's a pretty big story."

"Next step?" Delaney asked. "After that?"

"Not quite sure at this stage. Spain maybe. Or Bosnia. Not sure."

"I see. With Conchi."

"Oh yes," Smith said.

"She knows this?"

"Who? Fiona or Conchi?" Smith smiled wryly.

"Both. Either."

"Fiona, no. Not yet. Conchi, yes."

"Spain. Nice this time of year."

"It wouldn't be right away. There's still work to do here. And Conchi has her work left to do in Bosnia."

"Bosnia then."

"Not sure yet. We'll sort it out."

"Lots of unidentified bodies still in Bosnia."

"Perhaps they'll need some help from a slightly damaged middle-aged fingerprint man over there," Smith said with another smile, this one almost rueful. "That's who I am."

"They're always in demand, my friend. Lots of identification work left to do out there in the big bad world."

"Disaster victims," Smith said. "People not unlike myself."

"You're no victim, my friend," Delaney said.

"No?"

"No. I don't think so," Delaney said.

They agreed to meet in the afternoon at the Whale Bar. Smith said he needed to get back to work and needed more time to think. Delaney was glad of the unexpected additional time for thinking and resting.

Back at the hotel, he read a couple of agitated email messages from Rawson and listened to some Rawson voicemails. His editors at *International Geographic* were understandably agitated as well. There was little else of note on his computer screen or on his phone. Kate Hunter was maintaining her silence. Delaney was not sure when, or if, he would try to break that silence.

He slept for a while—in a hiatus, at that familiar point where a story, as a result of a reporter's intervention, begins to take on a new life of its own.

At 3 p.m. he showered and dressed and made his way past the smiling girls in the hotel lobby. All was quiet on the streets as his taxi made its way to the Whale Bar. The bar, too, was very quiet. Off-duty DVI teams had not yet filed in to swap stories.

A few people, not locals, were on high wooden stools, chatting to Prasan the barman. Only a couple of tables in the dimness down past the row of stools were filled. Smith was sitting at a small round table near the front, in a pool of warm sunlight that had formed on the floor below the plate-glass façade. Delaney was surprised, and not pleased, to see Conchi and Zalm sitting with him. This was to have been a working meeting, a meeting for private discussion about next steps—not for after-work drinks.

Smith sensed his displeasure.

"Conchi and Stefan are just going to have a fast welcome-back drink with us, Frank, and then we can get down to business."

Delaney looked over at Zalm.

"Jonah is being very mysterious, Frank. He hasn't told me a thing," Zalm said, raising his glass. "I'm still not to be trusted, it seems."

"All will be revealed in due course," Smith said.

"Will it?" Delaney said.

"You're in a very bad mood this afternoon," Conchi said.

"Yeah, I am," Delaney said.

"Have a drink," Zalm said. "I'll buy."

Zalm summoned Prasan. The barman came over, gave their table a wipe, and smiled broadly at them all.

"Welcome back to the Whale," he said to Delaney.

"Singhas again all around, I think, Prasan. Beer OK for you, Frank?" Zalm said.

"I'll have a small whisky with mine, thanks," Delaney said.

"He is in a very bad mood, Prasan," Conchi said. "Give him a very big whisky."

It was true that Delaney was beginning to feel irritated, uneasy, that valuable time was being lost with social niceties in tropical bars.

They drank, made small talk, wasted time. Delaney could see Smith watching him and trying to make silent apologies across the table for the delay.

"Frank Delaney is now going to make things right," Conchi said eventually, out of the blue. She seemed uncharacteristically giddy that afternoon. Perhaps she was in love. Perhaps it was the beer. "Then we can all get back to our normal work."

"Is our work normal, Conchi, my dear?" Zalm asked, red in the face from the hot sun streaming through the expanse of window glass.

Delaney fought back his feelings of frustration. He sat half listening to the chatter and looked idly around. Prasan was deep in conversation with the drinkers sitting at the bar. One of the patrons from the back tables, a fat man in a sweat-stained white mourner's outfit, headed to the toilets near the entrance.

A tall man, not a Thai, came in from outside and sat at the lone table between their own and the L-shaped bar. Too close, Delaney thought, becoming increasingly irritated, for any serious conversation to be had with Smith even when Conchi and Zalm decided it was time to leave. He began to doubt that any real progress would be made that day at all.

The new arrival had a close-cropped military haircut and wore big aviator's sunglasses with dark green lenses. He set down on the floor a black Nike sports bag he had been carrying. He nodded silently at Delaney, and then went up to the bar to order his drink. *Cop*, Delaney thought. *Or soldier. Tough guy.*

After about 15 more minutes, Conchi and Zalm finished their beers and got ready to go.

"So sorry, mischief boys, we will go now and leave you all alone," Conchi said.

"Good idea," Delaney said.

"Oh please, Frank Delaney, cheer up today, OK?" she said.

Conchi got up, looked around for her bag. It was under Smith's chair. Zalm stood up too.

"We will leave you two very serious people alone," Zalm said. "But maybe we'll have some dinner tonight, Jonah, OK?"

"We'll see, Stefan," Smith said. "I'll call you."

Then things began to happen very, very fast.

Delaney noticed that the tall drinker in aviator glasses had still not come back to his table. He instead sat on a bar stool, drinking his beer there and talking with Prasan.

As Conchi and Zalm made their preparations to leave, the aviator apparently decided it was time to pay and go as well. He quickly placed some Thai baht notes on the bar, drained his glass and strode toward the door. Delaney watched him as he went by. The man looked back over his shoulder from the doorway, and then he was out and hurrying across the street.

Conchi kissed Smith goodbye. Delaney also got a brief kiss

on the cheek. Zalm shook Delaney's hand. Then Zalm and Conchi started to move toward the door, hoisting shoulder bags. Sun poured through the window. All was silent for a moment.

Then Delaney saw the aviator standing on the other side of the street, looking in at them from a distance through the window of the Whale. Delaney watched him through the glass and the car and motorbike traffic beyond. Then he looked over to where the man had first sat down. The Nike bag was still there on the floor.

"That guy's forgotten his bag," Delaney said.

"What guy?" Smith said.

Suddenly, all was clear—all was in bright, sharp, sunlit focus. Prasan headed their way from behind the bar to wipe the table and collect empty bottles. Delaney looked out the window again and then back to the abandoned bag. He looked through the window again. He saw the aviator holding a cell phone in his left hand, tapping numbers with his right.

Delaney jumped up, knocking a chair over in his haste. He grabbed Smith by the shoulder and heaved him to his feet.

"Run!" Delaney shouted. "Out, out, out now. Fast!"

"What's up?" Smith shouted.

Delaney half dragged, half carried Smith to the door, staying very low.

"Out, out, out now!" Delaney shouted again. "Bomb, there's a bomb! Prasan, get down, down, get down now!"

When the bag exploded with a terrific boom and flash, time, for a split second, stood still just as witnesses and survivors of such bombings invariably say. Delaney and Smith had just cleared the doorway when the bag blew. Delaney felt the shock-wave on his back and the *whump* of hot air pounding his eardrums. Debris and shrapnel peppered his neck and back as he tumbled with Smith out of the Whale and into the street. The top of a bar table cartwheeled out with them.

The plate-glass window disintegrated into a million deadly

projectiles. Conchi and Zalm had made it well out into the street before the bomb went off. But they too were showered with flying glass and other chunks of debris. Delaney saw them both go down hard onto the road.

Delaney stayed on the sidewalk where he fell, crawling flat through bits of rubble toward Conchi and Zalm, still trying to drag Smith with one arm as he went. Passersby screamed and shouted and pointed. A local man was down on the sidewalk with them, moaning and holding his hands to a big bleeding gash on his temple. A motorbike had overturned on the road. No cars moved.

Delaney stopped crawling away from the Whale and lay on his side on the street. He didn't think he was very badly hurt. His neck and back were itchy with shrapnel hits and blood and sweat, but he didn't think he was going to die. His ears were ringing and he thought an eardrum might have burst.

Smith lay panting beside him. He was face down, flat on his stomach, but he was alive. In shock, probably, but alive.

"Jonah, Jonah," Delaney called out. "Are you OK?"

Delaney could hear his own voice only faintly, as if from a distance. Smith didn't answer. His ears, too, were likely damaged by the blast.

Delaney crawled over to where Smith lay. He shook his shoulder gently. Smith moaned, turned his head slightly and made eye contact. His eyes closed again. Delaney rolled over and looked again toward Conchi and Zalm. Conchi was trying to pick herself up from the gutter and the broken glass. She looked badly scraped up. Zalm, though, was lying motionless. Conchi managed to get to her knees. She tried to pull the Dutchman up and shake him conscious.

"Leave him, Conchi, leave him," Delaney shouted out. His voice was weak and dry and hoarse. "It's better not to move him."

"Jonah!" Conchi shouted. "Jonah!"

"He's OK," Delaney said. "He's OK."

"Jonah," she called out again. She sat back on the sidewalk, hugging her knees and crying.

In the distance, as he lay in the street, Delaney heard sirens coming, still far off. Two local policemen ran up to the scene, handguns drawn, staying low. They shouted to each other and to the crowd in Thai.

In English one of them shouted to Delaney: "Bomb? Bomb?"

Delaney heard the words as if from a great distance, as if in a dream.

"Yes," he said. "Bomb."

"Who are you?" the policeman asked, coming closer.

"Journalist," Delaney said. "Journalist."

EPILOGUE

Senior Minister Is Latest Victim in Widening German Spy Scandal

BERLIN, 28 May 2005 (Deutsche Press) – The growing scandal over the true identity of German super-spy Klaus Wolfgang Heinrich claimed another political victim on Wednesday with the sudden resignation of Interior Minister Edmund Heilbronner.

Heilbronner, 59, who is one of the most powerful ministers in the SPD government of Chancellor Gerhardt Schroeder, had until now been resisting repeated calls by some opposition parties and the media for him to resign in the wake of spectacular revelations in *Die Welt* newspaper on 30 April that Heinrich, long regarded as a hero for his many years of supposed work in the then East Berlin as a spy for the West, was in fact a Stasi double agent.

The *Die Welt* story, written by the newspaper's Political Editor Gunter Ackermann, revealed that some seven years after the fall of the Berlin Wall and Heinrich's subsequent installation in Bonn as a highly paid civil servant, his true identity was covered up when certain declassified Stasi files came to light. The story also reported that Heinrich did not die in a house fire near Bonn in October 2001 as previously reported, but in fact drowned in the tsunami disaster in Thailand on 26 December 2004.

In another revelation, the *Die Welt* article revealed that Heinrich had con-ducted a secret homosexual affair with BKA President Ulrich Mueller for at least several years while living in Bonn, and that the police chief had been forced to leave his post in disgrace in 2001 when the relationship was discovered. The Interior Minister and the BKA said at the time that Mueller had opted for early retirement in France, where he now lives. No other explanation was ever given.

Announcing his resignation on Wednesday to journalists at a packed news conference, Heilbronner insisted he had done nothing illegal and claimed that the decision to cover up the truth about Heinrich's Stasi affiliation and to subsequently provide him with a new identity in Thailand in 2001 had been taken by unnamed individuals from the previous CDU administration.

"My party came to power in 1998. That was after the Stasi files in question became known in certain circles and after the decision to hide the truth about Heinrich's work for Stasi," a defiant Heilbronner said, reading from a written statement. "It is the previous CDU government that did not take adequate care to check on Heinrich's past and the true nature of his activities in the years before he left East Berlin in 1990. It is the CDU that is responsible for this debacle."

"I am resigning my cabinet post today only because as Interior Minister I must take responsibility for the decision not to immediately reveal the security threat and potential blackmail threat posed by the homosexual relationship between Heinrich and Mueller when this became known in certain circles."

Heilbronner refused to say whether he had resigned voluntarily or had been ordered to do so by Chancellor Schroeder. He also refused to answer questions about whether he or any members of his government were aware, at the time Ulrich Mueller was forced to leave the BKA, of Heinrich's past as a double agent.

The Heinrich scandal comes when a federal election is on the horizon and opinion polls show Schroeder's SPD substantially behind the opposition CDU, led by the party's new leader Angela Merkel.

However, the CDU's party chairman Oskar Kaufmann, who served as senior adviser to former Chancellor Helmut Kohl before the previous government lost power in 1998, has also resigned over the Heinrich scandal. Kaufmann, 70, claims that so-called out of control elements in Germany's BND security service were responsible for the original decision in approximately 1997 to cover up Heinrich's work for Stasi and then to fake Heinrich's death in 2001 and set him up with a new identity in Thailand.

Kaufmann claimed when he resigned last week that these unnamed agents became alarmed in 2001 after it appeared the United States Central Intelligence Agency had deduced—using the recently decrypted "Rosewood file" the CIA had taken into its possession in the chaotic days after the fall of the Wall in 1989—that Heinrich continued to dupe the BND and the government for a number of years after his return to the West.

"No one who had served in the Kohl government at the time ever gave authorization in 2001 for Herr Heinrich to be provided with a new identity in Thailand or anywhere else," Kaufmann said in his resignation statement.

It is not clear why the Americans did not make public the truth about Heinrich if they knew it in 2001 or earlier. A U.S. Embassy spokesman in Berlin would say only that the developing spy scandal was "an internal German affair."

Both the SPD and the CDU have been resisting calls from the Greens and from political commentators for a full public inquiry. More resignations, and possibly criminal charges, are thought to be inevitable in the affair.

In a related development that could further tarnish reputations on both sides of the country's political divide, the BKA said on Monday that federal police now wish to question one Horst Reinhard Becker, who is a staff pathologist at the main army hospital in Frankfurt. Becker was detained last week by police in Phuket, Thailand, where he has been working on the German victim identification team established after the tsunami disaster that killed thousands of people, including many European tourists and expatriates.

The *Die Welt* article that revealed the Heinrich scandal alleges Becker falsified a German autopsy report to show incorrectly that Heinrich died in the Bonn fire in 2001. The article alleged that Becker then travelled to Thailand earlier this year to try to prevent proper identification of Heinrich's body after the tsunami. Becker was taken intro custody shortly after publication of the newspaper article but has so far not been charged with any offence.

In a press release, Thai Tsunami Victim Identification (TTVI) spokeswoman Ruth Connolly said: "The operation's joint commanders will undertake immediate inquiries into allegations by *Die Welt* and by an Interpol officer in Phuket that one or more members of the German team at the disaster site tampered with or removed material from a DVI file in order to hide the true identity of the individual in question."

The Interpol officer who made the Heinrich identification in Thailand, seconded Scotland Yard fingerprint expert Jonah Smith, was almost killed when a small explosive device was detonated in a popular bar in Phuket on 4 April. Neither the Thai police nor the DVI operation spokeswoman would comment on whether Smith may have been targeted by those trying to keep the Heinrich story a secret.

A 26-year-old Thai man working in the bar died in the bombing, and more than a dozen other people, including a Canadian magazine journalist on assignment in Phuket, were injured by shrapnel and flying glass.

Disgraced Former Policeman Shot Dead in Rural France

PARIS, 29 July 2005 (Newswire) – The disgraced former head of Germany's federal police agency, Ulrich Mueller, has been killed in an apparent botched burglary at his home in southern France, police said on Friday.

Police in the French town of Privas said Mueller, 68, was shot once at point blank range by a heavy gauge shotgun in a ground floor bedroom of his house in the hills outside Saint Lager Bressac in the Ardeche region. His body was found early on Thursday morning by a housekeeper when she arrived for work.

An investigation is underway, a police spokesman said, but detectives were proceeding on the assumption that Mueller, who was infirm and used a wheelchair, was shot after confronting an intruder in his home.

However, a local radio report said the housekeeper, Veronique Chagny, had told police nothing appeared to have been stolen and there were no signs of forced entry in the large house where Mueller lived alone.

Mueller retired to the Ardeche in 2001 after a long and successful career with the German federal police, known as the BKA. In April of this year, an article in the Germany's respected *Die Welt* newspaper, citing Mueller himself, an Interpol official and "a reliable Canadian source with inside knowledge of the situation," revealed that the BKA chief had been forced to resign when it became known he had a long-running homosexual affair with one of the former West Germany's most famous spies in the East.

The article alleged that the spy, Klaus Heinrich, had in fact for many years been a Stasi double agent.

French police dismissed suggestions Mueller may have been murdered in revenge for his providing information to *Die Welt*.

"There are many break-ins in the isolated houses of foreigners in rural France," Captain Laurent Chevrier of the Privas detachment said. "We have no reason to believe that Monsieur Mueller was murdered."

Also in April of this year, a Paris-based architect who had worked on the renovation of Mueller's home was seriously assaulted in the house by robbers. Pierre Rochemaure, 47, received serious head injuries from the beating and was in a coma for several days before eventually being released from a local hospital and returning to Paris.

There have been no arrests in connection with that incident. Police said it is too early to tell whether the perpetrators of the April break-in and beating may also have been responsible for the Mueller shooting.

The BKA press office in Weisbaden, Germany, said the police agency would have no comment on Mueller's death.

Scotland Yard Fingerprint Man Takes UN Bosnia Assignment

MetPolice Magazine

LONDON, 15 September 2005 – One of the most experienced fingerprint analysts in the Metropolitan Police Service, Jonah Smith, has landed himself another plum assignment, this time with the United Nations Mission in Bosnia-Herzegovina.

Smith was until recently seconded by Scotland Yard to Interpol headquarters in the picturesque French city of Lyon. Interpol in turn sent Smith to Thailand in January of this year to help in the massive international effort to identify bodies of victims in the tsunami disaster.

Although he is a Met civilian staffer, Smith has always showed a strong aptitude for investigative work, his colleagues say. While in Thailand, Smith used his police instincts to uncover a plot to cover up the true identity of a German national killed in the tsunami.

Smith became suspicious when he found that a DVI file had been tampered with but he was eventually able to positively identify the body in question as that of a former Stasi spy, using only poor-quality partial fingerprints. Solid police work by the Met's Detective Chief Superintendent Adrian Braithwaite, assigned to the Thailand operation as joint commander, led to the subsequent arrest of a pathologist on Germany's DVI team.

Smith has been on sick leave in sunny Spain since being injured in a bombing incident in Phuket in April just as the tsunami file affair was about to be made public. He received a broken arm, suffered multiple lacerations and lost most of the hearing in one ear as a result of that explosion.

Thai police have yet to make any arrests in connection with the bombing, which killed one person and injured a number of others. Smith brushes off continuing speculation that he may have been targeted because he was about to expose the coverup.

Fallout from media reporting of the tsunami file scandal has caused heads to roll in Germany, where the spy's true identity as a former double agent had been a well-kept secret for many years. Observers say the scandal could influence the outcome of the German federal election, scheduled for 18 September.

Smith says he is looking forward to his new challenge working with the UN mission in Bosnia and to a new stage in his career.

"For a fingerprint man, being able to help with any major forensic identification operation is an attractive prospect," Smith said at a small sendoff reception in London. "This sort of work is my life. But, for me, going to Bosnia at this stage is like a dream come true."

Frank Delaney, a veteran Canadian journalist who interviewed Smith in Thailand for an *International Geographic* feature story on the tsunami DVI operation and who was also injured in the Phuket bombing, attended Smith's sendoff event. Smith credits Delaney with saving his life in the blast.

"I think Jonah and I are kindred spirits, in a way," Delaney told *MetPolice Magazine*. "I suppose you could say that in the sort of lives we have, we're really always just looking for the same thing."

Canadian-born writer, journalist and broadcaster
Michael Rose has worked in senior roles for
major media organizations around the world,
including the CBC, *Maclean's*, and the
Reuters news agency in London.
From 2003 to 2006 he was Chief of
Communications and Publications for Interpol.
He draws upon that wealth of experience as a
journalist, foreign correspondent and traveller for
his Frank Delaney thriller series, which includes
The Mazovia Legacy and *The Burma Effect*, both
available from McArthur & Company.